Wavy pages and strine cobil 1/11 △A

True Colors

**Center Point
Large Print**

**This Large Print Book carries the
Seal of Approval of N.A.V.H.**

True Colors

Kristin Hannah

CENTER POINT PUBLISHING
THORNDIKE, MAINE

This Center Point Large Print edition
is published in the year 2009 by arrangement with
St. Martin's Press.

Copyright © 2009 by Kristin Hannah.

The text of this Large Print edition is unabridged.
In other aspects, this book may vary
from the original edition.
Printed in the United States of America.
Set in 16-point Times New Roman type.

ISBN: 978-1-60285-411-6

Library of Congress Cataloging-in-Publication Data

Hannah, Kristin.
  True colors / Kristin Hannah.
      p. cm.
  ISBN 978-1-60285-411-6 (lib. bdg. : alk. paper)
  1. Sisters--Fiction. 2. Washington (State)--Fiction. 3. Domestic fiction.
    4. Large type books. I. Title.

PS3558.A4763T78 2009b
813'.54--dc22

2008047216

For the women who have come into our family and brightened us with their presence: Debra Edwards John and Julie Gorset John.

For two friends, Julie Williams and Andrea Schmidt. You made me laugh in the craziest of times, and I thank you.

And, as always, to Benjamin and Tucker, without whom I would know so much less about life and love and joy.

Part One

Before

What is passion? It is surely the becoming of a person. . . . In passion, the body and the spirit seek expression . . . The more extreme and the more expressed that passion is, the more unbearable does life seem without it. It reminds us that if passion dies or is denied, we are partly dead and that soon, come what may, we will be wholly so.

—JOHN BOORMAN, FILM DIRECTOR

Prologue

1979

Fifteen-year-old Winona Grey stared out at the waterfront ranch that had been in her family for four generations, looking for something that had changed. Loss like theirs should leave a mark—summer grass gone suddenly brown, dark clouds that refused to lift, a tree split by lightning. Something.

From her bedroom window, she could see most of their acreage. At the property's back boundary, giant cedar trees stood clustered together, their lacy boughs draped downward; in the rolling green pastures, horses milled along the fence lines, their hooves beating the tall grass into muddy submission. Up on the hill, tucked into the deep woods, was the small cabin her great-grandfather had built when he homesteaded this land.

It all looked ordinary, but Winona knew better. A few years ago, a child had died in the cold waters along the Washington coast not far from here, and for months the tragedy was all anyone could talk about. Mom had taken Winona aside and warned her about invisible dangers, undercurrents that could drown you even in shallow water, but now she knew there were other threats lurking beneath the surface of everyday life.

Turning away from the view, she went downstairs, into a house that felt too big and quiet since yesterday. Her sister Aurora sat curled up on the blue and yellow plaid sofa, reading. Pencil-thin and bony at fourteen, Aurora was in that awkward stage that was neither quite childhood nor maturity. She had a small pointed chin and dark brown hair that fell long and straight from a center part.

"You're up early, Sprout," Winona said.

Aurora looked up. "Couldn't sleep."

"Yeah. Me, either."

"Vivi Ann's in the kitchen. I heard her crying a few minutes ago, but . . ." Aurora shrugged her skinny shoulders. "I don't know what to say."

Winona knew how much Aurora needed life to be steady; she was the peacemaker in the family, the one who tried to smooth everything over and make it right. No wonder she looked so fragile. No pretty words could soothe them now. "I'll go," Winona said.

She found her twelve-year-old sister hunched over the yellow Formica table, drawing a picture.

"Hey, Bean," Winona said, ruffling her sister's hair.

"Hey, Pea."

"Whatcha doing?"

"Drawing a picture of us girls." She stopped drawing and tilted her head to look up. Her long wheat-blond hair was a bird's nest of tangles and her green eyes were bloodshot from crying, and still she was beautiful: a perfect Dresden doll. "Mom will be able to see it from Heaven, won't she?"

Winona didn't know how to answer. Faith had always come easily to her before, been as natural and effortless as breathing, but no more. Cancer had come into their family and broken it into so many separate pieces it seemed impossible they would ever be whole again. "Of course," she said dully. "We'll put it on the fridge."

She walked away from her sister, but it was a mistake, that movement, and she knew it instantly. In this kitchen, memories of her mother were everywhere—in the handmade canary and blue gingham curtains, in the Mountain Mama magnet that clung to the refrigerator door, in the bowl of shells on the windowsill. *Come on, Winnie, let's go to the beach and look for treasures . . .*

How many times had Winona blown her mother off this summer? She'd been too busy to hang with Mom, too cool to scavenge the beach, looking for pieces of smooth broken glass amid the shattered oyster shells and drying kelp.

That thought sent her to the fridge. Opening the freezer door, she found a half gallon of Neapolitan ice cream. It was the last thing she needed, but she couldn't help herself.

Grabbing a spoon, she leaned against the counter

and started eating. Through the kitchen window, she could see the dirt driveway in front of the farm-house and the raggedy barn-red loafing shed in the clearing. Up there, her dad's beat-up blue truck was backing up to their rusted six-horse trailer. He got out of the driver's side and went back to the hitch.

"Tell me he's not going to the rodeo," Winona muttered, moving forward.

"Of course he is," Vivi Ann said, drawing again. "He was up at dawn getting ready."

"The rodeo? You're kidding." Aurora came into the kitchen, stood beside Winona at the window. "But . . . how can he?"

Winona knew she was supposed to step into her mother's empty shoes and explain why it was okay for Dad to get on with everyday life on the day after his wife's funeral, but she couldn't imagine forming a lie of that magnitude, not even to spare her sisters pain. Or maybe it wasn't a lie—maybe that was what adults did in this world, maybe they just went on—and somehow that was even more frightening, even more impossible to voice. The silence lingered, made Winona uncomfortable; she didn't know what to say, how to make this bear-able, and yet she knew it was her job to do just that. A big sister was supposed to take care of her siblings.

"Why's he getting Clem out of the pasture?" Aurora asked, taking the spoon from Winona and digging into the ice cream.

Vivi Ann made a sound that was part cry, part scream, and ran for the door, flinging it open so hard it cracked against the wall.

"He's selling Mom's horse," Winona said sharply. It irritated her that she hadn't figured it out first.

"He wouldn't," Aurora said, and then looked to Winona for reassurance. "Would he?"

Winona had no assurance to offer. Instead, she followed Vivi Ann's lead and ran. By the time she reached the parking area by the shed, she was out of breath. She skidded to a stop beside Vivi Ann.

Her father stood there, holding Clem's lead rope. Sunlight hit the sweat-stained crown of his cowboy hat, glinted off the saucer-sized sterling belt buckle he wore. His chiseled face reminded her of the nearby mountains: granite planes and shadowed hollows. There was no hint of softness there.

"You can't sell Mom's horse," she said, panting hard.

"You gonna tell me what to do, Winona?" he said, letting his gaze linger for just a moment on the ice cream.

Winona felt her cheeks redden. It took all her courage to speak up, but she had no choice. There was no one else to do it. "She loves . . . loved that horse."

"We can't afford to feed a horse that don't get ridden."

"I'll ride her," Winona promised.

"You?"

"I'll try harder than before. I won't let myself be afraid."

"Do we even got a saddle that'll fit you?"

In the excruciating silence that followed, Winona lunged forward and grabbed the lead rope from her father. But she moved too fast or spoke too loud—something—and Clementine shied, bolting sideways. Winona felt the sting of a burn as the rope yanked across her palm and she stumbled sideways, half falling.

And then Vivi Ann was beside her, controlling Clementine with a word, a touch. "Are you okay?" she whispered to Winona when the horse was calm again.

Winona was too embarrassed to answer. She felt her father moving toward them, heard the way his cowboy boots sank into the mud. She and Vivi Ann turned slowly to face him.

"You got no horse sense, Winona," he said. It was a thing she'd heard all her life from him. From a cowboy, it was as cutting a remark as was possible.

"I know, but—"

He wasn't listening to her. He was looking at Vivi Ann. Something seemed to pass between them, a piece of communication that Winona couldn't grasp. "She's a high-spirited animal. And young, too. Not just anyone can handle her," Dad said.

"I can," Vivi Ann said.

It was true, and Winona knew it. Vivi Ann, at twelve, was bolder and more fearless than Winona would ever be.

Envy hit her like the snap from a rubber band. She knew it was wrong—mean, even—but she wanted her father to deny Vivi Ann, to cut his most beautiful daughter down with the sharp blade of his disapproval.

Instead he said, "Your mama would be proud," and handed Vivi Ann the ragged blue lead rope.

As if from a distance, Winona watched them walk away together. She told herself it didn't matter, that all she'd wanted was to keep Clem from getting sold, but the lies were cold comfort.

She heard Aurora come up beside her, walking up the hill now that the drama was over. "You okay?"

"Fine."

"What matters is that he didn't sell Clem."

"Yeah," Winona said, wishing that was how she saw it. "What do I care about who rides a horse?"

"Exactly."

But years later, when she looked back on that week of her mother's death, Winona saw how that single action—the handing over of a lead rope—had changed everything. From then on, jealousy had become an undercurrent, swirling beneath their lives. But no one had seen it. Not then, at least.

Chapter One

1992

The day Vivi Ann had been waiting for—January 25—seemed to take forever to arrive. When it finally came, she woke even earlier than usual. Long before dawn had lightened the night sky, she threw back the covers and got out of bed. In the cold darkness of her room, she dressed in insulated coveralls and a woolen cap. Grabbing a pair of worn leather work gloves, she stepped into big rubber boots and went outside.

Technically she didn't have to feed the horses. Her latest ranch hand would do it. But since she was too excited to sleep, she figured she might as well do something useful.

Without a moon to guide her, she couldn't see anything except a ghostly silvered image of her own breath, but if there was one thing Vivi Ann knew in this world, it was the lay of her father's land.

Water's Edge.

More than one hundred years ago, her great-grandfather had homesteaded this property and founded the nearby town of Oyster Shores. Other men had chosen easier, more populated areas, places with easier access, but not Abelard Grey. He had crossed the dangerous plains to get here, lost one son to an Indian raid and another to influenza, but still he'd moved West, lured by a dream to this wild, secluded corner of the Evergreen State. The land he chose, one hundred and twenty-five acres tucked between the warm blue waters of the Hood Canal and a forested hillside, was spectacularly beautiful.

She walked up the small rise toward the barn they'd built ten years ago. Beneath a high, timbered ceiling, a large riding arena was outlined by four-rail fencing; twelve box stalls flanked the east and west sides of the structure. After she opened the huge sliding door, the overhead lights came on with a sound like snapping fingers, and the horses instantly became restless, whinnying to let her know they were hungry. For the next hour, she separated flakes of hay from the bales stacked in the loafing shed, piled them into the rusted wheelbarrow, and moved down the uneven cement aisles. At the last stall, a custom-made wooden sign identified her mare by her rarely used registered name: Clementine's Blue Ribbon.

"Hey, girl," she said, unbolting the wooden door and sliding it sideways.

Clem nickered softly and moved toward her, sneaking a bite of hay from the wheelbarrow.

Vivi Ann tossed the two flakes into the iron feeding rack and closed the door behind her. While

Clem ate, Vivi Ann stood beside her, stroking the big mare's silky neck.

"Are you ready for the rodeo, girl?"

The mare nuzzled her side as if in answer, almost knocking Vivi Ann off her feet.

In the years since Mom's death, Vivi Ann and Clementine had become inseparable. For a while there, when Dad had quit speaking and started drinking, and Winona and Aurora had been busy with high school, Vivi Ann had spent most of her time with this horse. Sometimes, when the grief and emptiness had been too much for Vivi Ann to handle, she'd slipped out of her bedroom and run to the barn, where she'd fall asleep in the cedar shavings at Clem's hooves. Even after Vivi Ann had gotten older and become popular, she'd still considered this mare her best friend. The deepest of her secrets had been shared only here, in the sweet-smelling confines of the last box stall on the east aisle.

She patted Clem's neck one last time and left the barn. By the time she reached the house, the sun was a smear of butterscotch-yellow light in the charcoal-gray winter sky. From this vantage point, she could see the steel-gray waters of the Canal and the jagged, snow-covered peaks of the distant mountains.

When she stepped into the shadowy farmhouse, she could hear the telltale creaking of floorboards and knew her father was up. She went into the kitchen, set three places at the table and then started breakfast. Just as she put a plate of pancakes into the oven to warm, she heard him come into the dining room. Pouring him a cup of coffee, doctoring it with sugar, she took it to him.

He took it from her without looking up from his *Western Horseman* magazine.

She stood there a moment, wondering what she could say that would start a conversation.

Dressed in his usual work clothes—well-worn Wrangler jeans and a plaid flannel shirt, with a saucer-sized silver belt buckle and leather gloves tucked in his waistband—he looked like he did every morning. And yet there was something different, too: a subtle collection of lines or wrinkles that aged his face.

The years since Mom's death had been unkind to him, sharpening his features and adding shadows where none belonged, both in his eyes and in the fleshy bags beneath. His spine had curved; it was the mark of a farrier, he said, the natural result of a lifetime spent hammering nails into horses' hooves, but loss had played a part in that curving of his spine, too. Vivi Ann was certain of it. The weight of an unexpected loneliness had reshaped him as surely as the hours he'd spent hunched at work. The only time he really stood tall anymore was when he was in public, and she knew how much it pained him to appear unbowed by his life.

He sat down at the table and read his magazine while Vivi Ann readied and served breakfast.

"Clem's made some awesome practice runs this month," she said, taking her place across from him. "I really think we have a chance of winning the rodeo in Texas."

"Where's the toast?"

"I made pancakes."

"Fried eggs need toast. You know that."

"Mix them in with the hash browns. We're out of bread."

Dad sighed heavily, obviously irritated. He looked pointedly at the empty place setting on the table. "You seen Travis this morning?"

Vivi Ann glanced through the window toward the barn. There was no sign of their ranch hand anywhere. No tractor out and running, no wheelbarrow by the barn door. "I fed the horses already. He's probably out fixing that fence."

"You picked another winner with that one. If you'd quit rescuin' every hurt horse between here and Yelm, we wouldn't need no help around here at all. And the truth is we can't afford it."

"Speaking of money, Dad . . . I need three hundred bucks for the rodeo this week and the coffee can is empty."

He didn't respond.

"Dad?"

"I had to use that money to pay the hay bill."

"It's gone?"

"The tax bill just came, too."

"So we're in trouble," Vivi Ann said, frowning. She'd heard it before, of course, had always known there wasn't much money, but for the first time, it really hit home. She understood suddenly why Winona was always harping about saving money for taxes. She cast an upward glance at her dad. He sat hunched forward, with his elbows on the table. Her sisters would have seen that as rude; Vivi Ann was sure she knew better. "Your back hurting you again?"

He didn't answer, didn't even acknowledge the question.

She got up, went into the kitchen, and got him some ibuprofen, setting the pills gently on the table between them.

His splayed farrier's hand closed over them.

"I'll find a way to get the money, Dad. And I'll win this week. Maybe as much as two thousand bucks. Don't you worry."

They finished the rest of the meal in silence, with him reading his magazine. When he was done, he pushed back from the table and stood up. Reaching for the sweat-stained brown felt cowboy hat that hung on a hook by the door, he said, "Make me proud."

"I will. 'Bye, Dad."

After he left, Vivi Ann sat there, feeling unsettled.

For most of her twenty-four years she'd been

like a leaf on the water, just floating along, following whatever current came her way. She'd tried changing direction a few times, but every attempt (like community college) had ended quickly, with her returning to this land.

She loved it here, plain and simple. She loved being around the horses, training them, and passing her expertise on to the bright-eyed girls who idolized her riding ability. She loved that everyone in town knew who she was and respected her and her family. She even loved the weather. Lots of folks complained about the gray days that followed each other, one after another, from November to April, but she didn't mind at all. No rain, no rainbows. That was her motto, and had been since she was twelve years old, a girl standing beside a freshly dug grave, trying to make sense of an incomprehensible loss. Then, she'd told herself that life was short and having fun was what mattered.

Now, though, it was time for her to grow up. Water's Edge needed her for once, instead of the other way around. She wasn't sure exactly how to make a change. Business and planning were hardly her strong suits, but she was smarter than people gave her credit for being. All she had to do was think about it.

But first she needed to borrow three hundred dollars from one of her sisters.

She'd tell them it would be a good investment.

Winona liked running the show. Any show; every show. And not from the sidelines, either. In college, all it had taken was one constitutional law class, and she'd glimpsed her future. Now, at twenty-seven, she had her life pretty much as she wanted it. Not completely, of course (she was unmarried, not dating, childless, and struggling with her weight), but pretty much. She was far and away the most successful attorney in Oyster Shores. It was common knowledge that she was fair, opinionated, and smart. Everyone said she was a good person to have on your side. Winona valued her reputation almost as much as she did her education. Dad and Vivi Ann might worship at the altar of their land, but Winona had a broader religion. For her, it was the community that mattered and the people who lived here. It was okay that Vivi Ann was the beautiful heart of town; Winona strove to be its conscience.

She reached for the intercom on her desk and pushed the button. "The council will be here in about ten minutes, Lisa. Make sure we have enough coffee."

Her receptionist answered promptly. "Already done."

"Good." Winona turned her attention to the slim pile of paperwork in front of her. There were a couple of environmental reports, a proposed short plat map, and a real estate sale contract that she'd written up.

It could save Water's Edge.

Well, perhaps that was a bit of an exaggeration; the ranch wasn't poised on the edge of financial ruin or anything. It was more like one of those pathetic starving horses Vivi Ann kept rescuing: limping along. Every month Dad and Vivi Ann barely made enough to keep the place running, and the taxes kept going up. This secret corner of Washington State hadn't been "discovered" yet by the yuppies who turned rugged waterfront lots into gold, but it was only a matter of time. Someday soon a developer would realize that their sleepy town sat on a spectacular stretch of beach that overlooked the Swiss Alps–like Olympic Mountain Range, and when that happened, Dad would find himself sitting on one hundred and twenty-five desirable acres. The rise in taxes would force him to sell the land or lose it, and no one seemed to notice the inevitability of this future except her. It had already happened all across the state.

She jotted notes down on her yellow pad, words to use in talking to him. It was imperative that he understand how important this was, how she'd found a way to save and protect him. Equally imperative was that she be the one to solve the problem. Perhaps then, finally, her father would be proud of her.

The intercom buzzed. "They're here, Winona."

"Send them into the conference room." Winona

slid the documents into a manila folder and reached for her blue blazer. Slipping into it, she noticed it had gotten tighter across the bust. Sighing, she headed down for the conference room.

Her office was housed in a large Victorian mansion on a corner lot in downtown Oyster Shores. She'd bought it four years ago and renovated it room by room. The entire downstairs was completed so far. She could hardly have people judging her public rooms and finding them lacking. Next year, she'd begin on the living quarters upstairs. She had saved up almost enough money.

In the hallway, she paused at a mirror just long enough to assess her reflection: A plump, pretty face, dark brown eyes set beneath arching black brows, full lips, the shoulders of an NFL lineman, and enough bust for three women. Her one outstanding feature—her long black hair—was pulled back from her face and held in place by a white and blue scrunchie.

Forcing a smile, she kept walking and turned into what had once been a ladies' sunroom. Floor-to-ceiling glass windows and a pair of antique French doors covered the back wall. Through the rectangular panes could be seen her winter-brown garden; and beyond that were the brick and wooden buildings along Front Street. In the center of the room was a long oak table. The members of the Oyster Shores city council sat around it, including her father, who wasn't technically a member, but was invited to every meeting nonetheless.

Winona took her usual place at the head of the table. "What can I help you with today?"

Beside her, Ken Otter, the town's dentist, smiled broadly. He always smiled broadly, saying it was free advertising. "We want to talk about what's going on at the reservation."

The reservation again. "I've told you before, it's not possible to stop them. I think—"

"But it's a *casino,*" Myrtle Michaelian said, her round face turning red at the very thought. "Prostitution is sure to follow. The Indians are—"

"Stop," Winona said firmly. She glanced around the table, eyeing each person for a long moment before she turned to the next. "First of all, they're Native Americans, and you don't have the legal right to stop them from building the casino. You can spend a lot of money fighting them, but you'll lose."

They argued on for a few moments, but the mention of spending money had pulled the wind from their sails. In the end, their dissent conked out like a dying engine and they rose to leave, thanking her for saving them money and helping them out.

"Dad?" she said. "Could you stay for a minute?"

"I got to be in Shelton in forty-five minutes."

"It won't take long."

He gave her a short nod, just a flick of the chin,

really, and stood there, arms crossed, while the council members left. When everyone was gone, Winona went back to her place at the head of the table and sat down, opening her manila folder. As she glanced over the paperwork, she couldn't help feeling a swell of pride. This was a good plan.

"It's about Water's Edge," she said, finally looking up. She didn't bother asking him to sit down. She'd learned that lesson well: Henry Grey moved when and where he wanted. Period. Trying to influence that only made the speaker look foolish.

He grunted something. She didn't think it was a word.

"I know how tight your finances are right now, but there are a lot of things at Water's Edge that need fixing. The fences are in bad shape, the loafing shed is starting to list, and someone's going to get lost in the mud in the parking area someday if we don't get a grader in there and lay some gravel. And don't even get me started on the taxes." She pushed the short plat map toward him. "We could sell off the ten acres along the road— Bill Deacon is ready to pay you fifty-five thousand dollars for it right now—or we could short plat it into two-acre parcels and double the price. Either way we can make enough money to tide you over for years. God knows you must be tired of shoeing seven horses a day, every day." She smiled up at him. "It's perfect, isn't it? I mean, you can hardly see those acres. You'll never miss them, and—"

Her dad walked out of the room, slamming the door shut behind him.

Winona flinched at the sound. Why had she allowed herself to hope? *Again.* She stared at the closed door, shaking her head, wondering why a smart woman such as herself kept stepping into the same mud puddle and expecting it to be dry. She was an idiot to still want her father's approval.

"You're mentally ill," she muttered to herself. "And pathetic."

The intercom on the table buzzed loudly, shocking her out of her thoughts.

"Luke Connelly on line one, Winona."

She pushed the red button. "Did you say Luke Connelly?"

"Yes. Line one."

Winona drew in a deep, steadying breath as she picked up the phone and answered. "Winona Grey."

"Hey, Win, it's Luke Connelly. Remember me?"

"Of course I remember you. How's Montana?"

"Cold and white right now, but I'm not there. I'm here, in Oyster Shores. I want to see you."

She caught her breath. "Really?"

"Everyone says you're the best lawyer in town—not that I'm surprised. I'm considering buying half of Doc Moorman's veterinary practice and I'd like to talk to you about the terms. Would that be okay?"

"Oh. You need a lawyer." She refused to feel disappointed. "Sure."

"Could you come over to the house tomorrow? I'm knee-deep in work over here. The last renters really left a mess. So, what do you say? We'll sneak a beer. It'll be just like old times."

"How about four o'clock? I hear that's Miller time."

"Perfect. And Win? I can't wait to see you."

She hung up the phone slowly; it was as if the air had thickened suddenly to water and resisted her movement. *I can't wait to see you.* She got up and left the conference room, walking down to the foyer, where Lisa sat behind an antique dining room table, typing a letter on her big green IBM Selectric typewriter.

"I'm going out," Winona said. "It's an emergency. I'll be back in an hour."

"I'll reschedule Ursula."

"Good."

Winona left her quiet office and walked down the sidewalk, following the cement strip two blocks to her sister's impeccably maintained brick rambler.

There, she opened the unstained wooden gate at Aurora's backyard and went up to the laundry room door to knock.

It took Aurora forever to answer, and when she finally did, she looked harried. A four-year-old child was on each hip; a boy and a girl. "You just missed Vivi Ann. She borrowed three hundred bucks for the rodeo. Said it was an investment."

29

"With a straight face?"

Aurora smiled. "You know Vivi. Good things just come to her."

Winona rolled her eyes at that, even though they both knew it was true. Their youngest sister often seemed to be standing in a ray of sunlight that excluded everyone else. "Did she leave for Texas?"

"Just now. I hope that old truck makes it."

"If it breaks down, she'll meet Tom Cruise at the gas station." Winona pushed past her sister and went into the small, cluttered laundry room, where stacks of folded clothes layered every surface. "Can we talk about me for a change?"

"Come on, kids," Aurora said behind her, "Aunt Winona is crazy today. Give her plenty of room. You never know when she'll blow."

"Very funny."

Aurora took Ricky and Janie upstairs and put them down for naps, or television; whatever mothers did with four-year-old twins in the late afternoon. Fifteen minutes later, she was down again.

"Okay, what's going on?" she said, standing in the middle of the living room. Today she was wearing tight black jeans, penny loafers, and a boxy jacket with oversized shoulder pads. Her straight brown hair was drawn back from her face in a French braid. Bangs poufed out over her forehead like a tiny awning.

Now that Aurora had asked directly, Winona found herself reluctant to reveal her true reason for racing over here. Stalling, she said, "I told Dad he should sell off the back ten acres or short plat them and then sell them."

"Yeah, well, you've got the learning curve of a lemming."

"Water's Edge is going under. Why else would Vivi Ann have to borrow entry money? And have you noticed how run-down the place looks?"

Aurora sat down on her new gray and mauve sofa. "You can't tell him to sell his land, Win. The man would rather sell his sperm."

"It's a few acres you can't even see, and it could give him financial security."

Aurora leaned back, drumming her long red fingernails on the glossy mahogany end table beside her. "You know you should talk to Vivi or me before you do something like that."

"I shouldn't—"

"I know. You think you're smarter than we are, and it's your responsibility to take care of everyone 'cause you're the oldest, but honest to God, Win, when you get a thing in your mind, you can't see the forest for the trees."

"I was just trying to help." Winona sat down on the salmon-colored brick hearth. A moment later she got up and went to the window. From here, she could see Aurora's child-friendly backyard and the houses behind it.

31

Aurora frowned. "I haven't seen you this jumpy since Tony Gibson asked you to go away for the weekend."

"We promised never to mention that."

"You promised. How can I forget the image of him stripping down to his women's panties?"

Winona couldn't take it anymore. She blurted out: "Luke Connelly called me today."

"Wow. That's a blast from the past. Last I heard he was off to vet school."

"He's back in town, and thinking of buying into Doc Moorman's clinic. He wants me to look over the documents."

"He called you as a lawyer?"

"That's what he said." Winona took a deep breath and finally turned to face her sister. "And that he was looking forward to seeing me."

"Does he know you had a crush on him?"

Crush. That was a pretty small word for what she'd felt, but she certainly wasn't going to tell Aurora that. Instead, she said, "I'm going to meet him at four tomorrow. Do you think you could help me look good? I know it's a herculean task, but—"

"Of course," Aurora said without smiling.

"What is it?" Winona asked. "You're giving me the something's-wrong look."

"I won't say anything. Okay, I'll just ask a question. It's about Luke, right? Just Luke."

"What do you mean?"

"Dad always wanted the Connellys' land. Don't pretend you don't know that. And he liked them."

"You think I'd go out with someone to get Dad's approval?"

"Sometimes I think you'd do almost anything for it."

Winona forced a laugh, but it didn't fly. Sometimes she worried about that, too. How far would she go for her father's approval? "This whole conversation is pointless because I'm fat. Luke won't want to go out with me. He never did."

Aurora gave her a sad, familiar look. "You know what amazes me about you, Win?"

"My keen intellect?"

"How wrong you are when you look in the mirror."

"Says the size six former cheerleader." Winona pushed to her feet. "Come over at three tomorrow, okay?"

"I'll be there."

"And Aurora? Don't tell anyone about this. Especially Vivi Ann. That stupid crush was a long time ago. I wouldn't want anyone to think it matters now. Hell, he's probably married with three kids."

"Your secrets have always been safe with me, Win."

The next afternoon, Winona stared at herself in the full-length mirror in her bedroom. These were not good fashion times for a woman of her size: shoulder pads, high-waisted slim-legged jeans, and cowboy boots were hardly helpful to her cause.

Aurora had done her very best, and Winona appreciated the effort, but some endeavors were simply destined to fail, and trying to slim her down was one of them. She kicked off her boots and actually felt some satisfaction when they thunked against the wall. Instead, she slipped on a pair of well-worn flats.

"He's going to think I haven't stopped eating since he left."

All the way to her car, and through town, she reminded herself that this was a business meeting with a man she used to know but didn't anymore. She absolutely should not tangle the past up with the present. Her crush on him had been a child-hood thing, not substantial enough to last.

She drove along the waterfront, past the touristy shops that lined the Canal, and turned left at the end of town. Here was the Water's Edge property line. She couldn't help noticing again how ragged the fences were looking. It reminded her again of yesterday's meeting with her father. Out at the highway, she drove south for a quarter of a mile and then turned onto Luke's land. Although the Grey and Connelly parcels were adjoining, Luke's land had been vacant for years; the grass, even in winter, was tall and clumpy. Alder trees had sprouted up like weeds in the past few years, giving the acreage a spindly, unkempt look. The old house, an L-shaped rambler built in the early seventies, was sorely in need of paint and the shrubbery around it had grown wild. Junipers tangled with rhododendrons, which peeked through azaleas.

She parked alongside his big dually truck and killed the engine. "He'll just want to give you the papers and say how nice it is to see you after all this time. Then he'll introduce you to his wife and kids." She took a deep breath and got out of the car.

The grass between her and the front door was soggy and brown. She left footprints that immediately filled with muddy water.

At the front door, she ran a hand through the hair Aurora had so meticulously curled and sprayed. Then she knocked at the door.

He answered almost instantly—and that was how quickly she knew she was in trouble.

He'd been tall in high school, but lanky and a little gawky. Those days were gone. He was tall and broad-shouldered and narrow-waisted—the kind of guy who went to the gym. His hair was still thick and mink brown, a perfect complement to his green eyes. "Win," he said.

And there it was: the smile that had always kicked the hell out of her heart.

"L-Luke," she stammered. "I came by for those documents . . ."

He pulled her into his arms and gave her the kind of whole-body hug she'd nearly forgotten existed.

"You think I'm going to let my best friend from high school just pick up some papers and go?"

He took her by the hand and led her through the house. It was like stepping into a time machine, being in the room that had changed so little in the past years. The same burnt-orange sculpted carpet was beneath her feet, the same brown and gold and orange plaid sofa hugged the wall, the same amber glass lamps with beaded switches sat on the end tables.

"The only thing missing is a black light," Luke said, grinning as he opened the avocado-colored fridge and pulled out a pair of beers. "It smells musty in here. I think the renters were smokers. Do you mind if we sit outside?"

"It wouldn't be the first time." She followed him out to the big cement patio that ran the length of the house. Off to the left, a barbecue was slowly rusting apart and dozens of dead geraniums sagged in flower boxes along the railing, but none of that could diminish the view. Like Water's Edge, this parcel of land looked out across the Canal—flat and silver on this late afternoon—and right at the saw-blade, snowcapped Olympic Mountain Range on the opposite shore. A thicket of trees provided total privacy between their properties. They sat in the rocking love seat that had once been Winona's favorite place in the whole world.

"I guess we should start with the basics," he said, opening his beer and leaning back to take a sip. "After we moved to Montana, I ended up going to WSU to become a vet. Big animals. Where did you go to school?"

"UW. Undergrad and law school."

"I thought you were going to run off and see the world. I was surprised to hear that you'd come back."

"They needed me at home. What about you? Did you ever make it to Australia?"

"Nope. Too many school loans."

"I know what you mean." She laughed, but when it faded, the day felt too quiet. "You ever get married?" she asked softly.

"No. You?"

"No."

"Ever fall in love?"

She couldn't help turning to him. "No. You?"

He shook his head. "Never met the right girl, I guess."

Winona leaned back, looked out over the view. "Your mom must hate that you've moved away."

"Nah. Caroline has four kids and no husband. That keeps Mom busy most of the time. And she knew I was getting restless."

"Restless?"

"Sometimes you have to go looking for your life." He took a sip of beer. "How are your sisters?"

"Good. Aurora met a guy named Richard a few years ago—a doctor—they have four-year-old twins. Ricky and Janie. I think they're all doing well, but it's hard to tell with Aurora. She wants everyone to be happy, so she doesn't talk much about what bothers her. And Vivi Ann's still the same. Spontaneous. Headstrong. She dives in first and thinks later."

"Compared to you, no one thinks enough."

Winona couldn't help laughing at that. "What can I say? I'm always the smartest person in the room."

They fell into a companionable silence, staring out over the untended field, drinking their beers, then, quietly, Luke said, "I think I saw Vivi Ann pulling out of the gas station yesterday."

Winona heard something in his voice, a little catch that put her on guard. "She was on her way to Texas. She makes a lot of money at weekend rodeos. And meets a lot of handsome cowboys."

"I'm not surprised. She's beautiful," he said.

Winona had heard that sentence from men all her life; they usually followed it up with: *Do you think she'd go out with me?* She felt herself stiffening, drawing back whatever feelers of hope she'd allowed foolishly to unfurl. "Stand in line," she muttered under her breath.

What had she been thinking, anyway? He was too damn good-looking for Winona; it was dangerous to let herself expect anything at all.

Especially now that he'd seen the beautiful Vivi Ann.

"It's good to be back," he said, bumping her shoulder-to-shoulder the way they used to when they were kids, when they were best friends, and suddenly her own warnings fell out of reach, clattered away.

"Yeah," she said, not daring to look at him. "It's good to have you home."

Chapter Two

All the next day, Winona told herself he wouldn't call, but still she looked longingly at the phone, jumping a little every time it rang.

One day.

That was all it had been since she'd sat with her once–best friend in a porch swing at night. One day. Of course he wouldn't call yet. Or at all. She was as big as a house, after all. Why would a man as good-looking as Luke Connelly want to go out with her?

"Focus, Winona," she said, looking over the paperwork he'd given her last night. She'd made plenty of notes—things she needed to discuss with him, precautions he should take to protect his interests. In addition to her legal opinion, she had some thoughts as to the viability of becoming Woody Moorman's partner; the man was well known to be a heavy drinker and he'd lost a lot of customers over the years.

When she'd made all her notes, she closed the Connelly file and opened the Smithson interrogatories. For the next few hours, she concentrated on work, until finally, at five o'clock, she shut down the office and went upstairs.

Usually she loved the evening news, but tonight she was restless, caught up in waiting for the phone to ring, and she couldn't stand it, so she threw on a pair of jeans, a white turtleneck sweater, and a thigh-length black vest.

A quick check of the weather told her it was one of those rare January evenings when the sky was plum-colored and cloudless. Bundling up, she decided to walk over to Water's Edge. The cold air might clear her head, and God knew she could use the exercise. It was less than a mile from one door to the other.

Pleased with her decision (it was so much better than watching TV alone), she headed down to Main Street.

Oyster Shores was set up like so many western Washington waterfront communities, in a T-bone pattern. The end of town was a four-block stretch of road that ran along the Canal's gray shoreline. That was where the touristy shops were located—the kayak rental place, the ice-cream shop, the fish bar, and several souvenir-type stores. In the four-block by seven-block radius between the Canal and the highway lay the bulk of Winona's childhood. She'd spent much of her youth in the library, reading Nancy Drew and Laura Ingalls Wilder; at Grey Park, she'd learned to play soccer and softball; on warm summer days, she and her sisters had often walked to King's Market for Pop Rocks and Tabs.

Even though she'd seen it all a million times, she couldn't help pausing at Shore Drive, drinking in the spectacular view. In other parts of the world, places more settled and less wild, a canal was a thin, lethargic strip of slow-moving water, a thing to be navigated at leisure in flat-bottomed boats. Not here; this was a wide and wild blue inlet of Puget Sound that ran inland for fifty miles, the only true fjord in the lower forty-eight states.

She turned left and walked out of town. As she passed the Waves Restaurant, the streetlamps came on, sent pretty golden patches panning out on the gray sidewalks and black pavement. In this cold season, when boats were scarce and tourists even scarcer, the street was still, maybe even a little forlorn. A mermaid wind sock hung limply from the flagpole in front of the Canal House Bed and Breakfast. In June the summer people would swarm these streets, taking over parking spots and cutting in line at the beach park boat launch, but for now it was quiet. The town belonged to the thirteen hundred people who called it home.

The ranch's entrance was indicated by a rough-hewn wooden sign, carved by Winona's great-grandfather in 1881. Passing it, she turned onto the long, rolling gravel driveway. On either side of her were green pastures lined in ragged four-rail fencing. Gullies of brown water bracketed the road. Dying black maple leaves lay stuck to the gravel, and potholes were everywhere, oozing gray rainwater. The place needed repairs.

Why wouldn't her father see that she could help him? She was going over the humiliating meeting with him—again—when she noticed Luke's truck.

She stopped and looked around.

There they were, on the porch, Luke and her father, talking together like old friends. She followed the wet, muddy driveway past the barn and down toward them.

As she approached, Luke laughed at something Dad had said.

Winona saw her dad smile and it actually brought her to a stop. It was like seeing the ocean turn suddenly red, or the moon go green. "Hey, guys," she said, stepping up onto the porch's bottom step. The old wood buckled beneath her weight, reminding her simultaneously that she was fat and the steps needed repair.

Luke reached out and put an arm around her, pulling her into a side embrace, out of which she stumbled a moment later feeling dazed. "If it weren't for Winona here," he said to Dad, "I never would have become a vet. She did most of my English homework in high school."

"Yeah, she's a brainy one, all right. Her latest big idea was for me to sell the land my family home-steaded."

Winona couldn't believe he'd bring that up in front of Luke. "I was just trying to protect your future."

Dad ignored her and looked at Luke. "When Abelard left Wales he had fourteen dollars in his pocket."

"Come on, Dad. No one wants to hear the old stories—"

"And Elijah lost his leg in the war and then came back to a dead wife and a dying son and land too wet to grow anything in, but he still managed to hang on to every acre through the Depression. He left his son every damned acre he'd inherited."

"Those were different times, Dad. We know that. We don't care if you leave us the same amount of land you inherited."

"How did I know you'd say that?"

"I didn't mean that. I just meant we want you to be comfortable. That's what matters."

"You can't understand loving this land like Vivi and I do. It ain't in you."

How easily he culled her from the herd and set her aside.

"The place looks great, Henry," Luke said into the awkward silence that followed. "Just like I remember. And I want to thank you for maintaining the fence. I'd like to pay you for that, by the way. Somehow Mom and I forgot to keep up on it."

Dad nodded. "I wouldn't take a dime from you, son. That's what neighbors do."

Son.

It was a tiny slice of pain, the way her father included Luke so easily, like sticking your hand in soapy water and finding a sharp knife blade. You didn't even realize you'd been cut until you drew back and saw the bead of blood on your skin.

"It's Vivi Ann who done most of it, anyway; her and whatever hand she's found to help her around here. This land is her soul." Dad looked at Winona when he said that.

"I hear she's a fine barrel racer."

"Best in the state," Dad said.

"I'm hardly surprised. I don't think I ever saw her when she wasn't on that mare of Donna's, riding at the speed of sound."

"Yeah," Dad said. "She and Clem are quite a team."

Winona held her tongue while Dad went on and on about Vivi Ann. What a great horsewoman she was, how everyone came to her for help, how men lined up to date her but she hadn't found the right fella yet.

Finally, Winona couldn't take it anymore. She actually interrupted the conversation to say, "I better go. I just came by to—"

"Oh, no, you don't," Luke said, taking her arm. "I want to treat you and Henry to dinner in town."

"I can't," Henry said. "I'm meetin' some of the boys down at the Eagles. But thanks."

Luke turned. "Winona?"

Don't think anything of it. He asked your dad, too. The advice rang clear in her head, but when she looked up at him, it left in a rush, and the worst emotion swept in to replace it: hope.

"Sure."

"Where should we go?" he asked.

"The Waves is good. On the corner of First and Shore Drive."

"Let's go." Luke reached out and shook Dad's hand. "Thanks again for everything, Henry. And don't forget my offer: if you ever need to use my pasture, just say so."

Henry nodded and went back into the house, closing the door solidly behind him.

"Asshole," Winona muttered.

Luke grinned down at her. "You used to call him a jerk."

"I've improved my vocabulary. I could think of a few more choice words, if you'd like." Smiling, she walked across the front yard and got into the passenger side of his big truck. The minute the engine turned over, the stereo came on loudly. "Stairway to Heaven" was playing.

She looked at him and knew they were remembering the same thing: the two of them at the Sadie

45

Hawkins Dance, moving together—or trying to— beneath a silvery disco ball.

"We sure showed those popular kids how to dance, didn't we?" he said.

She felt a smile start. Somehow, in the flurry of his return, she'd forgotten how they'd come together in that first year after her mother's death—a fat, quiet fifteen-year-old girl who lived in her own head and a gawky boy with a bad complexion who'd lost his father in a boating accident nearly a decade before. *It gets easier.* That was the first thing he said to her that she really noticed. Before that, he'd been just the son of her mom's best friend.

After that, for two years, almost everything he'd said had been right. Then he moved away, without ever even kissing her, and he hadn't called. They'd written back and forth for a while, but then that had been lost, too.

He pulled up in front of the Waves Restaurant and parked along the curb. A spotlight near the front door illuminated a yard full of ceramic gnomes that looked cute in the summer sun and oddly macabre on this winter evening. She led the way into the Victorian-home-turned-restaurant. On this evening, they were the only people under sixty in the whole restaurant, and the hostess led them to a corner table overlooking the Canal. Below, a discolored bulkhead held the water back, revealing a stretch of gray sand that was covered with broken white oyster shells and strands of bronze kelp. A tangle of harbor seals lay on the restaurant's wooden dock.

In moments, they had their drinks—him a beer, and her a margarita.

"To old friends," he said.

"To old friends."

Then he said, "Did you get a chance to look over the paperwork?"

"I did. As your lawyer, I'll tell you that everything looks to be in order. I'd make a few changes, but nothing major." She looked across the table at him and lowered her voice. "But as your friend, I'd tell you that Moorman doesn't have the best reputation. He's struggled with a serious drinking problem for years; well, actually, he hasn't struggled with it. Mostly he's given in to it. A few years ago he brought in a young vet to be his partner and word is that he screwed the kid pretty badly."

"Really?"

"Honestly, Luke, I think you'd do better to open your own practice. People around here would welcome you with open arms. You could set up an office in your house and fix up that four-stall barn on the property. Then, in a few years, maybe you'll be ready to build a new facility."

Luke sat back. "That's disappointing."

"I'm sorry. You asked for my opinion."

"Sorry? Are you kidding? I've always loved your mind. And I know I can trust you. Thanks."

She didn't hear anything after the word *loved*.

Vivi Ann was in the staging area, waiting her turn in the short round. There were only fourteen girls and women around her, all on horseback, who had also made the top fifteen. Run times were blaring through the PA system; tabulations were under way, starting with the slowest time and working to the top. She'd been in Texas for almost a week, and it had been one of the best rodeos in her life.

She leaned down and stroked the mare's sweaty neck. "Hey, girl," she said. "You ready to win this thing?"

The mare's heart was pounding like a jackhammer. Clem was ready.

Moments later, Vivi Ann heard her name through the giant black speakers and a jolt of adrenaline coursed through her, erasing everything from her mind but this moment.

Vivi Ann pulled her hat down low on her forehead. Clem leaped forward, bounding toward the gate. Vivi Ann tightened the reins, holding the mare back until they were positioned correctly for the first barrel.

Then she leaned forward and released Clem, and they were off, heads down, racing forward into the arena so fast that everything around them was a blur of sound and color. All Vivi Ann saw were the three barrels waiting for them in the dirt, set up in a bright yellow triangle. All the way through the pattern, around the barrels, she was kicking Clem's sides and urging her to go faster. The seconds passed with frightening speed, but Vivi Ann experienced it in a kind of slow motion—the way Clem snaked around the first barrel and then the second, and then they were hurtling forward for the last barrel, sliding sinuously around it and running back down the arena. When they passed the timer, Vivi Ann gently pulled back on the reins, bringing Clem to a bouncing trot.

She heard their time announced through the speakers and she grinned, then laughed.

14.09.

It would be a tough time to beat. She tried to do the math in her head, to see if she would win the average, but it was too difficult. She'd already won one of the two prior rounds. Only a couple of women even had a chance to beat her, and even so, it was unlikely. She had just run very close to a new arena record.

"Good job, Clem," she said, leaning forward to stroke the mare's neck. She slid out of the saddle and led the way back to the trailer. Giving Clem a bucket of water and some molasses-soaked oats, she unsaddled the mare and tied her to the side of the rusted old trailer.

Smiling, practically running, she headed up into the stands. Some of the other contestants were already there, especially those who had not made the top fifteen this time. Pam. Red. Amy.

"Nice run, Vivi," said Holly Bruhn, scooting sideways to make room.

Vivi Ann smiled. "Clem was hot for an old broad, wasn't she?"

"She sure was." Holly reached down into the ice chest beside her and produced a cold beer. "Here. But you can only drink it if your time holds."

"Ha!" Vivi Ann took the beer and tilted it to her lips.

Holly handed Vivi Ann a piece of paper. "This is for you."

Vivi Ann looked down at the flyer in her hands. It was the sort of thing she'd seen a hundred times in her life, maybe more. A list of barrel-racing events. The only new twist was that it was for a series of weekends, with a high-point money winner at the end.

"We're trying out a winter series," Holly said. "Now that the barn is up and running, we need to start generating some income. I'd love it if you'd come. Tell your 4-H girls."

And there it was: the idea. It came to her fully formed, so obvious a solution she couldn't imagine why she hadn't seen it before. "How many people have signed up?"

"So far we have about ninety. You can see the different fee schedules. And divisions for the kids, too. You have to attend four of the eight to be eligible for prizes, so you'll have to make all of the next events to qualify—since you'd be starting late, I mean."

"You're giving away money and prizes?"

Holly nodded. "Prizes at the end, money along the way."

"And you're still doing the team penning and roping jackpots?"

"Every Friday. It's starting slow—people are just discovering the arena—but every week is better than the one before."

From that moment on, Vivi Ann could hardly think of anything else. Even that afternoon, when she picked up the saddle and prize money she'd won, she was too distracted to say much. Instead of hurrying out with her friends, maybe line-dancing down at the local roadhouse, she loaded Clem into the trailer and headed for home. On the long drive up from Texas, while Garth Brooks sang to her, she looked at the idea from every angle, trying to find a flaw in her reasoning. But there wasn't one. She had finally come up with the answer her father needed.

She had come up with it. That made her smile almost every time she thought it.

Oh, she knew what people thought of her. Even her sisters, who loved her, saw her as a pretty decoration who could ride a horse like the wind but wasn't good at the heavy lifting in life.

Now, finally, she could show everyone that she was more than just a pretty face.

That thought, that hope, accompanied her on the lonely drive home. When she finally pulled into

Water's Edge at midnight on Saturday, she'd corralled all her ideas and figured out how to present them to the family.

She couldn't wait. They would all be so proud of her.

Pulling up to the parking area, she turned off the truck's engine and climbed out of the driver's seat, then went around to open the trailer door.

"Hey, Clemmie," she said, patting the mare's big hindquarters. "Are you as tired as I am, girl?"

Clem turned and nuzzled her side, nickering quietly.

Vivi Ann snapped the lead rope onto Clem's nylon halter and backed her out of the trailer. "No more stall for you," she said, leading her horse to the pasture and unhooking the halter. After smacking the quarter horse's butt, she watched Clem bolt away. Within seconds, the big mare was rolling in the grass.

Leaving the trailer to be swept out tomorrow, she closed the door and started toward the house, until she noticed that someone had left the barn door open.

She went inside, just to make sure everything was okay, and found a mess. The stalls were filthy and several horses were out of water.

Vivi Ann cursed beneath her breath and walked up the dirt and grass driveway toward her grandparents' old cottage. For years it had been used as a bunkhouse—for the men they hired to help out around the place. She knocked several times and got no answer, so she opened the door.

Inside, she found an even bigger disaster than had been in the barn. The small kitchen was piled high with dirty dishes and pans layered with drying food. Empty pizza boxes and beer cans covered the tables, and clothes lay across the sofa and chair.

She could hear a man snoring in the bedroom. Charging through the small living area, she shoved open the bedroom door and turned on the light.

Travis lay sprawled across the brass bed, asleep in his clothes. He hadn't even bothered to take off his cowboy boots, so there was dirt smeared on her grandmother's chenille bedspread.

"Travis," she snapped. "Wake up."

She had to say his name several more times before he rolled over and looked at her through bleary, bloodshot eyes.

"Hey, Vivi." He ran a hand through his close-cropped hair, making it stand up on end. His cheeks were chalky pale and dark shadows circled his eyes. There was no doubt in her mind that she was getting him at the tail end of a two-day drunk.

"The stalls are a mess, Travis, and the horses are out of water. Did you even feed them today?"

He struggled to sit up. "I'm sorry. I jus' . . . Sally has a new boyfriend." He looked as if he were going to start crying and Vivi Ann sat down on the bed beside him, unable to be angry. Travis and Sally had been in love since high school.

"Maybe you'll work it out," she said.

"I don't think so. She just . . . don't love me anymore."

Vivi Ann didn't know what to say. She didn't really know about the kind of love that tore you in half; except that she believed in it. "We're young, Travis. You'll find someone."

"Twenty-five ain't young, Vivi. And I don't want no one else. What am I gonna do?"

Vivi Ann's heart went out to him. She knew what she should do right now, what Dad or Winona would do, but she wasn't built that way. She couldn't just tell him to suck it up and get back to work. She'd learned early in life that a broken heart had to be treated carefully. It was a lesson every motherless girl knew. "I'll feed and water today but I want you to strip down every stall tomorrow, okay? There's fresh shavings in the loafing shed. Can I count on you?"

"Sure, Vivi," he said, already sliding back down to go to sleep. "Thanks."

She knew she couldn't count on him, but what else was there to do? With a sigh, she left the cottage, turning off the lights as she went. As she walked back down to the barn, fighting the wave of exhaustion that was trying to pull her under, it started to rain.

"Perfect."

Flipping up the collar of her jacket, she ducked her head and ran the rest of the way.

· · ·

On the first Sunday of every month the Grey family walked to church. It was a tradition begun generations ago; then it had been a necessity, a response to winter roads turned into muddy bogs by rain. Now it was a choice. Rain or shine they came together at the farmhouse in the midmorning and set out for town. It was important to their father, crucial even, that the Greys be respected in town, that their contribution to the creation of Oyster Shores be remembered. So they walked to church once a month to remind people that their family had been here when buggies couldn't navigate sawdust-covered winter roads.

This first Sunday in February, Vivi Ann got up an hour early to feed the horses so that Dad wouldn't know about Travis's recent breakdown. On this of all days she didn't want to listen to him complaining about her hiring skills, or lack thereof.

Not today, when she was going to surprise him with her perfect plan.

When she finished her chores, she returned to the house and showered and got ready for church. By the time she came downstairs, dressed in a white eyelet skirt and blouse with a wide belt and her good cowboy boots, the whole family was already on the porch.

Aurora and Richard were together, trying to keep the twins from breaking something, while Winona leaned against the porch rail, looking up at the pretty glass and driftwood wind chimes their mother had made.

Dad walked out into the yard and did his usual weather check. "Let's go."

They fell into formation, with Dad out front by at least ten feet, walking fast. Richard and the kids tried to keep up with him. The girls came together at the rear, walking elbow to elbow, as they'd done for the whole of their lives.

"I see Dad's setting his usual Bataan Death March pace," Winona said.

"I will never understand why I have to drive to the farmhouse to walk to church," Aurora said. It was a variation of the complaint she made each month. "How was the rodeo?"

"Great. I won a saddle and fifteen hundred bucks."

"Good for you," Winona said. "God knows this place could use some cash."

Vivi Ann smiled at that, imagining again her triumph when she revealed her plan to make money. For the first time, Winona would see how smart her youngest sister really was. "Did anything interesting happen while I was gone?"

There was an almost imperceptible pause. Then Aurora said, "Luke Connelly came back to town."

"The kid from next door? Wasn't he in school with you guys?" Vivi Ann tried to draw up a memory of him but couldn't do it. "What's he doing here?"

"He's a vet," Aurora answered. "Winona—"

"Is helping him out," Winona cut in.

Vivi Ann frowned; something seemed odd. It felt as if her sisters knew something she didn't. She glanced from one sister to the other and then shrugged. She had too much on her mind right now to sift through nuance for fact. "I don't really remember him. Is he good-looking?"

"You would ask that," Winona said crisply.

For the rest of the way, they kept up a steady stream of conversation. More than once Vivi Ann wanted to just blurt out her idea, but in an unusual display of personal restraint, she waited.

After the services, they milled among their friends and neighbors, gathering in the basement for coffee and muffins as usual. Luke Connelly's return was the topic of conversation. His unexpected reappearance brought up stories about the old days, back when Vivi Ann's mom and Luke's mom had been the prettiest girls in town. Ordinarily, Vivi Ann would have listened to those stories greedily—any mention of her mother was special—but today she had too much on her mind to relax and enjoy the conversations, and since Luke wasn't at church, she lost interest in him quickly.

A little earlier than usual she herded her family together and encouraged them to head home. "Before the rain hits," she said, and that was enough. They'd walked home in the rain often enough to know it wasn't fun.

Back in formation, they walked through town and turned onto their driveway. On either side of them were bright green pastures, their boundaries marked by four-rail fencing. At the end of the driveway sat their pretty yellow farmhouse, with its white wraparound porch. Behind it, the Canal, the sky, and the distant mountains were all muted by mist, turned gray so that it was all shadows within shadows.

Clementine whinnied at their approach and galloped toward them.

Vivi Ann hiked up her eyelet skirt and slipped between the fence rails.

"Not again," Winona said from behind her.

Laughing, Vivi Ann swung up onto Clem's broad back. Without a lead rope or bridle, she technically had no control of her mare, but her faith in Clem was absolute. She squeezed Clem's sides and the mare took off, running through the pasture toward the house. Vivi Ann leaned forward, hanging on to Clem's mane. Her eyes watered at the speed; her hair whipped across her face.

She loved this. Any second Clem could throw her or stop suddenly or veer so fast Vivi Ann couldn't hang on.

As they neared the house, she whispered, "Whoa, girl. Whoa," and stroked Clem's soft neck.

Vivi Ann was on the porch to greet her family when they finally arrived.

"Way to be a role model," Aurora said. "I hope you'll stop that when Janie starts lessons."

"She should be in lessons now," Vivi Ann said. "We were three when Mom started our lessons, remember?"

"You were three," Aurora said. "The prodigy. I was five and Winona—"

"Let's not talk about Winona and horses," Winona said.

Laughing at that, the three of them went into the house and headed directly to their stations: Vivi Ann on lead, with Winona doing whatever prep work was asked of her—usually cutting vegetables and making the salad—while Aurora set the table. The kids went upstairs to watch videos and Dad and Richard stood silently in the family room, drinking beer and watching whatever sport was in season.

For the next two hours the girls talked and joked and laughed as they got supper ready. By the time the pot roast was done, they'd finished off a bottle of chardonnay and opened another.

Sunday supper began as it always did, with Dad leading them in prayer. Immediately thereafter, the conversational free-for-all began. Vivi Ann tried to wait for a natural lull in the talking to pitch her idea, but now that she was seated, she couldn't wait any longer. Her enthusiasm was too high.

She just blurted it out: "I've been thinking about something. A way for the ranch to make some money."

Everyone looked up.

Winona frowned. Apparently she'd been in the middle of a story, but Vivi Ann hadn't noticed.

"In Texas I spent a lot of time with Holly and Gerald Bruhn. They just built that big arena down in Hood River, remember? Anyway, Holly is running a winter barrel-racing series. Eight weeks, every Saturday. They're giving away money and prizes."

"You always win those things," Aurora said.

"No," Vivi Ann said. "You don't get it. I want to run a series here at Water's Edge."

Dad shrugged. "Might work."

Vivi Ann grinned at the encouragement. "If it does, we could branch out to team pennings and ropings. Holly said last week they had over four hundred teams at the roping jackpot."

She had her father's attention now. "That costs money."

"I did some checking around. We could probably do it for about one hundred thousand dollars."

Winona laughed. "Is that all?"

Vivi Ann was surprised by that, and a little hurt. "We could get a loan. Mortgage the place."

That shut everyone up.

"We've never had a mortgage," Dad said.

"Times are changing, Dad," Vivi Ann said. "I really think we could make a go of this. All we'd need are some steers, a groomer, a new tractor, and—"

Winona was not smiling. "You're kidding, right?"

"Lord knows I'm tired of shoein' horses all day and worrying about taxes," Dad said, "and now that Luke Connelly is back we can use his acreage. We could keep the steers there, so we wouldn't need a big trailer."

Winona made a great show of rolling her eyes. "But if you can't make a mortgage payment you'll lose your property. You know that, right?"

"I ain't stupid."

"I didn't suggest you were," Winona said. "But this is crazy. You can't—"

"You gonna tell me what to do again, Winona?" he said. On that, he left the table and headed for the study, where he closed the door behind him.

Vivi Ann turned on Winona. "Way to be a bitch. You're just mad because it's not *your* idea. Miss Brainiac couldn't think of shit."

"And what happens if you suck at doing all this, Vivi? What happens if no one comes and Dad has to find a thousand bucks a month to cover this new mortgage? You going to stand by his side and watch him lose this place? It's all he has."

"What if he's already losing it?" Vivi Ann demanded, determined to stand her ground.

"It's just like Clem," Winona muttered, and Vivi Ann had no idea what her sister meant by that.

"You're just jealous that I came up with the idea," Vivi Ann said.

"Yeah, I'm jealous of your intellect," Winona snapped back.

"Come on, you two," Aurora said. "Let's not go down that road." She looked from one to the other. "It's a good idea. Can we figure out how to make it work?"

Chapter Three

In the past twenty-four hours, Vivi Ann had filled a spiral notebook with ideas. It didn't matter that her father hadn't agreed with her yet. She had no doubt at all that he'd come around to her way of thinking. So would Winona, once she got the bug out of her butt and stopped caring that it wasn't her idea.

"Vivi Ann? Are you paying attention?"

She looked up from her notes.

Ten eager faces stared back at her. The girls of the Bits and Spurs 4-H group were seated around the living room—on the blue and yellow plaid sofa, beside the wagon wheel coffee table, in clusters on the worn oak flooring. Their ages ranged from nine to sixteen, and they had a singular passion in common: horses.

For the next hour, the girls talked about their horses and the fair and the barrel-racing clinic Vivi

Ann was teaching next week. They were still talking and laughing and battering her with questions when Vivi Ann heard the first car drive up. Headlights flashed through the kitchen window and snapped off.

"Oh, no," someone whined when the doorbell rang. "Our moms are here to pick us up. Tell 'em we're still working, Vivi Ann."

She went to the door and opened it, surprised to find a stranger standing on her front porch. He was tall and lean, with a shock of precisely combed brown hair. He was good-looking in a starched, buttoned-down way; or maybe that was the impression she got from his yellow polo shirt and pleated khaki Dockers. "May I help you?" she said, struggling to be heard over the magpie din in the living room.

He swept her into his arms and gave her a bear hug that was as tight as it was surprising. When he said, "You don't remember me, do you?" it all clicked into place.

"Luke Connelly," she said when he put her down. "Back from the wilds of Montana."

He smiled. "I knew you'd figure it out if I picked you up."

She didn't quite know what to say to that. Did he have a memory of them that she'd misplaced? "It's good to see you again."

"You, too." He glanced past her to the houseful of giggling girls. "Why do I think your dad isn't home?"

"Sadly for you, you've missed him, but my Bits and Spurs 4-H Club would *love* to hear a real live veterinarian talk to them." She turned. "Wouldn't you, girls?"

A chorus of approval greeted her question.

Luke moved into the group easily, charming the girls as he talked to them about conformation and its importance in choosing a horse. He patiently answered questions until the girls' mothers began to show up.

At nine o'clock, when the house was quiet again, Vivi Ann grabbed two beers from the fridge and handed him one, saying, "You were a good sport about that."

"They treat you like a rock star."

"I know. Isn't it great?"

They sat down on the sofa and put their feet up on the coffee table. A log crackled in the fireplace and thudded off the grate, sending a shower of sparks flying.

"You don't really remember me, do you?" he said. "I waved at you at the gas station last week and you didn't wave back."

"I remember you, of course, but I don't *remember* you. You were the boy who lived next door, my mom's best friend's son. I was too busy with horses to spend any time with you. You moved when I was, what, fourteen?"

"About that. All I really remember about you is every time I saw you, you were on that little Welsh pony of yours, running like the wind. And later . . . it was your mom's quarter horse."

"I still spend most of my time on Clem, trying to reach Mach 1."

"How come you never went away to school like your sisters?"

She laughed. "Oh, I went away. I just came right back. Too much beer and too many boys and too few books. Besides, my dad needed me."

He took a sip of his beer. "My mom figured you'd be here; she even guessed you'd be the 4-H leader."

"How could she know that?"

"She said you were just like Donna. All heart."

"That's nice to hear. I don't remember Mom as much as I wish I did. What did you need to talk to my dad about?"

"Henry left a message that he wanted to talk to me about using my field. Do you know what that's about?"

Vivi Ann launched into her idea about the future of Water's Edge, from the first barrel-racing series to her hopes for team-roping jackpots, then she waited for his response.

"What's a jackpot, exactly?"

"It's like a rodeo with just one event, and the teams get more chances to compete. There are several go-rounds, or heats, I guess, and the guys can pair up in different combinations. Fifty guys can make up two hundred teams, or more. It gives everyone more chances to win."

"It sounds like a good idea."

"I think it is, if we can pull it all together. It'll take some money, which Dad doesn't really have. I'll get a chance to test it with the barrel racing series."

"Well, I'm a new vet in town. I could use some publicity, so how about I donate free vet services for the winner? One hundred and fifty bucks' worth."

Vivi Ann had never thought of sponsorship, but now that he'd said it she saw how natural a fit it was. She could get gift certificates from all kinds of local vendors to supplement her prizes. The feed store, the tack shop, the boot maker. "I'd say that's an ice-cream-worthy idea. Come on." She grabbed his hand and led him into the kitchen.

"Ice cream and beer? Does that go together?"

"Ice cream goes with everything. And thanks to Winona, we've got every flavor." She opened the freezer, revealing at least seven quarts of ice cream.

He looked them over. "Chocolate cherry."

"Perfect." She got his flavor and hers and scooped out two bowls. Then they went back into the living room.

"I was right. This beer tastes like crap now."

She grinned at him. "Don't worry. The ice cream won't last long."

"Will you have another beer with me?"

"Just try to stop me, Doc."

All that week, while Winona saw clients and read contracts, she thought about the future of Water's Edge. As much as she wanted to dismiss Vivi Ann's idea out of hand, she couldn't quite do it. Neither, however, could she embrace it, and on top of all of that indecision lay the irritating fact that *she* hadn't come up with the idea. In many ways, it should have been obvious. Finally, at eight o'clock in the evening she gave up and drove over to the ranch.

Knocking once, she went into the quiet house. A lamp in the kitchen was on; another one in the living room cast light on the plaid, skirted sofa and wagon wheel coffee table. She moved forward, crossed the honeyed oak floor, and stepped onto the oval blue rag rug that had been in this room for the whole of her life. "Dad?"

She heard the rattling of ice and saw him in his study, staring out across the backyard to the purple and black Canal beyond. She'd expected to find him there; it was where he always stood when he was unhappy. For the entire first year after Mom's death, he'd practically been rooted to that very spot. Only Vivi Ann, who'd never been afraid to take his hand and tug, had ever been able to make him move.

"Dad?"

He took a sip of his bourbon, and without turning said, "You come to tell me what to do with my own land?"

She knew right then how this would play out. He'd made his mind up and chosen Vivi Ann—again. Big surprise. Now Winona could either get on board or be shut out. It was an easy decision. "I've got money in the bank. It's probably enough for the steers and a bigger tractor. The chutes don't cost that much. Materials, mostly. We've got plenty of friends who'd be happy to help us build them."

He turned slowly to face her. "You want me to take your money?"

She couldn't tell if she'd touched him or offended him. Or maybe both. "Water's Edge is all of us, Dad."

She waited for him to answer, say something, anything, but he just stood there. It was one of a thousand times in her life she wished she knew him better. "At the very least, I can help. I can manage the finances, pay the bills. And I'll do the hiring. Vivi Ann makes the worst hiring choices I've ever seen. That Travis Kitt is a joke . . . and people in town are talking about how stupid it was to hire him."

"That's what they're sayin'?"

Winona nodded. "About the money—"

He gave her a hard look; there was something behind his eyes, a darkness that could mean any-thing—regret, sadness, anger. She didn't know, had never known, how to read his face. It was something Mom would have done someday, defined him for them, put him in some kind of context. Without that lesson, they had all been left in murky water, and Winona most of all. Before she could guard against it, worry tightened her stomach. She couldn't help thinking that she'd been wrong to offer her money to him.

"I ain't gonna take money from my daughter."

"But—"

"Go talk to Luke. He'll let us run steers on his land. See what he wants to charge us. And hire someone who'll stay. Make sure he knows his way around horses."

Before she could even come up with an answer, he was leaving her, just walking away.

He hadn't even thanked her for the offer.

A week later, on a cold gray day, Winona took her place at the end of the dining room table, seating herself in the chair that had once belonged to her mother. Aurora sat on the left side of the table, and Vivi Ann was on the right side.

Her father sat at the other end, his face still dusty from the day's work, his hair damp and flattened to his forehead by the hat that now hung on a hook by the front door. Only someone like Winona, who'd made a habit of studying his face for the slightest change or emotion, would have noticed the intensity of his gaze. She wasn't sure that he really wanted to go forward with Vivi Ann's plan, but he'd made up his mind, gone public with the news, so there was no way he'd back out. All that was left for Winona now was to protect him and his land to the best of her ability.

"Okay," Winona said. "I've gone over all the loan documents and the finances. The good news is that it didn't cost as much to get things started as we'd originally thought. All in all, we should be good borrowing fifty thousand dollars." She slid the paperwork toward her father. "The loan is collateralized by this property. If the monthly payments aren't made in a timely fashion the bank has the right to accelerate the note, demand full payment, and if none is forthcoming, begin foreclosure proceedings."

No one spoke, so Winona pushed another piece of paper toward him. "That's what you and Vivi Ann will need to generate in income to break even every month. If you'd like, I can act as financial manager for the first year or so. Pay the bills, watch expenses. That kind of thing. And, of course, I'll hire a full-time hand to help out around here." She glanced pointedly at Vivi Ann, then at her father. "I'll figure out a way to make sure he stays awhile."

"Thank God," Vivi Ann said, laughing. "We all know I suck at hiring."

Dad grunted something unintelligible and got up from the table. Without looking back, he headed into his study and closed the door behind him.

Winona sat there, irritated that once again she'd

let herself expect something from him. Gratitude at the very least.

"Don't worry about Dad," Aurora said. "You did a wonderful job. We see that, don't we, Vivi?"

"A fabulous job. Really," Vivi Ann agreed. "He's just scared. I say we celebrate with a little ice cream." She got up and hurried over to the kitchen. Claiming her favorite flavor, she went out to the porch.

Winona and Aurora followed her. Aurora picked her favorite—pralines and cream—and got two spoons.

Winona's favorite flavor wasn't there, so she took a pint of rocky road out onto the porch and stood with her sisters. They'd done this dozens of times over the years, come together on the porch, eating ice cream, and talking. "Hey, who ate my chocolate cherry?" she asked.

Vivi Ann answered, "Luke Connelly dropped by. I didn't even recognize him. He looked so different. Way cuter than I remember."

Aurora threw Winona a sharp look.

"What did he want?" Winona asked, hoping she sounded casual.

"To see Dad. The poor guy came during my 4-H meeting, so I made him talk to the girls. He was cool about it, though." Vivi Ann took another bite of ice cream and said, "He asked me out."

Winona knew she should just stand there and pretend it didn't hurt. It was what she'd always done around Vivi Ann, but this time she couldn't manage the pretense. "I gotta go. I've got a big day at work tomorrow . . . lots of papers to hear. Read. I meant read."

"Me, too," Aurora said. She wrapped an arm around Winona and led her down the porch steps toward their two cars. If Vivi Ann noticed anything odd in their behavior, she didn't remark on it; instead, she called out a goodbye and carried the ice-cream containers back into the house.

As soon as the door banged shut, Aurora turned to Winona. "Are you going to tell her or am I?"

"Tell her what?"

"Don't insult me. You have to tell Vivi Ann you're interested in Luke."

"And make myself look even more pathetic? No, thank you. I *knew* he wouldn't want me. Why did I let myself think otherwise? Who would want the fat girl when Michelle Pfeiffer is standing right there?"

"Tell Vivi Ann. She'll break the date and never make another one."

Winona could almost taste the humiliation of such a conversation; it would be bitter and sour at the same time, like a lime gone bad. "No way. Besides, Vivi Ann goes through men like I go through Post-it notes. Luke is way too quiet for her; you know she has a wild streak when it comes to men. It won't last long."

"You can't count on that. You have to tell her."

"No. And you have to promise not to say anything, either. I'd be mortified if Luke knew how I felt. Obviously he doesn't feel the same way." At Aurora's unconvinced look, Winona said, "Promise me." She knew that Aurora didn't make a promise lightly, and once made, she kept it.

"I'm not going to say anything. It's your life and you're a grown woman . . . but you're making a Godzilla mistake here. You've always had a chip on your shoulder about Vivi. This could turn it into a boulder. And it's not fair to Vivi, because she doesn't know a thing about it. She'd never hurt you if she knew."

"Promise me."

"I have a bad feeling about this, Win."

"Promise me."

"Oh, damn it, okay. I promise. And I won't say another word about it. Except I have a bad feeling about this. You're making a mistake."

"Thank God you didn't say anything," Winona said grimly. "Now let's go home."

In late February and March, rain pelted Oyster Shores. Mud oozed up through the pastures where the horses stood and pooled in brown bogs. Silver streams formed overnight, rushing in gullies on either side of the driveway. The poor purple crocuses that dared to peek up from the mud were soon pounded down by the rain.

The weather matched Winona's mood. Not perfectly, of course. A precise reflection of her emotions would have been a bank of swollen charcoal clouds gathering for a coming storm, but still it was a mirror. So much so that in April, when the sky caught its breath for a few moments and the pale, watery sun came out from its hiding place, she found herself missing the rain. The golden sun pissed her off.

The beautiful plum trees on Viewcrest burst into bloom, and all throughout her garden she saw signs of new life. The velvet-green start of tulips, the first lime-green buds on the tree branches, a row of butter-yellow daffodils. It was a daily reminder that the seasons were changing, that the steel-gray winter was giving way to a bright and shiny spring. Usually Winona loved this season of flowers, when pink blossoms floated through her yard like cotton candy bits, layering the ground, but this year time was not her friend. This year time was measured by the days Vivi Ann spent with Luke.

They had been together for almost three months now, and sometimes, when Winona lay in her lonely bed at night, she found herself counting the days Vivi Ann had stolen from her. Saturday nights at the Outlaw Tavern, dancing with Luke; Sunday mornings after church; evenings around the house, while Dad was there. Winona wasn't stupid, nor was she mentally ill. She knew these imagined moments had never belonged to her, that Vivi Ann had in fact stolen nothing, but still she felt cheated. Every day she woke thinking, *This will be the day she dumps him,* and she conjured scenarios in her mind to follow: how Winona would comfort him, hold his hand, and let him talk, how he'd finally turn to her and see the truth and be saved by it.

And every night she went to bed alone, thinking, *Tomorrow, then.*

One piece of knowledge, bone-deep and certain, kept her going: Vivi Ann didn't love Luke. For her beautiful, reckless sister, dating Luke was a lark, a way to pass the time.

All Winona had to do was keep hiding her feelings and wait for the inevitable breakup.

Now, on this Saturday night, she dressed for the last of the barrel-racing series events with care: black jeans, a long white tunic top, layers of stone-bead necklaces in bright colors, and black cowboy boots. Curling her hair and spraying it to hold, she put on plenty of makeup and then drove over to the ranch.

The driveway was full of truck-and-trailer combinations. Yellow light spilled from the barn's open end; she could see shadows moving back and forth across the light, breaking its beam. Vivi Ann's final barrel-racing event appeared to be a success.

Finding an open spot, she went to the barn and looked in. The honey wooden plaid of the new roping chutes and return alley lined one wall of the arena and the suspended announcer's booth was nearing completion. In the arena, there were at least twenty-two women and girls on horseback. One was racing around the first of three yellow barrels, the rider angled forward, kicking hard, yelling, *Ha!* loudly; the others were probably waiting their turn.

And Vivi Ann stood in the middle of it all, running the insanity like a beautiful, golden ringmaster. The women and girls hung on her every word, treating her like a movie star because she knew how to make a horse run around three barrels in under fourteen seconds.

Vivi Ann saw Winona and waved.

Winona waved back, even as she looked around for Luke. Assured that he wasn't in the arena, she walked down to the farmhouse and let herself in, calling out, "Hey, Dad."

"I'm in the study," Luke answered.

Smiling, she went to see him.

"Hey, there," he said, rising automatically. "You just missed your dad."

She smiled brightly. *Thank God.* "That's okay. I came by to get the bills."

"It's too late to be working," Luke said. "And it's a Saturday night. What do you say we have a beer?"

"You want to go to the Outlaw?"

"I told Vivi Ann I'd be here when she was done, so how about the Grey family back porch instead?"

"Of course," she said, forcing her smile to stay steady.

She got the beers and a warmer coat and followed him outside. On this late April evening, the air was cool but not cold, and as crisp as a new sheet of paper. Down at the bulkhead, a rising tide slapped against the cement and splashed over, dampening the grass. Along the weathered white railing, a row of collected shells reminded her of all the beachcombing they'd done as children.

They sat side by side with the ease of childhood friends, talking about their days. Luke told her about the foal he'd delivered and the wound he'd stitched up; she relayed a funny story about a client who wanted to buy a wolf pup for his son and didn't understand why an animal that lived around here could be considered exotic and therefore forbidden in town.

The more they talked, the more Winona felt that tightening in her belly ease. When she was with him it was easier to believe that there could be a future for them. Even her bitterness toward Vivi Ann softened to manageable proportions. In his presence she was like a stick of warm butter, slowly losing shape. "You said you came home because you were restless," Winona said, her words coming a little hesitantly. She didn't want to probe too deeply, but she'd been plagued by her desire to know everything about him. "What are you looking for?"

He shrugged. "My sister says I'm too romantic. That it'll be the death of me. I don't know. I just wanted something else. And all my life I heard stories about my dad and how he cleared this land by hand and found his place. I want to do something like that."

"I hardly remember your dad," Winona said. "Except that he was huge, and he had a voice like a grizzly bear. He used to scare me when he yelled."

Luke leaned back. "Did I ever tell you I quit talking when he died?"

"No."

"For a year. Third grade. I knew everyone was scared—my mom kept taking me to doctors for tests, and she cried all the time—but I just couldn't find my voice."

"What happened?"

"I got over it, I guess. One day I just looked at my mom across the dinner table and said, 'Pass the potatoes, please.'"

She looked at him, remembering how keen the loss of a parent could feel. It made her ache for the little boy he'd been, and she wanted to reach out and touch him, maybe say how alike they were. Instead, she looked away before he recognized the longing in her gaze. "What did Vivi Ann say when you told her about your dad?"

"Oh, Vivi and I don't talk about things like that."

"Why not?"

"You know Vivi Ann. She just wants to have fun. That's what I love about her. There are enough serious people in the world."

Winona felt as if he'd just cut her down, even if that wasn't what he'd intended. Here she was, right beside him, listening to his secrets, and still he didn't see her.

Men only cared about physical beauty. Her mistake had been in expecting more of him.

"Can I tell you a secret?" he asked.

She couldn't smile. The irony poked at her. "Of course. Secrets are always safe with a lawyer."

He reached into his coat pocket and pulled out a small blue ring box.

Winona wasn't exactly sure how she made herself move, how she reached out and took it from him. Her heart was beating so loudly she couldn't hear the rising tide anymore. Slowly, she opened the lid and saw a diamond ring inside. Moonlight caught its light, made it sparkle like a tiny star against the blue velvet. For a terrible moment, she thought she might be sick.

"I'm going to ask her to marry me," he said.

"But . . . it's only been three months . . ."

"I'm twenty-eight, Win. That's old enough to know what I want."

Something inside of her was dying, turning slowly to ash. "And you want Vivi Ann." Did he hear the brittleness in her voice? She didn't know, didn't care.

"How could I not?"

Winona had no answer for that. Everything came easily to Vivi Ann; love most of all.

"Tell me you're happy for me, Win," he said.

She looked right at him and lied.

Chapter Four

On the night of the barrel-racing awards banquet, Vivi Ann studied her work with a critical eye.

The main room of the Eagles Hall had been decorated from floor to ceiling. She'd hung streamers from the ceiling and draped all the tables in rented red-and-white-checked tablecloths. A table had been set up at the front of the room, with a podium and microphone at its center. Pretty spring flower arrangements—donated by a local florist—gave each table a festive look. On the walls were dozens of posters studded with eight-by-ten photographs of the barrel-racing series participants. In the back of the room, big speakers had been set up.

They were silent now, but soon they'd be pumping dance music into the place.

"What do you think?" she asked Aurora, who had spent most of the day working with her to set up the event. Outside, the weather had cooperated, giving them a bright, sunny late April day with not a rain cloud in sight.

"It's as good as this old place can look," she said.

Vivi Ann thought so, too. "Mae will be bringing the food over from the diner in about an hour."

Aurora put down her hammer and came over to Vivi Ann, hooking an arm around her. "You've done a great job, Vivi. The series was a success, and this banquet will really get everyone talking."

"I hope the girls bring their dads. The first team roping is only two weeks away. I want to get as many guys signed up as early as I can."

"You can't go anywhere in town without seeing a flyer. The ropers will come."

"They better. The barrel racing was a good beginning—it didn't cost much to do—but if the roping doesn't work, I'm screwed."

"Speaking of screwed, how is Luke?"

Vivi Ann laughed. "I never said I was screwing him."

"You never said you weren't. But really, Vivi, I saw you guys at the Outlaw last night. You looked pretty lovey-dovey."

"Everyone is lovey-dovey at the Outlaw. It's the tequila."

Aurora sat down on the table beside her and looked up. "Are you in love with him?"

Vivi Ann knew that she and Luke were a constant topic of conversation in town. Everyone accepted that he was in love with her. On their regular weekend night at the Outlaw Tavern, he told everyone who would listen that she'd stolen his heart over a bowl of ice cream. "One look and I just knew," he always said.

She had no idea what to say to that, how it was supposed to make her feel. She really liked Luke. They had a lot of fun together and lots in common.

But love?

How would she know? All she knew for sure was that they'd been together for nearly three months and he still acted nervous around her, still touched her cautiously, as if he were afraid that passion would break her. Last night, when he'd kissed her goodnight, she'd found herself wanting more, needing more. But how could you tell a good man that you needed him to be a little bad?

"You're not answering me," Aurora said.

"I don't know how."

Aurora gave her a look. "You just did."

Vivi Ann changed the subject before it plunged into murkier waters. "Where's Winona? She's been sort of distant the past few weeks. Have you noticed?"

Aurora got up and began rearranging the floral centerpiece. "What do you mean?"

"Is something going wrong at work? She told me she had better things to do than decorate the Eagles Hall."

"I think she's got some big case coming up."

"Luke said she's giving him the cold shoulder, too."

"You know Win. When she's wrapped up in something . . ."

"Yeah. I miss her around the house, though."

"You'll have to get used to that. You're with Luke now."

"What does that have to do with anything? You're married and I see you all the time. We still go to the Outlaw on Fridays together. Sisters trump men, remember? We made that pact a long time ago. Just because I'm dating someone doesn't mean I'll blow you and Win off. I'd never let a man do that to us."

She heard Aurora sigh. "I know. I told her that."

"You talked about this? What did she say? What's wrong?"

Aurora finally quit messing with the flowers and looked up. "I told her she needed to stop working all the time."

"Good. When she comes tonight I'll tell her the same thing."

"Uh. She's not coming."

"What?"

"This is your night." Aurora paused. "And you've had a lot of them. Just cut her some slack, okay? Let her figure things out. She's a little fragile right now."

"Winnie? She's as fragile as a jackhammer."

"Come on," Aurora said finally. "Enough talk about Win. Everything is ready here. Let's go get dressed."

Vivi Ann followed her sister to the Eagles' rest-room, where they'd left their evening clothes hanging on one of the stall doors. In the hustle and bustle of getting ready, she forgot all about Winona's hissy fit and concentrated on looking her best. She curled her long blond hair on big electric rollers and sprayed it all to stay in place. It only took a little makeup—mascara, blush, and lip gloss—to accentuate her features. Then she dressed in a flowy sleeveless polka-dot dress with a wide crystal-encrusted belt and her good boots.

For the next two hours, she was on top of the world. The banquet was a complete success. Twice the number of people she'd expected had shown up and everyone had had a great time. By the time she'd given away all of the prizes and thanked people for participating, she was already fielding requests for a fall series.

"Next time I'll give away a saddle," she told Luke as he swept her onto the dance floor. "We need really great prizes. And lots of cash. That'll keep them coming back. We could do two jackpots a month instead of one." She laughed at her own enthusiasm. It was like drinking too much cham-pagne, this feeling she had right now, and she didn't want it to stop.

When the banquet was finally over, and the place had been cleaned up and everyone had gone home, she still wasn't ready to leave.

"Let's go for a walk," Luke said, bringing her heavy woolen coat.

"That's a great idea." She snagged a half-empty bottle of champagne and carried it with her. Hand in hand, they walked through town. She kept up a steady stream of conversation. Caught up in the magic of her success, she was a little surprised to find that they were at the Waves Restaurant. It was closed down for the night, but Luke led her out to the deck, where they found an empty cast-iron table with two chairs. Sitting there, in the glow from a single outdoor light, with the Canal waves moving restlessly on the beach below, she said, "Did you see my dad smiling tonight?" She'd been thinking of it for hours, replaying it in her head so she would never forget it. "I know it meant a lot to him. He'd never say anything, but I know he's always felt that he didn't live up to his father's legend. If we make Water's Edge a viable business, it will be his way of leaving his mark on this land, of being another Grey that people remember."

"I think I know another reason your dad was smiling."

"Really?"

"I talked to him last night."

"And that's smile-worthy?" she teased, pouring champagne into the glasses she'd brought with them.

He reached into his coat pocket and pulled out a small box. "Marry me, Vivi Ann," he said, opening the box to reveal a diamond ring.

It was like getting popped in the head by a fast-ball; you knew instantly you should have seen it coming and ducked. She tried to think of how to answer, what to say, knowing that only a yes and tears would make him happy.

"It made your dad smile," he said.

Vivi Ann felt tears sting her eyes, but they were all wrong, not the kind he deserved at all. "It's so early, Luke. We've only just started dating. We haven't even—"

"The sex will be great. We both know that, and I respect you for wanting to wait until you're ready."

"Ready for sex is easy. This is . . ." She couldn't even finish her thought. It was impossible for her to do what he wanted, to put on that ring and seal her fate. She looked up at him, feeling sadness well. She'd thought—foolishly—that not sleeping with him would slow down their relationship, but it hadn't worked. He'd fallen in love with her anyway. "We hardly know each other."

"Of course we do."

"What's my favorite ice cream?"

He drew back, frowning. She could tell that it was sinking in, that he knew this was going wrong. "Chocolate cherry. Dark and sweet."

It was a question she asked every man who claimed to love her, a litmus test for how well they knew her. They always picked some sweet exotic flavor because that was how they saw her, but it wasn't who she really was. Most of the men she dated—Luke included—stared endlessly at her face, declared their love in the first few months, and never thought they needed more. "Vanilla," she said. "Inside, I'm plain old vanilla."

"There's nothing plain about you," he said softly, touching her cheek with a tenderness that only made her feel worse.

"I'm not ready, Luke," she said at last.

He looked at her for a long moment, studying her face as if it were a map he'd only just been handed, the terrain foreign. Then he leaned forward and kissed her.

"I'll wait," he promised.

"But what if—"

"I'll wait," he said again, cutting her off. "I trust you. You'll get there."

She wanted to say, *No. I don't think I ever will,* but the words wouldn't come.

Much later, when she stepped into the comforting quiet of the farmhouse, she looked longingly at her father's closed bedroom door, wishing that she had a mother to talk to about this. Moving tiredly, she went upstairs and got ready for bed, but before pulling back her comforter, she walked over to her window. The ranch lay in darkness before her, lit here and there by a moon that seemed as worn-out as she. She knew that just beyond a row of evergreens lay Luke's land, and she found herself wondering if that mattered. Not in the way her father cared, of course; in a deeper, more meaningful way of connection, of what it meant when two people grew up in the same place, knowing the same people, wanting the same things. Surely a property's border could be a boundary, but was it also a line of common ground?

She turned away from her window and climbed into bed, unable to stop her thoughts from spinning back to his proposal.

If only she could talk to someone about how she felt. Her sisters were the obvious choice, but she was afraid of what they would say. Would they listen patiently and shake their heads and say, "Grow up, Vivi. He's a good man."

Should that be enough for her? Was she wrong to want passion? To dream of something—someone— more? She'd always imagined love to be turbulent and volatile, an emotion that would sweep her up and break her to pieces and reshape her into someone she couldn't otherwise have become.

Was she a fool to believe in all that?

It felt as if something inside of Winona were slowly going bad, like a tomato left on the vine too long. In the past few days, she'd snapped at Lisa, lost a client, and gained five pounds. She couldn't help herself, couldn't control her emotions. She kept waiting for Vivi Ann to call her with the big news that she was engaged.

She wanted to believe that Vivi Ann would laugh at him, blow off his ridiculous proposal. God knew her baby sister wasn't ready to settle down, but Luke Connelly was a hell of a catch in this town, and Vivi Ann always got the best of everything.

By Tuesday afternoon, she was a wreck. This envy of hers was expanding, taking up too much space in her chest. Sometimes when she thought about everything Vivi Ann had stolen from her, she couldn't breathe.

Just when she thought her life couldn't get any worse, Lisa came on the intercom and said, "Hey, Winona. Your dad is on line one."

Dad?

She tried to remember the last time he'd called her at work and couldn't. "Thanks, Lisa." She picked up the phone and answered.

"That idiot Travis is gone," he said halfway through her greeting. "He left without sayin' a damn word and the cabin looks like a bomb went off in there."

"Isn't that Vivi Ann's problem? I don't do house cleaning."

"Don't get smart with me. Didn't you say you'd hire us someone?"

"I'm working on it. I've interviewed—"

"Interviewed? What are we, Boeing? All we need is someone who knows horses and ain't afraid of hard work."

"No, you need all that *and* someone who'll promise to stay for the summer. That's not easy to find." She'd learned that the hard way. Summer was rodeo season and all the men who'd answered their ads refused to commit to long-term employment. They were out of work, most of them, but cowboys were romantic in their way, seduced by the lifestyle, and they just had to follow the circuit. They all thought they'd hit it big at the next city.

"Are you sayin' you can't do it? 'Cause, by God, you should have told us that before—"

"I'll do it," she said sharply.

"Good."

He hung up so fast she found herself listening to nothing. "Nice talking to you, Dad," she muttered, hanging up. "Lisa," she said into the intercom, "I want you to take the rest of today and tomorrow off. I need those help-wanted ads posted at all the feed stores in Shelton, Belfair, Port Orchard, Fife, and Tacoma. And let's double the number of *Little Nickel* ads. From Olympia to Longview. Can you do that?"

"That's not exactly my idea of taking the day off," Lisa said, laughing. "But yeah, I can do it. Tom is working swing this week."

Winona realized how she'd sounded. "I'm sorry if I was snippy."

She folded her arms on her desk and laid down her head. She could already feel a tension headache starting behind her right eye.

She was hardly aware of the passing of time as she sat there, her face buried in the crook of her arms, imagining her life changing course.

She dumped me, Win . . .

Of course she did, Luke, come here. I'll take care of you . . .

Deep in the familiar fantasy, it took her a moment to realize that someone was speaking to her. She lifted her head slowly and opened her eyes.

Aurora stood there, eyeing her. "Quit dreaming about Luke. You're coming with me."

"He's going to propose to Vivi," she said, unable to turn up the volume on her voice.

Aurora's face pleated with pity. "Oh."

"Don't you have some play-nice advice for me?"

"I'm not going to say anything. Except that you have to tell Vivi Ann *now*. Before something bad happens."

"What's the point? She always gets what she wants." Winona felt that bitterness move again, uncoil from its resting place.

"That's poison, thinking like that. We're *sisters*."

Winona tried to imagine following Aurora's good advice, even chose the words she could use and turned them around in her head. All she could come up with was a perfect picture of herself as pathetic. "No, thanks."

Aurora sighed. "Well. She obviously hasn't said yes yet or we would have heard. Maybe Vivi Ann knows she isn't ready. You know how romantic she is. She wants to be swept away. When it comes to love, she'll either be in it from the start or out of it, and Luke hasn't rocked her world."

Winona let herself hope. It was a tiny flare of light, that hope, but it was better than the dark that preceded it. "I pray you're right."

"I'm always right. Now get up. Travis bailed in the middle of the night. We're going to help Vivi Ann clean the cabin."

"What if she shows off her ring?"

"You made this bed of lies; I guess you'll either crawl under the sheets or get the hell out of it."

"I'll go change."

"I'd change more than your clothes, Win."

Ignoring the jibe—or was it advice?—Winona went up to her bedroom and put on an old pair of jeans and a baggy gray UW sweatshirt.

In no time at all they were in the car, driving to the ranch.

Inside the cabin, they found an absolute shambles, with weeks' worth of dirty dishes on every surface and a pile of them in the sink. Vivi Ann was on her knees, scrubbing a stain from the hardwood floor. Even in her oldest clothes, with her long hair tied in a haphazard ponytail, and no makeup on, she managed to look gorgeous.

"You're here," she said, giving them both that megawatt smile of hers.

"Of course we came. We're family," Aurora said, putting the slightest emphasis on that last word. She elbowed Winona, who stumbled forward.

"I'm sorry I missed the banquet, Vivi Ann. I heard it was a great night."

Vivi Ann stood up, peeling off her yellow rubber gloves and dropping them beside the bucket. "I really missed you. It was fun."

Winona could see the vulnerability in her sister's eyes and knew that she'd hurt Vivi Ann. Sometimes all that beauty got in the way and Winona forgot that Vivi Ann could easily be wounded. "I'm sorry," she said, meaning it.

Vivi Ann accepted the apology with another bright smile.

"Did anything happen after I left?" Aurora asked.

Vivi Ann's smile faded. "Funny you should ask. I've been trying to figure out how to tell you guys. Luke asked me to marry him."

"He told me he was going to," Winona said. Her sentence seemed to fall off a ledge of some kind, landing in an awkward silence.

"Oh." Vivi Ann frowned. "A little warning might have been nice."

"It's not the kind of thing a woman usually needs a warning about," Aurora said gently.

Vivi Ann looked around the cabin. "He's so perfect for me," she said finally. "I should be over the moon."

"Should be?" Winona said.

Vivi Ann smiled. It was forced, though. "I don't know if I'm ready to get married yet. But Luke says he loves me enough to wait."

"If you don't think you're ready, you're not," Aurora said.

That awkward silence fell again.

"Right," Vivi Ann said. "That's what I thought. So let's get started cleaning this place up."

Winona felt her breath release in a quiet sigh. Maybe there was hope after all.

And she thanked God for that. Lately, she'd begun to wonder what terrible thing she might do if Vivi Ann married Luke.

A week and a half later, Winona sat in her father's study, at the big, scarred wooden desk that looked out over the flat blue waters of the Canal. On this crystalline day the trees on the opposite shore looked close enough to touch; it seemed impossible to believe that they were more than a mile away. She had just reached for the nearest bill— from the lumber store—when she heard a car drive up. A few moments later, footsteps thudded on the springy porch steps and someone knocked.

She pushed the bills aside and went to answer it.

A man stood on the porch, staring down at her. At least she *thought* he was staring down; it was hard to tell. A dusty white cowboy hat shielded the upper half of his face. He was tall and broad-shouldered, dressed in torn, dirty jeans and a Bruce Springsteen T-shirt that had seen better days. "I'm here about the job."

She detected a hint of an accent—Texas or Oklahoma, maybe. He took his hat off and immediately pushed back the long, straight black hair that hung to his shoulders. Skin the color of well-tanned leather made his gray eyes appear almost freakishly light in comparison. His face was sharp and chiseled, not quite handsome, with a bladelike nose that made him look vaguely mean, a little wild. He was lean, too; wiry as a strip of rawhide. Black tattooed Native American symbols encircled his left bicep, but they weren't from local tribes. These images were unfamiliar to her.

"The job?" he said again, reminding her that she'd taken too long to respond. "Are you still looking for a hand?"

"You know your way around horses? We don't want to train anyone."

"I worked at the Poe Ranch in Texas. It's the biggest operation in the Hill Country. And I team-roped for about ten years."

"You good with a hammer?"

"I can fix what's wrong around here, if that's what you're asking. I'm half white, too. If that helps you make up your mind."

"That hardly matters to me."

"You're above most folks, are you?"

She got the sense he was laughing at her, but nothing about him changed.

"You follow the rodeo circuit?"

"Not anymore."

She knew that her father wouldn't hire this man—a Native American—wouldn't approve of him at all, and yet their ads had been posted for more than a month now and the first roping jackpot was on Saturday. They needed to hire someone, and they needed to do it fast.

Taking off her expensive blue pumps, she stepped into Vivi Ann's oversized rubber boots, which were always stationed at the door. "Follow me."

She heard him behind her, moving slowly, his worn, scuffed cowboy boots crunching on the gravel. She refused to acknowledge her nervousness. It was an unfortunate by-product of the environment in which she'd been raised and she would not succumb. She was above judging people by the color of their skin. "Here's the barn," she said rather stupidly, as they were standing inside of it now.

He came up beside her, saying nothing.

The stall to their immediate left sported a big white poster board decorated with drawings and photographs and ribbons. In ornate, curlicue lettering it read: *Hi! I'm Lizzie Michaelian's horse, Magic. We're a great team. We competed at last year's Pee Wee Days and won a red ribbon for Fitting and Showing and a special mention for cleanest stall. We can't wait for this year's county fair.*

"Well, now," the man beside her said, "that's some homey shit."

Winona couldn't help smiling at that. Moving on, she showed him the tack room, wash stall, and hay storage. When they'd seen all that the barn and arena had to offer, she led him back out into the sunlight.

There, she faced him. "What's your name?"

"Dallas. Like the city. Dallas Raintree."

"Are you prepared to stay for at least a year?"

"Sure. Why not?"

Winona made her decision. That was the point, after all. This decision was hers to make. If Daddy didn't like him because of his skin color, it was time he changed. The more she thought about it, the more it seemed like her civic duty to hire him. And besides, men weren't exactly lining up for the job. If he'd stay for a while, why not? "Wait here." She turned and clomped back to the house, took off her boots, went to the study for a copy of the employment contract she'd written up, and then returned to him. "This job is for room, board, and five hundred dollars a month. You want it?"

He nodded.

Winona waited for more—something besides that stare, that stance—and then started up the hill toward the old cabin. "This way."

Up on the rise, she cut through the ankle-deep grass and went to the front door. "The porch needs work, as you can see. My sisters and I cleaned the inside, though." She flipped on the light and saw the old place, not as she usually saw it, through the sentimental prism of her family's history, but rather, the way it would appear to him.

Wide-plank cedar floors, scuffed and scarred by decades of use; a small living room with newly washed knotty pine walls and mismatched furniture—a faded red sofa, a pair of old wing chairs, Grandma's ancient coffee table—gathered around a river-rock fireplace, stained black from use; an alcove kitchen with 1940s appliances, wooden counters, and a blue-painted table with oak chairs. Through the door in the living room, she could see the bedroom, with its white iron bed piled with quilts. The only room she couldn't see from here was the bathroom, and the best she could say about it was that everything worked. The astringent scent of recently applied bleach couldn't quite camouflage the deeper smell of wet, decaying wood.

"Will this be okay?" she asked.

"It'll do."

She couldn't help staring at his harsh profile. His face was like broken glass, all sharp angles and hard planes.

"Here's our employment contract. You can get your lawyer to read it if you'd like."

"My lawyer, huh?" He glanced down at the paper, then at her. "It says you promise to hire me and I promise to stay, right?"

"Exactly. The term of the contract is one year." She handed him the contract and a pen.

He walked over to the table and bent down to write his name. "What do you want me to do first?"

"Well, I don't actually work here. My sister and dad run the place and they're both gone right now. Just get settled in and show up at the farmhouse tomorrow morning at six for breakfast. They'll tell you what to do."

He gave her the signed contract back.

She waited for something more, maybe a thank-you or a promise to do a good job, but when it was clear he had nothing more to say, she left the cabin. As she went down the porch steps and walked through the tall grass toward the gravel road, she heard him come out onto the porch.

She wouldn't turn around to check, but she was sure just the same: he was watching her.

The Grey sisters had spent Friday nights together forever, and tonight was no different. As usual, they met at the Blue Plate Diner for a quick meal and then walked down Shore Drive to the Outlaw Tavern. Men could come and go in their lives—and meet them at the bar—but dinner with the three of them was set in stone.

Tonight, they were surrounded by the familiar late spring crowd. A few tourists were here, recognizable by the brightly colored designer clothing and their shiny SUVs parked out front. The locals, on the other hand, sipped lemonade, talked quietly while reading the newspaper, and didn't bother even looking at the laminated menus. Most of them ordered Gracie's famous meatloaf, which hadn't actually been on the menu since the early eighties.

Winona reached over for one of Vivi Ann's french fries. "I hired a ranch hand today," she said, wondering what Vivi Ann would think of Dallas Raintree.

Vivi Ann looked up. "You're kidding. Who is he?"

"A guy from Texas. Says he knows his way around horses."

"What was he like?"

Winona considered how best to answer that, then said only, "I don't know. He didn't say much."

"Cowboys," Aurora muttered.

Vivi Ann looked disappointed. "Like meals with Dad aren't quiet enough. I don't think he and Travis said more than twenty words to each other in all the meals we had together."

"Believe me, you're lucky," Winona said. "To me, Dad is—"

"We're not going there tonight," Aurora said firmly. "This is our night to remember we're sisters." She gave Winona a pointed look.

They paid the bill and left the restaurant.

In the warm, lavender evening, they strolled down Main Street.

"It's too bad Luke couldn't come with us," Winona said, trying to sound casual. Lately she spent a lot of time doing just that: trying to act normally around Vivi Ann.

"He had an emergency out in Gorst. Colicky mare."

They turned on to Shore Drive and walked along the waterfront. Streetlamps came on all at once, creating a yellowy carnival atmosphere on the street.

Gradually the pavement ended, turned into gravel. Here, there were no well-swept sidewalks, no pots filled with flowers hanging from streetlamps, no merchants looking to sell souvenirs. There was just a rocky bit of road that led to a big parking lot. On the water side was Ted's Boatyard and the alley that led to Cat Morgan's ramshackle waterfront house. To their right, stuck back in a weedy lot, was the Outlaw Tavern. Multicolored neon beer signs decorated the windows. Moss furred the flat roof and grew in clumps on the windowsills. Beat-up trucks filled the parking lot.

Inside the tavern, they wound through the familiar crowd and around the stuffed grizzly bear that had become the tavern's mascot. Someone had hung a bra from his outstretched paw. Smoke blurred everything, softened the tawdry edges. Behind them the band pounded out a barely recognizable version of "Desperado."

When they reached the bar, the bartender poured three straight shots and set them in front of three empty stools.

"How's that for service, girls?" Bud said.

Aurora laughed and sat down first. "It's why we never miss a Friday night."

Chapter Five

The Outlaw Tavern was filled with the regular Friday night crowd. While the band played a watery, slowed-down version of "Mamas, Don't Let Your Babies Grow Up to Be Cowboys," couples line-danced across the parquet floor. Vivi Ann sat at her usual barstool, swaying to the music. She had a nice buzz going. Swiveling on her seat, she looked for someone to dance with, but couldn't find anyone who wasn't already paired up. Aurora and Richard were back at the pool tables playing a game with some friends, and Winona was deep in conversation with Mayor Trumbull.

Vivi Ann was about to turn back around to the bar when she noticed the Indian standing by the cash register. Anyone unknown would have stood out in this crowd of locals, but she was certain that this guy would be noticeable in *any* crowd. With his long hair and dark skin and hawkish features, he looked a little like Daniel Day-Lewis in that upcoming movie, *The Last of the Mohicans.*

He caught her looking at him and smiled.

Before she could turn around or pretend she hadn't seen him, he was coming toward her. She wanted to look away, but she couldn't make herself move.

"You wanna dance?"

"I don't think so."

He smiled, but it didn't quite change the harshness of his face. "You're afraid. I get it. Nice white girls like you are always scared."

"I'm not scared."

"Good." He reached for her hand, took it in his. She noticed the roughness of his skin—so different from Luke's—and the possessiveness of his grip as he pulled her onto the dance floor and into his arms. The way he did it surprised her; even more surprising was the tiny thrill she felt.

"I'm Dallas," he said at a lull in the music.

"Vivi Ann."

"You got a boyfriend? That why you keep looking around? Or you afraid the neighbors won't like you dancing with an Indian?"

"Yes. No. I mean—"

"Where is he?"

"Not here."

"I bet he treats you like some kind of pretty little treasure. Like you'll break if he's too rough."

Vivi Ann drew in a breath and looked up at him. "How do you know that?"

He didn't answer. Instead, he pulled her close and kissed her.

For a split second—she was sure it was no longer than that—Vivi Ann felt herself giving in.

103

Then someone was pulling her away from Dallas. A group of men crowded forward, pushing her out of the way. They were muttering angrily to themselves and each other, but it was Dallas who held her attention. He looked deadly calm, and when he smiled, she thought: *Someone's going to get hurt.*

"Get on outta here. Vivi Ann don't need trash like you." That was from Erik Engstrom, her third-grade boyfriend.

"Stop it," Vivi Ann yelled. Her voice was like a rock breaking through glass, catching everyone's attention. "What's *wrong* with you?"

"We were just standin' up for you, Vivi," Butchie said, fisting his hands.

"You're idiots, all of you. Go back to your tables."

Grudgingly, the crowd dispersed, walked away. She was left alone with Dallas.

"I'm sorry about that," she said, looking up at him. "We don't get many strangers here."

"I can see why." Smiling as if it had all meant nothing, he leaned toward her, whispered, "Nice kiss," in her ear, and then he walked away, leaving her standing alone beneath the hot lights, feeling unsettled.

"What happened?" Winona said a minute later, coming up so fast she was out of breath. "I came back from the bathroom and someone said—"

"I danced with a guy. Big deal."

Aurora sidled in close. "Way to pick 'em, Vivi. Very classy."

Vivi Ann didn't know what to say. Her whole body felt odd, like an engine idling too fast. "Don't be a bitch, Aurora."

"Me? Never. I know how much you love a man with tattoos." Aurora laughed. "And an Indian, too."

"She danced with an Indian?" Winona asked sharply. "With tattoos? What did he look like?"

"Hot," Aurora said immediately.

Vivi Ann looked away, unwilling to see the judgment in Winona's gaze. "Dallas somebody."

"Like his name matters," Aurora said. "How was the kiss?"

"She kissed him?" Winona said. "In front of everyone?"

Vivi Ann would have sworn her sister was smiling when she said it. "Come on," she snapped. "I need a drink."

Aurora laughed. "I'll bet you do."

When Vivi Ann woke the next morning she felt edgy and restless, and, worst of all, aroused. Putting on her robe, she went into the bathroom and brushed her teeth, then headed down the hallway.

Her father stood by the fireplace in the living room, watching her come down the stairs.

Winona was beside him, already dressed for

work in a blue dress that was stretched tight across her chest.

"Good morning," Vivi Ann said, tightening her robe's belt around her waist.

"It don't look good from where I'm standin'," her father said. "My daughter makin' out with some Indian in front of God and everyone."

She missed a step. She'd known he would hear about it, of course. In a town like theirs, what she'd done was certainly gossip-worthy. She'd just thought she'd be able to tell him her version first. Whatever her version was. "It was nothing, Daddy, really. Tell him, Win. The gossip will die down in no time."

"They were drinking and dancing," Winona said. "You know how she flirts when she's drinking."

"Win!" Vivi Ann said, shocked by her sister's disloyalty. "That's not true—"

"Fire him," Dad said.

"What do you mean, fire him?" Vivi Ann asked.

"We can't. He signed a contract." Winona looked right at her. "You were sucking face with our new ranch hand last night."

This was coming at Vivi Ann too fast. She felt as if she were suddenly in a boat that was taking on water.

"I'm ashamed of you," her father said.

Vivi Ann was shaken by those hard words. She'd never heard them from him before, never imagined it to be even possible that she'd shame him. Years of connection seemed fragile; for the first time she wondered if his love was as conditional as her sisters always said it was, and that frightened her. He was the bedrock, the solid ground of their family. A crack in that was inconceivable.

While she was trying to figure out what to say, someone knocked on the door. She knew who it would be. "Did you tell him?" she asked her sister.

"Half the town was there, Vivi," Winona said, and she should have looked angry, but in that strange, surreal moment, as Vivi Ann's panic poked through, she thought Winona looked pleased. And she hadn't answered the question, not really.

The door opened and Luke stood there, dressed in his Dockers and a plaid flannel shirt, as if this were an ordinary morning visit. But his hair was damp and unbrushed.

She moved toward him, desperate suddenly to undo all of this. "Tell them none of this matters, Luke. You know we love each other." When he said nothing, her panic increased. "We're getting married. Tell Daddy there's nothing to worry about."

"You're engaged?" Dad said.

Vivi Ann turned to her father. "We were waiting for the right time to tell everyone."

Dad finally smiled. "Good. This is over, then. Our first jackpot is startin' in two hours and we got plenty to do to get ready. I'll go talk to our new man, tell him what's what. He'd best mind his *p*'s and *q*'s from now on or I'll fire him. I don't care about no contract."

As soon as he left, Vivi Ann started to pull away from Luke, but he took hold of her hand and wouldn't let her leave.

"Did you kiss him back?" he asked.

"Of course not." She felt Winona watching them from across the room.

He tilted her chin up. She knew the second before she saw his face that it would be creased with worry, that those clean, honest eyes of his would be colored by doubt. She knew, too, that he would believe her because he wanted to.

"Are we okay?" he asked.

"We're fine."

"You've made me the happiest man in Oyster Shores."

It should have been a romantic moment.

But already she knew she'd made a mistake.

You've made me the happiest man in Oyster Shores.

The sentence kept coming back to Winona, playing and replaying. She saw the whole tragic scene in slow motion: Vivi Ann coming down the stairs, her beautiful face registering surprise when she realized what was happening . . . Dad, turning on Vivi Ann for once, telling her he was ashamed . . . and then Luke walking in, his eyes shadowed with doubt and heartbreak.

Winona had wanted to go to him, say, *She always breaks hearts,* and be there for him. She'd even dared to imagine that, to hope for it. Then . . .

We're getting married.

Three words that turned everything around, three words that returned the luster to Vivi Ann's reputation, three words that made the old man smile.

Winona sat in the living room, still as a stone, hearing their conversation but not really listening. She could get the drift of it without the words. They were no doubt exchanging the honeyed words of new fiancés everywhere. Stuff about love and ceremonies and dreams.

They seemed to have forgotten she was here, or they didn't care. She was just another piece of bulky furniture in the room.

She got up slowly, schooled her face into impassivity, and went to them. She almost paused, almost uttered a wooden congratulations, but as she approached them, Luke pulled Vivi Ann into his arms and kissed her.

It was the first time Winona had seen them really kiss, and she stopped, unable to look away.

And then she was moving again, across the living room, onto the porch, and to her car. She drove too fast up the driveway, surprised to find that she was crying as she came to Orca Way. She wiped her eyes impatiently and turned right.

A block later she hit the brake and came to a sudden stop, right there in the middle of the street.

We're getting married.

How could Luke and Dad be so stupid? Couldn't they see that Vivi Ann was acting out of desperation, chewing off her foot to get free of the trap of their disappointment?

"Don't think about it," she muttered aloud. She had to find a way not to care. Aurora was right. Winona had always known that. Sisters trumped men. She *had* to stop wanting Luke or it would destroy them all. But how did you go about such a thing? All the rationalizations in the world hadn't worked. A seed of discontent had been planted deep inside of her, and even now she could feel it putting down roots.

Hours after the roping had ended, Vivi Ann sat on the arena's rail, staring down at the loamy brown dirt. The last twenty-four hours had been among the worst of her life. Gossip about her behavior last night had swept through town like a brush fire. News of her engagement to Luke had put out the flames, but people were watching her closely, whispering as she passed.

"Hey."

She glanced to her left.

Dallas stood in the barn's open doorway, a tall shadow against the tangerine evening light behind him. In the muddy bog of this day, she'd almost forgotten about him. Almost.

"How long have you been standing there?"

"Long enough."

Easing down from the rail, she walked toward him.

"Anyone ever tell you you don't know how to run a jackpot?"

She sighed. That should be obvious to everyone by now. "Did you get something to eat?"

"Yep." He tipped his hat just enough so that she could see his eyes. They were gray as the Sound in winter. Unreadable. "So who's gonna fire me? You or Daddy?"

It had been one day and already she was sick to death of hearing about that kiss. "It's 1992, Dallas, not 1892. I'm the one who is in trouble for it, not you."

"I tarnish your shiny reputation?"

"Something like that. I actually figured you'd quit after that fiasco at the bar."

"I look like the kind of guy who quits?" He moved toward her. "Or maybe you figure all Indians are shiftless. Is that why your friends came after me for kissing you?"

"No one cares that you're In—Native American. It was about me. I was Pearl Princess, for gosh sakes. Four times. And everyone likes my boyfriend. You could have been as white as Dracula and they still would have wanted to kick your ass."

"Pearl Princess, huh?" He moved closer, smiling. "You must have some special talent, then, like tossing flaming batons or singing elevator music?"

"What I have is a boyfriend. A fiancé," she corrected, tilting her chin up. "Did you get that part?"

"This fiancé," Dallas said, whispering now, leaning close. "He know you kissed me back?"

Vivi Ann pushed past him and walked away, saying over her shoulder, "Tomorrow is Sunday. I don't suppose you go to church, but we do, so I don't make breakfast, and it's the only day I feed the horses. Come to the house at four p.m. sharp or I'll toss your supper to the gulls."

When she got into the house, she found her father waiting for her. "Perfect," she muttered, taking off her boots and setting them by the door. She definitely did not want to talk to her father. What would be a good topic? The gossip about last night? Her engagement? The botched roping? Dallas?

"I'm going to bed, Dad. We'll talk tomorrow." Keeping her head down, she headed for the stairs. She was halfway up when she heard him say:

"You stay away from that Indian."

She said nothing and kept moving. In the bathroom, as she brushed her teeth and changed her clothes, she remembered his admonition.

That Indian.

She'd heard the change in her father's voice when he said it, the distaste and the prejudice, and for the first time in her life, she was ashamed of him.

Still, she knew it was good advice.

Chapter Six

May came to the Canal in a burst of sunshine. All along the shore, preparations were made for the coming summer. Awnings were unrolled and washed and readied for use, barbecues were repaired, and trips to the nursery became commonplace. Overnight, the planters on porches and decks bloomed with color. Everyone knew it was illusory, this palpable proof of the coming heat, but no one cared. A couple of sunny days in May could tide the locals through a rainy June.

For the first few days, Vivi Ann did her best to ignore Dallas Raintree. She woke earlier than usual and set out breakfast for the three of them, but she made sure not to be there at six when Dallas stopped by. Each morning she left a list of chores on the kitchen table for him, a list she knew her dad added things to, and by suppertime (which she also avoided) those chores were always finished. Even her father, who judged people harshly, had to admit that Dallas "knows his way around a ranch." By the end of the week, amazingly, no one cared about Vivi Ann's tavern transgression anymore. The tidal surge of her wedding plans had washed all that away.

Oh, people still gossiped about it, pointed to Dallas when he walked into the Outlaw Tavern or the feed store, but none of it mattered anymore. Henry Grey had accepted him as the new ranch hand, and that ended any discussion. When asked in town, Dad was heard to say, *Coulda surprised me, but the Injun turned out to know ranchin'*, and that was the end of that.

Vivi Ann wished she could forget it so easily.

He was in the barn now, on this bright afternoon, standing in the open doorway, sweeping dust and dirt and bits of straw into the sunlight.

It was too late to pretend she hadn't looked at him, so she smiled—more a gritting of her teeth, really—and walked toward him.

"Could you go to the feed store and get some psyllium? We're out. Chuck will know what to give you and he'll put it on our tab. Do you need my truck?"

"A truck I got."

"Good," she said, meaning to walk away.

He smiled.

She hesitated a moment longer and then forced herself to move. She thought she heard him laughing softly behind her, but she refused to turn around.

Just then a big black SUV pulled into the lot and parked. Six preteen girls tumbled out, giggling and talking all at once. Mackenzie John ran toward her. "Are we late?"

"Nope. Go get saddled. I'll meet you all in the arena."

The girls rushed off.

Vivi Ann heard the car door open and close behind her and she knew what that meant.

Julie John sidled up to her, bumping her hip to hip. She was a tall, beautiful woman with spiky blond hair and a ready smile. "Where is he?"

"Who?"

"Christian Slater. Who do you think? *Him*."

Vivi Ann knew it was pointless to pretend confusion, so she tilted her chin a little, just enough to indicate direction.

Dallas was by the shed now, forking cedar shavings into a rusted wheelbarrow.

"Wow." Julie paused, maybe even sighed, then said, "You be careful, Vivi."

"I've been hearing that a lot lately."

"Yeah, well. I'd listen if I were you. Your engagement is the talk of the town. People thought you'd never settle down, and Luke is a great guy."

"I hardly need you to tell me that."

"Really? Because I know about that wild streak of yours. Remember when you were all hot for that transfer student in tenth grade? The guy who got in trouble for drinking at the homecoming game? What was his name?"

Vivi Ann pulled away.

"Just be careful. That's all I'm saying."

"I will. Thanks." Vivi Ann left Julie standing

alone in the parking lot. As she walked toward the barn, she could feel both of them looking at her—Julie and Dallas—but she didn't glance at either one. Instead, she strode purposefully into the arena and began her lessons.

"Your posture is lovely, Mackenzie," she said. "Keep your heels down, remember? And Emily, today we're going to work on your lead changes for the fair. So I want you to collect your mare. You remember how to do that? First you sit deep in the saddle . . . Good. Now bring her head in by drawing back the reins . . ."

One lesson followed another all day, and the constant activity kept Vivi Ann focused. When the last lesson had ended, she rubbed the crick in her neck and walked back to the house, where she made a pot of spaghetti sauce, put it in a Crock-Pot to simmer, and went upstairs to shower.

She was downstairs pouring herself a glass of wine when someone knocked at the door.

He was right on time.

Steeling herself, she opened the door. "Hello, Dallas."

She waited for him to say something, but he just stood there staring down at her. It was the first time she'd really allowed herself to look at him, and she noticed a jagged, nearly invisible scar that ran along his hairline, from temple to ear. It was crooked and uneven, as if a drunk seamstress had stitched it up with an ordinary needle and thread;

she couldn't help wondering how he'd been injured. Without thinking, she traced the ragged lines with her fingertip. She was about to ask him how he'd gotten this scar, but before she could ask the question, he said quietly:

"Be careful, Vivi Ann. I might touch you back."

She jerked her hand away from him.

"You sure you want to stop?" he said. There was laughter in his voice, and something else, a knowing that irritated her.

She turned away, walked into the kitchen saying, "There's spaghetti sauce on the stove and noodles in the strainer in the sink. Help yourself."

She knew he was still there, watching her, so she went to the phone and called Luke, who answered almost immediately.

"Thank God, Vivi," he said. "I've been going crazy waiting for you to call. I thought . . . maybe . . ."

"There's nothing to worry about," she said too sharply. "How about a drink? I need to get the hell off this ranch."

"Perfect," he said. "I'll pick you up at eight. And Vivi: I love you."

She knew what she was supposed to say, what he wanted to hear, but she couldn't do it. Instead, she whispered, "Hurry, Luke," and hung up.

Slowly, she turned to face Dallas again and saw the way he was smiling.

"Good idea, Vivi Ann. Run off to that pretty boyfriend of yours. He looks like one of those lapdog men who like the leash. See if he can scratch your itch."

"I do not have an itch."

But even as she said it, she knew suddenly it was a lie.

And Dallas knew it, too.

The Outlaw was quiet on this weekday night. A few haggard-looking regulars sat on barstools, nursing their drinks. Most were smoking. In the back, a couple of older women with long, permed hair were shooting pool. A pair of Native American men stood back by the restroom door, drinking beers. The jukebox thumped out an old Elvis tune.

Vivi Ann let Luke lead her to one of the small, varnished wooden tables to the left of the bar.

"Margarita?" he asked.

She nodded absently, said, "Rocks. No salt."

When he walked away, she sighed, trying to listen to the music, but she couldn't rid herself of Dallas's voice. His words banged around in her head like stones in a coffee can. Clanging and discordant.

Be careful, Vivi Ann . . .

I might touch you back.

As if conjured by the course of her thoughts, he walked into the Outlaw. Across the smoky interior, their gazes met, and she caught her breath.

Then Luke was back, sliding into view and blocking Dallas out.

"Here you go," he said, setting a pale green margarita down on the wobbly table. "Look who I found playing pool."

Winona stepped in beside him. "Hello, Vivi Ann."

There was something in Winona's tone, an acidity that bore considering, but Vivi Ann didn't care. Frankly, Winona had been a bitch lately, and Vivi Ann was tired of trying to figure out what she'd done wrong to her sister. And all she could think about was Dallas anyway.

She leaned sideways to look at the door, but he was gone.

A quick survey of the tavern revealed that he hadn't stayed.

She stood up. "I need something out of my purse. I left it in your car. I'll be right back."

"I can get it for you—"

"No. Talk to Winona. I know how much you guys like each other." She patted Luke's shoulder as if he were a—

lapdog.

"It'll only take a second." She refused to look at Winona, whose frown had deepened.

"Okay," Luke said. "Hurry back."

Feeling guilty and yet unable to stop herself, Vivi Ann rushed out of the tavern. The parking lot was empty.

He hadn't waited for her.

She ran out to the street and saw him. He was at the corner by Myrtle's Ice Cream Shop. He tilted his head for a moment as if he were listening to something, then he walked into the dark alley beside it.

"Stay here, Vivi," she said aloud. "This is trouble." But when he moved, she followed, staying far enough back that he couldn't hear her. The alley was one of the few places in town Vivi Ann had never been, not even as a kid. It was narrow and dark and thick with litter: beer cans, empty booze bottles, cigarette butts. At the end of it, she paused and peered around.

Cat Morgan's ramshackle bungalow sat on a lozenge of land that clung to the shoreline by dint of will. The yard was a mess and so was the house. Duct tape crisscrossed several broken windows and the front door hung askew. Moss furred the roof and turned the chimney a sick, nuclear-waste green. Over the years, Vivi Ann had heard dozens of shocking stories about what went on in this house.

Music pulsed into the night, a hard heavy metal song Vivi Ann didn't recognize. Through the dirty windows, she could see people dancing.

Dallas went up to the front door and knocked.

The door swung open and Cat Morgan walked out. She wore a black velvet halter top that showed off her big boobs and tight black jeans tucked into silver cowboy boots. Hair the color of newly minted pennies fell in wild curls on either side of her heavily made-up face, and a dozen or so sterling bracelets encircled her wrist.

"Hey," Dallas said.

Cat said something Vivi Ann couldn't hear, then motioned for him to come inside. The screen door banged shut behind them.

Vivi Ann stood there a moment longer, waiting. When it was clear that Dallas wasn't coming out, she headed back toward the nice part of town. In less than three minutes, she was in the Outlaw again, seated across from Luke and Winona.

Safe. Like always.

"I've been wanting to talk about our wedding," Luke said. "And now we're all together. Is this a good time?"

She worked up a smile. "Sure, Luke. Let's talk about it."

"I am telling you, Aurora, something's wrong."

"Wow, big surprise. Here's what's wrong, Win: you're an idiot. Even with your continent-sized brain, you didn't get what was happening right in front of you and now you're screwed. Your little sister is engaged to the man you love."

"I never said I loved him."

"And I never said my husband was boring, but you knew, just like I know about Luke."

Winona sat back and pushed off. They were in the hanging porch swing at her sister's house. The old chains creaked at the movement. "She doesn't love him, Aurora."

"So, what are you going to do?"

121

"What can I do? It's over."

"It's not over till it's over. All you have to do is tell Vivi Ann the truth. She'll make it go away. She won't marry him. I guarantee it."

Winona stared out at her sister's shadowy yard. It was ten o'clock on a weeknight and most of the neighboring houses were dark. Oyster Shores closed up early in the spring. "So all I have to do is admit that I love a man who thinks I'm a good lawyer and a great friend, and tell my beautiful younger sister that my happiness is more important than hers, and—just to add a cherry on the sundae of this humiliation—let Dad know that we won't be getting Luke's land by marriage after all, because pathetic Winona got in the way."

"Jeez, when you put it that way . . ."

"It *is* that way. Maybe I could have done something at the start. I'll admit I screwed up, but it's too late now. I just have to suck it up."

"Do you think you can quit being such a bitch? While you're sucking it up, I mean?"

"I haven't been a bitch."

"Really? Trayna said you bit her head off the other day. And last Sunday after church, you didn't even look at Luke and Vivi. And then there was the barrel-racing banquet you missed. People are going to notice."

Winona sighed. "I know . . . I want . . ." She couldn't even put it in words, this new need of hers. Its darkness embarrassed her. She didn't just want Luke to suddenly love her. That wasn't enough anymore. She wanted it to hurt Vivi Ann, to make her understand—for once—how it felt to lose.

"It's us, Win," Aurora said quietly, reaching for her hand. "The Grey sisters. You can't let Luke mean more than we do."

"I know," she said, and it was true. She *did* know what was right here, what she had to do. She just couldn't do it, and the realization of that hurt as much as the rest of it. Self-control had never been her strong suit. Before, that had meant only that she ate too much and exercised too little. These days, though, her emotions were as uncontrollable as her urges. Sometimes, in the middle of the night, when she found herself hoping some terrible tragedy would befall Vivi Ann (not a death or anything, but something bad enough that Luke would leave her), Winona wondered what she was capable of. "Just watch Vivi Ann, okay? You'll see she doesn't love Luke."

"Ah, Win," Aurora said. "You don't get it. The point is, he loves her."

"He wouldn't if he knew the truth."

Aurora was staring at her now; even in the pale glow of the porch light, her worry was obvious. "You wouldn't do something stupid, would you?"

Winona laughed. It only took a little effort to pull off. "Me? I'm the smartest person you know. I never do anything stupid."

Aurora immediately relaxed. "Thank God. You were starting to sound sort of *Single White Female.*"

"You know me better than that," she said, but much later, when she was home alone, thinking back to the Outlaw, remembering how Luke had looked at Vivi Ann, Winona worried about herself, too, worried about what she would someday do.

From the dining room, Vivi Ann could see the yard, the barn, and the paddock. In the pink light of this early morning everything looked soft and a little surreal.

She told herself she was setting the table, just as she always did, that she wasn't waiting at the window, but when Dallas came into view she recognized her own lie. Schooling her face into neutral, she opened the door. "Hey," she said, wiping her hands on a pink rag. It was the first time she'd been here for breakfast with him and even as she did it, stayed, she knew she was making a mistake.

Be careful, Vivi Ann.

"You gonna leave the dang door open all morning?" her dad said, coming up behind her.

"Come in, Dallas. Have a seat," she said, leading him toward the table.

Vivi Ann served breakfast and sat down between them. When Dad finished his prayer, they each began eating.

Vivi Ann had eaten breakfast in silence for most

of her life. Her dad and cowboys in general were not the most talkative bunch, but this morning it grated on her nerves. She knew Dallas was watching her when she said, "The next roping is coming up. I'm going to need some flyers posted."

"I c'n do that," Dallas said. "Just tell me where you want them."

She nodded. "And that leak in the loafing shed—"

"I fixed that yesterday."

She looked at Dallas, surprised. "I didn't write it down."

"What makes you think I can read, anyway?"

Dad made a sound at that, a kind of snort, and kept reading his magazine.

She forced her gaze away from Dallas's face and looked at her father. "Can you come to Sequim with me today?"

"I got a full schedule, Vivi," Dad said, cutting his ham steak. "Six horses to shoe. Last one's all the way out to Quilcene. You got a horse needs rescuin'?"

She nodded.

"I could help you," Dallas said.

"No, thank you. My fiancé can help me," she said.

"Whatever you say."

She pushed back from the table and went to start the dishes. By the time she was finished, they were both gone and the house was empty again.

For the next five hours she worked tirelessly:

teaching lessons, training the Jurikas' mare, and making up flyers. At eleven-thirty, she returned to the house and made lunch, half of which she wrapped up and put in a picnic basket; the other half she left on the table, wrapped up for Dallas. Then she went over to the yellow Princess phone in the kitchen and called Luke, who answered almost immediately.

"Hey, there. I want to kidnap you today," she said. "I've got an abused horse to rescue in Sequim. We could have a picnic on the beach."

"Damn. I wish you'd called earlier. I just committed to go out to the Winslow place. Their filly is limping."

"Are you sure?"

"Sorry. We're still on for dinner, right?"

"Of course."

"See you at seven."

She hung up the phone and walked outside. Standing on the porch, she saw Dallas turn the tractor toward her. When he saw her, a smile spread across his face, and she knew he'd expected her to come looking for him.

"I don't have any choice," she said aloud, to herself. "It's just work."

She crossed the parking area and stopped beside the tractor.

"It turns out I do need your help picking up that horse," she said. Without waiting for him to answer, she headed over to the truck and climbed in. Ten minutes later, when she'd hitched up the six-horse trailer, she honked the horn impatiently.

As soon as he climbed into the passenger seat, she shoved the gearshift into drive; the truck lurched forward and they were off.

"You know how to load a skittish horse?" she asked after a long while.

"Yep."

Miles passed in silence.

They were coming into Sequim when he spoke again. "Your first jackpot was a joke. You know that, right?"

Vivi Ann didn't know what she'd expected from him: maybe some half-baked sexual innuendo or a silky smooth come-on. Maybe even a comment about Luke. But this . . . She frowned. "So I've heard. Repeatedly. Not that anyone has actually tried to help me."

"I'll help: Your prizes were too expensive, you had too many go-rounds, and your entry fees were too low. Most of all, you aren't building up a mailing list. You need more regulars. I could teach roping. You wouldn't have to charge much. The point is to get the guys used to coming here. Word will spread fast."

She could see instantly how all that would work; she should have figured it out herself. "How do you know that?"

"We did it on the Poe Ranch. We'd have six hundred teams or more for a jackpot."

"And you could do that? Teach roping?"

"I'd need a horse."

"That's not a problem."

Vivi Ann glanced out at the field along the highway, watching the breeze cartwheel through the tall grass, and thought about how quickly things could change shape. A little wind, a little information . . .

"Thanks," she said after a while. There was probably more to say, but she didn't know what it was and he didn't seem to care anyway.

"I'm surprised someone didn't tell you all this before now."

She came to Deer Valley Road and slowed, waiting for her chance to turn left. "People don't take me seriously. They think I'm a Barbie doll. All blond hair and a plastic, empty head."

"That explains Khaki Ken."

She couldn't help smiling at that, but her smile only lasted until he said, "I don't think you're empty-headed."

She glanced at him in surprise and then forced her gaze away. "Thanks," she said, turning onto the hill and shifting gears. The old truck and trailer shuddered and groaned before gathering speed again.

"How many horses have you rescued?"

"Ten or eleven, I think. I took in the first one when I was twelve."

"Why?"

Again, Vivi Ann was surprised. No one ever asked her why. "It was the year my mom died."

"It help?"

"Some." She eased onto a rutted, potholed road that snaked through a thicket of giant evergreens. Slowing, she maneuvered around the biggest of the holes, until they came to a clearing with a pretty little log house, a four-stall barn, and a small fenced pasture. There, she parked. "The Humane Society found this gelding in a really bad way and brought him here. Hopefully the people who did this to him are in jail. Whitney Williams—she owns this place—is at work, but she knows we'll be here." She grabbed a lead rope from the back of the truck and headed for the barn. "Wait here."

Inside, the barn was dusty and dark. At the last stall door, she paused. The black gelding melted into the shadows; all she could really make out were the bared, yellowed teeth and the whites of his eyes. His ears lay flat back and he snorted, blowing snot and air.

"Whoa, boy." Vivi Ann opened the stall door and took a cautious step forward. The horse reared and lunged at her, striking out with his front hooves.

She sidestepped easily and snapped the lead rope onto his halter as his hoof banged into the wooden door.

It took her another quarter hour to get the terrified horse out of the dank, smelly stall and into the sunlight; then, finally, she saw the scars.

Wherever he'd been whipped or cut deeply enough, the hair had grown back in white.

"Son of a bitch," Dallas muttered beside her.

Vivi Ann felt the start of tears and dashed them away before Dallas could see her weakness. No matter how many times she did this, she never quite got used to seeing wounded horses. She thought of Clementine, and how the horse had saved her when she'd needed saving, and it broke her heart to think how cruel people could be. She tried to stroke the horse's velvety muzzle, but he yanked back from her touch, his eyes rolling wildly. "Let's get him loaded and out of here."

"If it upsets you so much, why do you do it?" Dallas asked later, when they were on the road again.

"I should just let them suffer because it's painful to help?"

"You wouldn't be the first to do that."

"This particular horse—his name is Renegade— was the state Western Pleasure equitation winner just four years ago. I saw him win that day. He was magnificent. And now they say he can't be ridden. They were going to put him down before he hurt someone. As if it's his fault he's violent."

"Pain can turn an animal mean."

"You sound like you know what you're talking about."

His voice lowered. "He could hurt you."

"I can take care of myself."

"Can you?"

Suddenly, strangely, Vivi Ann didn't think they were talking about Renegade anymore.

She focused on the road, saying nothing until they were home again, parked in the gravel lot, and unloading Renegade. "Dinner will be a little late," she said, letting the horse loose in the grassy paddock behind the barn. She knew from experience that horses like Renegade needed to be alone. Sometimes they were so broken they could never run with a herd again.

Dallas came closer. "Don't worry about me. I'm taking Cat Morgan to dinner."

"Oh. Well." She took a step back, telling herself she wasn't disappointed. "I guess I'd better get to the house." But she didn't move. She wasn't even sure why until he closed the distance between them.

For a moment she thought he was going to kiss her, and in spite of everything, she wanted him to, but then he whispered against her ear, "We both know Cat isn't the one I want."

Chapter Seven

After dinner at the Waves Restaurant, Vivi Ann and Luke drove back to the farmhouse. The noises of an early June night were all around them, floating through the truck's open windows—

motorboats chugging onto their trailers after a day spent on the flat waters of the Canal, kids laughing in the park along the shore, dogs barking. There was so much going on in town it should have been easy to overlook the silence in the truck, but Vivi Ann noticed every pause, every breath. In the weeks since she and Dallas had rescued Renegade, she felt as if her life had been suspended somehow, as if danger were nearby and she had to be careful, be on her guard against it always. There was a pressure building inside her, heating up.

She looked at Luke, and the smile he gave her was everything a man's smile should be: clear and bright and honest. It should have made her want to smile back, to say something romantic, but the longer she looked into his eyes, the more trapped she felt. The whole of her life with him was suddenly here with her, sitting in his truck, and it was small and unassuming. Not what she wanted for her life at all. She wanted passion and fire and magic. Maybe her mistake had been in not sleeping with Luke. In the beginning, she'd held back because he was serious and she wasn't and she hadn't wanted sex to trap her into a false love, but now she was trapped anyway, and the irony was that he believed their lack of intimacy was a signal of love, a proof of it in some way. Maybe if sex was great with Luke, she'd be swept away and tumble into love . . .

And stop thinking about Dallas.

As soon as they parked in front of the farmhouse and got out of the truck, she went to him, reaching out. "I want to want you, Luke. Right now." She'd meant to say simply *I want you,* but it was too late now to take it back.

She pressed her body against him, rubbing wantonly, and pulled her shirt off, tossed it aside. "Come on, Luke . . ." she pleaded. "Make me crazy . . ."

He kissed her deeply and then drew back, looking down at her. "This isn't how our first time should be. Let's go back to my place."

Vivi Ann felt a wash of disappointment. All that kissing, and nothing. It was as she'd thought: this good, handsome, loving man would never start a fire inside of her. She made herself smile. "You're right. Our first time should be special. Rose petals and candlelight." She bent down for her shirt and put it back on. "And not on a night when I've had one too many glasses of wine."

He put an arm around her and led her toward the house. "I guess I'll have to keep a closer eye on you, remind you that two's your limit."

I bet he treats you like some kind of pretty little treasure.

She couldn't answer, but when they were on the porch, standing in front of the door, and Luke kissed her goodnight, it was all she could do not to cry.

"What's wrong, Vivi?" he asked, pulling back.

"You know you can talk to me about anything, right?"

"I'm just tired, that's all. Everything will be better tomorrow."

He accepted that and kissed her goodnight again. With a sigh, she watched him walk back to his truck and drive away. Then she went into the house and climbed the stairs to her bedroom.

There, she stared out across the darkened ranch, saw moonlight on the barn roof. She was just about to turn away when a flash of bone-white color caught her eyes. A cowboy hat.

Dallas was out there right now, standing by Renegade's paddock, watching her. He'd seen her take off her shirt . . .

She turned away from the window and went to bed, but it was a long time before she fell asleep.

On a sunny afternoon in mid-June, Winona got the call she'd been waiting for: "Winona?" he said. "I need to talk to you about Vivi Ann. Can you meet me at Water's Edge tonight? I'll be in the barn after seven."

She managed somehow to get through the remainder of her workday, writing deposition questions, reading through real estate contracts, seeing clients, but her mind kept going off-road, thinking about that phone call.

He's going to end it. Finally.

Then he'd turn to her for comfort.

When her last client left and Lisa closed up the office, Winona went upstairs to her shambles of a living space. Up here, away from the public eye, her floors needed refinishing, her wallpaper had peeled away, revealing water-stained Sheetrock, and rust coated too many of the fixtures. Ignoring all that, she chose her clothes carefully and dressed in a long velour tunic and jeans. Curling her hair, she sprayed it away from her face and let it tumble down her back. When she looked as good as possible, she left the house and drove out to the ranch, surprised to find the parking lot full of truck-and-trailer combinations.

Finding a parking spot up near her granddad's cabin—beside Dallas's beat-up old Ford truck—she walked down the long grassy driveway to the barn.

Inside, she found a hive of activity: men on bulkily muscled quarter horses, galloping along the rail, throwing well-aimed ropes at running steers; boys, practicing their throws on fake steers; women in the bleachers, clustered together, talking and smoking and drinking beer. And at the center of it all, clearly running the show, was Dallas Raintree. He was helping a man right now, telling him to keep his elbow up to flatten his loop, showing him how.

She found Luke sitting in the stands. "What's all this?"

He took a sip of his beer. "Dallas is giving a

roping clinic. It's been going on for hours. Thirty-five bucks apiece."

Winona studied the arena, counted the men on horseback and the boys practicing with the roping dummy, and did the math. "Wow."

"Everyone here has already signed up for the jackpot tomorrow," he added. "And the women want a barrel race next Saturday."

She sat down by Luke, scooted as close as she dared. It wasn't much, just sitting by him, but it was all she had these days. "I was surprised when you called. You've been too busy with Vivi Ann lately to get in touch with me." She hoped she didn't sound bitter.

"I'm sorry about that. Actually, I wanted to talk to you about Vivi Ann. I hope that's okay. I'll understand if you say no. There's that sisters' code."

"It's okay. Vivi Ann knows we were friends before you two fell in love." She stumbled only briefly over the difficult sentence. "So tell me what's wrong."

"Vivi Ann is acting strange lately."

Of course she is. She doesn't love you.

Winona turned to him, saw the pain and confusion in his eyes, and her heart ached for him. He was no match for Vivi Ann, who treated love as if it were made of stone and hearts as if they were spun glass. She reached over and took his hand. Suddenly it felt as if there was an opening, a crack in the connection between Luke and Vivi Ann. "I love my sister. It's impossible not to. She's like sunshine, but . . . she's selfish, too. Headstrong. Settling down isn't really in her. Maybe she's afraid. Or not ready."

"Sometimes I have trouble believing she really loves me," he said.

"Vivi Ann's emotions are transparent. If she loves you, you'll know it to your bones."

He didn't hear the warning in her words. "I should have said 'what the hell' the other night and dragged her over to the grass and made love to her."

Winona didn't understand. "She wanted to have sex outside?"

"Right in front of the farmhouse. But she wouldn't look me in the eyes. She seemed . . . frantic. I shouldn't have worried about all of that, though, right? I love her and I should have showed her how much."

Winona felt the dying of opportunity; it shriveled up inside, left her feeling small and dry. He wasn't looking to her for comfort. Nothing had changed. Vivi Ann could treat him like crap, and still he loved her. "Yeah. Sure."

"I mean, who cares who might be watching? We're in love."

"Sure," Winona said dully, wishing he hadn't called after all. "Who could be watching anyway?"

As she said it, her gaze fell on Dallas.

• • •

At dawn on Saturday, while Dallas and Dad were gathering the steers from the back field, people began pouring in to Water's Edge. By the time the jackpot officially began at eleven o'clock, almost three hundred teams had entered. Vivi Ann began her day long before the sun came up and didn't stop until the event was over.

Finally, when the last go-round had been run and the prizes had been handed out, she got a glass of lemonade from the fridge and leaned against the warm side of the barn.

The parking lot was a blur of people. Cowboys and their families were busy loading up their horses, putting away their tack, folding up their chairs. The snake of traffic had begun; trucks and trailers moved in a steady stream up the gravel driveway toward town.

Today's jackpot had been more than simply a success. That word was too small and ordinary. This had been a bonanza. A triumph. At last count, they'd earned well over two thousand dollars. And that didn't even count the profits they'd made selling food at the snack shack.

Winona came up beside her, leaned against the barn. Sipping Diet Coke from a plastic cup, she said, "You're avoiding me."

"Why shouldn't I? You've been a real bitch lately. Would it kill you to just say congratulations, Vivi? Way to go? The jackpot kicked ass today."

"I would have said all of that earlier . . . if you hadn't been avoiding me."

"I'm not avoiding you. I just don't want to hear it."

"Hear what?"

"You know."

"He loves you," Winona said quietly, "and he might not see that something's wrong, but I do."

Exactly the words Vivi Ann had been avoiding. "I'm marrying him, aren't I?"

"Yeah. And why is that?"

"Are you asking as his friend or my sister?"

"What difference does it make?"

"Plenty."

Winona seemed to consider that, and then said, "Okay. Let me be your sister for a minute. About Dallas. I'm worried—"

"You're always worried." Vivi Ann pulled away from the barn. "I've got to go, Win. All this craziness is upsetting the animals." She practically rushed for the barn door and ducked inside. At Clem's stall, she opened the door and went inside, resting her forehead on the mare's soft neck. "She's right, Clem, something is wrong and I don't know what to do about it."

Her horse nickered and gently nudged her thigh. Vivi Ann scratched her ears and whispered, "I know, girl. I'll do the right thing."

Then she left the stall, bolting it behind her, and went out the barn's back door and into the falling twilight.

Renegade was at the fence, running wild, galloping back and forth around the paddock, skidding to a stop at either end and pivoting to start again.

"Whoa, boy," she said, going to him. "It's okay. The roping is over. It'll be quiet again soon." She reached out to touch his silky neck, but he reared up and spun away. "It's okay, boy," she said, trying to soothe him with her voice.

"I can't get you out of my head," Dallas said softly from behind her.

She turned. This was what she'd been looking for, why she was here, although she hadn't admitted it to herself until right now. She tilted her chin just a little, waiting . . .

The kiss was like nothing she'd experienced before. It lifted her up and twirled her around and plunged her to the ground. She clung to him as she'd never clung to another human being in her adulthood, as if he alone could save her.

"Vivi Ann!"

She heard her name being called as if from underwater, far away. It came again before she returned to herself and reality.

"I have to go," she said, pushing Dallas away.

He grabbed her elbow, held her close. "I want you," he said in a low voice. "And you want me."

She wrenched free and ran back along the side of the barn. In the parking lot, she found both of her sisters as well as Richard and Luke; they were all waiting for her.

"There you are," Winona said, her sharp gaze scanning the area behind them. Was she looking for Dallas? Did she suspect something? "We thought we'd go out and celebrate the jackpot's success."

"Oh," Vivi Ann said, trying to look casual. "Sounds great."

Later, at just past one o'clock in the morning, Vivi Ann sat on the top porch step, with a sister on either side of her. She had a nice little buzz going, but unfortunately it wasn't enough to muddle her mind. "Who wants to do tequila straight shots?"

"No, thanks," Aurora said. "I need to get home. Richard said he'd wait up for me."

"Win?" Vivi Ann said. "You in?"

"Are you kidding? I'm exhausted."

Vivi Ann put her hands behind her and leaned back, looking past the porch roof to the night sky. On the rise behind the barn, a light came on, a little yellow firefly of color amid the darkness.

I want you . . . And you want me.

She turned to Aurora, who sat beside her, studying the tiny flags on her scarlet nails. "Aurora, how did you know Richard was the one?"

Aurora cocked her head just enough to make eye contact. In the orangey porch light, her face was a mask of light and shadow. "Because he asked."

"That's it? Because he asked you to marry him?"

"No. Because he asked me everything. Was I

141

warm enough? Did I like the movie? Where do you want to go for dinner? Richard is . . . kind. Like Luke." Aurora gave her a little jut of the chin that was its own question. "I dated a lot of unkind men before—you all remember Dylan and Mike. Anyway, I was tired of being hurt when Richard came along."

"Why don't you just admit it, Vivi?" Winona said. "You don't know if you love Luke."

"She knows if she loves him," Aurora said. "And she knows if she doesn't. What she's asking is if she should settle."

"Settle?" Winona said sharply. "That's ridiculous. It's Luke Connelly we're talking about."

Aurora looked at Winona. "You're *her* sister," Aurora said. "Don't forget that, Win."

"How could I?" Winona muttered. "You two remind me often enough."

"It's been the three of us since Mom died," Aurora said, still staring at Winona as she spoke. "Pea, Bean, and Sprout. We can get pissed off at each other and scream and shout and cry—that's okay, that's being sisters. But we stick together. And right now Vivi Ann is asking us some hard questions. Perhaps things should have been said months ago, but they weren't, and now we live with that. You understand? We live with it." She turned and looked at Vivi Ann. "Here's the truth, Vivi: there are worse things than marrying a decent man and hoping to be content."

"What about passion?" Vivi Ann said quietly.

"Passion fades," Aurora said. She tried to smile, but it was false, that smile, and her eyes said something else entirely.

For the first time Vivi Ann wondered if Aurora wore all that makeup as camouflage, to hide the unhappiness of a dull marriage. "But there are better things, too. Is that what you're saying?" As she said it, she couldn't help glancing up at the hill, at that yellow dot.

"Are you sure you want to marry Luke?" Winona said. "If you don't, it's okay. Just admit it."

Vivi Ann forced a smile. How could she admit what she didn't know? It was insane to want Dallas the way she did. There was no way it would last. She'd just have to quit thinking about him. "I'm just nervous, that's all. Marriage is such a big deal."

Winona was watching closely, like a hunting dog on point. She didn't look convinced. Had she seen Vivi Ann's involuntary glance at the cabin?

But Aurora said, "That's only natural," and the conversation landed safely.

"Well, I'm beat," Vivi Ann said. "Thanks for the help today." She hugged each of her sisters, then walked them to their cars and watched them drive away. When they were gone, she went inside the house. At her bedroom window, she looked at the small yellow light burning in the trees. He was up there. Waiting.

"I just won't go," she said as she got ready for bed.

Chapter Eight

Throughout the rest of June, Vivi Ann woke at dawn and made breakfast for three, leaving the meal on the table. Every day she mumbled excuses to her father about why she couldn't stay for the meal. Instead, she focused all her efforts on running Water's Edge, and the ranch was becoming more successful than she could have imagined. All of the stalls were full now, and there was a waiting list. Vivi Ann's classes and clinics were full, too, as were Dallas's. For the first time in her father's life, he was shoeing horses only when he felt like it. The rest of the time he spent working on the ranch, doing things that had been overlooked for years—like painting the fences and repairing the dock.

Vivi Ann should have been on top of the world, and in many ways she was. She felt stronger these days, more sure of herself. The only problem was Dallas.

Whenever she saw him, or thought of him, she mentally repeated her vow: *I won't go to him.* She used these words as a talisman. When she saw Dallas out by the fence, wearing a sweat-dampened T-shirt, hammering a new nail in place, and then looking up suddenly, smiling at her—

I won't go to him.

Or when he paused in mucking out a stall and rested a tattooed bicep on the pitchfork's handle, staring at her—

I won't.

It had taken a toll on her, all that concentrated avoidance. More than once in the past month she'd had to make excuses for her odd behavior. Several times she'd told Luke and her sisters that she felt sick, and, in the way of lies, it had become the truth. By mid-July, a headache had taken up permanent residence in her left temple, and longing had tightened her chest until sometimes she could barely breathe. No matter what she told herself or how fast she moved during the day, her desire for Dallas remained, growing along with her guilt.

She was a wreck. She expected her sisters to comment on her uncharacteristic silences, but they didn't seem to notice. Now the family was gathered in the living room on a Saturday night, waiting for Richard to show up so they could go to the Silverdale Fairgrounds. Tonight was the last night of the county rodeo, and for the first time in years, Vivi Ann hadn't entered. She was simply too busy to barrel-race anymore.

"What do you think of that, Vivi Ann? Vivi?"

She looked up, realizing too late that she hadn't been paying attention and everyone was looking at her.

"Do you feel okay?" Aurora asked.

"I've got a headache," Vivi Ann answered, rubbing her temple.

"Do you want some aspirin?"

"No, thanks."

"Maybe you should bag the rodeo," Winona said, watching her. Lately Winona was *always* watching her. "It'll be a late night and you don't want to miss church in the morning."

"But Luke is supposed to meet her there," Aurora said.

That did it. She couldn't handle seeing her fiancé. It was becoming harder and harder to be with him. Every quietly respectful kiss made her want something more. Someone else. She couldn't stand how guilty she felt every time he told her he loved her.

"Winona is right," Vivi Ann said. "The last thing I need tonight is to stay out late. Maybe some sleep will help. You all better go on without me. Tell Luke I didn't feel well."

"You sure?" was Dad's contribution to the conversation. It wasn't much, just two words that reminded her the Grey family always went to the Silverdale rodeo together. Another thing she couldn't make herself care about lately. "I'm sure."

And with her father's nod, it was over.

When Richard finally arrived, Vivi Ann walked them all out to his huge Suburban and said goodbye. Back in the house, she poured herself a glass of wine and ran a nice, hot bath.

She stretched out in the claw-foot tub and leaned back against the slick porcelain. The sweet scent of lavender drifted up from the water. One by one, the muscles in her body relaxed, until she felt completely languid. By nightfall, she'd had a few glasses of wine and the headache was gone. Best of all, she hadn't allowed her mind to drift toward Dallas at all.

Much later, when it was quiet and dark and she was in bed reading, she noticed a noise. At first it sounded like the beat of a heart: pa-*dum,* pa-*dum,* pa-*dum.* Nice and even and slow.

She sat up, listening. It was a horse, running along the fence line. Coyotes?

Putting on a robe, she got up and hurried to her bedroom window. The dark ranch lay stretched out before her. Even with the moonlight, it took her a while to locate the running horse. Renegade.

He was only a shadow from here, moving along the rail in an easy lope. She sensed him more than saw him; all she could really make out was a hat, colored by the moon to look like bone, set on hair too dark to be seen.

She knew she shouldn't go, just as she knew she would. Tightening her terrycloth belt, she went down the stairs and crossed the yard, careful to stay in the shadows.

Dallas was riding Renegade bareback.

Only riding seemed too ordinary a word. Vivi Ann couldn't believe how effortless he made it look, how he cued and turned and guided the gelding with movements so slight she couldn't see how he did it.

"Hey, boy," Dallas said quietly. "You remember all this, don't you? A champion doesn't forget."

Vivi Ann stood hidden in the shadows for almost an hour, unable to look away, until finally she heard Dallas say, "Whoa, Renegade."

The horse came to an abrupt stop and Dallas slid off in a single fluid motion. Exchanging the bridle for a halter, he petted the horse for a while, and then walked away, up the hill.

At his cabin, a light came on. Like the Dungeness Spit lighthouse that both showed mariners the way home and warned of dangerous shoals.

And then she was moving, following him. With each step, she told herself that this was a mistake, coming up here, that she was seeing something in him that wasn't there, but none of that mattered now. It felt inevitable, this moment, this succumbing, as if the choice had been made long ago.

Without bothering to knock, she opened his cabin door and saw him standing by the sofa, drinking a beer. "Just once," she said, hearing the cracked pleading in her voice, the fear and the excitement. Everything about this night felt impossible, as if she'd found this place that lay parallel to the real world, that had all its tastes and smells and desires, but none of its rules. In this new world she could be brazen and sexy and bold. Just for this one night. "We'll do it once and get it out of our systems. No one will ever know."

"I'll be your dark secret, huh?"

Vivi Ann nodded, moved toward him.

He swept her into his arms and carried her to the bed, where he pushed the pile of her grandmother's quilt aside and laid her down. Wrenching his Levi's open, he shoved the jeans down his bare legs and kicked them aside, then pulled off his shirt.

Scars covered his chest; one ended in a coil of puckered flesh at his rib. Moonlight softened the marks, made them look silvery and almost pretty, but she'd seen enough abused horses to know what she was seeing. "My God, Dallas . . . what—"

He kissed her until she couldn't breathe any-more, couldn't claim to own even the smallest por-tion of her body. He took it all from her, forced her to want him with a desperation that was so raw it hurt. When he pulled off her clothes and rolled her beneath him, she opened herself up shamelessly, crying out his name and clinging to him. Nothing mattered except his body and hers and how alive he made her feel.

Vivi Ann woke in the middle of the night, wanting him again. She rolled over to kiss his shoulder and discovered that she was alone in bed.

She pushed the pile of covers away and reached for the robe that lay in a heap on the floor.

She found Dallas on the porch, sitting on the top step, drinking a beer.

She sat down beside him. "Did I wake you up? Kick you in the head or something?"

"I don't sleep."

"Everyone sleeps."

"Do they?"

It was a reminder not only that she didn't know him, but that she was a small-town girl in a big world. She stared out over this ranch that suddenly looked unfamiliar. She knew she should get up, say thanks for the great sex, and go back to her life. But even as she imagined forming those hard, sharp words, she remembered the softness of his tongue on her body, the way he'd made her cry out in pleasure.

"I should go," she said finally.

He just sat there, staring out over the fields. "Take off your robe, Vivi."

She shivered at the way he said it. In some distant part of her (grown smaller in the space of this one night; the old Vivi Ann) she wanted to deny him. She had to get back to the house. Come dawn, she'd be missed. "We said just once," she whispered, hearing how hollow she sounded, how unconvincing.

"You said it. I didn't."

He was on his feet in an instant, standing in front of her, untying her robe.

"This is crazy," she said, feeling the terrycloth slide down her body.

"Crazy," he murmured, kissing her throat, the swell of her breasts, the valley between.

"Just once more," she said, closing her eyes.

The last thing she heard before he kissed her was laughter.

The next morning, when Vivi Ann woke in her own bed, feeling bruised by last night's passion, she knew she'd been changed. All her life she'd pretended to be wild, while really she'd been safe and protected. Riding a horse at breakneck speed was nothing, easy; all she'd ever had to do was yank back on the reins and her mount would slow to a stop.

There were no reins to pull back on now, no way to slow down with Dallas. She might not know him well—at all, really—but she knew that there were only two speeds available to them. Stop or run.

And she had to stop.

She got out of bed and dressed for church. With her hair drawn back from her face and caught up in a white scrunchie, and in her ankle-length jean dress with a wide belt, she looked absolutely normal.

She went downstairs, left a plate of food in the fridge for Dallas, and then went to find her dad. Together they walked out of the house and up to the truck. "How was the rodeo last night?"

"Luke was worried about you. He said he was gonna call."

"Really? I must not have heard the phone. Are you still going to Jeff's house after church?" It was all she could think to ask. She wanted to change the subject.

"Yep."

They drove to church in silence. Outside, in the parking lot, they met up with Luke and the rest of the family and went to their regular pew, where Vivi Ann felt hemmed in, trapped as she was between Luke and her father. All through the service (*God's path for us is righteousness; sin is the bend in the road that will lead us astray if we are not ever vigilant against its dark temptations*), she felt exposed, guilty. She was sure that any minute Father MacKeady would point to her and shout out, *Sinner!*

When the service was over, she bolted from their pew and rushed down to the relative peace of the church basement, where refreshments and coffee were being served. There, she moved among her friends and neighbors, trying to let their voices drown out the roaring noise of her own guilt. All the while, as she talked to friends and made silly jokes and sipped coffee, she was thinking: *Dallas.*

Just that, his name. Over and over again.

Every passing minute tightened something in her, until she began to think that she might break apart. Only he could loosen her.

Maybe just once more.

"There you are," Luke said suddenly, putting an arm around her and drawing her close to his side.

Then Winona and Aurora showed up.

"Let's go," Aurora said. "I'm starving."

Vivi Ann let herself be swept along by Luke and her sisters as they left the church and walked the two blocks to Winona's house.

There, they gathered in the living room for mimosas and homemade cinnamon rolls. The whole house smelled of spices and scented candles. Everywhere Vivi Ann looked there was a pretty little decoration, a possession. Was that what life was supposed to be—a search for things to own, a decorating of otherwise empty rooms? She went to the sunroom and stared out at the garden, which was a riot of tamed, clipped color. Every plant had been shaped to match Winona's precise vision.

It should have been beautiful, and was, in a controlled way that wasn't what Vivi Ann wanted at all. It was like their mother's garden had once been—tended with care and planted with precision, rows that were even and straight and true.

She glanced sideways, wishing she could see the ranch from here, wondering what he was doing now. Behind her, she could hear her sisters talking to her, but it was just noise. She remembered last night in vivid detail, wanting it—him—again.

"Vivi? Are you listening?" It was Winona, and she was practically yelling.

"We're talking about where to have your reception," Aurora said sharply.

Slowly, Vivi Ann turned around and found them all staring at her. "Oh. Sorry. I was looking at the garden. It's so pretty, Win."

Luke pulled her into his arms. "I'm worried about you, baby."

"We all are," Aurora said.

"The ranch is too much for her," Winona said. "Maybe we need another hand to help out."

They were closing in on her—Aurora, who saw too much, was frowning, while Winona, who wanted too much, looked pissed off. And there was Luke . . . whom she wanted to love, should love . . . but couldn't. They were gathering forces, giving each other concerned glances, and she knew she should feel enfolded by the concern, comforted, but instead she felt claustrophobic. All she wanted to do was run up to the cabin again and be with Dallas; that need terrified her. She had to stop this madness *now,* before it burned her to ash. "Maybe we should go somewhere, Luke. Just the two of us. See how we get along twenty-four hours a day."

"They call that a honeymoon," he said, smiling. "I was thinking of Paris. I know how much you want to see the world."

"Do I?"

She could envision their trip in the smallest detail: they'd have a moderately priced hotel room—maybe with a view of the Eiffel Tower if they were lucky—and they'd base their dining decisions on recommendations from a tourist guide. They'd see every sight the City of Lights had to offer, and they'd talk easily while they walked down the Champs-Élysées or along the Seine. Everything would be romantic, but there would be no ripping off each other's clothes in impatience, no days spent naked in bed making love. "I really don't feel well," she said, feeling Winona's narrowed gaze on her. Vivi Ann was careful not to look at her sisters.

"I'll walk you home," Luke said.

"No," Vivi Ann said sharply, then softened her tone with a smile. "Please." She heard the tinny desperation in her voice and there was nothing she could do about it. If she stayed here another minute, she'd explode. "It's a beautiful day for a walk."

"Let her go," Winona said, surprising them all.

"You sure?" Luke asked Vivi Ann.

"I'm sure." She pressed up onto her toes and gave him a quick kiss, pulling back before he could deepen it. "See you all later."

She was careful to walk slowly, as if she really felt bad. Outside, she kept up the pretense, walking down First Street toward the water. It wasn't until she came to the corner and ducked into the shade of an old tree that, finally, she could breathe.

And there he was, standing in front of the Waves Restaurant, looking recklessly out of place amid the gnomes in the yard. He wore his dusty white cowboy hat drawn low on his head, so low that even with the sunlight shining down on him she couldn't make out his eyes. The bold black tattoos stood out on his tanned bicep, a sharp contrast to the overwashed gray cotton of his T-shirt.

She pretended not to see him and kept walking, but when she heard his footsteps following her on the sidewalk across the street, she walked faster.

At Water's Edge, she went inside and shut the door, hearing it click; a brass mechanism that separated her from a world she hadn't even known existed before. "Dad? Are you here?"

There was no answer.

Alone in the house, she stood there, waiting.

Then she heard footsteps on the porch . . .

The door handle began to turn.

He came into the house like a hot summer wind. She stumbled sideways and hit the dining table. He pinned her against the heavy wood, pressed his hips into hers, and kissed her so long and so hard she couldn't breathe enough to tell him to stop. She felt his hand slide up her bare leg, balling the fabric of her skirt in his fist. His hand slipped into her underpants.

She fumbled at the buttons of his jeans, ripping them open, shoving them down to his knees. Her hands were desperate on his body, pushing, pulling; her need was so intense she couldn't remain quiet, and when he pushed her back onto the table and thrust deep inside her body, she cried out his name.

When it was over, and she'd come back to herself, she felt shaky and off balance. She lay there, with her skirt bunched up around her waist and her panties around her ankles, on her mother's dining room table. And she knew she should be ashamed. "This is crazy," she said quietly. "I can't live with it. The lying . . ."

He touched her face with a gentleness that surprised her. "It won't last long, Vivi. We both know that. In the end, you'll marry Khaki Ken and no one will ever know about us. So come to my bed."

"Okay," was all she could say. It was the wrong answer—immoral and hurtful and wrong—and still she took his hand.

Chapter Nine

That summer, Vivi Ann learned to lie. Throughout the rest of July and August, she worked long hours at the arena, sometimes alongside her father, but more often on her own, teaching lessons or training horses or scheduling the many uses of the barn. She celebrated her twenty-fifth birthday at one of her own barrel races, and for the first time in her life she over-heard someone say she was dedicated.

Dallas had taught her a lot about running a ranch. Water's Edge now hosted some of the best jack-pots and clinics in the western half of the state. Ropers and barrel racers and cutting teams came regularly to compete for money and prizes. Afterward, they went home and told their friends and more people came.

During the hot, sunny days, Vivi Ann made sure to be her old self. The Pearl Princess. She still cooked three meals a day and served each one at the dining room table to two men who rarely spoke. At first she'd been careful at these meals not to make eye contact with Dallas, afraid that her father would see that which she tried so hard to conceal, but in truth, her dad hardly paid her any attention either way.

And thank God for that, because she was addicted to Dallas; it was as simple—as com-plex—as that. At least five nights a week she went to his cabin in the middle of the night. They tum-bled into her grandmother's brass bed like horny teenagers, making love until dawn.

Or maybe it wasn't making love. Maybe it was just sex. She wasn't sure and, to be honest, she didn't care. He was booze and heroin and cigarettes, all wrapped into one: the bad habit she couldn't quit. She learned to exist moment-to-moment, always on the lookout for an opportunity to be with him.

Like now.

It was a gorgeous Friday night in late August: the opening of the Oyster Days festivities. Preparations for the parade and street dance and charity auction had been under way for weeks. In years past, Vivi Ann would have been knee-deep in all of it; this year, though, she'd made one excuse after another until this morning Aurora had come over and taken her hand and led her to the truck, saying simply, "Enough."

So Vivi Ann was on Main Street with her sisters, going over the final details. There were people everywhere, hanging banners, putting up signs, setting up booths, and the police were beginning to block off various streets for Sunday's parade. Down at the end of the street, the band was warming up. "Testing one, two, three . . ." rang through the darkness.

Vivi Ann had done it all a hundred times, and yet tonight it grated on her, irritated her. The band was too loud, the to-do list too long, and Winona was watching her every move like a lioness on the hunt in tall grass.

"What?" Vivi Ann finally snapped at her.

"You're a little testy today," Winona said. "Luke says you never want to talk about the wedding. Why is that?"

"Why do we always have to talk about Luke?" Vivi Ann said. "I'm sick to death of wedding plans and I'm sick of your constant nagging. Go find yourself a damn boyfriend and leave mine the hell alone."

"Maybe you're the one who should leave Luke alone."

Aurora was between them in an instant, the referee. "We're in public, you two."

"But Vivi Ann loves to be the center of attention, don't you, Vivi?" Winona said.

Vivi Ann couldn't take this crap now. "Look, Win—"

"No, *you* look. You just take and take and take, and you don't think about anyone else, do you? You don't care about anyone except yourself."

"Winona, don't," Aurora warned.

"Don't what? Don't tell Miss Pearl Princess the hard truth?" Winona looked at her. "You're spoiled and you're selfish and you're going to break Luke's heart and you don't even care. And then he won't be able to love anyone else, because *you'll* always be there first." On that, Winona turned on her heel and shoved her way into the crowd, disappearing.

The accuracy of Winona's attack left Vivi Ann shaken. "She's right," was all she could say when it was over. She felt sick to her stomach; ashamed and afraid.

"I know she didn't mean all that. I'll go talk to her."

Vivi Ann knew she should go with Aurora, find Winona and work this out, but God help her, when

160

Aurora said, "We'll meet you at the street dance," Vivi Ann thought of Dallas.

She knew where he would be. He spent his Friday and Saturday nights at Cat's. Everyone in town knew that. The gossip was that he played a mean game of poker, and that he outdrank every man there.

"You should go to the street dance," she said aloud after Aurora had left. But she couldn't follow her own advice. The need for him was a fire in her blood. She started walking toward the waterfront, trying to keep in the shadows. Fortunately there was so much going on in town that no one seemed to notice her.

At the end of the alley, Cat Morgan's house sat like a drunken old man on the edge of the sea, leaning and haggard-looking. The porch was askew, the windows still duct-taped. But she could see the party going on inside; shadowy people danced in front of the open windows. Music— AC/DC or maybe Aerosmith, something with a thudding beat—pulsed so loudly she could hardly hear the waves slapping at the bulkhead.

Vivi Ann had never in all her life gone up to the front door of this house. There were two kinds of people in Oyster Shores: those who went to church on Sundays and those who partied with Cat Morgan. This house was off-limits to people who cared about their reputation. From the moment Cat had first come to town about ten years ago, she'd carved out this place for herself on the fringes of respectable life. Everyone knew she hosted parties with booze, sex, and drugs, but she paid her taxes and stayed where she belonged: in the dark. Mothers used her as a cautionary tale with their impressionable daughters. Watch out for boys and booze or you'll end up like Cat Morgan.

Steeling herself, Vivi Ann crossed the uneven, scrubby patch of lawn and went up to the front door.

"Tell me that ain't Vivi Ann Grey comin' up my steps."

The shadows on the porch were so thick that it took Vivi Ann a moment to make out who had spoken. Then she caught a glimpse of fake reddish hair.

Cat stood in the corner of the porch, smoking a cigarette. Dressed in tight black jeans and a tuxedo jacket cinched at the waist with a glittering silver belt, she looked like she belonged on an *Urban Cowboy* soundstage. Shadows accentuated the lines on her face. Vivi Ann had no idea how old she was—maybe forty?

"I'm . . . uh . . . looking for Dallas Raintree. He works for me. We have a sick horse."

"Sick horse, huh?" Cat took a long drag on her cigarette and exhaled smoke. "I think you'd need a vet for that."

"Would you mind getting him for me? I'm in kind of a hurry."

Cat eyed her for a long moment, then finished her cigarette and put it out. "I'll tell Dallas about the sick horse. I'm sure he'll come a-runnin'. That man has a soft streak for animals."

Vivi Ann thanked Cat and walked back through town to her truck, then drove home and parked deep in the trees by his cabin.

In Dallas's bedroom, she stripped out of her clothes and climbed into bed, waiting impatiently.

Only a few minutes later, she heard a truck screech to a stop outside, then a metal door banged shut.

Dallas pushed open the cabin door so hard it cracked against the wall, making the whole room shudder. "What in the *hell* were you thinking?"

"I told her I was looking for you. What's wrong with that?"

"Get out of here, Vivi. We're done."

She didn't understand. "Why are you being like this?"

"Just leave, Vivi. I got enough regrets."

She climbed out of bed, followed him, grabbed his arm. "Dallas, please—"

He grabbed her wrist so tightly she felt it bruise. "Go back to Khaki Ken and the church group and all those people you care about."

"What if I care about you?" The question was out before she could stop it.

"Don't be a fool, Vivi Ann."

"I love you, Dallas." For the first time in her life, those words came effortlessly.

"Ah, Vivi," he said, gentling his hold. "You're so naïve . . ."

She smiled up at him, knowing what she had to do now. Those words had changed everything, just as they were supposed to. "Kiss me, Dallas," she whispered. "You know you want to."

On this first night of Oyster Days, the streets were crowded with people, tourists and locals alike. A band was set up in the bank's parking lot. The stage was elevated, allowing the musicians to look out over the throng dancing to their music, all the way to the row of food and craft vendors, to the lights along Shore Drive.

Winona was trying to be a good sport, but she was so angry that even dancing with Luke was no fun.

"Do you think I should take waltzing lessons for the reception?"

She rolled her eyes at that. "Have you had any indication that Vivi gives a shit about this wedding?"

"She's not one for ceremonies. She likes quiet events."

"Are you kidding me? *Vivi?*" Before she could say more, someone pushed up between them.

"Sorry, guys," Julie John said. "Our foal, Peanut, is colicky, I think. Kent is walking him, but we're worried. I'm sorry, Luke. I know you're having fun, but—"

"Don't worry about it," he said. "I can be at your house in fifteen minutes. Tell Kent to keep up the walking. Whatever you do, don't let Peanut lie down." He turned to Winona. "Tell Vivi I'll come find her when I'm done."

After they left, Winona stood there staring out at the crowd, feeling more alone than should have been possible in this town of hers.

"There you are," Aurora said a moment later, coming up beside her. "I've been looking all over for you."

"Trying to make peace again, Aurora? I think you're in the wrong family for that."

"You can't keep going like this, Win. We're falling apart because of you."

"Do you think I don't know that?" Winona said, feeling as if the admission were tearing something inside of her, something that had always been intact before. "She's my sister, and I love her, but . . ."

"You love him, too. I know. But you have to live with it somehow. You chose this."

Winona shook her head. "Not this. If she loved him, I could accept it. I could maybe get past it."

"Could you?"

She pulled away. "I'm out of here. Tell Luke and Vivi Ann I said good luck and have fun." She was running now, feeling the start of tears.

What was wrong with her? Why couldn't she let go of this? The jealousy was killing her and hurting the thing she cared most about: her family.

I'm worried about what you'll do. Aurora had voiced that fear long ago, and it came back to Winona now.

"Winona?" someone called out.

She came to a breathless stop on the sidewalk and wiped her eyes, then turned—smiling—toward the speaker.

Myrtle Michaelian stood there. "Your father is making a scene at the Eagles Hall. I think someone should drive him home." Myrtle frowned at her. "Are you okay, honey?"

Winona swallowed hard. "Sure, Myrtle. Why wouldn't I be?" She turned away and walked briskly toward the Eagles. Before she'd even stepped through the door and into the smoky interior, she heard her dad telling one of his many Vivi-Ann-is-perfect stories in a slurred voice.

"Come on, Dad," she said, taking his arm. "It's time to go home."

He was too drunk to put up much of a fight. She guided him out of the building and into her waiting car. "You should cut back on the whiskey, Dad."

"Saysh the girl who eats everything in sight."

Winona said nothing more to him on the drive to the ranch. There, she helped him into his room, watched him collapse on the bed and start snoring.

"You're welcome," she said, pulling off his boots and covering him with a blanket.

Sighing, she left the house and returned to her

car. As she drove up past the barn, she noticed Vivi Ann's truck parked deep in the trees by Grandpa's cottage. Dallas's truck was there, too.

If the moon had been smaller, or its light muted by clouds, she might not have noticed it at all. No one would.

Winona slammed on the brakes and sat there, staring at the trucks parked side by side. In that moment, memories locked into one another, brush-strokes of color formed a solid image. She remembered several times Vivi Ann had been missing or hadn't shown up as she'd promised to. And all the while Luke waited for her, trusting her.

Could it be that Vivi had lied to them all?

The kiss. Had it been the start of something?

Driving onto the grassy road, she parked up beside the trucks and went to the front door, opening it without a knock, calling out, "Hello?"

She saw them in a rush of images: Dallas, naked in the bed, lying on his side . . . with a chest full of ugly, misshapen scars, and a tattooed arm slung possessively around her sister. Even from here, she could see the way they looked at each other, touched each other; the whole cottage smelled of sex and lust and candle wax.

He sat upright at her entrance, looked right at Winona.

Vivi scrambled to cover her nakedness. "I can explain."

Winona wanted to laugh. She held it back by

sheer force of will. This was it. The end of Vivi and Luke. "Really? I doubt that."

"She won't understand," Dallas said. "You can see that by looking at her."

Vivi Ann wrapped herself in Grandma's pink quilt—ruined now—and stumbled out of bed. "Winona, please, let me explain . . ."

"Explain to your fiancé."

"I will, Win. I swear. I'll make this right. I know you're disappointed in me—"

"Don't bother talking, Vivi. She's too jealous to hear you." Dallas got up and stood beside Vivi Ann, naked, as bold as brass.

She felt his stare like a beam of light, slicing through her, seeing too much. She backed away from him, from them. "Jealous? Dream on."

He picked up a pair of black boxer shorts off the floor and put them on. "I know about wanting, Winona, believe me, I do. You're sick with it."

She turned away from them and ran back to her car. She heard Vivi Ann behind her, calling for her to stop, to come back, but she kept moving, slamming her car door shut. Starting the engine, she stared for a moment through the dirty window at her sister, wrapped in an antique quilt, standing on the porch.

Winona hit the gas and drove away, thinking as she came to the barn that it was finally done.

After twenty-five perfect years, Vivi Ann had fallen.

Dallas came up beside Vivi Ann on the porch.

She turned to him. Her eyes were wet with tears and she was shaking, but even with all of that, she felt relieved, too. "No more sneaking around now. I'll tell Luke and it will be done."

"Are you crazy? Winona is probably driving to his house now."

"No, she won't. We're sisters."

He touched her face. "You're wrong."

She kissed him softly. "Don't look so worried. This will be okay. I'll go talk to Luke and be back in no time. You'll be here, right?"

"I'll be here," he said, but he didn't look happy about it.

Winona went home and poured herself a straight shot of tequila.

Downing it, she poured a second, and then a third.

It was over.

Finally.

Vivi Ann would lose Luke now for sure.

Unless she lied. The thought of that sank through Winona, made her feel slightly sick—it was true. Her gorgeous, beloved sister could do what she'd always done: smile and shrug and get her way. If Dallas were gone tomorrow, Vivi Ann could marry Luke and everything would seem okay. Dad would walk his perfect youngest daughter down the aisle, hand her off to Luke, who'd take her hand and put his ring on her finger and swear to love her forever. No one would ever know the truth.

She got to her feet and paced the room, trying to think it through, but the tequila she'd drunk made it hard to think straight. What should she do now? She was so caught up in all of it that she barely heard the doorbell, and then Luke walked into the living room.

Winona froze. The sight of him right this minute, standing in front of her, with his bright, honest smile, was more than she could bear. She felt tears burn her eyes. She wanted him like she wanted air, and yet even now, with what Vivi Ann had done, she couldn't reach out. They were sisters, after all.

He pulled her into his arms, held her as if it meant something. "You're drunk," he whispered, smiling. "I thought you'd wait for me."

She stared up at him. "A little." Feeling reckless, she reached up and touched his face. She'd wanted to touch him like this for so long. "You came back for me."

He smiled. "I was looking for Vivi. Have you seen her?"

Always Vivi.

She drew back, trying not to cry. It hurt so badly, and she was so tired of being hurt.

"Have you seen her? She was supposed to meet me. I'm going crazy, looking—"

"You want to find Vivi Ann? Try Dallas's cabin."

170

"What?" He pulled away. In his eyes she saw confusion turn to shock, and then to anger.

She reached for him, desperate to hold on, to make him understand. *She* was the one who loved him; she was the one he could trust. "I *told* you she'd break your heart."

He stormed out of her house, slamming the door shut behind him. Winona heard the sound of a car door slamming shut on the street, then the starting of an engine, a squealing of tires on the pavement.

Only then did she realize what she'd done.

Chapter Ten

A s Vivi Ann drove to Luke's house, she tried to figure out what she'd say.

I'm sorry. I never meant to hurt you.

I never expected to do anything like this. It just happened . . .

It all sounded so pedestrian, so soap opera, but the truth was no better. How could she put into words this passion she had for Dallas? It was so much more than sex. In his arms . . . in his bed . . . she felt whole. It made no sense, even she knew that, but it was true nonetheless.

At Luke's house, she parked the truck and ran inside, searching room by room, calling out his name.

He wasn't home.

Of course he wasn't. He was in town somewhere, standing in the crowd, waiting for her. At his kitchen counter, she stopped and took off her engagement ring leaving it on the avocado-colored tile. Then she went back out to her truck and drove to town. As she passed the gas station, an ambulance came up behind her, sirens blaring, lights flashing.

She pulled over, then eased back onto the road, driving slowly through town, looking for Luke's truck. She was nearing the bowling alley when she happened to glance to the left. In the distance, she could see the start of Water's Edge, the shadowy rolling pastures. Red and amber lights flashed up from the darkness. The ambulance was at her house.

Vivi Ann hit the gas hard and sped home. At the rise, she parked and jumped out. She was running across the grass when two paramedics came out of the cabin, rolling a gurney between them. Dallas lay strapped on the narrow bed.

She skidded to a stop beside him. His right cheek was cut open. One eye was swollen and turning black.

"Hey, Princess," he said, wincing, trying to smile.

"Oh, Dal . . . I'm sorry—"

"We've got to get him into the ambulance," said one of the paramedics, and she nodded and stepped back.

"I'll meet you at the hospital," she promised.

"Don't."

She leaned down and kissed his good cheek.

"It'll be ugly in there, Vivi . . ."

"It's my fault. I shouldn't have lied."

There was no time to say more. The paramedics rolled him to the ambulance, loaded him in, and drove off.

In the sudden, quiet darkness, Vivi Ann stared at her grandfather's cabin, trying to find the strength she needed to face Luke.

When she was ready, she went up to the front door and stepped inside.

Only it wasn't just Luke. He stood near the kitchen sink, flanked by Winona and Dad.

Vivi Ann's step faltered, but she kept going, walked up to them.

"I'm sorry, Luke. I went to your house to tell you—"

"Too late, Vivi," he said.

"But—"

"Your chickenshit boyfriend didn't even fight back." He pushed past her and walked out of the cabin. The door banged shut behind him.

Vivi Ann stood there, hearing his truck start up and drive away. In the silence that followed, she looked at her father and Winona. "I'm sorry, Daddy. You must have felt like this when you met Mom—"

He smacked her across the cheek so hard she stumbled sideways.

"You'll be at the parade tomorrow, with this family, and by God, you will not disgrace me again."

Vivi Ann sat in her grandmother's wing chair all night. If she slept at all it was a catnap here or there. Mostly she stared out the window at the darkened expanse of Water's Edge.

You'll be at the parade. You will not disgrace me.

There was no doubt at all about what that meant. Her dad was reminding her that she was a Grey and as such was expected to align with her family. He knew, as she did, that she could be forgiven for this affair, even for hurting Luke. It would not be pretty, or come without pain, but forgiveness could be granted in time. Things were done a certain way in Oyster Shores and everyone knew the rules. All she had to do was repent and return home in acknowledgment of her sin.

His ultimatum had been a reminder that family bonds were strong. For all her life, she'd taken that fact as a bedrock truth; indisputable. Last night, though, she'd glimpsed a fragility that was new to her, a fault line running beneath the surface of their family. Never before had she considered that it might all be conditional, that if a wrong choice was made, a misstep taken, the once-solid ground could crack in half and let them fall.

Her choice now was clear: Dallas or her family.

It was like having to choose between an arm and a leg, lungs and a heart.

At last, dawn came to Water's Edge, spilling over the steel-gray Canal and illuminating the snowcapped mountains on the opposite shore. She went to the barn and fed her horses, then returned to the cabin, where she sat on the porch, watching.

She was there when Dad left the house and walked over to his truck.

Did he glance up here? She couldn't be sure. But he drove away without once slowing down as he passed her truck. Soon he would be pulling up to the diner, where he'd meet his friend for breakfast; then, at noon, he'd drive to Grey Park. The family always met in the same spot before every town gathering. There, the various pieces came together to make up the whole. He cared deeply that they all showed up to things together, a subtle reminder that they were a family that mattered in this town. Her dad would meet Aurora first (she was always early) and then Winona.

The pain at that thought surprised her, so she pushed it aside. Her sister had betrayed her last night; it was a thing that had to be dealt with. Later.

Now it was time to make a decision. She could go back to her family or she could go to Dallas.

She wished it were a difficult choice, but the truth was that she wanted Dallas Raintree.

It had always come down to that, from the very

first time he reached for her hand and led her onto that dance floor.

She got dressed and went to her truck. As she drove out of town, she could hear the start of the parade, but by the time she reached the gas station it was gone and the world was quiet again, leaving her time to think, to worry.

Would he still be there?

Did he even want her? He had never said the word *love* to her.

At the hospital, she found him in his room, standing at the window, looking out. When the door opened, he turned to her. "Go away, Vivi. We're done."

She crossed the room, went around the bed, and approached him. Her gaze moved along his face, his injuries, pausing at every stitch and bruise. He'd have a new scar along his cheekbone because of her. "You should have defended yourself."

"Should I?"

"You did nothing wrong. I was the one who was engaged."

"Leave me, Vivi Ann."

"Tell me you don't want me and I'll leave."

"I don't want you."

She saw the lie in his pale gray eyes. "What's my favorite ice cream?"

"Vanilla. Why?"

"Marry me," she said, surprising herself.

"You're crazy."

"We've been crazy from the start."

Time slowed down for a moment. She realized how much she wanted him to say yes and she was afraid. All her life, she'd gotten what she wanted. What if that meant she would lose it now, when it mattered most?

"Say something," she pleaded.

Winona heard her front door bang open and knew exactly who it was. She sat down on the end of her bed, waiting.

Aurora came around the corner in a cloud of Giorgio perfume. "What the fuck?"

Winona was dressed for the parade, but even with her curled hair and heavier-than-usual makeup, she knew she looked bad. A sleepless night always showed in the eyes. "You heard."

"Are you kidding? Everyone has heard. And thanks for letting me hang out there alone, by the way. When Myrtle Michaelian spilled the beans, I told her to quit spreading lies."

Winona sighed. "It was ugly last night."

"What happened?"

"Vivi's been screwing Dallas Raintree."

Aurora sat down in the chair by the window, sighing. "Jesus. I guess that explains a lot. How did Luke find out?"

Winona studied her ragged fingernails. She'd chewed them down to the quick last night. "When I got to the cabin, Luke was kicking the shit out of

Dallas. He just stood there and took it, too, smiling the whole time like he liked it. I ran down and got Dad to stop them. But when Vivi Ann came back, he slapped her across the face and called her a disgrace."

"He slapped her?" Aurora frowned.

Winona could see that her sister was fitting the pieces together. Before she could find a hole, Winona said, "It's probably all for the best."

"What do you mean?"

"Better that Luke finds out now that she doesn't love him. And God knows she can't go around screwing a guy like Dallas. She had to know she'd get caught. She should get caught. It's disgraceful."

Aurora went very still. "What did you do, Winona?"

"What do you mean?"

"You told Luke, didn't you? I *knew* it was all going to go to crap when you wouldn't tell Vivi Ann the truth."

Winona got to her feet. "Don't be ridiculous. Let's go to the parade. Vivi Ann will be there. Dallas will be gone and everything will be fine. You'll see."

"You think Vivi Ann will show?"

"Where else would she go?"

"What if she doesn't forgive you?"

Winona didn't answer that. Instead, she shuffled Aurora out of the house and toward the sidewalk. As they walked to Grey Park, she tried not to think

178

about last night, but Aurora's words had brought it all back. Now she couldn't forget anything . . . her agonizing jealousy, her desperate longing, the surge of bitterness . . .

She'd raced to the cabin after Luke, wanting to take back what she'd done, but when she'd gotten there, she'd seen him beating Dallas up, and she'd gone for help, pulling Dad out of bed.

Luke is beating Dallas up. You have to come.

Luke . . . beating up Dallas? Why?

Because Vivi has been screwing him.

That was the moment, of all of them, that played over and over in her mind. She could tell herself it had been a heat-of-passion decision, but she couldn't quite believe it. She'd *wanted* her dad to know the truth.

When they turned the corner and came to the park her grandfather had donated to the town, she saw her father standing alongside Richard and the kids. They stood beneath a gorgeous madrona tree. For more than fifteen years they'd met here at the start of every town party or parade. It was a tradition their mother had begun, back when she'd had three small girls and a horseback 4-H group to corral. But today, as they stood there, all that mattered was who was missing.

Every minute that passed was an aftershock that rattled the foundation of their family, cracked it just a little more. Finally, at 11:55, Dad walked over to the trash can on the street, threw his empty plastic glass away, and turned to them. His face, always craggy and a little cold, looked older. "I guess she made up her mind, then. Let's go."

Aurora looked at Winona in confusion. She was chewing on her flag-painted acrylic fingernail like a rabbit with a carrot. "We can't just leave. She'll be here. Won't she?"

Winona had to admit it: she was shaken by this. It wasn't what she'd expected.

"Come on," Dad said sharply. He was already to the corner, making the turn.

Winona didn't know what else to do, so she followed.

She stood beside her dad for the next two hours, waiting every minute to see Vivi Ann move past her on some float or ride past on Clem.

But her sister never showed.

"This is trouble," Aurora said when the last entry in the parade moved past them. "Big trouble. Tell me the whole story. Why did you—"

Winona walked away. "I'll talk to you later, Aurora," she tossed over her shoulder.

By the time she got to her car, she was practically running to avoid the gossip on the streets. She jumped into her car and drove out to Luke's house. He would be the only person who would understand and appreciate what she'd done. She found him exactly where she'd expected to: sitting on his porch, staring out. Cuts and dried blood marked his left hand.

"Hey," she said.

He barely acknowledged her, just tilted his chin a little.

She sat down on the seat beside him, her heart aching for how hurt he felt right now. It was the same pain she'd felt since he first turned to Vivi Ann. "I'm here for you."

He didn't answer, didn't even look at her, and something about that made her nervous.

She started to put her arm around him. "It's all for the best, really. If she didn't love you, you had to know that. Now you can go forward."

He pushed her arm away.

"Luke?"

"Why did you tell me?"

"What? You had to know. What she was doing with that man was wrong. I knew how hurt you'd be."

"Exactly." He got up and walked over to the porch railing, putting as much distance between them as was possible. With his back to her, he stared out at his land.

"It's not *my* fault, Luke. I wasn't sleeping with him. I didn't cheat on you and break your heart. What she did was wrong. Of course she got caught. I'm the one who is trying to help you. Look at me, Luke."

He didn't turn around. "Just go, Winona. I can't talk to you now."

She didn't know how to react. None of this made sense to her. "But—"

"Go. Please."

It was the *please* that grounded her. She'd come to him too soon; that was all. Of course he wasn't ready for comforting yet. But he would be. Time healed all wounds. She just had to be patient. "Okay. I'm available anytime, though. Just call me if you need a friend."

"A friend," he said, putting a sharp, strange emphasis on the word.

She was halfway to the door when his voice stopped her.

"Was she at the parade?"

"No," she said bitterly, looking back at him. "She chickened out."

"Did she? You think?" He sighed, and still he didn't turn around. "You shouldn't have told me."

"It broke my heart," she said quietly, "seeing them in bed together. I knew what you'd think."

"I love her."

"Loved," she corrected, reaching for the door. "And you didn't even know her."

Vivi Ann and Dallas got married in the Mason County Courthouse, with a justice of the peace presiding and a law clerk as witness. After the ceremony, they climbed into the truck and turned on the radio. The first song that blared through the speakers was Willie Nelson's "My Heroes Have Always Been Cowboys," and Vivi Ann laughed and thought: *That will be our song.*

All the way out of town and deep into the Olympic rain forest, they talked. When the sky turned dark and the road began to twist and turn, thrusting deep into the old-growth trees, they came to the lodge at Sol Duc, and there they rented a cabin.

"I guess we're just a cabin couple," Dallas said as he carried her over the threshold and into the piney-scented room. For four days they stayed in bed, making love, caressing, talking. Vivi Ann told Dallas everything there was to know about her— when she'd lost her virginity and to whom, how it had felt to lose her mother, why she loved Oyster Shores so much, and even what foods she despised. The more she talked with him, the easier he laughed, and it became a new addiction for her, this needing to make him smile.

On the fifth day, they hiked up the beautiful, rugged trails to the famous Sol Duc Falls. There, completely alone in the wild old-growth rain forest, with the sound of the falling water thundering around them and the air full of spray, they made love in a small clearing at the base of a two-hundred-year-old cedar tree.

"I'm wise to you, you know," she said when they were done, resting her back on the mossy nurse log behind them.

He pulled out his pocketknife and began idly carving a heart in the tree's ridged bark. "Oh, really?"

"I've told you everything there is to know about me and you haven't told me a thing. Every time I ask you a question you kiss me."

"That's all that matters." He carved his initials, then began on hers.

"But it isn't. We're married now. I have to be able to answer questions about you."

"Are we signed up for *The Newlywed Game* or something?"

"Don't make a joke. I'm serious."

He finished the carving and put down his knife, looking at her finally. "If you saw someone standing on the edge of a cliff and you thought they were going to jump, what would you say?"

"I'd tell them to back away before they got hurt."

"Step back, Vivi."

"How can it hurt me to know you?"

"You might not like what you find out."

"You have to trust me, Dallas, or we won't be able to make this thing work."

"Okay," he said after a long silence. "Ask your questions."

"Where were you born?"

"Big surprise: Dallas, Texas. My mom and dad met at a diner down there. She was living on the reservation with her sister."

"What's her name?"

"Her real name was Laughs Like the Wind. Her husband called her Mary. She's dead now."

"And your dad?"

"Alive."

She touched the scars on his chest. In the fading light, they looked silvery, like skeins of broken fishing line embedded in his flesh. "How did you get these?"

"Electrical cords and cigarettes. The old man didn't like to look for weapons."

Vivi Ann flinched at that. "And your mom, did she—"

"That's enough for now," he said quietly. "How about we talk about something that really matters?" he asked when she leaned against him.

"Like?" She stared up through lacy evergreen fronds at slices of the purple sky.

"Winona."

Vivi Ann sighed. They might not have talked about this in the past few days, but she'd thought about it. "She couldn't stand what we—what *I* was doing to Luke and she snapped. Win's always been a very black-and-white, right-and-wrong girl. I know I should be mad at her, and I am, but in the end, she helped me. How can I stay mad at someone when I'm married to you?"

"So you want to go back," he said.

"It's where I belong," she said quietly. "Where I want you and our children to belong."

"It won't be easy. People will talk."

"They always do, and I've finally given them something to talk about."

"I love you, Vivi," he said, and in his voice was

a surprising intensity. It scared and thrilled her at the same time. "I won't let anyone hurt you. Not even Winona."

She laughed. "Don't worry, Mr. Raintree. We Greys are ranchers. We know how to mend our fences."

On the first Saturday in September, Winona woke well before dawn and dragged her tired ass to the ranch. On the way there, she picked up Aurora, who managed to look completely put together at this ungodly hour.

"I can't believe she's still not home," Aurora said as they pulled up to the farmhouse.

"She wants us to sweat a few bullets. It's working, too. Dad is realizing how much he needs her around here."

"That's not how she thinks."

"You're assuming she does think."

Aurora rolled her eyes. "God, you can be a bitch. So, after all this, how's Luke? Has he promised his undying love yet?"

Winona slammed on the brakes hard enough to shut her sister up. "The cookie dough is in the fridge. Make as many as you can, and then take all the food to the cook shack."

"Aye, aye." Aurora got out of the car and disappeared into the house.

Winona found her dad in the arena, grooming the dirt for today's jackpot. She waved at him and headed up into the announcer's booth, where she started setting up the PA system.

For the next few hours, she went through her list of tasks, making sure the barrier was set up, the timers were in place, the steers were brought in, their horns were wrapped, and the microphone worked. By ten o'clock she was in the announcer's booth again, surrounded by entry forms, trying to organize the teams for the first go-rounds. Worse than all that was the handicapping. Each roper had a skill level, assigned by the roping association, and all those numbers had to be added up, handicapped, and assigned to the right team so that the roping results would be fair. You needed a damned Ph.D. in math to figure it all out.

The door to the announcer's booth opened with a little puff of dust and her dad stood there, looking irritated. "What's takin' so long, Win? You got seven years of college. Do the danged math."

"I can't figure it out."

"Them colleges are a waste." He grabbed the cash box off the plywood desk and left the booth.

Winona followed him out to the parking area, where dozens of men on horseback were gathered.

"What's up, Henry?" Deke asked, tipping the cowboy hat back on his head.

"We're closin' up today," Dad said. "Everyone gets their money back. The handicappin' is too much for Winona."

She felt her face heat up.

He opened the cash box and had just begun to count out the money when another truck pulled into the lot. Winona was so focused on her own humiliation that it took her a second to realize that people were whispering Vivi's name.

Winona looked up sharply, peered through the crowd.

It was Vivi Ann's truck, all right.

The men on horseback twisted in their saddles to look. Winona's first thought was: *Thank God.* Then she saw Vivi Ann and Dallas come forward, holding hands as if they were just an ordinary pair of lovers come to watch some team roping, and Winona knew this was going to be bad. In worn jeans and a wrinkled T-shirt, Vivi Ann managed to be so beautiful it almost hurt to look at her, and if she was sunlight, all glittering and golden, Dallas was shadow, cool and dark.

The crowd was eerily quiet, aware completely of what was going on. They were unsure of how to respond, especially the men, who tended to let women lead on matters such as these.

"Hey, Dad," Vivi Ann said as if nothing were new. "Do you need my help?"

Dad paused just long enough to prove his anger, but not long enough to show a schism in the family. "You're late," he said, thrusting the cash box at her.

And just like that, Vivi Ann moved back into her place. The cowboys smiled down at her instantly, welcomed her home, while Dallas moved easily among them, giving advice to some of the younger guys.

Winona couldn't believe it. All of that—the sex, the lying, the slap—and still Vivi Ann could waltz back into Water's Edge and be welcomed.

Winona marched over to the cook shack, where Aurora was busy flipping burgers.

"You will not believe what just happened."

Aurora turned to her. "What?"

"Vivi Ann came home. And she's with Dallas."

"Have they been together this whole time?"

"Who am I? Carnac the Magnificent? I don't know, but they looked lovey-dovey."

"This is going to be bad. Did you tell her you were sorry?"

"Me? She's the one who started all this."

"No," Aurora said sternly. "You're the problem."

"How do you figure that? Did I fuck Dallas Raintree while I was engaged to Luke? Please, enlighten me with your superior brainpower, Aurora."

"Luke is a friend, Winona. Vivi is family. When the chips were down, you chose Luke. The whole town knows it. How long did you wait before you told him and Daddy?"

"I'm not listening to this," Winona said as she walked out of the cook shack.

In the arena, she felt suddenly conspicuous. As she looked around, she wondered what people were saying about her part in this. Once she began to worry about her reputation, she couldn't stop. Climbing to the highest row of bleacher seats, she sat in the shadows until the roping ended and then went to the cook shack.

"That's what the whole town is saying, huh? That I told Luke?"

Aurora turned off the griddle and wiped it down. "There are no secrets in a town like this."

"It's not fair. I did the right thing. People will see that in the end."

Aurora sighed. "I'm going to find Vivi Ann. You coming? Or are you hiding out?"

Winona bit back a mean retort and followed her sister out to the parking area. The trucks and trailers were pulling out, moving up the driveway in a multicolored snake of traffic. When they were gone and the parking lot was empty of vehicles, Winona and Aurora were by the fence and Dad was standing near the loafing shed. All of them waiting.

Vivi Ann and Dallas strode toward them, hand in hand.

The five of them stood there, in the purplish falling night, surrounded by black fields and the sounds of horses moving back and forth along the fence and the tide ebbing back toward the sea.

"He ain't welcome here," Dad said.

Dallas moved closer to Vivi Ann, put his arm around her. "We got married."

No one spoke; it felt for a moment as if time had stopped. Vivi Ann looked directly at Dad. "I want us to belong here, Dad, to keep running the ranch, but if you don't want us . . ."

Winona knew then that Vivi Ann was far from dumb. She'd painted their father into a corner to get her way.

"I don't suppose I have much choice now, do I?" he said. On that, he turned and went into the house, closing the door hard behind him.

Aurora moved forward and hugged Vivi Ann. "He'll come around. Don't worry."

Vivi Ann clung to Aurora. "I hope so."

Aurora gave Dallas an awkward hug and then headed for her car. As the BMW's engine roared to life, Winona stood there, too shaken to speak.

Vivi Ann moved toward her, but didn't let go of Dallas's hand; it was a reminder that they were a couple now. Together. "How do you want to handle this, Win?" she asked quietly.

"I only told Dad because Luke was beating Dallas up." Winona heard the crack in her voice and it pissed her off. She sounded weak when she wanted to be strong. "I was trying to *save* Dallas."

Dallas stepped forward then, as if he belonged there, as if he had a place between the sisters. "You wanted everything she had," he said.

"That's not true," Winona said, but she knew—they all knew—that it was.

"You did me a favor, Win," Vivi Ann said, "even

though you meant to hurt me. The truth is, I don't care about all that crap now. I've found the man I love and we're on the ranch. Nothing else matters to me."

She was right. Somehow, impossibly, Vivi Ann had broken all those rules, and a good man's heart, she'd slept with a stranger and brought him home, and *still* she'd paid no price. *Golden.*

"I know that forgive and forget isn't your forte," Vivi Ann said, "but it's the only way we have now. I can do it. Can you?"

Winona was as backed into the corner as her father had been. There was nothing she could say now except yes. Anything else would make her look petty and spiteful. "Of course," she said, surging forward to give her sister a lackluster hug. "Forgive and forget."

Chapter Eleven

Some things couldn't be forgotten, no matter how hard you tried. Humiliation. Loss. Jealousy. They were buoyant emotions that kept popping to the surface. In the end, you grew too tired to keep them submerged. Winona knew: she'd tried. She kept trying, but sometimes, like tonight, the effort seemed unbearable.

When she heard the doorbell ring, her first thought was: *What if I just don't answer?*

It rang again.

There was nowhere to hide in your own family.

Turning away from the sink, she headed for the door and opened it.

Aurora stood there, dressed and ready to go. She had teased her brown hair into a poufy banana-clipped ponytail and painted her face with layers of color. Shoulder pads emphasized her small waist, which was circled by a wide, rhinestoned leather belt. Her denim dress looked plain by comparison. "Don't give me that sucked-on-a-lemon look. Let's go."

Wordlessly, Winona followed her sister out to the road where her car was parked. Climbing into the Beemer's backseat, she wished she were anywhere but here. "This is a stupid idea," she said.

"Your opinion is noted," Aurora said.

Winona made a great show of sighing and crossing her arms. "Where's Richard?"

"He's working late tonight. He'd rather eat his shoe than come with us."

"I can relate."

"I'm so not interested in your theatrics."

They turned into Water's Edge and drove up to the cabin.

At the front door, they knocked, and in moments Vivi Ann answered.

"Phew," Aurora said, "they aren't naked."

Winona rolled her eyes. "It's not even dark out."

"What you know about hot sex is equivalent to what I know about beekeeping," Aurora said curtly. To Vivi Ann she said, "We're going to the Outlaw."

"Of course you are, it's Friday," Vivi Ann said.

Dallas rose instantly and moved in behind Vivi Ann, putting his hand possessively around her waist.

Aurora studied him, her eyes narrowing. "Do you love her, Tattoo Boy?"

"It seems I do, Junior League wannabe."

Aurora smiled at that. "Then take her to the Outlaw. This is how it's done."

"She's right," Winona said sharply. "The best way to stop the gossip in town is to show them how happy you are."

Dallas stared at Winona. "You don't look too happy, Winona. I guess you like the gossip about Vivi."

"In your vast experience at judging my moods, you mean."

"I don't know . . ." Vivi Ann said. "Luke might be there."

Dallas took her in his arms. "We don't have to do anything you don't want to."

The softness of his voice surprised Winona. No wonder he'd sucked her sister in. Especially Vivi Ann, who saw the best in everyone.

"You can't avoid him forever," Aurora pointed out.

At last, Vivi Ann nodded. "Give us a minute,"

she said, taking Dallas's hand. When they disappeared into the bedroom, Winona said, "If I hear sex, I'm out of here."

"You would be," Aurora said with a laugh.

Fifteen minutes later, the Grey sisters and Dallas pulled up to the Outlaw and parked.

They went in one after another. When Dallas came in—last—there was a noticeable ripple in the room. People looked up, drinks paused in midair, conversations halted. Even the drummer missed a beat.

Winona noticed that their friends couldn't look away from Vivi Ann and Dallas. They came together by the bar, ordering drinks. Once they were served, the four of them turned in unison to face the crowd. In the background, "The Dance," played on the jukebox.

The first person to approach them was Luke.

"Here he comes," Aurora muttered. "Ex-fiancé at one o'clock."

"He knows how it's done, too," Winona said, forcing herself not to move toward him.

Dallas moved in closer to Vivi Ann, took her hand in his.

"Hey, Vivi," Luke said.

The bar fell quiet. The only sounds came from the back of the room, where one ball hit another on the pool table.

"I heard you got married," Luke said woodenly. "Congratulations."

"I should have been honest with you," Vivi Ann said to him.

"I wish you had been."

Winona studied every detail of his face, the way he closed his eyes for just a second before he spoke, the frowning around his mouth. She expected him to say something else, something cutting and cruel—the kind of thing Vivi Ann deserved for what she'd done—but the longer she stared, the deeper she saw. Luke wasn't angry with Vivi Ann.

He still loved her. Even after all of it.

"I'm truly sorry," Vivi Ann said.

Her sister kept talking, piling meaningless words on top of each other, while everyone else listened and smiled and accepted. It turned to a roar of white noise in Winona's head, so loud she couldn't hear anything beyond the beating of her own heart. She was so caught up in her own thoughts, her own bitter disappointment (what about karma? what about paying for your sins?), that she hardly noticed when it was over.

The music came back on. People moved onto the dance floor.

She blinked and looked around for Luke.

Dallas was watching her and something in those eerie pale gray eyes made her uncomfortable. He let go of Vivi Ann's hand and moved toward her. Winona noticed the sexy, loose-hipped way he walked and recognized the motive behind it. Not that it would ever work on her.

"Poor Luke," Dallas said in a silky voice that made her nervous. "I'll bet he needs a shoulder to cry on."

"You don't know me."

"I know you," he answered, smiling now.

Winona thought then: *He's dangerous*. And Vivi Ann had brought him into their family. It proved to Winona that she'd been right to try to protect Vivi Ann from this man. "You'd better not hurt her," she said. "I'll be watching you."

"She might forget what you did, Winona, but I haven't. You betrayed her, pure and simple. So you remember this: I'll be watching *you*. She might forgive. I won't."

Winona sat in her car, parked outside the police station.

She shouldn't go in. She knew that. Some things were better left unknown.

If only she were the kind of person who could ignore information. But such feigned ignorance was impossible for her to achieve.

Once an idea got in her head she was like a crocodile death-rolling its prey. And suddenly she was worried that Dallas was actually dangerous.

She got out of the car and walked toward the station, opening the door. Inside, the place was empty but for a few uniformed officers walking from one office to another.

At the receptionist's desk, Helen looked up

from filing her hot-pink nails. "Hey, Winona."

"Hey. Is Sheriff Bailor in? I'd like to see him."

"Course he's in. You've got an appointment, dontcha? He's in his office. Go on back."

Winona walked down the busy hallway and found Sheriff Albert Bailor in his office, eating a breakfast sandwich.

"Hey, Winona," he said, wiping his mouth with a napkin. "Have a seat."

She didn't bother with small talk. It was a skill she'd never really mastered anyway. "I need to do a background criminal check on someone."

"This the Indian?"

"Yes."

"I had the same questions myself when Vivi married him. To be honest, I expected you in here before now." He left the room and came back a few moments later with a file, which he set down on his desk. "I'll be right back. Nature calls."

As soon as he was gone, Winona opened the file. *Dallas Raintree, DOB 5/05/65.*

She scanned through his criminal record, reading charges, arrests, and convictions. There were almost a dozen theft or possessing stolen goods charges, two assault charges that were pled down, an assault and battery conviction, and a couple of weapons charges. A notation was made that his juvenile record was sealed per court order and that he had, on several occasions, been ordered to undergo psychiatric evaluations. It appeared that he'd been a juvenile the first time such a recommendation was made.

"Holy shit," Winona said.

"Holy shit is right," Al said, coming back into the office, closing the glass-topped door behind him.

Winona looked up at him. "What does all this mean?"

Al sat down at his desk. "I read it as your brother-in-law is a man with a bad temper and not much respect for the law. And somethin' bad happened when he was a kid. There are a lot of psychiatrists' reports in there. More'n a few think he's unstable." He leaned back. "Rumor is that you're the one who hired him. I would have expected you to do a background check."

She gritted her teeth. "What can I do now?"

"Now?" Al shrugged. "He's married to your sister, Win. There's nothing to be done now."

"Is he dangerous?"

Al looked at her. "Under the right circumstances, we all are. You just keep your eye on him."

"I will," Winona promised.

In late November, an icy wind blew across the Canal, whipping the normally calm waters into a whitecapped frenzy. Waves smacked against the cement and stone bulkheads along the shore; foamy water sloshed onto the well-tended yards, turning the green grass brown. All at once, the birds disappeared, taking their early morning song and afternoon chatter with them. Bare trees shivered in the cold, their last multihued leaves plucked away by the wind. Those same leaves now lay in slimy, blackening piles in the ditches on the sides of the road.

As if a memo had been sent to the trendy East Side, the tourists stopped coming. No boats dotted the Canal, no motors were heard purring in the afternoons. Instead, the portable docks were pulled ashore for the season and the permanent ones were shut down, their water spigots covered and turned off. All up and down the shoreline, barbecues were hauled off the decks and placed in garages for the winter months; planters full of precious, fragile flowers were taken in, too. Without sunlight, everything looked washed out, especially when it was raining, and it was almost always raining. Not hard, pounding storms, rather a steady, thready mist. On the day after Thanksgiving, the Bits and Spurs 4-H Club members and their families gathered at Water's Edge to make wreaths. It had been a tradition for years. Vivi Ann had always been a part of it, first as her mom's helper, then as a 4-H member, and now as the leader.

The event went from morning to night, and to be honest, she had never enjoyed it more than this year, and when it was all over and the day was done, she and Dallas walked up the spongy road to their cabin. "I saw you talking to Myrtle Michaelian," Vivi Ann said.

"She held on to her purse the whole time. I think she was worried I'd steal it."

Smiling, she opened the door and went inside.

The cabin smelled like Christmas. Dallas had set up a small, perfect tree in the corner near the fireplace and draped several of the leftover boughs along the mantel. "Merry Christmas," he said.

Vivi Ann was surprised by him yet again. All her life men had lined up to give her things; they'd wowed her with presents wrapped by salespeople and paid for by credit cards. But this, a simple, sparsely decorated tree, meant more to her than any of that because she knew her husband didn't care about Christmas. He'd done this for her because *she* cared.

"That friend of yours—Trayna at the drugstore—helped me pick out ornaments."

Vivi Ann laughed at the image of scary-looking Dallas following Trayna around, picking out angels and elves. She loved him so much she couldn't stand it.

"What's so funny? Did I do something wrong?"

"No, Dallas Raintree. You did something right." She took him by the hand and led him into the bedroom, and there she showed him in a dozen ways how much she loved him.

Afterward, they lay in bed, staring at each other. Through the open door, she could see their first Christmas tree, twinkling in the darkness.

"I thought you'd hate today," she said.

"No."

"Did you do corny stuff like that when you were a kid?"

"No," he said, and this time his voice was quiet. She knew she'd struck a nerve.

"Is there anyone you want to invite for Christmas?"

"You keep asking the same question in different ways, Vivi," he said. "There's no one. Just you."

She didn't see how that was possible, how a person could be as alone as he implied. She angled onto one elbow and looked at him. "What happened, Dallas?" It was the first time she'd ever asked the question directly.

"He killed her," he said quietly. "I guess that's what you want to know so bad. Beat her up for years and then shot her one night."

"Were you—"

"Yeah. I was there."

It all clicked into place for Vivi Ann then: the scars on his chest, the anger he sometimes couldn't control, the trouble sleeping. She imagined him as a boy, listening to things no child should hear, seeing terrible images. No wonder he didn't want to talk about his past. She scooted closer and took him in her arms, holding him with the whole of her body, her heart and soul, trying somehow to impart her childhood to him.

He was holding her so tightly she knew their conversation had reopened an old wound. The look he gave her was a terrible, beautiful combination of happiness and pain, and she wondered suddenly if that was what he lived with, that unbearable duo. She kissed his lips, then his cheek, and then, at his ear, she whispered, "We're going to have a baby."

He said nothing, just pulled her more tightly into his arms and held her.

"Are you ready?" she asked.

He drew back just enough to look at her, and the love in his eyes was all the answer she needed.

If Winona had been keeping her memories in manila file folders, she would have labeled the Christmas of 1992 as the second worst in Grey family history; only the year their mom died had been worse.

She'd tried to pretend that everything was okay. She'd shown up at the farmhouse to decorate for the holidays. She'd schlepped up and down the attic stairs, carrying down the dusty ornament boxes until she was sweaty and tired. Working alongside her sisters, she'd said all the right things. *Look, Vivi, it's the Life Savers clown you made at Bible camp in fourth grade . . . and here's Aurora's favorite angel with the broken wing.*

But none of it had felt right. Aurora and Vivi Ann had laughed and joked and fought over what Christmas album to play, while Winona felt increasingly distant. She knew it was wrong of her, that she needed to put aside the old grudges, the bitterness, and go on with their everyday life. She couldn't seem to do that, though.

The problem was Dallas. He was like a tumor in the body of their family, and only she detected the malignancy.

It didn't matter that he acted like he loved Vivi Ann (*acted* was the key word, to Winona's mind) or that he was doing a great job at the ranch. What mattered was that he couldn't be trusted. The police reports on his past were proof positive. He would hurt her family somehow.

Anyone sitting at this table for Christmas dinner should have seen that. Everything was in its usual place, looking sparkling and perfect. Daddy was dressed up in new dark blue Wrangler jeans and a crisp white shirt, buttoned all the way to the throat. Aurora and Richard and the kids looked like they'd just stepped out of the Nordstrom catalog, and Vivi Ann was an image of golden beauty in her green velvet dress.

And then there was Dallas, sitting beside his wife, looking uncomfortable and vaguely irritated by the goings-on. Winona watched him from beneath lowered lashes. His long hair and pale blue shirt didn't soften him at all; quite the contrary. Getting dressed up only made him look more dangerous.

If Winona could have thought of a way to reveal this truth, she would have, but Dallas was smart. He didn't push his way into things; he didn't demand his share. He waited on the sidelines, pretending to be willing to work for whatever he got. The cowboys had accepted him and the women in town had begun lately to talk about the "great love" of Vivi Ann and Dallas. Even Aurora refused to hear about his criminal past and told Winona to let it go.

Vivi Ann clinked her fork against her wineglass, drawing everyone's attention.

Winona looked down the table toward her sister, as she was supposed to, and several facts registered, clicked into place like the firing sequence in a handgun: Vivi Ann was even more beautiful than usual, radiant, even, and she was drinking water.

"We're pregnant," Vivi Ann said, and her smile lit up the room.

Winona experienced the announcement in a strange, slowed-down way, as if she were underwater or behind a wall comprised of wavy glass block. She saw everyone except her father leap to congratulate Vivi Ann; she heard the squeals and cries, saw Aurora hug Vivi Ann and start to cry.

Winona knew she needed to move, to join in, but she couldn't. She just sat there. Once, when she was little, she'd tried barrel racing. Bathed in the rare glow of her dad's encouragement, she'd climbed onto Clem's big back and kicked hard. She'd barely hung on around the first barrel, and on the second she'd lost her grip. She still remembered how that felt: the letting go, the sliding sideways in the saddle, losing her stirrup. For a second before she'd fallen, she'd known it was coming, and the fear of that moment was how she felt. From now on, no matter what, Dallas would be a part of this family. The cancer of his presence had just metastasized.

She glanced sideways and found Dallas looking at her. She shifted uncomfortably in her chair and lifted her wineglass in a toast. "Here's to Vivi Ann . . . who now will have a baby . . ." *Too.* She tried not to think about her own loneliness, but it was impossible to ignore. Here she was, the oldest sister and the only one unmarried and childless.

After that, the evening passed for Winona like a movie without sound. She did all the things that were expected of her—she cleared the table and washed the dishes with her sisters, she put on their favorite Elvis Christmas album and danced in the kitchen, she read "The Night Before Christmas" to her niece and nephew—but none of it felt real.

"You're not very good at pretending to be happy."

Winona hadn't even heard him approach. It seemed that sneaking up on people was a particular skill of his. She turned slightly, found Dallas beside her, sipping his beer. "I've never been good at pretending to be anything," she answered. "And you don't fool me for a second. I've seen your record."

"She's happy, you know," he said.

"What about you? I wouldn't peg you as the daddy type."

"You don't care how I feel about anything."

It was a relief to be understood, not to have to pretend. "You're right."

"And why is that?"

"This family was happy before you got here."

Dallas glanced around the room; his gaze stopped on Aurora and Richard arguing quietly by the tree, and then moved on to Dad, who was well into his third bourbon and staring at an old picture of Mom. "Was it?" he asked. "So you were *happy* that Vivi was dating your boyfriend."

"He wasn't my boyfriend."

Dallas gave her a knowing smile. "That was the problem all along, wasn't it?"

"Fuck you."

He laughed. "Is that a traditional holiday greeting?"

She pushed past him and walked away. For the rest of the evening, she tried to be her old self, surrounded by the people she loved, but he was always there, on the fringes, watching them, watching her.

Winona counted the days until Luke returned from his Montana vacation. They had spoken on the phone on Christmas Day, and he'd sounded better. Finally. Their friendship still felt fragile these days, not quite healed, but Winona was trying to be patient. He needed time, that was all. He'd come around. For Luke, she would be patient.

The evening he got home, she made a date for them to go see a movie.

In these winter months night came early, so that by the time she left work, got dressed, and drove to his house it was already dark out. When he opened the door, she threw herself into his arms and hugged him tightly. "I'm so glad you're back."

He eased out of her embrace and led her into the living room, where a fire glowed in the hearth and Christmas lights still twinkled on the tree she'd helped him decorate. While she sat down, he went into the kitchen and came back with two glasses of wine.

"Booze. Thank God," she said, taking her glass and scooting sideways to make room for him. Kicking off her slouchy ankle boots, she put her stockinged feet up on the coffee table. As was usual lately, he said little. It fell to her to keep up the conversation. "You have no idea how weird these holidays have been. Dallas ruined every-thing and no one can see that. I keep wanting to grab Vivi by the shoulders and shake her until she sees what I see. Maybe I can figure out a way to mail her his criminal record. That should wake her up."

"Really, Win," Luke said, sighing. "Do we have

to have this conversation every time we're together? It's getting old. They're married."

"And now they're going to have a baby."

"She's pregnant?"

"Already. Even I'm surprised, and I usually expect the worst."

Luke got to his feet and walked over to the fire, staring down at it.

"A baby," he said, in a sad, soft voice.

Winona could have kicked herself. It was one of her worst traits, the way she could focus so much on the minutiae that she completely missed the big picture. She kept thinking he'd be over Vivi Ann by now. She got up and went to him. "I'm sorry, Luke. I wasn't thinking. I shouldn't have told you about it like that."

He glanced away from her, looked past the tree to the rainy black night beyond the window. "I can't do it."

"Do what?"

"I thought I could stick around and watch Vivi Ann love someone else, but I can't."

"But . . ." Winona didn't know what to say, how to frame her sudden fear into a cogent appeal. "You can't leave . . ."

"What else can I do, Win?"

She felt like one of those old Eskimo women who'd been set out on an ice floe. She knew that if she didn't reach out, grab for him, she would float away, alone. "Luke, please . . ."

"Please what?"

She swallowed hard, battling her own fear. It was terrifying to tell him the truth—she wasn't ready; he wasn't ready—but there was no choice anymore. She dared to touch him, take hold of his wrist. "I know you're not ready to hear this, Luke, but . . . I love you. If you'd just try, we could be happy together."

She saw his answer before he spoke. In the silence, with a fire crackling beside them, she saw his surprise. Then came the pity.

Her stomach twisted in on itself. She had handed her assassin a knife and bared her chest. If there were any way to stop him from speaking the words aloud, she would have done it, but the wheel was already turning.

"I love you, too," he said, lowering his voice to add, "as a friend."

She pulled away from him and turned her back. "That's what I meant," she said dully, though they both knew it was a lie.

"I think I'll go back to Kalispell," he said, staying by the fire.

"Maybe you can find a nice skinny girl there," she said, reaching down for her coat.

He came to her then, took her by the shoulders, and turned her around. "Winona, you know it's not about that. It's just . . ."

Try as she might to control her tears, they came anyway, stung her eyes. *Pathetic.* And in that instant, she was the fat girl begging for her mother's horse all over again. "I get it, Luke. Believe me. I get it."

The following Monday, she heard from Aurora, who'd heard from Julie: Luke had moved back to Montana.

Chapter Twelve

On the water, time passed in currents, rippling closer and closer to the shore. In winter, the waves were bolder, angrier, tipped in white; wind whipped them into a frenzy and rain fell almost daily. Color faded the landscape. Even the evergreens lost some of their rich hue, appearing black against the gray sky, gray clouds, and gray water.

Sunlight changed all that, and in May, when the rains paused, bright pink and purple azaleas bloomed overnight, and everywhere was lime-green new growth—on the lawns, in the shoots of fragile leaves along the roadsides. At night the sound of frogs croaking to one another was so loud that all through town, people got up in the middle of the night to shut their windows.

In June, the summer people came back. Along the banks of the canal, docks began to reappear, as did the boats that were tied alongside them. The diner extended its hours and added a few trendy vegetarian sandwiches to the menu, and the seasonal shops reopened. Hanging baskets of purple lobelias and red geraniums were returned to their hooks on the streetlamps.

Vivi Ann noticed every change. For years, it seemed, she'd taken all that for granted, seen each alteration in the seasons as nothing more than the passing of time.

Her pregnancy had changed her perspective. Now she marked time in the smallest increments— a day, a week, sometimes even an hour. It wasn't just her body that was changing, either. Everything felt different lately. She had never been as excited for anything as she was for the arrival of this baby. She was equally terrified. On a daily basis she missed her mother, and not in the ephemeral, little-girl way that she'd always missed her. That ache had turned into a hot, sharp pain. She had so many questions and no way to get the answers she needed.

Her fear—a new thing—ran deep and dark. At night, when she lay in bed with Dallas, listening to him sleep, she worried that she was too selfish to be a good mother, too immature to guide another human being through life. She worried, too, about his or her Native American heritage and how she would help her child to feel accepted by both worlds. In the ten months since her marriage, she'd learned very little about the man she loved. He loved her—that was obvious—but the rest of his emotions he kept in close check. Anger was the only thing that sometimes came to the surface, and on the rare occasions when she saw that side of him, she was afraid.

Remember, he'd told her once when they were fighting, *abuse can make an animal mean. I tried to warn you.* He'd wanted to push her away; she saw that now. The only thing in the world that scared him was their love.

He didn't understand, really, that she didn't just love him. She lived for him. He was still the addiction she couldn't shake.

"You're zoning out again," Aurora said, taking a french fry from Vivi Ann's plate. "Hot sex this morning?"

Vivi Ann laughed, and rubbed her swollen belly. "You were the one who told me that passion faded."

"Yeah, well. Then you met Tattoo Boy."

"I can't believe how much I love him. You know that, right?"

"The surprising thing is how much he seems to love you. He watches you like a hawk. Sometimes I think he can't stand to be away from you."

Vivi Ann heard the wistfulness in her sister's voice, and realized how familiar that tone had become. "Do you want to talk about it?"

"About what?"

"Richard. What's wrong?"

213

Aurora's well-made-up face crumpled at that. "I thought I was hiding it."

"That must be lonely."

Aurora's eyes filled with tears. "I like him. And he likes me. Maybe that's okay, enough. But I've seen what you and Dallas have and now I don't know. Should I just . . . walk through life? And there are the kids to think about. I don't want them to grow up like we did, with this hole in the family where someone should be."

Vivi Ann reached across the table and laid her hand on top of Aurora's. "Everyone thinks Winona's the smart one of us, but it's you, Aurora. You . . . see things, you pay attention. You'll make the right choice."

"Maybe I don't want to choose."

Vivi Ann knew all too well how seductive that idea was. "Not doing anything is a choice, too. Not a good one. Trust me. Winona's still pissed at me for hurting Luke. And she's right. It's the only time in my life I've ever been purposely cruel."

"No one can hold a grudge like Winona, that's for sure."

"Sometimes I think she hates me."

"Believe me, Vivi, the person Winona hates is herself. She's spent her whole life trying to get blood from a stone and because she doesn't know how to give up, she can't stop. She keeps waiting for something from Dad that she'll never get."

"That's because she needs words, and he can't do that."

Aurora sighed. "Vivi, you have a different dad than I do, that's all I can say. To you, he's like one of those horses you rescue."

"He *is* like that, Aurora. He loves us."

"If he does, Vivi, it's a pathetic, watered-down version, and God help any of us if we ever need him to show it."

"I saw him cry once," Vivi Ann said. It was a memory she'd never been able to share before.

"Dad?"

"That last night, when Mom's hospital bed was in the living room and we slept in sleeping bags on the floor."

Aurora's smile was unsteady. "She wanted us with her."

Vivi Ann nodded. "I woke up in the middle of the night and saw Dad sitting by her bed. Mom said, 'Take care of my garden, Henry. Love them, for me,' and he wiped his eyes."

My garden. The fragile moment bound them; they were Bean and Sprout again, a pair of little girls sitting at the kitchen table with their mom, making seashell-encrusted Kleenex boxes for the bathroom.

"What did you say to Dad?"

"Nothing. I pretended not to be awake. And when I woke up again, she was gone."

"It could have been dust in his eyes."

"It wasn't."

Aurora sat back.

Vivi Ann looked down at her swollen belly. "I miss her lately all the time. I want to—" She gasped in surprise as a cramp squeezed her abdomen. Hard. She had just gotten her breath back when another one hit; this one hurt even more.

"Are you okay?" Aurora asked, leaning forward.

"No," Vivi Ann gasped. "It's too early . . ."

Vivi Ann had never been one of those people who thought about the bad things that could happen in life. When she heard people say, *Life can turn on a dime,* she usually smiled and thought: *Yes. It can always get better.* On the rare occasions when morbid thoughts did cross her mind, she pushed them away quickly and focused on something else. She'd learned early on that optimism was a choice. When asked about the buoyancy of her outlook she replied jauntily that good things happened to good people, and she believed it.

Now she knew why people often frowned at that answer. They knew what she had not yet learned: Optimism was not only naïve. Often it could be cruel.

Bad things did happen, even when you did everything right. You could get married when you fell in love, conceive a child in the bed of that love, give up every habit that endangered your child, and still give birth six weeks early.

"Can I get you anything else?"

Vivi Ann roused herself enough to open her eyes. She wasn't sure how long she'd been lying here with her eyes closed, replaying it all in her head. "Have Dad and Win come by yet?"

Aurora stood by her bed, looking sad. In the last few hours her sister's poufed-out bangs had fallen flat across her face and her makeup had faded. Without all that, Aurora looked thin and worn-out. "Not yet."

Vivi Ann smiled as best she could. "It means a lot that you've been here for all of this, Aurora. I forgive you for stealing my birthday tiara."

Aurora brushed the still-damp hair away from Vivi Ann's face. "I never stole your stupid tiara. You're the princess in the family."

"I wish they'd let me see him again. He's so tiny." That last word broke a piece of her control away; fear rushed through the crack. She reached over to the bedside table and picked up the pretty pink scallop shell she'd kept in her purse for years. It was as close to her mother as she could get.

"Don't go down that road," Aurora said. "You're a mom now. He needs you to be strong for him."

"I'm afraid."

"Of course you're afraid. That's what parenting is. From now on you'll always be a little afraid."

"Couldn't you lie to me? Tell me it's a bed of roses?" Vivi Ann closed her eyes, sighing tiredly.

All this honesty was crippling. The truth kept

banging around in her head: *thirty-four weeks . . . undeveloped lungs . . . complications . . . we'll see if he makes it through the night.*

She heard the doorknob turn and opened her eyes. Had she fallen asleep? For how long? She looked around the room for Aurora or Dallas, but they were gone. The room was empty. They'd given her a private room, which would have been great if she didn't know why. They wouldn't put her in a room with another new mother because Vivi Ann's son might not make it. She knew this without being told.

Then Winona and Daddy walked into the room. Vivi Ann felt tears well in her eyes. The fear she'd been holding back spilled over when she looked at Winona. No matter what had happened between them, Win was still her big sister, her mom in a way, the one who always made things right. Vivi Ann hadn't realized until this moment how much she'd needed her. "Have you seen him, Win?"

Winona nodded, coming over to the bed. "He's beautiful, Vivi."

Dad's big, rough hands curled around the bed's metal rails, looking like old roots against the shiny metal. Up close she could see how hollow his face looked; how tightly he was controlling his emotions.

It was a look she'd seen on his face all her life, or at least since Mom's death. "Hey, Daddy," she said, hearing a catch in her voice.

The change on his face was as subtle as cold butter turning soft around the edges on a warm day, but in it, she saw everything that mattered. It was how he used to look at her, back when she was his favorite little girl who could do no wrong, and he was the ground beneath her feet. Winona would have wanted words to go with that look, and Aurora wouldn't have noticed the change at all, but Vivi Ann knew what it meant: he loved her. And it was enough.

"He's too small," she said, starting to cry. "They say he might not make it."

"Don't cry," Winona said, but she was crying, too.

"He'll make it," Dad said, and his voice was firm now, the voice of her youth, gone in the years since Mom's death and suddenly back. It reminded her in a painful flash of who they all had been with Mom between them.

"How can you be so sure?"

"He's a Grey, ain't he?"

Vivi Ann smiled at that. A Grey. There were generations of strength behind that name. "Yeah," she said quietly, feeling hopeful for the first time.

It meant so much to Vivi Ann that they were here, that even after all that had happened, they were a family. She talked for a while and then closed her eyes just for a minute. When she opened her eyes again, the room was dark and they were gone.

She hit the bed control and angled up to a seated position. Shadows darkened the room, but a shaft of moonlight came through the window, illuminating her husband, who lay slumped in an uncomfortable plastic chair. In the ethereal, uncertain light, it took her a moment to see his face.

"Oh, Dallas," she said.

He got up slowly and walked toward her, pushing a hand through his long hair as he moved. "You should see the other guy."

At her bedside, he stopped.

She was glad for the shadows suddenly, wished it were even darker in here. As it was, the contrast of pale light and shadow only highlighted the damage: his cheeks were pale and hollow but for the dark, bloody gash right above the bone; one eye was swollen shut and looked to be a sick, yellowing color. He lifted his right hand, showing her his battered knuckles, how caked they were by dried, black blood.

"Where have you been?" she asked.

"Cat's."

"Who started the fight?"

"I did."

Vivi Ann looked in her husband's eyes, and saw how damaged he'd been by his father, and how scared he was about being a father himself. There was so much about him she didn't understand, like what you were left with after being beaten with electrical cords or locked in a dark closet or after watching your father murder your mother. But she knew about going on, and she knew about love. "Aurora tells me that from now on we'll always be afraid. Apparently it's part of parenting."

Dallas said nothing to that, just stared down at her as if he were waiting for something.

"You can't go beating people up every time you're scared; I guess that's my point."

"What if I'm not up to this?"

"You are."

"Lots of people . . . cops, judges, shrinks . . . they said I was like my dad. Ask Winona. She dug up my record, and she's right about one thing: it isn't pretty."

It was the clearest picture of his past she'd ever gotten: she imagined him as a young boy, abused for a long time and then suddenly alone in the world, being told by adults that he was bad to the bone. *Abuse can make an animal mean.* Had they dared to say that to a little boy who'd been hurt?

She reached up, gently touched his wounded cheek. "You love me, Dallas. That's how you're different from him."

It was a long time before he nodded, and even then, he didn't smile.

"So no more beating up strangers because you're scared, okay?"

"Okay."

"Now take me to see our son. I've been waiting all day for you."

221

He helped her into a wheelchair and tucked a blanket around her, then rolled her down to the neonatal intensive care unit. There, they spoke to the night nurse, who made an exception to the rules and showed them to the tiny incubator where their son lay sleeping.

Emotions overwhelmed Vivi Ann. Love. Terror. Grief. Hope. Joy. Love most of all. She thought she was too full to feel anything else, but then she looked up at Dallas.

"My grandfather's name was Noah," he said quietly.

"Noah Grey Raintree," she said, nodding at the sound of it.

"I didn't know it would feel like this," Dallas whispered. "If anything happens to him . . ." He didn't finish the thought and Vivi Ann didn't try to help him.

There was nothing to say. She reached out for her husband's hand, hoping together they could find the kind of hope that once she'd taken for granted.

On the fifteenth of July, people began showing up at Water's Edge, uninvited. Each person came with a specific task to do. The 4-H chapter cleaned out the horses' stalls; the Future Farmers of America helped Henry feed the steers; the Women's Equestrian Drill Team took over Vivi Ann's lessons. The word had gone out last week: Noah was coming home at last. And the town rallied to help out Vivi Ann.

She was stunned by her neighbors' help and grateful for their prayers. In the last six weeks, she and Dallas had been living separate lives, making sure that one of them was always at the hospital. Although she hadn't told people how difficult it had been, obviously they knew.

"It's time," Aurora said, coming up beside her.

"Are you ready?" Winona asked, following close behind.

Vivi Ann hugged them both tightly. Her emotions were so close to the surface right now she was actually afraid she would start crying. "Thank everyone for today, will you?"

"Of course," Aurora said.

Just then Dallas's primer-gray Ford truck came out from behind the barn and drove slowly through the parking area toward them. It was an old, rounded model that had seen better days, but the engine worked perfectly. He pulled up in front of them and parked.

Vivi Ann thanked her sisters again and opened the truck's heavy door. It screeched and rattled, then slammed shut behind her. On the ripped leather bench seat, the robin's-egg-blue car seat looked bizarrely out of place.

"You ready, Mrs. Raintree?" Dallas said, giving her the first true smile she'd seen in more than a month.

"I'm ready."

For the next two hours, as they drove down the twisting, tree-lined highway behind a steady stream of RVs and campers, they talked about everyday things—the new school horse that was giving the kids problems, Clem's aching joints, what to award for prizes at the next barrel race—but when they finally arrived at the hospital, Vivi Ann reached over the car seat and held his hand, unable to think of anything to say.

"Me, too," he said, and together they walked through the parking lot and into the bright white lobby of Pierce County's biggest hospital.

In the past weeks they'd become like family within these walls, and they stopped and talked to plenty of nurses, volunteers, and orderlies along the way to the pediatric wing.

There, Noah was waiting for them, swaddled in a blue thermal blanket and wearing a teacup-sized cap over his shock of wild black hair.

Vivi Ann took him in her arms. "Hey, little man. You ready to come home?"

Dallas put an arm around Vivi Ann and drew her close. They stared down at their son in silence and then carried him out of the hospital.

It took Vivi Ann a ridiculous amount of time to get him into the car seat, so much that she was laughing by the end of it.

All the way home, she found herself cooing to him, talking to him in a high-pitched voice that bore no resemblance to her own. He responded by spitting up all over himself.

"Note to self," she said, laughing. "Keep diaper bag handy." Looking for a tissue or a wad of drive-in napkins, she clicked open the glove box.

She heard Dallas say, "Don't!" sharply beside her, but it was too late.

The glove box lid flipped open and she saw what he'd wanted to hide.

A gun.

She started to reach for it, but he said, "It's loaded," and she drew back as if stung.

"Why in the hell do you have a loaded gun in your truck?"

He pulled over to the side of the road and parked. They were just past Belfair, at the rounded end of the Canal, where the low tide exposed hundreds of feet of oozing gray mud. Docks jutted out into it, waterless on either side. Boats lay angled on the ground, waiting for the tide to lift them up again.

"You don't know what my life was like before you."

It scared her, that simple declaration of a different world; she'd known it all along, but in her naïveté, she'd thought of him as a wounded, abused child. Vulnerable. This was new. This reminded her that he hadn't been a kid for a long time; that he'd grown into a man that sometimes she hardly knew. Against her wishes, she remembered the fight he'd started at Cat's, and the steely look in his eyes when a fight had almost started at the Outlaw. And the criminal record he'd told her about. Stealing cars had sounded almost romantic, reckless, but now she wondered. "Okay, but I know what it's like now and you don't need to keep a loaded gun in your car. Jesus, Dal, a kid could find it—"

"The truck is always locked."

"You're scaring me."

"I am who I am, Vivi Ann."

"No," she said. "That may be who you were. You're different now. Get rid of it. Promise me."

He released his breath; she knew then he'd been holding it, waiting. Leaning past the car seat, he reached out and closed the glove box. "You'll never see that gun again."

Chapter Thirteen

In the two years since Noah's birth, the gossip about Vivi Ann and Dallas died down. Not away, of course; it was simply too entertaining to release altogether, but other transgressions by other lovers had come along to replace it. The only people who seemed determined to hang on to the old animosities were Winona and Dad, and Vivi Ann understood their concerns. In time, though, she knew it would be forgotten completely.

Tonight, beneath a twilight sky the color of a bruised plum, she stood at the paddock fence, watching kids chase after a greased piglet at the annual Water's Edge Halloween party. Noah was in her arms, dressed for the party in an orange pumpkin outfit. Aurora stood on her left side; Winona was on her right. A pirate and a witch, respectively.

"Remember the first time you and I went after a greased pig, Winona?" Aurora said. "All the rest of the kids were behind us by a mile."

"I'm sure people said to one another in awe: 'Wow, that fat girl sure can hang on to a pig,'" Winona said.

"Ooh," Aurora said. "Someone is feeling sorry for herself tonight. I thought it was my turn."

"You always think it's your turn," Winona said, sipping her beer.

"Have you spent any time with Rick and Jane lately? They're the Children of the Corn. And Richard is losing his hair so fast I need to bring a vacuum to the dinner table. Top that, Miss Town's Best Attorney."

Winona turned to her. "You actually think it's better to be fat, childless, and single?"

"Uh. *Duh.* Again, I point to my offspring and husband. It's not like I'm married to that hot tattoo guy."

Vivi Ann laughed. "He is hot. And you're not fat, Win. You're bigboned."

"Lies and pretense," Winona muttered. "The new family motto."

Vivi Ann recognized the irritation in her sister's voice and knew Winona was having one of her bad days, when nothing made her happy.

"On that note," Vivi Ann said, "I'm going to go find my husband. This mermaid costume is itching like crazy, and it's time for my little man to go to bed."

Saying goodbye, she carried Noah through the crowded parking lot, weaving in and out of people who were standing around talking. She heard snippets of conversations; they were the same words she always heard at a gathering like this. A mixture of local gossip; who was screwing whom, who was late on their mortgage, whose kid had gone off the deep end. All she really cared about was that she and Dallas were no longer on the top of the rumor menu.

As she neared the barn, she found kids and dogs running around in the dark, squealing and barking. The salty tang of the sea air was sharpened by the smell of wood smoke and barbecuing hamburgers.

The arena was dark except for dozens of strategically placed Chinese lanterns that hung from the rafters. A portable dance floor had been placed over the dirt and every step taken on it sounded like thunder. Over in the corner, a local band was playing a popular mix of seventies and eighties music. People danced, while teenagers bobbed for apples and dug through bowls of cooked spaghetti, looking for grape eyeballs.

"Do you see Daddy?" she asked Noah, who sleepily babbled something that ended with, "Go Dada."

"Uh, Vivi Ann?"

Turning, she saw Myrtle Michaelian dressed in a pink polyester princess outfit. Her plump features were outlined in bright color: blue eye shadow, rosy pink blush, red glittery lipstick. A cheap tin tiara sat on her head amid a pile of graying curls.

"Hey, Myrtle," Vivi Ann said. "Great costume."

"Where's your husband?"

"I was just looking for him. Why?"

"Well . . . I don't usually trade in gossip . . ."

Vivi Ann kept from gritting her teeth by sheer force of will. While it was true that the gossip about their affair had faded, Dallas was still a man to be watched in Oyster Shores. Especially by the older, more conservative people like Myrtle. They didn't like the way he drank too much, fidgeted in church, played poker for money, and (perhaps most of all) that he didn't seem to care about their opinion of him. "I'm sure I already know whatever you're going to say."

"Really?" She leaned forward, whispered loudly, "Last Saturday I was closing up late and I saw Dallas and that Morgan woman walking across the street. They got into that beater car of hers and drove away."

Vivi Ann nodded. She'd heard this story in one form or another for two years; Dallas and Cat had been seen together at the minimart, at the gas station, at King's Market buying beer. "They're just friends, Myrtle."

"I'm only saying this, Vivi Ann, because your mama can't. She was a good friend, and if she were here, she'd tell you that no good can come of giving a man that kind of freedom."

"I love my husband," Vivi Ann said. To her, that was answer enough. She loved her husband and she trusted him. So what if he let off a little steam drinking and playing poker once a week at Cat's? The small-minded gossip meant nothing to her. She knew her husband too well to be jealous.

"I love my dog," Myrtle said crisply, "but I keep him chained up when the bitch across the street is in heat."

Vivi Ann couldn't help laughing at that. "Thanks for the heads-up, Myrtle. I'll keep a closer eye on my husband."

"You do that."

Still smiling, Vivi Ann left the barn and went up the hill to their cabin. In the past year, Dallas had added on a big wraparound porch as well as about eight hundred square feet of space, which they'd turned into a new kitchen, nursery, and bathroom. New French doors ran the length of the living room, framing the majestic Canal view and leading the way out onto the white porch.

In the back bedroom, decorated with horses and cowboy hats, she changed Noah's diaper, put him into his dinosaur pj's, and lay him down in his crib. "Goodnight, little pumpkin."

Out in the living room, she found Zorro standing beside her new sofa. He stepped sideways and turned on the stereo. His cheap black polyester cape caught on something and he pulled it free with a muttered curse.

She smiled. "You said you never dressed up for Halloween."

"I said there was no Halloween when I was a kid. That's different."

He came so close she could feel his breath on her cheek, smell the whiskey he'd drunk. He brought up one gloved hand, let his finger trail down her exposed throat, down to the valley between her breasts.

"Myrtle Michaelian says you're being a very bad boy lately. She saw you up to no good with Cat."

"The gossip never stops in Mayberry. What did you tell her?"

"I told her I like bad boys."

He picked her up and carried her to their bed, kicking the door shut behind him. "Trick or treat, Mrs. Raintree?"

She laughed when he dropped her onto their bed. Moonlight came through their window and illuminated half of his sharp face, turned half of his hair blue. "I think I'll take a treat, Mr. Raintree. If you're up to it."

On Christmas Eve morning, Vivi Ann rose well before dawn and began making cookies. At some point Noah woke up and she brought him into the kitchen with her. He laughed and played with his plastic dinosaurs in a mound of sugar cookie dough. When he realized how good the dough tasted, he giggled and threw the toys aside and started eating.

"Oh, no, you don't." Wiping her floury hands on her apron, she scooped him up and held him on her hip while she cleaned up the kitchen. It was like carrying a seizing cat; he kept reaching and twisting and crying, "Mo', Mama, mo'."

She carried him into their newly expanded bedroom. Sunlight poured in checkerboard beams through the French doors, landed in streaks on the wide pine floorboards, which glowed like streaks of fresh honey. "Get up, sleepyhead," she said to Dallas. "Your son needs changing." She dropped Noah alongside Dallas, who mumbled something and rolled over.

"Look, Noah, Daddy's playing hide-and-seek."

Noah giggled and clambered over Dallas, falling like a slinky on the other side of him. "Dada?"

Dallas's arm came out from under the covers and coiled around the little boy. Noah immediately settled down, as he always did around his dad, and snuggled in close, resting his cheek on his father's tattooed bicep. Closing his eyes, he started sucking his thumb and fell quiet.

Vivi Ann stood there a moment, drinking in the sight of them. From birth they'd been a pair; when Noah got hurt, it was Dallas he wanted, and when he woke in the middle of the night, crying over a bad dream, it was Dallas who calmed him. Oh, Noah loved Vivi Ann, followed her around like a puppy dog and kissed her good morning and fell asleep in her arms, but he was a daddy's boy and everyone knew it.

Smiling, she went into the bathroom and took a shower. By eleven, she'd boxed up the cookies, wrapped up the fudge, and dressed for church.

"Dallas," she said, trying to waken him. "You were supposed to get Noah ready."

He rolled over onto his back. With Noah tucked protectively in the curl of his arm, he came awake slowly. "I don't feel good."

She sat down beside him, noticing how dull and glassy his eyes were. A few beads of sweat dotted his hairline. She reached down, pressed the back of her hand to his forehead. "You're burning up."

"It's that stupid play group. Every time I drop Noah off there, I get sick. I think there's something wrong with me."

"There's nothing wrong with you. I'll get you some aspirin."

When she came back, he was asleep again. She jostled him awake, made him take two aspirin and drink a glass of water.

"I was so excited about today," she said.

"The Grey Christmas Eve tradition," he said. "Ugh."

"What? You don't like shopping all day, having dinner at the Waves, going to a movie, and then ending it all with night services at church?" She pushed the damp hair away from his eyes, let her touch linger on his face.

"I'd rather eat my own boots."

"I thought you'd want to help me find something for Noah."

"I made him a dreamcatcher. My mom made me one when I was about his age." He smiled. "I kept it a long time."

"What's a dreamcatcher?"

"Indian thing. You hang it over your bed and it keeps the bad dreams away."

She touched his bare, damp chest, letting her fingertip trace the ugliest of his scars. It was an oblong-shaped pucker with pink edges. "Okay, Mr. Raintree, because I love you, I'm going to tell my sisters you're sick today, but tomorrow is Christmas morning and we're going to Dad's. So if this is some kind of Ferris Bueller trick, you only get one day off."

"It's no trick."

She leaned down and kissed him, germs and viruses and all. "I love you, Dal."

"I love you, too."

She reached over for Noah and picked him up. Taking him into his bedroom, she changed his diaper and put him in a red and green flannel shirt, OshKosh overalls, and his coat. Then she went back to Dallas, put a cool, wet rag on his forehead, and kissed him goodbye.

The following morning, Vivi Ann woke just as dawn was beginning its gentle rise from the horizon.

Rolling over, she faced her husband. She hadn't known before that your whole world could sometimes be found in another person's face, that creases could seem like valleys to be explored; lips a mountain range.

She leaned closer, pressed her naked body to his in the way she'd done so many times before. "Merry Christmas," she whispered against his lips.

"Merry Christmas." His voice was gravelly and low, as if he'd been yelling all night, or smoking cigars.

"How do you feel?"

"Better."

They lay there for a while longer, and then Vivi Ann kissed him one last time and got out of bed. Almost from that moment on, they were both in motion. They took showers and got dressed. While Vivi Ann readied Noah for the big gathering down at the farmhouse, Dallas fed the stock and checked the water in the fields. By the time he returned, the fullness of daylight had settled across the pastures, catching in the puddles and drops from last night's rain and giving everything a silvery sparkle.

Vivi Ann packed the truck with food and presents.

"Oh. There's one more thing," Dallas said as they were heading out. "Just a second." He went into the bedroom and came out a moment later carrying a big pink-wrapped box. She could tell he'd wrapped it himself—the Scotch tape was at odd angles and covered every possible seam. The white foil bow was hanging on by a thread.

"You know we open presents at Dad's," she said. "Just put it in the truck."

"Not this one."

She laughed. "What is it? Edible underwear? Or a nightgown that doesn't quite cover my nipples?"

"Open it."

The way he was watching her caused a little shiver to skip down her spine. She took the package from him and carried it over to the sofa. He scooped Noah up from the floor and sat down next to her.

The sight of him beside her, holding the son who looked so much like him, was all the present she could ever want, and all the future, too. Still, eagerly she unwrapped the box and found another, smaller one inside of it, and then a small one inside of that. By the time she got to the smallest package, she was pretty sure she knew what it was and her heart was beating quickly.

She glanced at him, caught the intensity of his gaze, and opened the box.

Inside was a beautiful diamond ring. The stone was small but brilliant and set amid an antique-looking gold filigree.

"I'm sorry I couldn't afford one when we got married." He took the ring out and slid it onto her finger, butted it up against the plain gold band she'd worn since their wedding day more than three years ago.

She held his gaze. "I never needed a diamond."

"I wanted to give you one."

"It's perfect."

Holding hands, they went out to the truck and drove down to the farmhouse.

Vivi Ann stood back, looking at the house. White Christmas lights embellished the eaves and glittered along the porch's handrails. Through the front window, the decorated tree cast prisms of multicolored light through the ancient glass.

Inside, the party had already begun. The Glen Campbell Christmas album—a family staple—was on the turntable, pumping music into the house. Ricky and Janie were running around, playing hide-and-seek with their dad, while Aurora and Winona worked in the kitchen. Dad was by the fireplace, drinking bourbon already, and looking at a photograph of Mom.

Aurora greeted them at the door. In her green leggings, high-heeled ankle boots, and red velvet tunic, she looked like an elf come to life; her jewelry ran on some kind of battery pack and came on and off in bursts of light. "There's my gorgeous nephew." She reached out for Noah and carried him over to the tree.

"The usual carnival," Dallas said, looking around at all the Christmas knickknacks.

Richard chose that moment to join them. In his tan Dockers, cinched high on his waist and drawn tight by a brown belt, with his blue plaid shirt tucked in, and his stockinged feet, he managed to look as he always did, both ready to stay and ready to leave at the same time. "Dallas," he said, nodding. "I heard you've been working miracles with the Jurikas' new colt."

"He's a hell of an animal," Dallas said. "Just last week . . ."

Vivi Ann squeezed her husband's hand and wandered into the kitchen. Winona was at the counter, rolling squares of dough into crescent rolls. She looked up at Vivi Ann's entrance and paused. "Hey."

For a second, Vivi Ann felt time peel back. With the pale winter sunlight coming through the windows, wreathing her sister's full, beautiful face, Vivi Ann remembered another time in this kitchen . . .

I'm drawing something for Mommy, she'd said, feeling about as small and forgotten as a child could. That was what she recalled most about her mother's funeral: feeling invisible. But Winona had seen her, had bent down beside her and touched her head and said, *We'll put it on the fridge.*

Vivi Ann had assumed back then that they would always be connected, she and Win, that nothing could rend two sisters apart.

That was before she'd known about passion, of course. And though Winona wouldn't admit it, Vivi Ann knew that their reconciliation was imperfect. Winona still didn't trust Dallas, and she hadn't entirely forgiven Vivi Ann for hurting Luke. In Winona's world, everything was black and white. Justice most of all. And she thought Vivi Ann had been rewarded for doing the wrong thing.

Vivi Ann reached out suddenly, took Winona's hand, and spun her in time to the music. It was a flick of a switch, that movement, a spinning back to the seventies, when dancing in the kitchen had been a normal part of Christmas morning.

Come on, garden-girls, Mom used to say, dancing all by herself, *I need some swing partners.*

Aurora skidded into the room, pushing her way between them and taking the lead. "No way you bitches are dancing without me. You *know* I'm the one with all the rhythm."

"Comes from all that pumping of your hips you did in high school," Vivi Ann said, laughing.

It was funny how a song, or a dance, or a look passed between sisters could give the whole of your life back to you. The rest of the day passed in a blur of familiar snapshots: opening gifts, sipping wine, coming together in smaller groups to talk, watching Janie and Ricky ride their new bikes in the yard and Noah walk around with ribbons stuck to his hair. They had so much fun that even their dad's drunken sullenness couldn't take the shine off the day.

At the end of the meal, as the girls had just finished serving pie and retaken their seats, Dallas stood up. "My son will grow up with this." He made a motion with his hand, a gesture that included all of them. "Thank you."

Vivi Ann gazed across the table at her husband.

"My Dada," Noah said in her lap, grinning.

"Yeah," she said quietly. "That's your daddy."

In no time they went back to talking at once and cracking jokes and commenting on the various pies. After dinner, Vivi Ann tried to talk everyone into a game of charades. "Come on, you guys. It'll be fun . . ."

Then the doorbell rang and Sheriff Al Bailor walked in.

"Hey, Al," Aurora said, pushing back from her chair to greet him. "Tell Vivi Ann we are not playing any games. We're still sober, for God's sake."

"I'm sorry to bother you all on Christmas," Al said, taking off his hat and working its brim with his blunt fingers.

Dad stood up. "What's the problem, Al?"

"Cat Morgan was murdered last night."

Dallas came slowly out of his chair. It was impossible not to notice how pale he'd gone. "What happened?"

"Well," Al said, looking down the table, "that's what I've come to find out. Where were you last night, Dallas?"

Chapter Fourteen

LOCAL WOMAN FOUND SHOT TO DEATH IN OYSTER SHORES HOME

In the early morning hours of December 25, local woman Catherine Morgan was found shot to death in her home on Shore Drive. The forty-two-year-old woman was discovered by a neighbor, who immediately contacted police.

Investigators are continuing to gather evidence at the scene. Sheriff Albert Bailor has reported only that the death "appears suspicious," and that they are "following all leads." Sources outside law enforcement confirm that Ms. Morgan was shot in the chest at close range and that there was no sign of forced entry at her residence. Reports of sexual assault remain unconfirmed at this time. Anyone with information is asked to contact Sheriff Bailor.

—William Truman
Oyster Shores Tribune

Vivi Ann got out of bed slowly. In the last forty-eight hours she'd learned how to move quietly, to be both there and gone at the same time. Wrapping her terrycloth robe around her, she walked out into their living room and found Dallas exactly where she'd expected him to be: slouched over the kitchen table, rereading the newspaper accounts of the murder.

She put a hand on Dallas's shoulder, felt him flinch. He cocked his head and looked up at her. There was a wildness in his eyes that made her want to draw back, but she knew how close to the edge he was and how much he needed her to keep him steady. She knew, too, that he was waiting for her to ask him if he'd done it. The whole town was talking about his connection to Cat. Rumors were running rampant about his late-night visits, his trips to the store for beer with her at his side. They knew this, both of them, although they hadn't spoken of it.

"Today's the funeral," she said quietly. "We need to get Noah to the babysitter at eleven."

"I don't think I should go."

"You have to go. People are talking—"

"You think I give a shit what these small-minded bastards say?"

"I think we have to care."

"I should leave. Just leave. I never should have stayed."

She grabbed his arm then, pulled him up to face her. "Don't you *dare* say that."

"They'll come after me for this, don't you know that?"

"No, they won't. It's just gossip. They need facts to make an arrest. It'll go away."

"Ah, Vivi," he said tightly. "You're so naïve . . . This will destroy us."

He turned away from her and went into the bathroom and closed the door. She stood there a long time, staring after him. Her hands were trembling and she felt close to following him, but she didn't.

They'll come after me for this. He sounded so sure, as if he knew something she didn't.

She wanted to brush it off, tell herself it meant nothing, but she couldn't do it. Taking a deep breath, she walked through the shadowy cabin and went outside.

His gray truck was parked deep in the trees. Through the morning mist it looked like an old elephant, fallen to its knees in the shade. She slipped into the rubber boots by the door and clomped through the muddy grass. Opening the passenger door, she stared at the glove box, feeling panic rise like the fog around her. Reaching forward, she clicked it open.

The gun wasn't there.

She didn't know whether to be disappointed or relieved, but fear remained, settled into a hard knot in her lungs. Moving stiffly, she closed the truck back up and went inside.

She found Dallas in the bathroom, dripping wet, wearing a towel slung low on his hips.

"Where's your gun?" she asked, watching him closely.

He sighed. "I gave it to Cat."

Vivi Ann closed her eyes. It felt as if everything were draining away—blood, hope; life.

"You told me to get rid of it, remember? And she had that guy who was harassing her last year."

"That's why you're sure they'll come after you."

"It's why I'm afraid." He reached out, touched her chin. "Go ahead and ask me, Vivi. I know you want to."

She heard the desperation in his voice, saw it in his eyes. All his life he'd been let down, and he expected it of her, but she knew him. *Knew* him. She knew how he looked at his son when he was sleeping and how he talked about their family. There was darkness in her husband's past; but those days were behind him. Love wasn't a surface emotion for Dallas, nor was friendship. No matter what he'd done wrong before, she knew he wouldn't kill Cat. "I don't have to, Dallas. I know you're innocent."

He seemed to deflate before her eyes. Saying nothing, he looked away.

"Now get ready. We've got to go to your friend's funeral."

For the next two hours, they went through the morning routine in silence, except for Noah's nearly constant babbling.

At eleven o'clock, Aurora and Richard showed up, looking glum and concerned. Vivi Ann and Aurora stared at each other for a long moment, neither speaking, and then they all got into Richard's rain-spotted black Suburban. They dropped Noah off at their house, along with Janie and Ricky and the sitter, and then drove to the church.

There, the pews were almost full of black-clad mourners.

Throughout the short, impersonal service, Vivi Ann held Dallas's hand. She could feel his tension; sometimes he squeezed her hand so tightly it hurt. When the funeral was over, she got to her feet, pulled him up awkwardly beside her. Together, they merged into the aisle and went downstairs, where food filled the table and no one would make eye contact with Dallas or Vivi Ann. As usual, the women had baked their way to goodbye. People stood around, talking in small groups. There were no pictures of Cat set up on easels around the room, no sounds of weeping.

"Hypocrites," Dallas muttered beside her. "Look

at them. Those women crossed the street to avoid her if they could."

"Don't," Vivi Ann said sharply.

Aurora, Richard, Dad, and Winona came up to them, closed in tightly. Vivi Ann felt a wave of gratitude for their support, but she could see by her dad's face that he was not happy about being here.

And then, suddenly, Al was there, in uniform. "Come with me, Dallas Raintree," he said in a loud, showy voice. "You've got some questions to answer."

Vivi Ann clung to her husband's hand. "Come on, Al. You can't believe—"

Dallas pulled free of her. "Of course he believes it."

Al took Dallas by the arm and led him away. The crowd parted, stunned into an uncharacteristic silence by the drama unfolding in front of them.

Vivi Ann followed Al and Dallas through the crowd, pleading with Al to be reasonable, but he didn't answer, just dragged Dallas out into the parking lot and drove away.

Vivi Ann opened her purse and fumbled through the junk inside for her keys. Then she realized that she hadn't driven here. She looked back for Aurora and saw people gathered together on the church steps, watching her. "He didn't do it," she yelled at them. Her voice cracked like an egg and the emotions she'd been trying to control spilled out. She knew she was crying and she couldn't stop, couldn't even manage the strength to turn away.

Aurora came up to her, put an arm around her. Winona was next. Together her sisters shielded her. Vivi Ann noticed that her father held back, staying where he was.

"Come on," Winona said. "We'll take you home."

"Home?" Vivi Ann looked at them incredulously. "Take me to the police station. I need to be there for him when he's done."

Aurora and Winona exchanged a look.

"What?" Vivi Ann demanded.

"You're making a scene," Aurora said firmly. "Let's walk toward the car."

"What if I refuse?"

"Then I'll break one of your legs," Aurora said, smiling at the crowd, saying loudly, "She's fine now. No need to worry."

"We'll take you to the police station," Winona said, and Vivi Ann let herself be led away.

The drive to the police station was over so quickly there wasn't much time to talk, and Vivi Ann didn't know what to say anyway. As soon as they parked along the curb, she got out of the car and ran into the station.

"I'm here to get my husband, Helen."

The woman she'd known since childhood wouldn't look at her. "He's being questioned, Vivi Ann. Albert says he'll return him as soon as he can. You can wait in the lunchroom if you want, but it might be a while."

Aurora and Winona came up behind her and led her down to the lunchroom. There, they sat in molded plastic chairs at Formica tables, drinking bitter coffee from a vending machine. For the first two hours they talked about nothing; each tried to make conversation, but the black and white wall clock kept ticking past the minutes.

"You know about this stuff, Winona," Vivi Ann finally said. "What are they doing?"

"Questioning him, but don't worry. He's too smart to confess to anything."

Vivi Ann looked at her. "Innocent people make mistakes all the time. They think they have nothing to hide."

"You need to be prepared for the worst here," Winona said evenly.

"You've been waiting for this, haven't you, Win? You can't wait to tell me you were right."

"Vivi, don't," Aurora said. "We shouldn't fight now."

"I *was* right," Winona said. "If you'd listened to me in the beginning, we wouldn't be sitting in the police station right now. I told you Dallas would cause trouble. He's been on the wrong side of the law his whole life."

"Get out of here, Winona," Vivi Ann snapped. "I don't want you with me."

"Vivi, you don't mean that," Aurora said.

"Dallas always said you were jealous of me. He was right, wasn't he? You're probably loving this."

"Just because I knew this would happen doesn't mean I'm loving it. What did you expect, with a man like him?"

"Of course you don't understand. The only thing you know about love is how it feels not to have it. Has any man ever said he loved you?"

"Vivi—" Aurora warned.

"No. I want her out of here, Aurora. *Out.* If she thinks he's guilty, she can go." Vivi Ann knew she was screaming, that she was hysterical, but she couldn't rein in her emotions.

Winona grabbed her purse and got up from the chair. "Fine. You want to be alone on this, go for it."

Aurora reached for Winona. "She doesn't know what she's saying, Win—"

But Winona was already walking toward the door, yanking it open.

"You shouldn't have done that," Aurora said when the door banged shut.

"I couldn't listen to any more."

Aurora got up slowly, sighing, and got them each another cup of burnt, old-tasting coffee. Doctoring both cups with lots of fake creamer and sugar, she sat down by Vivi Ann. "This is going to get ugly," she said.

"It already is."

"No," Aurora said, stirring her coffee. "I don't think we've seen the start of ugly yet."

Hours later, Al finally walked into the lunchroom, looking worn-out and a little sad.

Vivi Ann got to her feet. "Where is he?"

"He failed the polygraph, Vivi Ann," Al said.

"I watch *L.A. Law.* Those results aren't admissible," Aurora said, standing beside Vivi Ann.

Vivi Ann thought she'd been afraid in the parking lot, or when she'd seen the empty glove box and then found out what he'd done with his gun; she'd been wrong. That previous emotion was nothing compared to this, as different as falling was to flying.

"We arrested him, Vivi," Al said. "Murder. You'd best find him a lawyer."

Aurora swore beneath her breath. "Great time to piss off Winona."

On the way home, Winona came up with one stinging comeback after another: *Of course you know about love. If I'd gone slumming like you, I could have gotten laid, too.* Or: *He doesn't love you. Why can't you get that through your head? Oh, wait. I know the answer: you're blond.* Or: *If that's love, I'd rather have the swine flu.*

At her house, she yanked the door open and went inside. The Christmas decorations were still up: the brightly festooned Douglas fir in the corner, the reindeer and sleigh on the coffee table, the ridiculously hopeful mistletoe hanging from the archway between rooms. She wrenched the mistletoe down and shoved it in the trash can, and then sat down in her window seat, staring out at the rain falling on the bare trees. From here, she could see people walking through town; they were probably doing some after-holiday shopping or coming home from church, as if this were a normal winter day.

But it wasn't normal, might never be normal again.

With a sigh, she went into the kitchen and found a quart of ice cream in the freezer. Taking it back to the sunroom, she sat down, eating and thinking. With every passing moment, she felt her resolve harden: she would not let Dallas Raintree destroy this family. Vivi Ann's passion for him had already cost them all too much. And now there was the Grey name to consider, too. Already people were saying that they'd been fools to let him into their home.

She wasn't sure how long she sat there, but it was long enough that the weather changed. The rain stopped and a hesitant sun peeked through the bank of gray clouds.

She heard a knock at the door, but didn't answer. There was no one she wanted to talk to right now.

A moment later, Vivi Ann walked into the sunroom. Already, Winona could see changes in her sister: the panic lurking at the edges of her mouth, the desperation in her green eyes, the knotting together of her hands.

"You caught me," Winona said, taking another spoonful. "I'm stress-eating."

"You didn't answer, so I came in."

251

"I didn't want to see anyone. I especially didn't want to see you."

Vivi Ann moved into the room, took a seat opposite her.

"I'm sorry, Pea," she said quietly; Winona knew she was using the old nickname as a kind of shorthand reminder of all that they were to each other. Sure, they fought and said things they didn't mean, but they were sisters. In the end, what mattered were not the breaks in the chain, but the links.

Winona took another bite. "How do you think Mom knew what we'd look like when she gave us those nicknames?"

"What do you mean?"

"You're the bean, right? How did she know I'd be the round, fat pea?"

"They were just the veggies that grew in her garden, Win. That's what she saw, what she wanted: us growing up together."

"You were too young to know what she wanted." Winona put the empty ice-cream container on the floor at her feet, with the spoon handle sticking up inside of it.

"I know she wanted us to stick together when times got tough."

"Says the girl who just threw me out."

"I said I was sorry."

"Of course you are. They arrested him, didn't they?"

Vivi Ann nodded.

"And you just realized that he needs a lawyer, so here you are."

Vivi Ann leaned forward. "It doesn't matter that he failed the polygraph, right?"

"He failed a polygraph?"

"Yeah, but even I know that's not admissible."

"They might not be admissible, but they're reliable. And he failed."

"He's innocent," Vivi Ann said stubbornly.

"He has no alibi. He was sick, remember? Even though he was fine the next morning."

"I'll do anything, Winona. Please. Just help me save him."

Winona stared at her younger sister, seeing how close she was to breaking. Vivi Ann had probably never begged for anything before, but Winona knew how that felt, that pathetic desperation, how your need warred with your ego, and you wanted to shout, *Fuck you,* even as you whispered, *Please.* "He needs a criminal defense attorney, Vivi. A good one. I'll handle his arraignment if you want me to, but after that I'd be in over my head. I'm just a small-town civil lawyer—"

"I don't care about all that. What he needs is someone who believes in him. That matters more than experience."

And there it was, the thing Winona had thought about as she sat in her window seat staring out at the rain, the thing that would break their bond, but there was no way to avoid it. "I heard about the fight he got into at Cat's," she answered quietly, knowing her words would hurt Vivi Ann and unable to change that. This pain was inevitable. It had been moving this way slowly, advancing on them, probably from the moment Dallas took the job at Water's Edge.

"What do you mean?"

"The night you had Noah, Dallas picked a fight with Erik Engstrom. Word was he almost killed him."

"We thought Noah would die that night. He was scared."

"He's dangerous, Vivi. Everyone but you can see that," Winona said evenly. "I tried to tell you . . ."

"Is that what this is about? I told you so?"

"No. I'm trying to protect you. I'm trying to be a good big sister."

"Do you actually think he killed her?"

"It doesn't matter. This thing will break your heart, Vivi Ann. You're not strong enough to—"

"Doesn't matter?"

Winona wasn't saying the right things, or in the right way, to make Vivi Ann understand. "I'm sorry, Vivi Ann. What I mean is, my opinion doesn't matter. I can't help Dallas. I'm not experienced enough. And there's probably a conflict of interest. He needs—"

Vivi Ann stood up. "You keep talking," she said. "I didn't hear anything after 'it doesn't matter.' Believe me, Win, I got your point loud and clear.

You think I'm married to a murderer." She turned and ran for the door, trying twice before she wrenched it open.

"Vivi, wait, please—"

Winona ran across the porch and out into the yard, but her sister was already gone.

Chapter Fifteen

After a long and sleepless night, Vivi Ann woke up tired. Still, by nine o'clock she was dressed in the only suit she owned and heading out to her truck, with Noah squirming in her arms. Now more than ever he needed her to be strong, and she would be. Her son would someday hear about all of this and say, *Mommy, what did you do while Daddy was in trouble?* and she would say, *I never stopped believing in him and I made everyone in town see how wrong they were.*

All her life she'd been dismissed by people because of her beauty, considered naïve because she saw the best in everyone. Finally she would show people that her innate optimism wasn't a weakness or an ignorance or even a flimsy kind of hope. It was made of steel and she would wield it like a sword. Driving through town, she passed Grey Park, and saw the sign—LAND DONATED BY ELIJAH GREY

IN 1951. For the first time, she thought not about her family's prominence in this community's history, but rather about their durability in the face of adversity. Her great-grandparents had traveled the Oregon Trail in a covered wagon, making their way through countless dangers. Her grandparents had hung on to this land through the Great Depression and two wars.

The land was still theirs because they'd refused to give up or give in. That tenacity was in her blood and she would call on it now.

On the street in front of the diner, she parked and got Noah out of his car seat. As she headed to the restaurant, she felt people watching her, shaking their heads. Their whispers pissed her off, renewed her determination to prove her husband's innocence. As expected, she found Aurora at the diner with Julie and Brooke and Trayna, having coffee.

At her entrance they all looked up and their expressions of pity said it all: *Poor Vivi, such a fool.*

"Hey, Vivi," Julie said, sliding sideways in her booth. Her silver bangle bracelets tinkled at her wrists. "You're just in time for breakfast."

"Thanks, but I can't. Aurora, you still okay with taking Noah for the day?"

"Sure."

"Why?" Trayna asked. "Are you going to the jail?"

"Not yet. I need to go to Olympia to find a good lawyer. I got some names out of the phone book."

Brooke frowned. "Winona—"

"Won't help."

"She said no?" Julie asked, frowning.

"Yeah. Be sure and spread it around: Winona turned her back on us." She kissed Noah's plump cheek and handed him off to Aurora, along with his diaper bag.

Noah went to his aunt happily, immediately playing with her beaded necklace.

"You want me to come with you?" Aurora asked. She'd made the same offer last night when Vivi Ann called her.

"I love you for offering, but no. I need to start doing things on my own. I have a feeling there's going to be a lot of that in my future." She started to leave.

Julie's hand on her wrist stopped her. "Not everyone thinks he's guilty," she said.

"Thanks, Jules."

All the way to Olympia, Vivi Ann practiced what she would say, how she would convince a stranger to take her husband's case. At the first address, she strode into the squat brick building, gave the receptionist her name, and waited impatiently. Almost twenty minutes later, James Jensen came out to meet her.

She smiled brightly when he finally appeared. "Hello, Mr. Jensen. Thank you for seeing me on such short notice."

"When one is looking for a criminal defense

attorney, it's often a rush. Here, come into my office and sit down."

For the next twenty minutes, Vivi Ann gave him the facts of the case, at least as much as she knew. She was careful to be professional and unemotional; she didn't want to look like one of those women who stupidly believe the best of their husbands. When she'd exhausted the limited facts, she talked about what a wonderful husband and father Dallas was. Then she waited for him to speak.

At last, he looked up.

She had waited for that look. Now he would ask if Dallas was innocent and she'd nod and tell him how she knew that to be true.

"So, Mrs. Raintree. I would need a thirty-five-thousand-dollar retainer. Then we could get started."

"A . . . what?"

"My fees. In advance. Not all of them, of course; just enough to get started. A case like this requires a lot of manpower—private detectives, lab work, motions. The discovery alone is often mind-numbing."

"You haven't asked if he did it."

"And I won't."

"I don't have that kind of money."

"Ah. I see." His flat, pudgy palm made a muffled thumping sound on the wooden desk. It reminded her of a closing door. "There are some good public defenders."

"But they won't care like a private attorney would. Like *you* would."

He lifted his hands, palm up. "Such is the system. I will hope that you can get the money together, Mrs. Raintree. From what you've told me, and what I've read in the newspapers, your husband—who, as you know, is no stranger to American jurisprudence—is in serious trouble." He stood up, shuffled her to the door with the ease of one who was experienced in this action. "Best of luck to you," he said, and closed the door between them.

In the next four hours, five attorneys told her the same thing. Their offices and personalities were different, but the deal was always the same: a large retainer up front or no lawyer.

The last lawyer she'd seen, a lovely young woman who seemed genuinely interested in Dallas's fate, had said it most clearly. "I can't take on a case of this complexity for free, Mrs. Raintree. I've got children to feed and a mortgage to pay. I'm sure you understand. I'd be happy to handle the arraignment, but if you want me to file a notice of appearance on behalf of your husband, I'll need a substantial retainer. At least twenty-five thousand dollars."

There was only one option left: she needed to find twenty-five thousand dollars.

She drove home from Olympia at twilight, turning onto the Canal road just as the last rays of sunlight were polishing the winter waters to a silvery sheen and the snow in the mountains had turned lavender-gray.

When she pulled up in front of her father's house it was full-on dark. She found him in his study, with a drink in his hand, reading a newspaper. All the way home from Olympia she'd practiced what she'd say, how she'd say it, but now none of that mattered. He was her father and she needed his help. It was really that simple.

She sat down in the chair opposite him. "I need twenty-five thousand dollars, Dad. You could take out a second mortgage on the ranch, and Dallas and I would pay you back. With interest."

He stared down at his newspaper so long she started to worry. It took all her self-control to sit there, waiting patiently. Her whole world hung in the balance, but she knew not to prompt him. He might be a little taciturn sometimes and judgmental, but most of all, he was a Grey, and in the end that would be his answer.

"No."

He said it so quietly she thought she'd imagined it. "Did you just say no?"

"You never shoulda married that Indian. Everyone knew that. And you never should have let him spend so much time at the Morgan place. It disgraced us."

Vivi Ann listened in disbelief. "You don't mean this."

"I do."

"Is that how you take care of Mom's garden?"

He looked up at her. "What did you say?"

"All my life I made excuses for you, told Win and Aurora that Mom's death broke you, but it isn't true, is it? You're not who I thought you were at all."

"Yeah, well, neither are you."

Vivi Ann got to her feet. "You told me the old stories a million times, made me proud to be a Grey. You should have warned me it was all a lie."

"He's not a Grey," Dad said.

Vivi Ann was leaving, at the door, when she turned around to say, "Neither am I. Not anymore. I'm a Raintree."

Vivi Ann walked up the hill toward her cabin. At the barn, she stopped, unable to keep moving. The ranch she loved so much was still and cold; winter-bare trees lined the driveway, looking stark and lonely against the gray skies and brown fields. She could see a few dying leaves still clinging stubbornly to their places on the branches, but soon they'd be gone, too, let go. One by one they'd tumble to the ground, where they would slowly fade to black and die.

She felt like one of those lonely leaves right now, realizing suddenly, fearfully, that there was no group around her. She'd clung to something that wasn't solid after all.

Without her father, she didn't even know who she was, who she was supposed to be. She walked into the cold, dark barn and turned on the lights. The horses immediately became restless, whinnying and stomping to get her attention. She didn't pass the stalls slowly or with care. For once she walked straight to Clem's stall and opened the door, slipping inside. The fresh layer of salmony-pink cedar shavings cushioned her steps, made her feel absurdly buoyant.

Clem nickered a greeting and moved toward her, rubbing her velvety nose up and down Vivi Ann's thigh.

"It's always been you and me, girl, hasn't it?" she said, scratching the mare's ears. She leaned forward, slung her arms around Clem's big neck, and pressed her forehead against the warm, soft expanse of hair, loving the horsey smell of her.

Two years ago, maybe even last year, she would have reached for a bridle right now, would have jumped on Clem's bare back and headed for the power lines trail. There, they would have run like the wind, fast enough to dry Vivi Ann's tears before they fell, fast enough to outrun this emptiness spreading inside her.

But Clem was old now, with creaking joints and aching legs. Her days of riding like the wind were over. Unfortunately, her spirit was young and Vivi Ann knew the mare waited patiently to be ridden again.

"Too many changes," Vivi Ann said, doing her best to sound strong, but halfway through the sentence, it hit her all at once—her father's simple *no;* Winona's refusal to help; Noah's plaintive bedtime cry last night of *Dada?* and the kiss Dallas had given her just before they left for Cat's funeral. She hadn't known then it would be their last one for a long time, but he had. She remembered what he'd said so quietly that morning, dressed all in black, with his gray eyes so impossibly sad: *I love you, Vivi. They can't take that.*

She'd laughed at him, said, "No one is trying to take it away. Trust me."

Trust me.

She wondered now if she'd ever be able to laugh again, and then, in the stall with this horse that was somehow her childhood and her spirit and her mother all wrapped up in one, she cried.

This part of the county had been economically devastated by decreased logging and dwindling salmon runs. In the heart of downtown, several storefronts were empty, their blank, blackened windows a reminder of the people and revenue this community had lost. Dirty, dented pickup trucks, many with FOR SALE signs in the back window, lined the street, gathered in front of the taverns on this Thursday afternoon.

Vivi Ann stood on the sidewalk, staring up at the gray stone courthouse. Behind it, the lush green hills of the Olympic National Forest rose into a cloud-white sky. It wasn't raining yet, but it would be any moment.

Tightening her hold on her purse, she headed up the stone steps toward the big double wooden doors.

Inside, the place was even more decrepit-looking. Tired wooden floors, peeling walls, people in cheap suits moving up the stairs to the courtrooms and down the hall to various closed doors. She walked over to a harried-looking receptionist and smiled. "I'm here to visit someone in jail," she said, embarrassed.

The woman didn't even look up. "Name?"

"Vivi Ann Raintree."

"Not yours. The inmate's."

"Oh. Dallas Raintree."

The woman punched some keys into her bulky beige computer, waited a few moments, then said, "P Cell. Visitation begins at three and ends at four." She pointed one stub-nailed finger down the hall. "Second door on your right."

"Th-thank you." Vivi Ann began the long, slow walk to the jail. When she got there, another receptionist was waiting for her.

"Name?"

"Dallas Raintree."

"Not the inmate's. Yours."

"Vivi Ann Grey Raintree."

"Identification, please."

Vivi Ann's hands were shaking as she opened her purse and extracted her driver's license from the wallet. The receptionist took it, wrote some things in a logbook, and handed it back.

"Fill out this form."

As she stood there, Vivi Ann heard people come up behind her, forming a line of sorts. It forced her to write faster. "Here you go," she said, handing the sheet back to the receptionist.

"Over there," the receptionist said, tilting her chin without looking up. "Put all your personal items in one of those lockers. No purses, wallets, food, gum, keys, et cetera. The metal detector is at the end of the hallway. Next."

Vivi Ann walked down the quiet corridor. At the end of the steel-gray lockers, she stowed her purse, and then headed toward the metal detector. A huge uniformed guard stood by the entrance, with his booted feet planted apart and his arms loose at his sides. He wore a gun on each hip.

She handed him the locker key and moved cautiously through the detector. Since she'd never flown anywhere, this was the first time she'd ever been through one of these devices and she wasn't quite sure how it should be done. Slowly made sense, so she inched forward. A high beeping alarm sounded; Vivi Ann's heartbeat kicked into high gear. She looked around; now there were three uniformed guards around her. "I—I don't have anything on me."

A woman guard came forward. "Over here. Spread your legs."

Vivi Ann did as she was told. Even though she knew she was fine—had to be—she was afraid. Sweat broke out on her forehead.

The guard passed a flat black paddle in front of her. It beeped again at her bra and at the buckle on her shoe.

"You're fine," the guard said. "That way."

Vivi Ann moved forward again, to another desk, where her hand was stamped and a VISITOR tag was hung around her neck. She followed another uniformed guard down another hallway to a door marked VISITATION.

"You got one hour," he said, opening the door.

Vivi Ann nodded and walked into the long, low-ceilinged room. A row of Plexiglas cut the space in half; on either side were cubicles. Each one had a black telephone receiver and a chair.

She went to the last cubicle on the left and sat down. The fake glass was clouded with thousands of fingerprint smudges.

She wasn't sure how long she sat there, alone, but the wait felt endless. At one point another woman came in, took a seat at the opposite wall. Through the distorting series of Plexiglas cubicles, their gazes met and then looked away.

Finally, the door opened and Dallas was there, wearing an orange jumpsuit and flip-flops, his long hair falling lank across his bruised face.

He came over to the cubicle, sat down on his side of the dirty Plexiglas. Slowly, he reached for the receiver.

She did the same. "What happened to your face?"

"They call it resisting arrest."

"And did you?"

"Oh, yeah."

She didn't know what to say to that, so she said, "I'm looking for a good defense attorney. It takes so much money, though. I'll keep trying. I can't—"

"I've already signed the pauper's affidavit and met with the lawyer assigned to my case. You're not going into debt to save me."

"But you're innocent."

The look he gave her was so cold that for a second he was someone she didn't know. "And that's what I'm going to teach you in the end. Cynicism. When this thing is over you won't know what to believe so you'll believe in nothing. That will have been my gift to you."

"I love you, Dallas. That's what matters. We have to stay strong. Love will get us through."

"My mom loved my dad until the day he killed her."

"Don't even *think* about comparing yourself to him."

"You're going to hear all about it before this thing is over, how he abused me, burned me with cigarettes, locked me up. They're going to say it made me mean. They're going to say I had sex with Cat, that I—"

Vivi Ann pressed her hand to the glass. "Touch me, Dallas."

"I can't," he said, and she could see how that admission ate him up inside and made him angry. "Love isn't a shield, Vivi. It's time you saw that."

"Touch my hand."

Slowly he brought his hand up, pressed his palm against hers. All she could feel was the slickness of the Plexiglas, but she closed her eyes and tried to remember the heat of his skin against hers. When she had the memory close, and could hold it to her chest, she opened her eyes. "I'm your wife," she said into the receiver. "I don't know who taught you to run, but it's too late for that now. We stand and fight. And then you come home. That's how it's going to be. You get me?"

"It makes me sick to see you in here, touching this dirty glass, talking into that phone, trying not to cry."

"Just don't pull away. I can take anything but that."

"I'm scared," he said quietly.

"So am I. But I want you to remember that you're *not* alone. You've got a wife and a son who adore you."

"It's hard to believe that in here."

"Believe it, Dallas," she said, swallowing the tears she refused to shed. "I won't ever give up on you."

All that winter and for the following spring, the upcoming trial of Dallas Raintree dominated town gossip. It was such a juicy bit of steak, with lots of fatty flavor. There was the big question: Did he do it? But in truth that didn't get much play. Most folks had made up their minds when he was arrested. Respect for the law ran high in Oyster Shores, and they figured a mistake was unlikely. Besides, they'd known from the minute he walked into the Outlaw Tavern, with his inked-up bicep and shoulder-length hair, and his looking-for-a-fight gaze, that he was trouble. The fact that he'd gone after Vivi Ann was proof enough he didn't know his place. She'd been suckered in by him, pure and simple. That was the talk anyway.

Winona had spent the last five months in a holding pattern. It was obvious to everyone that her sisters were no longer speaking to her. Dallas's arrest had broken the once-solid Grey family into two camps: Aurora and Vivi Ann vs. Winona and Henry. Sympathy ran high for all of them. The general consensus was that Dad and Winona had made an uncharacteristic mistake in hiring Dallas in the first place. While no one believed Dad should have paid for a private lawyer (*Why throw good money after bad* being the most common expression of this point), they believed he was wrong to let his family break up over it.

Winona had carefully planted the seeds of her own defense: that she wasn't a criminal defense attorney and couldn't represent Dallas; that she longed to reconcile with Vivi Ann and waited for the day when her baby sister would return to the fold; and most convincingly, that Vivi Ann had always been headstrong and would learn in time that she'd made a terrible mistake in believing in Dallas. On that day, Winona always said, "I'll be there to dry her tears."

It was true, too. Every day of her estrangement with her sisters was a nearly unbearable burden on Winona. For the first few months she had tried to bridge the gap, repair the damage, but each of her attempts at reconciliation or explanation had been ignored. Vivi Ann and Aurora would neither speak to her nor listen. They didn't even sit in the family pew at church anymore.

By mid-May, when the rhododendrons burst into plate-sized blooms and the azaleas in her yard were bright with flowers, she was hanging on by a thread, waiting for the trial to begin. When it was over, and Dallas was convicted, Vivi Ann would finally face the ugly truth. Then she would need her family again. And Winona would be there, arms open, waiting to take care of her.

On the first day of the trial, Winona woke up early, dressed in a suit, and was among the first spectators allowed into the gallery of the court-room. As she watched the poor defense attorney enter the room, dragging his file boxes toward the defense table, she knew she'd done the right thing in declining to represent Dallas. She could never have handled a trial of this magnitude. Last week she'd watched voir dire and several of the pretrial motions and known without a doubt that she would have been in over her head with this trial. Although, to be honest, she had her doubts about the defense attorney's competence, too. He'd allowed a couple of local residents on the jury, which didn't seem smart to Winona.

She went to a place in the third row and sat down, hearing people file in behind her. The gallery filled up in no time. Everyone in town wanted to be here today. The whispering was as loud as a rising tide in the wood-paneled room.

On the right side of the courtroom, at the front table, sat the assistant prosecuting attorney, Sara Hamm, and her bright-faced young assistant. On the left side, at the defense table, sat Roy Lovejoy, the attorney assigned to Dallas's case. Winona had tried her best to get information out of the prosecuting attorney's office, but everyone had been close-mouthed during the discovery process. All she knew was what everyone knew: that the rape charge had been dropped and the murder charge remained. The media hadn't been much help, either. The murder of a single woman in a small town in a rural county didn't warrant much in-depth coverage. Sensationalism about Dallas's and Cat's unsavory pasts abounded; true facts were harder to come by.

At eight forty-five, Vivi Ann and Aurora walked into the courtroom, holding hands.

In a loose-fitting black suit, Vivi Ann looked incredibly fragile. Light gilded her ponytailed hair, softened the thinness of her face. She looked like a piece of bone china that would crack at the slightest touch. Aurora looked as grim and determined as a bodyguard. They passed Winona without making eye contact, and took seats two rows in front of her.

Winona fought the urge to go to them. Instead she straightened, folded her cold hands in her lap.

And then two uniformed guards were bringing Dallas into the courtroom.

He wore a pair of creased black pants, a pressed white shirt, and a black tie. The months in jail had left their mark on him; he was thinner, sinewy, and when he looked at Winona, she froze, heart thumping.

Vivi Ann stood up, rising like a white rose from a messy garden, and tried to smile at Dallas.

Before Dallas was seated at the defense table, the guards removed his restraints.

Judge Debra Edwards entered the courtroom, wearing her flowing black robes. She took her place on the bench and looked at the attorneys. "Are the parties ready to proceed?"

"Yes, Your Honor," the lawyers said in tandem.

The judge nodded. "Bring in the jury."

The jurors filed into the courtroom in quiet order; all of them stared openly at Dallas. Several were already frowning.

Sara Hamm stood up. With that simple act, she commanded attention. An imposing woman in a crisp blue suit with a needle-thin white pinstripe, she looked professional and calm. She smiled at the jury and moved toward them confidently. "Ladies and gentlemen of the jury, the facts in this case are simple and straightforward." She had the voice of a fairy tale witch: smooth and honeyed on the surface but with a layer of steel beneath. Winona found herself leaning forward, hanging on every word.

"During the course of this trial, the state will prove beyond a reasonable doubt that Dallas Raintree feigned an illness on Christmas Eve of last year to avoid having to attend church services with his family. While his wife and child were away, he went to Catherine Morgan's home and he killed her.

"How do we know this beyond a reasonable doubt? The answer is evidence. Mr. Raintree left a trail behind him that investigators were able to follow. First and most obvious was his long-term association with the victim. Several eyewitnesses will testify as to Mr. Raintree's regular weekend trysts with Ms. Morgan. These evenings have been described as 'rowdy, drunken, lewd' gatherings that went on long into the morning. But association doesn't equal murder. For that we have to look to the physical and forensic evidence. Of which there is plenty."

Sara held out a photograph of Cat Morgan; in it, she was sitting on her porch, smiling at the camera. In the next photograph, she was slumped against a bloody wall, naked, a torn dark bullet wound in her chest.

Several jurors flinched and looked away; others glared at Dallas. Sara Hamm strolled in front of the jury, pausing now and then in front of the female jurors as she went on, describing the crime in excruciating detail. When she was finished with that, she turned to the jury again.

"The state will introduce evidence that the gun used to kill Catherine Morgan was owned by Dallas Raintree. Experts lifted his fingerprints from the weapon. That alone could be enough to establish his guilt beyond a reasonable doubt, ladies and gentlemen, but the state has even more proof. An expert from the Washington State Crime Lab will use hair samples gathered from the scene to place Dallas Raintree in Catherine Morgan's bed that night, and an eyewitness will testify that he left her house at just past eight o'clock that evening. The medical examiner has placed Ms. Morgan's death at somewhere between six and nine-thirty on the twenty-fourth. DNA samples from the crime scene will establish that Dallas Raintree is the same blood type as the man who had sex with Ms. Morgan just before her death.

"Coincidence? Hardly. When all this evidence is put together, the answer is inescapable. Dallas Raintree, who had a very public affair with Catherine Morgan before his marriage, went back to the affair sometime thereafter. After an argument of some kind, things went wrong for the lovers. Evidence will show that they fought for control of the gun. And Dallas Raintree won that fight. He shot her in the chest at point-blank range and then went home to his wife, celebrating a cozy Christmas while Catherine Morgan lay dead in her house. Ladies and gentlemen, this is a common-sense case. There is no doubt, reasonable or otherwise, that Dallas Raintree murdered Catherine Morgan in cold blood, and at the conclusion of the evidence I am confident that you'll find him guilty of this heinous crime. The mistake Ms. Morgan made on that dark Christmas Eve night was in believing that the defendant was her friend and letting him into her home. She died for that mistake, ladies and gentlemen. Let's not compound it now. Let's make sure that Dallas Raintree is never able to hurt anyone again." She returned to her seat and sat down. "Thank you."

Winona sat back in her seat, finally releasing the breath she'd been holding. She glanced up at the clock, seeing that it was nearly ten-thirty. The hour and a half Sara Hamm had been talking had flown by. But it was the jury that captured her attention. Almost all of them were staring at Dallas through cold, angry eyes.

Dallas's attorney rose. He appeared nervous and ill-put-together next to the elegant prosecuting attorney, and when he spoke his voice cracked and he had to clear his throat. Winona wondered how many murder trials he'd done. "Ladies and gentlemen of the jury, you have just heard the story the state would like you to buy; it is a collection of circumstances that appear to fit together like a puzzle, but upon closer examination create only a portrait of reasonable doubt. Dallas Raintree *was* sick that Christmas Eve. He never left his home that evening, and he certainly never killed the woman he identified as a friend. A good friend, but not a lover. Evidence will show that Catherine Morgan had lots of men in her life. Additionally, the DNA evidence left at the scene does not identify Dallas Raintree as the man who had sex with Ms. Morgan. Experts will testify that the sample was too small to be tested. And the matching of his blood type is meaningless; forty percent of the population shares that blood type. The state has arrested the wrong man. It is as simple as that. Dallas Raintree is innocent." With a nod to the jury, a kind of head-bobbing exclamation point, the man returned to his seat and sat down.

Winona couldn't believe it. Lovejoy's opening

had taken less than fourteen minutes. A look at the jury convinced her that he hadn't swayed one mind, not after the prosecutor's brilliant blow-by-blow account of the crime.

She saw Vivi Ann frown at Aurora, who shrugged.

Winona wasn't sure what to make of it. She didn't know much about criminal law and knew very little about trials, but the defense attorney seemed to be making a crucial mistake.

The judge looked at the prosecuting attorney. "Ms. Hamm, you may call your first witness."

The rest of the day and all of the following afternoon were taken up with the slow lacquering of facts, layer by layer. The prosecuting attorney brought in a series of crime scene witnesses, from Sheriff Bailor, to his deputy, to the dispatcher, to the photographer, to the medical examiner. In total, they confirmed everything that Sara Hamm had promised in her opening. Somewhere at or around five on the afternoon of Christmas Eve, Cat Morgan let someone into her home, presumably someone she knew, given that there was no evidence of forced entry. Several disreputable-looking witnesses testified that Dallas was at Cat's every Saturday night and repeated the speculation that they'd been lovers. Photographs of the bedroom revealed evidence of a fight; a lamp was knocked over and broken, a picture had fallen off of the wall. Defensive wounds on Cat's palms suggested that she'd fought her attacker and her prints on the gun suggested that she'd actually fought for control of the weapon.

Winona sat in the gallery day after day, riveted by the slowly expanding web of circumstance and fact. She learned more than she ever wanted to know about fingerprint analysis, DNA testing, and blood types. The prosecution introduced one expert after another, proving bit by bit their assertion that Dallas's fingerprint had been found on the gun (which had once belonged to his father—a convicted murderer himself) and that his blood type matched the sample left at the scene. The defense argued that the semen sample had been too small to run a DNA test on, and that the blood type match was meaningless, and, perhaps most importantly, that two unidentified prints had also been found on the weapon. But the damage had already been done.

On the morning of the fourth day of trial, the prosecuting attorney called Dr. Barney Olliver, a forensic criminologist. After presenting more than an hour of testimony about his credentials and testing methods, Sara got to the point. "Dr. Olliver, we've established that you are an expert on hair analysis. Were hair samples recovered from the crime scene?"

"Indeed."

Ms. Hamm moved to admit a series of hair samples found at the scene, and then said, "I know this is complicated scientific testimony, Dr. Olliver, but could you explain your findings to this court?"

"Certainly. May I go to my boards?" he asked, indicating four large easels.

The judge nodded.

For the next hour, Mr. Olliver explained everything there was to know about hair sample analysis, including itemizing the hairs found at the scene, textures, thicknesses, cuticles, and more.

Winona could see the jury losing interest, taking idle notes, until the prosecuting attorney said, "And of the nine pubic hairs found at the scene, which you examined and subjected to your rigorous testing methods, did any match the defendant's?"

"Objection!" Roy said, coming out of his chair. "The use of the word *match* is misleading."

"Sustained," the judge agreed.

Dr. Olliver barely paused. "Of the nine pubic hairs found at the scene, six were microscopically consistent with the defendant's."

"Meaning that, judged side by side, by a trained professional doctor, Mr. Raintree's pubic hairs were scientifically the same as the killer's?"

"Objection. Sidebar," Roy said, shooting out of his seat.

Winona watched as the attorneys approached the bench, argued back and forth, and then retreated.

Ms. Hamm said, "Dr. Olliver, is it your expert

testimony that Dallas Raintree's pubic hairs are microscopically consistent with those found at the scene?"

"It is."

Roy came forward when the prosecutor sat down. "You cannot *prove* that the pubic hairs found at the scene came from Dallas Raintree, can you?"

"I can testify that the hair samples when viewed at the tiniest microscopic level are entirely consistent with Mr. Raintree's."

"But not that they *in fact* came from him."

"Not conclusively, no, but as a medical professional—"

"Thank you," Roy said. "You've answered my question."

Ms. Hamm stood up. "Dr. Olliver, is it your considered medical opinion that the hair samples found at the scene could have come from Mr. Raintree?"

"Yes, it is."

"Thank you."

The rumor in the courthouse on the fifth day of trial was that the prosecution's star witness was expected to testify. Speculation ran rampant; everyone was trying to guess who it would be. Excitement was a buzzing, tangible presence as people walked into the courtroom and took their places in the gallery.

Winona sat in her regular seat, watching her sisters walk past her.

This week had taken a toll on Vivi Ann; she moved slowly down the aisle, no longer able to look anything other than weary and afraid. Her blond hair, usually so shiny and cared for, hung in a lank, boardlike sheath down her back. She'd given up on makeup, and without color, her face appeared wan and pale. Her green eyes looked startlingly bright by comparison.

Winona longed to be beside her, helping Vivi Ann, but she wasn't welcome there.

The judge walked into the courtroom and took her seat at the bench. As soon as the jury was seated, the proceedings began.

"The state calls Myrtle Michaelian."

A wave of whispers moved through the courtroom, so loud that the judge reminded the gallery to be quiet. Winona was as surprised as everyone else. She'd been certain that the star witness would be one of the seedy men who frequented Cat's house on the weekends.

Myrtle walked into the courtroom, trying to look confident, but the attempt only emphasized how frightened she was. Already her hair was damp with sweat. In her floral polyester dress, she looked like an aging legal secretary.

"State your name for the record."

"Myrtle Ann Michaelian."

"Your address?"

"One-seventy-eight Mountain Vista Drive, in Oyster Shores."

"How do you make a living, Ms. Michaelian?"

"My parents opened the Blue Plate Diner in 1942. I took over management in 1976. My husband and I opened our Ice Cream Shop in 1990. That's down on the end of Shore Drive."

"And where is the ice-cream shop in relation to Catherine Morgan's home?"

"Down the alley. You go right past us to get to her place."

"Please speak up, Ms. Michaelian."

"Oh. Yes. Sorry."

"Were you working at the ice-cream shop on Christmas Eve of last year?"

"I was. I wanted to make a special ice-cream cake for the evening service. I was running late, as usual."

The people in the gallery smiled and nodded. Myrtle's tardiness was well known in town.

"Was Oyster Shores busy that night?"

"Heavens, no. Everyone was at church by seven-thirty. As I said, I was late."

"Did you see anyone that night?"

Myrtle gave Vivi Ann a sad look. "It was about eight-ten. I was almost ready to go. I was putting the finishing touches on the frosting when I looked up and saw . . . saw Dallas Raintree coming out of the alley that leads to Cat's house."

"Did he see you?"

"No." Myrtle looked miserable.

"And how did you know it was the defendant?"

"I saw his profile when he passed under the streetlamp, and I recognized his tattoo. But I already knew it was him. I'd seen him there before at night. Lots of times. I'd even told Vivi Ann about it. It was him. I'm sorry, Vivi Ann."

"No further questions," Ms. Hamm said.

Roy rose and asked about Myrtle's eyesight, which wasn't good, whether she'd had her glasses on (she hadn't), and whether Dallas had looked directly at her. He made valid points: the man hadn't looked at her; it had been dark; his face had been partially hidden by a cowboy hat. Lots of men had been known to come and go from Cat's house, and at all hours of the night. And white cowboy hats and Levi's were hardly noteworthy in these parts.

But none of it mattered to the jury, Winona could tell. Myrtle's testimony had done the last thing necessary: she'd placed Dallas near the scene on the night in question, when he'd told his wife he was home in bed with a fever. No one in that courtroom believed Myrtle was lying. In fact, when she finished testifying she was crying and apologizing directly to Vivi Ann.

The trial went on for another two days, but everyone knew it was just limping along. Dallas never took the stand in his own defense.

In the last week of May, the defense rested and the case was handed over to the jury.

They deliberated for four hours and found Dallas guilty. He was sentenced to prison for life, without the possibility of parole.

Chapter Sixteen

"Tell him, Roy," Vivi Ann said as they sat at the table in the small room across from the courtroom. "We can appeal this. That hair evidence was bogus science, and so what if he's type O blood? And Myrtle *couldn't* have seen him because he wasn't there. It's all circumstantial. There were other prints on the gun. We'll appeal, right?"

Roy pulled away from the wall. He'd been standing as far from them as he could in the room, to give them a few precious moments before they came to take Dallas away. "I'll file an appeal after sentencing. Probably next month. We have plenty of grounds."

"Tell her what's real in this world, Roy," Dallas said.

"It's difficult to overturn a conviction, it's true. But it's too early to give up," Roy said, yet she could see how tired he was, how dispirited.

Vivi Ann stood up and faced her husband. She

knew she needed to be strong for him, for them, but she felt herself weakening. "I understand why it's hard for you to believe in things." She stared at his face, trying to memorize every crease and line, so she could call on his image at night when she lay alone in their bed. "But I *can* believe. Let me. Lean on me. I'll show you . . ."

He closed the distance between them, kissed her with a strange gentleness. She knew what it was, what it meant. "Don't kiss me goodbye," she whispered.

"It is goodbye, baby."

"No."

"You were more than I ever hoped for. I want you to know that."

A knock at the door sounded like gunfire in the quiet. Roy crossed the room, opened the door.

Aurora stood there, holding Noah, who pointed immediately at Dallas and said, "Dada."

"Christ," Dallas said softly.

Aurora brought Noah over and put him in Dallas's arms. He clung to his son, pressing his lips to the silky black hair, breathing in deeply. "Tell him I loved him."

"You tell him," Vivi Ann said, dashing away tears with her sleeve. "We'll visit you every Saturday until they let you out."

Dallas kissed Noah's pudgy cheek and then pulled Vivi Ann closer. For one heartbreakingly perfect moment, they were together, the three of them, like it was supposed to be, and then he drew back.

He placed Noah in Vivi Ann's arms and said, "I won't let him see me in prison. Never. If you bring him I won't come out of my cell. I know what it's like for a kid to have his old man behind bars."

"But . . . how will he know you?"

"He won't," Dallas said, then he turned to Roy. "Tell them I'm ready to go now."

Vivi Ann wanted to throw herself at him, to block his path and cling to his leg and beg him not to go, but she couldn't make any part of her move. "Dallas," she whispered, crying so hard now he was a blur of black and white, a sliver of movement against the wooden wall. She didn't blink or breathe or wipe her eyes, afraid that at the smallest movement, he'd disappear. "I love you, Dallas," she said.

"Love Dada," Noah agreed, nodding and pointing.

At that, Dallas broke. She saw it as clearly as if an arm had simply been snapped off or his spine had cracked. "Get me out of here, Roy," he said.

And then he was gone.

Every Saturday for the rest of the summer, Vivi Ann went to the prison to visit Dallas. The remainder of her time she spent working at the ranch. She went out of her way not to talk to her father; she left a list for him at the barn when she needed something done.

Now it was the final night of the county fair. For the past few days, she'd lost herself in the familiar routine. Her 4-H Club had brought twelve girls this year, ranging in age from eleven to fifteen. From the moment Vivi Ann pulled her truck and trailer into the shorn, grassy field behind the horse barns, she was in motion. It took a herculean effort to keep the girls—especially the younger ones—on schedule for their classes, so that each one was dressed, mounted, and on deck during the class before theirs. Vivi Ann was constantly running back and forth between the barn and the arena, with Noah in her arms or holding her hand, trying to keep up with her. There were mothers there, too, of course. Julie and Brooke and Trayna were just as busy, doing the girls' hair, polishing their horses' hooves, fixing gear that broke at the worst time. By Sunday night, everyone was dusty and exhausted and exhilarated.

Everyone except Vivi Ann. She was just dusty and exhausted.

Closing her eyes, she leaned back against the stall door behind her. All she had to look forward to now was going home, crawling into her empty bed. Every night for the whole summer, she'd rolled over in her sleep and reached for Dallas. She didn't know which bothered her more—reaching for him or knowing that some night it would stop.

Sighing again, feeling older and more tired than should have been possible for a twenty-nine-year-old woman, she dragged her tack trunk over to the truck and put it in the bed.

She stood in the grassy field, empty of trucks now except for her own. She could see the sparkling lights of the midway from here, the giant glittering spool of the Ferris wheel against the black sky, and hear the distant, recognizable song of the calliope.

She used to love the fair. Now even the word *fair* mocked her. Everywhere she looked lately, she saw injustice. Nothing was fair; not really.

For all the years of her life, this had been a special weekend, a time of coming together for the Grey girls.

She and her sisters had always closed the fair together, turning this last night into a journey through their common past. They'd walked shoulder to shoulder down the midway, eating scones smothered in local marionberry jam and picking at pink clouds of cotton candy, and talking. They'd done that most of all.

. . . look, Aurora, that's where you got your first kiss, remember?

. . . that quilt looks exactly like the one Mom made for the Bicentennial, doesn't it?

. . . Speaking of the Bicentennial, whatever happened to my Bobby Sherman watch? I know one of you witches stole it . . .

She knew her sisters were down there, going their separate ways for the first time. For months,

Winona had been trying to reconcile with Vivi Ann, but she ignored every pathetic attempt. Vivi Ann couldn't look at Winona without wanting to smack her in the face.

She reached into her pocket and pulled out the Xanax Richard had prescribed for her. The little pills had become her best friend lately. Popping one into her mouth, she swallowed dryly and then went to the barn, where Noah lay sleeping in a portable crib. She scooped him up, held him a little too tightly, and carried him over to the truck.

At home, she put him to bed and took a long, hot bath. As was usual lately, she let herself cry in the bathtub, and when it was done, and she'd dried off, she was okay again, able to keep walking, breathing, living. Believing. That was the hardest part of all, the believing that his appeal would be granted and all this would be over. Every time the phone rang, she caught her breath, thinking: *It's happened.* And every day, when the call didn't come, she popped another pill and kept moving. Slowly, perhaps, but she moved, and in this cabin, where memories of Dallas were everywhere, each forward step was a triumph.

She crawled into their bed, took two sleeping pills, and waited for the sweet relief of sleep.

It seemed that she'd just closed her eyes when the phone rang.

She clawed out from the oozy comfort of sleep and reached sideways, feeling for the phone. By the time she found it, she was sitting up. "Hello?" she answered.

"Vivi Ann? It's Roy."

She was instantly alert. Glancing at the clock, she noticed that it was 8:40 in the morning. She'd overslept again. The first lesson of the morning started in twenty minutes. "Hey, Roy. What happened?"

"The appellate court affirmed his conviction."

The words hit her so hard she couldn't breathe. "Oh, no . . ."

"Don't lose hope yet. I'll file a petition for rehearing and a petition for review with the Washington State Supreme Court."

Vivi Ann struggled to believe in that, but hope had become a slippery thing, hard to hold on to.

"And . . . uh . . . don't bother going to the prison on Saturday."

"Why not?"

Roy paused. "When Dallas got the news about the decision, he went a little nuts. They've got him in solitary for a month."

"Did he hurt anyone?"

Roy paused again, and in the silence, the answer came loud and clear.

"It's killing him," she said. *And me, too.*

"It won't help him to start fights."

Vivi Ann heard Roy's words, but all she could think about were her visits to the prison, sitting across the plastic glass from Dallas, who was dressed in his orange felon's jumpsuit, and the things he'd told her. The way his cell door popped open automatically four times a day, with a buzzing, clicking sound, for meals and one hour of exercise; the way it felt to look out from the yard and see grass through razor wire; the way the prisoners congregated by color and how you had to stay with your own kind but he was half of two groups and belonged in neither; the way "the girls"—guys dressed in as close to drag as their jumpsuits would allow—trolled for takers while bullies looked for victims; and the way it felt to believe you'd never see the stars again, never ride a horse at night, or hold your son.

"Will anything help, Roy?" she asked, hearing Noah's voice come through the baby monitor. As always, he called out for his daddy. She closed her eyes in pain. She couldn't help wondering if one day Noah would forget about his father and go on without him. Or would he always remember, and always keep reaching out for a man who wouldn't be there?

"Don't give up yet," Roy said.

"I won't."

She couldn't imagine a moment when that would be possible. As much as believing in hope hurt, not believing would hurt even more.

Vivi Ann hardly noticed the changing of the seasons. As the golden summer of 1996 slid slowly into a cold and rainy autumn, she struggled to act like her old self. To keep moving forward. Aurora showed up on an almost daily basis to make sure that she was rarely alone, but even her sister couldn't help. Vivi Ann felt as if she were trapped in a cold bubble, suspended. Every day she woke up depressed, alone, but she rose anyway and went about her daily chores. She gave lessons and trained horses and hired a new ranch hand. Thoughts of Dallas came and went, hurting both on arrival and departure; she gritted her teeth and didn't slow down. Every night when she finally crawled into bed, she prayed that tomorrow she'd get good news about his appeal.

She knew that people were worried about her. She could see it in their sideways glances, hear it in the way they whispered as she passed. Once, their gossip and concern would have mattered to her. No more. In the eleven months since Dallas's arrest, she'd learned a little something about optimism. It was an acidlike emotion, eating through everything. To believe in hope meant she had to hang on to that alone. There was no room inside of her to care about anything else.

On this cold, brown late November evening, she gave her last lesson at four o'clock, fed the horses, and returned to her cabin.

There, she found Noah on the rug in front of the fireplace, playing with a pair of Teenage Mutant Ninja Turtle action figures.

He looked up at her, grinning gummily. "Mommy," he said, opening his arms.

Vivi Ann felt a spasm of guilt. The truth (which she'd told no one and never would) was that the sight of her son's face was almost more than she could bear these days. That was why she paid this thirteen-year-old girl to watch him during the afternoons. Every time Vivi Ann looked at Noah, she wanted to cry.

"How was he?" she said, reaching into her pocket for some cash.

"Great. He loves Tigger."

How could Vivi Ann not have known that? "Great."

Through the living room window, headlights shone, illuminating everything for a moment.

"My mom's here. See you Monday after school?"

"You bet." Vivi Ann watched her leave and then stared down at her son. At almost three and a half, he was the spitting image of his father, right down to the long black hair. Vivi Ann hadn't been able to cut it. "Hey, little man," she said.

He got up and toddled toward her, talking non-stop. She scooped him into her arms and carried him into the bathroom, where she opened the medicine cabinet. Taking a Xanax, she waited to feel better. Soon, the sharpness of her pain would dull.

Talking to Noah about nothing, she took him into the kitchen and made dinner. When it was finished, she bathed him and read him stories until he fell asleep in her arms.

When she'd put him to bed, she returned to her empty, silent living room and sat there alone, staring down at the diamond ring on her finger.

"Tomorrow will be better," she said aloud, trying to take comfort in that. "The court will probably give us their answer. Maybe it's in the mail right now."

A knock at the door startled her. She had been so deep in her thoughts—dreams, actually—she hadn't heard anyone drive up. Before she could even stand, the door opened, and Aurora stood there, backlit by the glow from her headlights.

"Enough," Aurora said, closing the door behind her.

"Enough what?"

"Get dressed. We're dropping Noah off with Richard and we're going to the Outlaw."

Aurora crossed the room, sat down beside Vivi Ann. Gone were the shoulder pads and glitter of the early nineties; in their stead, Aurora had moved on to the Meg Ryan sweetly frumpy look of baggy pants and T-shirts. Cropped hair, now dyed reddish brown, framed her small face and gave her a pixie-like look. "You can't keep going on like this. It's killing you, Vivi. You're just tranquilizing yourself to get through the days."

"And your point?"

"My point is that you have to get back on the

horse. Or at least the barstool. I won't take no for an answer, and you know what a bitch I can be."

Vivi Ann didn't want to go to the Outlaw, where all her old friends would stare at her sadly and try too hard to be friendly. They all thought she should have let Dallas go by now, "moved on," and it bothered them that she hadn't. Fashion and music and television shows continued to change, but not Vivi Ann. Her life had paused. Still, the thought of another night spent alone, staring at nothing and remembering too much, didn't sound so good, either.

"If you can't do it for yourself, do it for me," Aurora said, her smile melting a little. "Richard is hardly talking to me these days. It's like . . . I don't know. I'm going a little crazy. I need to laugh," she said quietly. "And I know you do, too."

Vivi Ann saw the truth Aurora was hiding, or hadn't faced. Her sister's brown eyes were dark with the sorrow that came from a crumbling marriage.

There was plenty of sorrow to go around these days, it seemed.

"We could stop off at Winona's house, maybe see—"

"No," Vivi Ann said. All her life she'd been a forgiving person, but not on this. She didn't see how she could ever forgive Winona for turning her back on them when they needed her most. "But I'll go."

She got up and went into her (their) room, and found a pretty, out-of-date Laura Ashley dress with a ruffled collar and flounced skirt. Not bothering with makeup, she anchored her hair off her face with a headband and slipped into her caramel-colored cowboy boots. At the last minute, she put a pill in her pocket. Just in case.

Then she got Noah out of bed and went into the living room. "I'll follow you," she said to Aurora. "The car seat is in the truck."

Noah squirmed and cried when she put him in his car seat.

"It's okay, little man. You're just going to go visit boring Uncle Richard. Don't worry—you'll fall right asleep."

She followed Aurora to her house, dropped Noah off, and walked with her sister down First Street.

Vivi Ann tried to keep talking, but as they turned on Shore Drive, she felt her stomach tightening up. Memories came at her.

"I don't know if I want to do this," she said as they approached the tavern.

You wanna dance?

"But you will." Aurora took her hand and led her inside.

The usual weekend night crowd was here, playing music and pool, line dancing, laughing, and talking. Vivi Ann could feel them looking at her, whispering.

"They haven't seen you here in almost a year. That's all it is," Aurora said.

Vivi Ann nodded, smiling as naturally as possible. Holding her head high, she walked straight to her old barstool.

"Tequila straight shot," said Bud, sliding it across the bar to her. "On the house."

"Thanks." Vivi Ann downed the drink and ordered another, drinking it as quickly. She scanned the crowd, seeing Butchie and Erik in the corner with their wives, and Julie and Kent John in the back playing pool. Winona was on the dance floor with Ken Otter, the dentist who'd recently divorced his wife.

"I hear they just started dating," Aurora said, following Vivi Ann's gaze.

"Lucky him," Vivi Ann said bitterly.

The band finished one song and started another. It took Vivi Ann only a note or two to recognize it: "Mamas, Don't Let Your Babies Grow Up to Be Cowboys."

Vivi Ann ordered another straight shot and drank it down, but it didn't help to get rid of this titanic sense of loss.

And then she saw Winona coming her way.

"I gotta go," she muttered.

"Don't—" Aurora said, reaching for her.

Vivi Ann pulled free and ran stumbling through the crowd. Outside, she could breathe again, but that wasn't good enough. She needed to be gone from here, away from this place where he was everywhere.

She ran back to Aurora's house and went straight

to her truck, leaving Noah asleep in Aurora's safe, memoryless house. At Water's Edge, she hit the brake so hard she lurched forward, smacked her breasts into the steering wheel when she parked.

To the left lay her cabin and the bed she'd shared with Dallas.

To the right lay the house where she'd grown up, and inside was her father, once her safe place and idol; now, nothing. Without him and her whole family, she felt lost, but there was no help for that. He and Winona had made their choice a year ago when they turned their backs on Dallas.

Dallas.

Vivi Ann made a little sound, a thin moan of pain. Stumbling forward, she went into the barn, down the aisle to Clem's stall. Flipping the latch, she pushed the heavy wooden door open.

"Hey, Clem," she said, stepping into the darkness and closing the stall door behind her.

Nickering softly, Clem limped over to her, nudged her with her graying, velvety muzzle.

"I haven't spent the night with you since Mom died, have I, girl?"

Clem nickered again, rubbing her nose along Vivi Ann's thigh.

And just like that, at her horse's touch, Vivi Ann fell apart. Everything she'd been trying to hold in came pouring out. She slid down the stall wall and slumped in the cedar shavings, bowing her head to her knees.

Winona was at the stuffed grizzly bear's outstretched paw when she saw Vivi Ann glance at her, see her coming, and run out of the Outlaw. She paused just a moment, stumbled as disappointment washed through her.

All of this was so unlike Vivi Ann. They'd always fought and made up and gone on; sisterhood was like that, a quilt made up of all the scraps, good and bad. Sighing, she walked over to Aurora, who stood there alone, staring at the open door, sipping her strawberry margarita.

"I can't stand this anymore," Winona said. "What are we going to do?"

"We?" Aurora's voice was icy but dull, and in that lack of luster Winona knew there was an opening.

"You hate it, too."

"Of course I hate it."

"What do we do?"

Aurora turned to her. "Take his appeal. Help her."

Why didn't anyone understand? "I won't be any help to him, don't you get that? I'm a small-town attorney. I don't know anything about criminal appellate work."

Aurora's gaze was steady and more than a little sad. "You're the one who doesn't get it, Win. We're sisters. At least we used to be." On that, she set down her half-empty margarita and walked out of the tavern.

Winona stood there in the smoky darkness, surrounded by friends and neighbors. Alone.

Winona and her father spent Christmas Eve together. She got to his house early and decorated all by herself. She went up to the attic, found the worn, creased cardboard boxes marked *Xmas,* and carried them down to the living room.

There, it was quiet. There were no sisters laughing together, drinking wine, and arguing about what holiday movie to watch while they decorated. No wonder Winona had put off the decorating until this late date. She'd known how it would feel.

Still, she refused to skimp on any tradition, and so she decorated the house from stem to stern, using everything in the boxes. She curled fresh cedar boughs up the banister and tied them in place with glittery gold ribbons. She put the miniature Christmas scene along the mantel: fake snow, tiny people with cars and carriages and replicas of downtown storefronts. As a girl, her favorite part had been to fit the tiny oval of mirrored glass on top of the cottony snow to make a minuscule skating lake. The girls had fought over that job for years . . .

Winona refused to think about that. Instead, she poured herself another glass of wine, put dinner on the stove, and cut herself a big piece of cake.

She'd used food to tide her over for most of the

past few months. Whenever she'd felt depressed, she'd gone into the kitchen. Now she had probably ten dozen cookies in Tupperware containers in her refrigerator, and she'd gained at least fifteen pounds since Dallas's arrest.

Don't think about that, either.

She went into Dad's study, finding him there. He was holding a drink and staring out at the Canal. The view was crisp on this cold, late December day—purple mountains crowned in pink snow, steel-blue water, gray shoreline. The few docks that could be seen from here were thick with sleeping seals. Seagulls lined the railing, one after another, like yellow-beaked bowling pins.

"Hey, Dad," she said, coming up behind him.

"Hey," he said without looking at her.

She was trying to think of something else to say when the phone rang. Grateful for the interruption, she said, "I'll get it," and ran to the wall phone in the kitchen. "Hello?" she said, slightly out of breath.

"Merry Christmas Eve," Luke said.

"Luke!" she said, smiling for the first time all day. Yanking the long cord out behind her, she sat down at the breakfast table and put her feet up. "How's Montana?"

They didn't talk as easily as they once had. Their conversation was punctuated with lengthy silences, things unsaid. Still, he told her about the house he'd bought a few weeks ago and how it was going with his new partner. She told him a funny story about her recent date with Ken Otter and said it was what she had expected, dating a thrice-divorced dentist. "It's better than being alone though."

There was a pause, then he said, "How is she?"

"Is that why you called? To ask about Vivi Ann?"

"It's about you," he said. "I know how much it's killing you to be on the outs with her. Quit waiting for a chance and go up and make one. Just walk up to the house, knock on the door, and say you're sorry."

"Can we talk about something else, please?" Winona said, and for the next hour they talked about ordinary things, and when they ran out of topics, he said, "Well. I just wanted to say Merry Christmas."

"You, too, Luke," she said, hanging up.

But as she walked away from the phone, his words stayed with her, echoed. Aurora and Richard had taken the kids skiing for the holiday, probably because they knew the loneliness that would lurk at Water's Edge this year, and so she knew Vivi Ann and Noah were up there alone.

Could she do it? Just walk up to the cabin as if it were a journey back in time? She tried to think it through, imagine it rationally, but the truth was that once she'd had the thought, she couldn't let it go. Longing sank its hooks deep in her heart, and she grabbed her coat from the closet by the front door and slipped into it. Walking carefully, avoiding puddles that floated on the gravel road, she walked up to Vivi Ann's cabin and knocked on the door.

Vivi Ann answered instantly, looking awful. Her hair was a rat's nest of tangles, as if she'd been obsessively scratching her scalp, and her face was red and blotchy. Her eyes were watery and blood-shot, and she was unsteady on her feet, almost drunken. "What do you want?"

Winona was momentarily taken aback by the sight of her sister. "I . . . I wanted to talk. I know you're pissed at me, but it's Christmas Eve, and I thought—"

"You're here to gloat, aren't you? You know his appeal was denied."

"I'm sorry."

"Sorry? You think I want to hear that you're *sorry?*" Vivi Ann moved forward, lurched a little. "You sat in that courtroom every day, listening to the evidence, Winona. My supposedly brilliant sister. Did you question any of it? He *was* sick on Christmas Eve. I took his temperature . . ."

"You think Myrtle was lying?"

"I think she was mistaken. She *had* to be, and that hair evidence was crap. Even you can't believe Dallas was screwing Cat while he was married to me." Vivi Ann's eyes were glassy and a little wild-looking, and Winona felt a flutter of fear. Something was wrong here.

In the back of the house, Noah started to cry.

"Answer me," Vivi Ann snapped. "Do you think he was screwing Cat? You saw us together."

Winona saw how desperately Vivi Ann was trying to convince her. She knew that all she had to do was pretend to agree, and maybe they could begin to mend their breach.

But sometimes, if you loved someone, you had to be strong, had to say the thing that needed to be said. Clearly, Vivi Ann was falling apart. Losing it. Winona might not know much about the criminal justice system, but believing in miracles within it couldn't be good.

She moved toward her sister. Vivi Ann looked like one of those skittish abused horses of hers, terrified and ready to bolt. "This is killing you, Vivi," Winona said as gently as she could. "Believing in something that will never happen—"

"He *will* be released."

"I *did* sit in that courtroom and I saw the truth you're trying to ignore. He—"

"Don't say it, Win."

"You know it, Vivi. You must. He's guilty. You need to—"

Vivi Ann slapped her across the face so hard she stumbled back. "Get out of my house. We're done talking. Forever."

Chapter Seventeen

The years ground slowly forward.
   1997.

1998.

1999.

Aurora tried to make peace within their family numerous times, but Vivi Ann had no room in her shrunken heart for forgiveness, and in truth, she didn't try to make space. Her father and Winona had wounded her too deeply. Every Saturday, Vivi Ann dropped Noah off with Aurora and drove two and a half hours to the prison, so that she could sit behind a dirty Plexiglas window and talk to Dallas through a heavy black receiver. Roy filed one motion after another, each one a beacon of hope that crashed on the rocks. She felt as if she were tied to a wicked seesaw where every high and low took a little more of her soul away. And when Roy finally called to say that the last state appeal had been denied, he'd added quickly, "But don't worry, I'll go federal." So she'd tried again to keep believing, and the months kept passing.

The only way she'd found to survive was to numb herself to everything else. She popped Xanax like jelly beans during the daytime, and they allowed her to move forward, to smile and talk and pretend to be in an ordinary world. Aurora was her anchor in that attempt, her steadying hand. Still, when Vivi Ann was alone at night, she drank too much and either held her son too tightly or not at all. Sometimes she just sat there, swaying to the music in her head, hearing Noah crying or calling out for her, and trying to remember how it had felt to touch Dallas, to hold him. The memories were leaking away, and without them, she had nothing to ward off the numbness, and so she gave in, falling into a deep and troubled sleep on the sofa.

On several of her Saturday visits she'd missed things—Noah's first tricycle ride, his preschool's winter party, even his fourth birthday. She'd told herself at the time that he was young, that if she told him his birthday was Sunday he'd believe her—and he had—but she'd seen the way Aurora looked at her, so full of pity, and Vivi Ann had had to turn away. That night, after all the party decorations were in the trash, she'd taken so many shots of tequila that she'd missed her lessons in the morning.

Now it was October 1999; a Saturday. Almost four years after Dallas's arrest.

She sat in the prison parking lot, staring through the windshield at the gray walls. Rain assaulted the windshield, falling so hard and fast the glass seemed alive, almost flexible. Through this distortion, she could see the imposing concrete mass of

306

the maximum-security prison. She'd seen the collection of buildings in all kinds of weather, and even in full sunlight, with the green landscape and blue sky surrounding, it looked grim and menacing. The rain made the prison look dismal and forlorn, huddled against the hillside instead of standing defiantly in front of it.

She went through the routine of checking in on autopilot, barely noticing anymore how frightening it was to be in here. All she really noticed these days was the noise—the clanging of doors, the clicking of locks, the distant hum of raised voices.

She took her usual place on the left-side cubicle, waiting.

"Hey, Vivi," he said when he sat down across from her.

At last she smiled. For all the apathy in her everyday life, she couldn't escape the fact that here, with him, she felt alive. As crazy as it was, she was glad to see him, to be near him, even if they couldn't touch. She said his name and it was like a prayer, had almost become one. She reached into her pocket and pulled out the newest photograph of Noah. In it, he was a bright, shiny six-year-old, wearing a baseball cap and holding a bat, grinning.

Dallas stared down at it, touched the glass as if for once it wouldn't stop his hand.

Vivi Ann knew what he saw: a boy. The years of

Dallas's incarceration could be seen on the changing face of his son. Noah was taller, thinner; he'd left babyhood behind this year. And he'd stopped asking about the daddy he didn't remember.

"He misses you," Vivi Ann said.

"Don't do that," he said. "We don't have much left. Let's at least be honest."

She should have known better than to lie to him. They were separated now, kept apart by razor wire and Plexiglas and concrete, but the connection between them was as strong as ever. "If you'd let me bring him to see you—"

"We've had this discussion. He doesn't need to see me like this. It's better if he forgets me."

"Don't say that."

They fell silent after that, staring at each other through the dirty plastic, holding on to big black phone receivers, with nothing to say. She wasn't sure how long it went on, their quiet, but when the end-of-visiting-hours alarm buzzed, she flinched.

"You look tired," Dallas said finally.

She wanted to pretend not to know what he was talking about, to lie to him again—this time with a confused smile—but she knew he saw the truth on her face, in her weary eyes. In the years of his imprisonment it had grown increasingly difficult to pretend there was a different future waiting for them. They had both lost weight; Roy said last month that they looked like a pair of walking skeletons. Dallas's face, always sharp, had grown hollow and gaunt. The veins and sinews in his neck were like tree roots protruding just beneath the soil.

Time had left its mark on Vivi Ann's face, too; she could see the changes in her mirror every morning. Even her hair had grown dull and stringy from too few cuttings and too little care. She was thirty-two, but looked nearly a decade older than that.

"It's hard," she said softly.

"Are you still taking those pills?"

"Hardly ever."

"You're lying," he said.

She looked at him, loving him so much it was a physical pain in her chest. "How do you get through it?"

He leaned back. They rarely did this, rarely left the path of pretend and stepped onto the hard cement of reality. "When I'm out in the yard, I find a place that is empty, and I stand there and close my eyes. If I'm lucky, the noise will sound like hoofbeats."

"Renegade," she said.

"I remember riding him at night . . . that night."

Their eyes met; the memories were vibrant, electric. "That was our first time . . ."

"How do you get through it?"

Pills. Booze. She looked away, hoping he didn't notice. "Out on the porch, I have one of the wind chimes my mom made. When she was sick, she gave them to me and said that if I listened closely, I'd hear her voice in their sound. And I did. I do." She looked at him again. "Now I hear you, too. I wait for the wind sometimes . . ."

She fell silent. That was the thing about memories; they were like downed electrical cables. It was best to stand back.

"Have you heard from Roy?" she asked.

"No."

"We'll hear soon," she said, wanting to believe it, trying to. "The federal court will hear your case. You'll see."

"Sure," he said. Then he stood up. "I gotta go."

She watched him hang up the phone and back away.

"I love you," she said.

He mouthed the words back to her, and then he was gone. The door clacked shut behind him.

She sat there alone, staring at his empty cubicle for so long that a woman came up and tapped her on the shoulder.

Mumbling an apology, Vivi Ann got up and walked away.

The drive home seemed to take longer than usual. As one mile spilled into the next, she tried to remain steady. There were so many things she couldn't think about these days, and if she really concentrated, she could hold back the fear. During the daylight hours, at least. The nights were their own kind of hell; even overmedicating herself only worked some of the time.

In town, she eased her foot off the gas and slowed down. All around her, she saw proof that while she'd been suspended in the gray-black world of the criminal justice system, life here had gone on. The trees along Main Street were riots of autumn color; the first few of the dying leaves had begun to fall. The Horsin' Around Tack Shop was advertising their yearly sale and the drugstore had a window display full of ghosts and pumpkins.

Trick or treat, Mrs. Raintree?

She flinched and hit the gas. The old truck coughed hard and lurched forward.

At the ranch, she pulled up into the trees and consulted her watch. It was three o'clock. That gave her one hour to feed the horses and be at Aurora's in time to pick up Noah.

Noah.

There was another truth she tried to avoid. She was becoming a useless parent. She loved her son like air and sunlight, but every time she looked at him another piece of her heart seemed to fall away.

She would have to change that. Tomorrow she'd stop taking the Xanax and get back to the business of living. She had to, whether she wanted to or not.

Feeling a tiny bit better with this goal (she'd made it before, but this time she meant it; this time she'd really do it), she headed for the loafing shed, where they kept enough bales of alfalfa for a week.

Opening the door, she pulled out the wheelbarrow and stacked it with flakes of hay.

In the barn, she snapped on the lights and began feeding the horses, going from stall to stall. Here, she found a measure of peace again, and she was very nearly smiling when she unlatched Clem's stall door.

"Hey, girl, have you missed me?"

There was no answering nicker, no whisper of a tail whooshing from side to side.

Vivi Ann knew the minute she stepped onto the fresh shavings.

Clementine lay crumpled against the stall's wooden wall, her massive, graying head lolled forward.

Vivi Ann stood utterly still, knowing that if she tried to move she'd fall to her knees. It took work just to breathe. In that moment, in the cool, shadowy familiarity of this barn that had always been her favorite place in the world, she remembered everything about this great mare. Their whole lives had been lived together.

Remember when you stepped in that hornet's nest . . . when you jumped the ditch and I landed in the blackberry bushes . . . when we won State for the first time?

Swallowing hard, Vivi Ann moved forward and dropped to her knees in the pale pink shavings at Clem's belly. She reached out and touched the mare's neck, feeling the coldness that shouldn't be there. There were so many things to say to this great animal—her last real link to her mother—but none of that was possible now. Vivi Ann's throat felt swollen; her eyes stung. How would she go on without Clem? Especially now, when so much had been lost?

She scratched Clem's graying ears. "You should have been out in the sunlight, girl. I know how much you hate this dark stall."

That made her think of Dallas and the cell he was in, and loneliness and grief overwhelmed her. She lay down against her mare, curling into the fetal position against her comforting flank, and closed her eyes.

Goodbye, Clem. Tell Mom I said hey.

Time kept going; inching, lurching, slowing, but always moving. The year 2000 drained away in a blur of gray and empty days and endless nights. Noah had started kindergarten at five (too early, Vivi Ann thought; she should have held him back a year, would have if Dallas were here, but he wasn't), and T-ball at six and soccer at seven. She missed all of his Saturday games; it was just one more thing to feel guilty about. Aurora always offered to come with her to the prison, but Vivi Ann refused the offer. She could only do it alone.

Then, finally, in the first week of September 2001, she got the call she'd been waiting for.

"Mr. Lovejoy would like to see you today."

It was good news. Vivi Ann knew it. In all the years of Dallas's imprisonment, never before had Roy asked Vivi Ann to come to his office for a meeting.

Thank you, God, Vivi Ann thought as she got ready that morning. That sentence cycled through her mind, gaining the speed of a downhill racer, until she could hardly think of anything else.

On her way out of town, she stopped at the school and picked up Noah. After all that they'd been through, he deserved to be there on the day they got the good news.

"I'm going to miss recess," Noah said beside her. He was playing with a pair of plastic dinosaurs, making them fight on the front of his bumper seat.

"I know, but we're going to get news about your daddy. We've been waiting so long for this. And I want you to remember this day, that you were here for it."

"Oh."

"Because I never gave up, Noah. That's important, too, even though it was really hard."

He made sound effects to go along with the dinosaurs' epic battle.

Vivi Ann turned up the radio and kept driving. In Belfair, the town at the start of the Canal, she drove to Roy's office, which was housed in an older home on a small lot beside the bank.

"We're here," she said, parking. Her heart was beating so fast she felt light-headed, but she didn't take one of her pills, not even to calm down. After today, she'd never take one again. There would be no need, not once their family was together. Helping Noah out of his seat and taking him by the hand, she walked up the grass-veined cement path to the front door.

Inside, she smiled at the receptionist. "I'm Vivi Ann Raintree. I have a meeting with Roy."

"That's right," the receptionist said. "Go on through that door. He's expecting you."

Roy sat at his desk, talking on the phone. Smiling at her entrance, motioning for her to sit down, he said something else into the phone and hung up.

Vivi Ann put Noah on the sofa behind her, told him to play quietly; then she took a seat opposite Roy's desk.

"You made it over here in record time," he said.

"I've been waiting years for this phone call, haven't I? Haven't we?"

"Oh," Roy said, frowning. "I should have thought of that."

"Thought of what?"

"What you'd think."

Vivi Ann felt herself tensing. "You called to tell me his federal appeal has been granted, right?"

"Technically it's a writ of habeus corpus, but no, that's not my news."

Behind her, Noah's voice grew louder, as did the clacking together of his dinosaurs, but Vivi Ann couldn't hear much of anything over the sudden roar of white noise in her head. "What is your news?"

"I'm sorry, Vivi Ann. We were denied again."

Slowly she closed her eyes. How could she have been so naïve? What was wrong with her? She knew better than to believe in hope. She took a deep breath, released it, and looked at him.

She knew she looked calm and composed, as if this new setback were just another bump in a bad stretch of road. She wouldn't let herself fall apart until tonight. She'd had years of practice at waiting, pretending, hiding. "May I have a glass of water?"

"Sure. It's right there."

She got up, walked carefully to the pitcher of water set up on the sideboard. Pouring herself a glass, she reached into her pocket and pulled out a pair of pills, swallowing them before she turned around. "Does Dallas know?"

"Yesterday," Roy said.

Vivi Ann sat down, hoping the numbness would come fast. She couldn't stand what she was feeling. "What now? Who do we appeal to?"

"I've done everything I can on his case, pled every argument, filed every motion, sought every appeal. I'm not a public defender anymore—you know that. I've been doing all this pro bono, but there's nothing more I can do. You could get another lawyer, say I was incompetent, and hell, maybe I was. I would help you in that if you wanted." He sighed. "I don't know, Vivi. I just know we're done now. I'm sorry."

"Don't say that." She heard the shrill desperation in her voice, the sharp edge of anger, and tried to soften it with a smile. "I've been hearing that for years, from everyone. I'm tired of it. We need you, Roy, to prove his innocence."

Roy glanced away.

In that furtive look, Vivi Ann saw something. "Roy? What is it?"

"Nothing. I just . . . had a heart-to-heart with Dallas this week. Finally."

"You know he's innocent, right, Roy? You've said it to me a million times."

"I really can't comment on that anymore."

Now she was afraid. Was Roy implying that Dallas had confessed to him? She got to her feet and stood there, looking down at him. "I can't take this shit, Roy. Please. Don't screw with my head."

He looked up slowly, his eyes sad. "Talk to Dallas, Vivi Ann. I've made arrangements for you at the prison for tomorrow."

"That's it? That's what you have for me after all these years?"

"I'm sorry."

She spun away and went to Noah, grabbing his hand and dragging him out of the office and down the steps and into the truck.

All the way home, she replayed it in her head,

trying to change it, soften it. At Aurora's house, she shoved Noah at her sister, saying, "I can't deal with him tonight."

She heard Aurora calling out to her, telling her to come back, but she didn't care. Fear was like a great black beast standing in her peripheral vision and she was desperate to get away, to get numb.

When she finally got home, she slammed the door shut behind her and went straight to the medicine cabinet. She took too many pills—who cared? anything to numb the pain—and washed them down with tequila.

Crawling into bed, she pulled the covers up and tried not to think about Dallas or Noah or the future. If she thought about any of it, she'd fall apart. And so she lay there, woozy, cottony, staring out the window at the ranch until night fell; after that, she stared at nothing until she was part of it and she couldn't feel anything at all.

The next morning, feeling like a piece of old, dried-out leather, she climbed out of bed, took a scalding-hot shower, and went to the prison.

"Vivi Ann Raintree to see Dallas Raintree," she said formally, although by now she was known around here.

The woman at the desk—it was Stephanie today—smiled. "Your lawyer scheduled a contact visit today."

"Really? No one told me that."

Normally she would have been thrilled at the

idea of a contact visit. In all the years she'd been coming here, she'd only had a few. But now she knew why it had been scheduled. It was Roy's parting gift to her, a signal that the end had come.

She went down to the metal detector. Once she was through it, a big man in uniform said brusquely, "This way." He stamped her hand and gave her an identification tag to wear around her neck.

She followed him down a wide, gray hallway. Doors opened and closed automatically, swinging wide slowly and clicking shut with a loud thud behind them. The noise seemed to grow closer and louder with each new open door, until Vivi Ann was in the prison itself, the part where the prisoners were housed.

At last, the guard led her into a room at the end of the last hallway. It was small, without windows or cubicles. A uniformed guard stood in the corner opposite the door. He took note of her arrival but didn't move or nod.

In the center of the room was a large wooden table, scarred and scratched from years of use. Several molded plastic chairs were pushed up to it. She went to the table, sat down, and scooted close, waiting. On the wall, the minutes ticked past.

Finally, the door in the back of the room buzzed and swung open. The guard turned slightly to face the door.

Dallas hobbled into the room; his wrist and ankle

cuffs were linked to chains cuffed together around his waist.

She got to her feet, waiting, unable to believe they were this close again after all these years.

He shuffled over and she took him in her arms, holding him tightly, feeling how thin and bony they'd both grown.

"That's enough," the guard said. "Take your seats."

Vivi Ann reluctantly let him go. He hobbled back to the opposite side of the table and sat down.

He slid back in his chair, putting his feet forward. His hair was really long now, almost past the curl of his shoulder.

She reached into her pocket and pulled out the latest picture of Noah, handing it to him. In it, their son was sitting in a big western saddle on Renegade, waving to the camera. "You should see your son ride. He's going to be as good with horses as you are."

Dallas took the photograph in a trembling hand. "We're not good for each other, Vivi."

"Don't say that. Please."

"I tried to be good enough for you."

She swallowed hard. "What did you tell Roy?"

"It doesn't matter anymore." He was so still it was almost as if he wasn't breathing, which made no sense because she was gasping like a sprinter, unable to catch her breath.

"You know what I loved most about you, Vivi? Y'never asked if I killed her. Never."

She went to him, pulled him into her arms, and kissed him, wanting to *feel* him, touch him, but all she tasted were her tears. "Don't you try to tell me you did it, Dallas. I won't believe you. And don't you dare give up. We're in this together. We have to keep fighting—"

"Back away," the guard said, moving toward them.

Through the blur of her tears, Vivi Ann could see that Dallas was smiling. It was the same sexy, easy, come-hither smile he'd given her all that time ago at the Outlaw Tavern on the night they'd met. "You should have married Luke."

"Don't," she said, but it was barely a whisper, that plea.

The guard opened the door and led Dallas out.

And when she looked down, she saw the photograph of Noah still on the table, and she knew he had given up.

Saturday after Saturday, as September turned into October, and then into November, Vivi Ann went to the prison and signed in. She sat in a cubicle, alone, watching the minutes of her life tick away.

Dallas never came out to see her again. Her weekly letters were returned unopened. In December, six years to the day after his arrest, he sent a postcard that read: *Give Noah my truck and tell him the truth.*

The truth.

She didn't even know what that meant. Which truth? That his parents had loved each other, or that it had ruined all of them, that love? Or did he mean to imply, as Roy had, that he had confessed to Cat's murder (she would never tell her son that, and she wouldn't believe it, either). She didn't know. All she knew was that she was past falling apart these days. It had been bad going to prison to see him all those years. Now not seeing him was worse. She'd thought until today that it couldn't get worse.

Then the mail had come. When she saw the big manila envelope from the prison, she tore into it, thinking, *Thank God.*

PETITION FOR DISSOLUTION OF MARRIAGE.

Nothing had ever hurt like that, not even losing Mom or Clem. Nothing.

She'd gone straight to the medicine cabinet for her pills and took too many, washing them down with tequila. Then she crawled into bed and closed her eyes, praying to God that she didn't dream . . .

"Mommy. Is it time yet?"

"Mommy?"

She lifted her heavy head from the pillow.

Noah stood beside her bed. "We gotta go to Sam's house, remember?"

"Huh?"

His face pursed into a frown that was becoming familiar. "The party starts at three o'clock. All the other moms know that."

"Oh . . ." She shoved at the covers and stumbled out of bed. Moving slowly—her head was pounding and her body felt as if it had been stuffed with cotton—she tried to take a shower, but her hands were so numb she couldn't turn the faucet on. Instead, she ran her fingers through her lank, dirty hair and made a sloppy ponytail. Dressing seemed to take forever; her focus was off and her fingers were trembling and her balance was shot. Finally, though, she got herself into a pair of old gray sweats, cowboy boots, and a flannel shirt. "Less go, little man," she said, trying to smile, thinking that maybe she'd slurred the words.

"Where's the present?"

"Huh?"

"It's his *birthday,* Mom."

"Oh. Yeah." She walked unsteadily around the house, wishing this fog in her head would go away. She found a nearly new halter on the kitchen counter (what the hell was it doing there?) and wrapped it up in the comics section from last weekend's newspaper. "There. He got a new horse, right?"

"That's a dumb present."

"It's this or nothin'."

He sighed. "Fine."

They went outside, into a falling rain, and headed for the truck.

It took her too long to strap him into his bumper seat, and by the time she finished, she was soaking wet. Her shaking fingers were so slick she had trouble grasping the wheel.

Rain pummeled them, turned the windshield into a river. The wipers could barely keep up.

She hit the gas. Driving through town, she tried to focus only on the road in front of her; it was impossible to see. The world looked watery and bleak, insubstantial, like the last time she'd gone to the prison to see Dallas . . . when she'd kissed him and begged him not to give up on her, on them . . . she'd come out into the rain on that day, too, had—

"Mommy!"

She blinked and tried to focus. She was in the wrong lane; a car was coming at her fast, its horn honking.

Swerving hard, she felt the truck lurch sideways and careen over the sidewalk. She slammed on the brakes but it was too late, or too hard. The truck skidded through the wet grass and crashed into a tree.

She hit her head on the steering wheel so hard that for a second she didn't know where she was. The taste of blood filled her mouth.

Then she heard Noah's screaming.

It seemed to come at her from far away, that high-pitched, hysterical sound. Somewhere deep inside, she reacted to that scream, wept for it, but her head was so fuzzy that she couldn't make sense of it all.

"Mommy!"

With shaking hands, she undid her seat belt and unhooked his bumper seat. Noah launched himself into her arms, sobbing against her neck.

Slowly, slowly, she began to feel him in her arms, to realize what had just happened. She clung to him, breathing in his little boy scent. For so long, she'd held back from Noah, been afraid of him, but now her love for him came rushing back like water through a storm drain, almost drowning her. "Oh, my God," she cried. "I'm so sorry . . ."

He looked up at her, sniffling, his eyes dark with tears. "Are you okay, Mommy?"

"I will be, Noah. I promise you."

Vivi Ann put the truck in reverse and backed away from the scarred and dented tree trunk. The truck's engine idled too fast, revved when she hit the gas, but it backed up, dropped down from the curb.

Her whole body was shaking as she drove; still, she tried to hide that from her son, who was back to playing with his dinosaurs as if nothing had happened. But he'd remember this; she was sadly certain of it.

She drove to the party and dropped him off, holding him so tightly he squirmed to be free.

"I love you, Noah," she said, wondering how long it had been since she'd let herself say those three words.

"Love you, too, Mommy."

Straightening slowly, she watched him walk up

to the front door. In another life—the one she'd once imagined for herself—she would have walked up with him, held his hand the whole way, and then joined in with the other mothers inside, organizing games and handing out cupcakes.

Now she stood here, alone and separated from her own life.

It had to stop.

She went back to the dented, smoking truck and climbed into the driver's seat.

What a joke that was: her in the driver's seat. She'd been a passenger for years, but what was she going to do? What *could* she do? The answers seemed too big to grasp, too far away to see clearly.

The only thing she knew for sure was that she needed help. She couldn't handle being alone anymore.

And Winona's house was across the street.

She got out of the truck and walked to her sister's property line, standing at the closed white picket fence. Rain pelted her, blurred her vision, but it couldn't obscure the sudden knowledge of what needed to be done. Noah deserved more from her.

Finally, with a heavy sigh, she walked up to Winona's front door.

"Winona? Your sister, Vivi Ann, is here to see you."

Winona had been waiting for that sentence so long that when it finally came, she stood upright immediately, almost forgetting to tell Lisa to send her in.

She stood there, uncertain, hopeful, afraid, trying to think of what to say. Then Vivi Ann opened the door and walked in, and Winona was so taken aback that she couldn't say anything at all.

Vivi Ann wasn't just crying; she was sobbing. Great, gulping tears that shook her shoulders and ravaged her pale, drawn face.

Winona went to her, opening her arms instinctively.

Vivi Ann shrank away, stumbled over to the couch, and collapsed onto it.

Winona took the chair opposite her, sat stiff and erect, barely breathing, waiting. For once she needed to keep her mouth shut and not speak first. It was torture. She had so many things to say to her sister, words she'd hoarded for years, polishing like the bits of beach glass their mom had loved.

It seemed silent forever. Then, quietly, Vivi Ann said, "I almost killed Noah and me today."

"What happened?"

"That's not what matters." She looked away. Stringy, lank hair clung to her face; tears fell from her bloodshot eyes. "I want to get the hell away from here, but I don't have anywhere to go."

"Don't run away from us," Winona said. "We're your family. We're Noah's family. We can get through this."

"Dallas isn't going to get out of prison. You were right about that. And now he wants to divorce me."

"I was wrong about a lot of things, Vivi," Winona said. They were the words she'd waited too long to say.

"I know you think I'm crazy for loving him, and you hate me for hurting Luke, but I need advice, Win." Vivi Ann looked up at that.

"I don't hate you for hurting Luke," Winona said, sighing. "I hated you for being loved by him."

Vivi Ann frowned and wiped her eyes. "What?"

"I've loved Luke Connelly since I was fifteen. I should have told you."

It was a long time before Vivi Ann spoke, and when she did, her words came slowly, as if she were finding them one by one in the dark. "You loved him. I guess that makes it all make sense. We Greys," she said. "We aren't lucky in love, are we? So, what do I do, Win?"

Winona had known the answer to that question for years, had waited for it to be asked of her, and imagined her response a hundred times. And yet, now that the time had come, she finally understood how cruel the truth was and she couldn't say it.

"Tell me," Vivi Ann said, and in her broken voice, Winona knew that Vivi already understood the answer; she just needed her big sister's help to admit it.

"You need to stop being Dallas's wife and start being Noah's mother. And those drugs are killing you."

"Noah deserves so much better than the mother I've been."

Winona went to her finally, took her youngest sister in her arms, and let her cry. "You'll get over this, I promise. We'll all help you. Someday you'll even fall in love again."

Vivi Ann looked up, and in her gaze was a sadness so deep Winona couldn't touch the bottom of it. "No," she said at last. "I won't."

Part Two

After

I wanted you to see what real courage is,
instead of getting the idea that courage is a man
with a gun in his hand. It's when you know
you're licked before you begin but you begin
anyway and you see it through no matter what.
—ATTICUS FINCH, FROM HARPER LEE'S
TO KILL A MOCKINGBIRD

Chapter Eighteen

2007

There were places that changed with the times and others that remained stubbornly the same. Seattle, for example, had become all but unrecognizable to locals in the past decade. The combination of dot-com ingenuity and designer coffees had turned the once REI-garbed, nature-loving inhabitants of that beautiful big town into honest-to-God urbanites. The sound of construction was ever-present; huge orange cranes dotted the changing skyline like giant birds of prey. Every day there was a new high-rise shooting up into the gray underbelly of the sky. Restaurants with flashy fusion menus and unpronounceable names lined the boomtown streets, creating instant neighborhoods where before there had been only buildings and street signs. The famed Space Needle and the once-renowned Smith Tower, now the bookends of the city instead of its proud twin masts, looked smaller and older each day.

Vivi Ann had grown up, too. She was thirty-nine years old, and most of her youthful optimism and energy had been lost. A few times a year, when she felt especially alone, restless, and edgy, she drove into the city. With a cover story firmly in place—buying tack at an auction or looking at a horse for sale—and babysitting secured, she tried to find solace in dark bars, but on the rare occasions when she let a man take her home, she ended up feeling dirtier and more unhappy than when she'd begun.

And always, she came back to Oyster Shores, where nothing ever changed. Oh, houses had been built, property values had risen, but it was still relatively secret, this hidden patch of warm water in a cold-water state. A few years ago Bill Gates had built his summer compound on the Canal and the locals had been abuzz with worry that other millionaires would follow and tear down their old, comfortable houses to put up McMansions along the shore, and it had happened—was happening—but slowly.

Many of the same stores lined the same streets, albeit with better signs, thanks to all that summer money. There were a few more restaurants, a few more bed-and-breakfasts, and a new three-screen movie theater, but other than that, not much had been added. Flowers still bloomed in window boxes along Main Street and hung from baskets on the streetlamps along Shore Drive.

The biggest difference in town was actually Water's Edge. The ranch had grown more successful than she'd ever imagined. Two ranch hands worked full-time on the place, and the arena was rarely empty. It had become the social heart of the town, so much so that Vivi Ann had to work hard to schedule time with her sisters.

Now she sat at the diner, at her favorite booth, with Aurora across from her. They were surrounded by the usual pre–Memorial Day lunch crowd; locals sitting here and talking quietly among themselves. In a week's time, when the holiday hit, this place would be packed with tourists.

"I heard there's a new banker in town. Not bad-looking is the word," Aurora said, tucking a lock of newly blond hair behind her ear. In the past months, she'd chosen Nicole Kidman as her personal fashion icon, which meant she ironed her dyed wheat-blond, chin-length hair, and wore enough sunscreen to be safe in the event of a nuclear blast.

"Really?" Vivi Ann answered. They both knew she didn't care. "Maybe you should go after him."

"It's been twelve years," Aurora said, meeting Vivi Ann's gaze head-on.

As if she didn't know exactly how long it had been since Dallas's arrest. There were still nights she couldn't sleep and days when she beat herself up over signing those divorce papers. Sometimes, in the still of the night, she wondered if he'd been testing her; if he'd wanted her to prove her love by refusing to give up. "Can we talk about something else, please?"

"Sure." Aurora paid the check and they walked

out together, into the sunlit day. "Thanks for meeting me for lunch."

"Are you kidding? I love playing hooky. Next time I'll dress up."

"You? Ha."

"I know how you hate to be seen with a woman wearing fifteen-year-old jeans."

"It's a small town. My choices are limited. If I weren't with you, I might have to join the Women's Auxiliary again and hear how stupid I was to let Richard go. Like I was supposed to not care that he was screwing his nurse."

Vivi Ann linked arms with her sister. It had been four years since Aurora's acrimonious divorce, but no one knew better than Vivi Ann how long some wounds could take to heal. She knew Aurora felt foolish for failing to see her husband's infidelity. "How are you doing? Really?"

"Some days are better than others."

"I know that song," Vivi Ann said. She, of all people, knew that a thing could be talked about only so much. Then, finally, you had to let it go. Everything that needed to be said about Aurora's divorce had been. So she said, "How's work?"

"I love it. I should have taken a job a long time ago. Selling jewelry might not be curing cancer, but it keeps me out of the house."

Vivi Ann was just about to say more when her cell phone rang. Reaching into her purse, she pulled it out, flipped it open, and answered.

"Vivi? This is Lori Lewis, from the middle school. Noah is in the principal's office."

"I'll be right there." Vivi Ann snapped the phone shut with a curse. "It's Noah," she said. "He's in trouble at school."

"Again? You want me to come with you?"

"No, thanks." Vivi Ann gave Aurora a quick hug and then hurried over to her new truck. Jumping in, she drove three blocks and parked on the street.

At the secretary's desk, she smiled tightly. "Hey, Lori."

"Hi, Vivi," Lori said, leading her toward the principal's door. Opening it, she said, "Noah is in with Harding now."

"Thanks," Vivi Ann said, stepping past the secretary.

Harding rose at her entrance. He was a big man, with a paunch that strained the buttons of his short-sleeved white dress shirt. Baggy brown polyester pants rode beneath his protruding belly, held in place by taut suspenders. His fleshy face, folded by distress into basset hound lines, was showing signs of emergent beard growth. "Hello, Vivi Ann," he said. "I'm sorry we had to pull you away from the farm. I know how busy you are these days."

She nodded in affirmation and glanced over to the corner, where her almost fourteen-year-old son sat slumped, one booted foot stretched forward. A column of jet-black hair fell across his face, obscured one green eye—the only trait he'd inherited from her. Otherwise, he was the spitting image of his father.

When she got closer, he tucked the hair behind his ear and she saw the black eye it had shielded, and the cut along his jaw. "Oh, Noah . . ."

He crossed his arms and stared out the window.

"He got in another fight at lunch. Erik, Jr.; Brian; and some other boys. Tad had to go to the doctor's for an X-ray," Harding said.

The lunch bell rang and the floor beneath them shook with movement. Raised voices bled through the walls.

Harding pressed the intercom, said, "Send Rhonda in, please." Then he looked at Noah. "Young man, you've run out of rope with me. This is the third time you've been involved in a fight this year."

"So it's a crime to get beaten up around here, is that it?"

"I have several students who say you started it."

"Big surprise," Noah said bitterly, but Vivi Ann knew him well enough to see the hurt beneath his anger.

Harding sighed. "If it was up to me, I'd suspend him, but Mrs. Ivers seems to think he deserves one last chance. And since there's only two weeks of school left, I'm going to agree with her." He looked at Vivi Ann. "But you need to get a tighter leash on this boy, Vivi Ann. Before he hurts someone like his—"

"I can do that, Harding."

The door behind them opened, and Rhonda Ivers walked into the room.

"You may go, Noah," Harding said, and Noah was on his feet in a flash.

Vivi Ann grabbed his arm as he tried to pass her, yanked him around to face her. He was now eye to eye with her; tall and gangly. "You come straight home after school. Do not pass Go. Do not collect two hundred bucks. Got it?"

He wrenched free. "Yeah, yeah."

When he was gone, Harding said, "I hope you know what you're doing, Rhonda." Giving them each a pointed look, he added, "Have your meeting here. I need to keep an eye on the lunch crowd."

Rhonda waited for him to leave and then took a seat behind his big metal desk. Amid the piles of paper stacked on top of it, she looked frail and birdlike. She wore the same hairstyle and type of clothing she had some twenty years earlier when she'd tried to teach Vivi Ann to appreciate *Beowulf*. "Sit down, Vivi," she said.

Vivi Ann was so tired of this; it felt as if she'd been battling one invisible foe after another for twelve years. Ever since Al had asked Dallas what he'd done on that Christmas Eve night.

"We all know Noah's story," Mrs. Ivers said when Vivi Ann sat down. "And his problem. We understand why he's acting out, why he's unhappy."

"You think he's unhappy? I thought . . . I hoped it was just normal teenage angst."

Rhonda gave her a sympathetic smile. "You know the kids make fun of him?"

Vivi Ann nodded.

"He needs a friend, and perhaps some counseling, but that's for you to decide, of course. I'm here because he is going to fail Language Arts this year. I've done the calculations and there's no way he can make up all the lessons he's missed."

"If you hold him back a grade it will just compound his problem. Then they'll think he's stupid as well as . . . different."

"Such was my analysis." Mrs. Ivers pulled a black and white bound composition book out of her bag and slid it across the desk. "That's why I'm giving Noah this one opportunity to save his grade. If he'll fill this journal with *honest* writings this summer, I'll pass him on to high school."

Vivi Ann felt a wealth of gratitude for this woman she'd once called Mrs. Eyesore. "Thank you."

"Don't be so quick to thank me. This will be hard work for Noah. I'll require eight pages a week all summer. I'll meet with him each Monday to give him that week's topic. We'll begin next week before school. Say seven-fifty in my classroom? In late August, I'll grade his work. I will not read his personal entries except to ascertain that it's his own original work. Is that understood?"

"Perfectly."

Mrs. Ivers smiled at last, a little sadly. "It can't be easy on him."

The past was always close in a town like this, like a layer of new snow on deep mud; noticeable. "No," Vivi Ann said, reaching for the empty journal. "It's not easy."

By the time Vivi Ann returned to the ranch, it was almost time for her afternoon lessons. She passed her dad in the arena, where he was roping with a couple of buddies. The hired hands—day workers now; no more live-in help for Water's Edge—were working the chutes. Waving, she went into the arena office and began creating flyers for next month's cutting series.

In the past years, Water's Edge had grown financially successful, but beneath the overhead lights inside the barn, little had changed. The arena still boasted rows of wooden bleachers and a series of gates and chutes for roping; three big yellow barrels were pushed to one side; they'd be pulled out and positioned for tonight's barrel-racing jackpot. Inside the barn, horses had chewed down the wood wherever they could, leaving the slats scalloped. Cobwebs hung thick in the corners and flyers studded the walls with color, advertising stuff for sale, classes and clubs to join, and veterinary and farrier services. The arena schedule had been set for a long time now, too. She still ran a few jackpots a month, as well as a longer barrel-racing series; still taught lessons and trained horses. In addition, several clubs rented out use of the place regularly—drill clubs, 4-H Clubs, and horse shows. Once a month, kids with special needs came to ride. The only real difference was Vivi Ann herself; she no longer barrel-raced. She'd never been able to bring herself to replace Clem.

For the next four hours she worked nonstop. After school, the 4-H Club showed up, and she surrounded herself with girls still young enough to love their horses more than any boy and committed enough to practice what they were taught. She felt like a rock star around them, idolized and adored. Soon, she knew, these girls would grow up, sell their horses, and move on. It was the circle of life in these parts: horses came first, then boys replaced them and took the lead. At some point later on, those girls came back as women with daughters of their own and started the cycle all over again.

At the end of the day, she turned off the overhead lights, checked the horses one by one, and then went down to the farmhouse, where she found her father sitting in his favorite rocking chair on the porch. As usual lately, after a long day spent working the ranch, he was sitting on the porch, drinking bourbon and whittling a piece of wood.

He had aged in the past decade, remarkably so. His face, always craggy, had hollowed out, and his once-wild hair had thinned to a cottony fuzz. Bushy white eyebrows grew in tufts above his black eyes.

He was seventy-four, but he moved like an even older man. They never spoke of what had happened all those years ago, he and Vivi Ann, never brought up the arrest that had broken their family's spine and split them in half.

They spoke of ordinary things now, sometimes barely looking at each other; it was as if part of their lives had frozen over and couldn't be found. But Vivi Ann had learned that things didn't always have to be talked about to be resolved. If you pretended long enough and hard enough that everything was fine, in time it could come to be true, or nearly so.

No one in town spoke of what happened all those years ago, either, not to Vivi Ann. There was a tacit agreement made by all to forget.

Unfortunately, it was Noah's life that everyone in their farmhouse and in town ignored so pointedly. The adults, anyway. The kids had obviously made no such pact.

"Hey, Dad," she said, coming up the stairs. "We need another load of hay. Can you call Circle J?"

"Yep. I sent that new hand over for bute, too."

"Good." She went into the house and cooked dinner for him and the hands, leaving the meal in the oven on low heat. The three men ate catch-as-catch-can these days; Vivi Ann cooked in the farmhouse, but rarely sat down to eat with the men. Her life was up in the cottage these days, with Noah. When she was done, she returned to the porch.

She was about to walk past her father when he said, "I hear Noah got in another fight today."

"The busybody express," she said, irritated. "They tell you who started it?"

The past was between them now, as visible as the wide white planks at their feet.

"You know who started it."

"Your dinner is in the oven. Tell Ronny to wash his dishes this time."

"Yep."

She walked out across the parking lot and driveway (paved since 2003) and stopped at the paddock behind the barn. Renegade whinnied at her approach and hobbled toward her, his knobby, arthritic knees popping at each step.

"Hey, boy." She rubbed his graying muzzle and scratched behind his twitching ears. It flashed through her mind suddenly: *Does he still dream of riding Renegade?*

Pushing the thought aside, she headed up toward her house. Renegade followed on his side of the fencing, limping and struggling until the start of the hill, where he gave up and stood there, watching her go.

She was careful not to look back at him as she went up the final rise to her cottage. When she opened the door, she knew that Noah was home. A pounding, pulsing beat of music rattled the knotty pine walls. She drew in a deep breath and released it slowly. Lord knew anger wouldn't aid her now.

At his bedroom door, she paused and knocked. It was impossible to hear an answer above the music, so she opened the door and went inside.

His room was long and narrow, a recent addition to the cabin. Posters of bands covered his walls—Godsmack, Nine Inch Nails, Korn, Metallica. He had his own computer in the corner and a television hooked up to an Xbox.

Maybe that was the problem; she'd given him too much and asked too little in return. But she was always trying to make up for what he'd lost.

He was sitting on his unmade bed, with a wireless controller in his hand, making some animated biker-looking chick kick a guy in the balls.

"We need to talk," she said to his back.

When he didn't respond, she went over to the TV and turned it off.

"Damn it, Mom. I was just about to beat that level."

"Don't swear at me."

He gave her a sullen look. "If language is such a big deal, maybe you and your sisters could start setting a better example."

"You aren't going to turn this around," she said. "Not this time. What was the fight about?"

"Gee, lemme think. Global warming?"

"Noah . . ."

"What do you think it was about? What's it *always* about? That puke-for-brains Engstrom called me Injun boy and his assface friends started doing a rain dance. So I punched him out."

Vivi Ann sat down beside him. "I would have wanted to clean his pimply clock, too."

He glanced at her through the curtain of his greasy hair.

Vivi Ann knew how desperate he was for someone to take his side, to be his friend and support his actions. It broke her heart that she couldn't fill that role. Once, she'd thought they'd be best friends forever; that youthful naïveté was no more. He was a fatherless boy; he had to have a mother who made the rules. "Every time you hit someone, you prove them right."

"So what? Maybe I *am* just like my old man." He threw his wireless remote at the wall. "I *hate* this town."

"Noah—"

"And I hate you for marrying him. And I hate him for not being here . . ." His voice broke on that and he stood up, moving quickly away from the bed.

She went to him, took him in her arms the way she used to, but he shoved her away. She stared at his back, saw the defeated slope to his shoulders, and knew how wounded he'd been by those ugly words in the schoolyard.

"Believe me, I know how you're feeling."

He turned. "Oh, really? You know how it feels to have a murderer for a father?"

"I had one for a husband," she said quietly. "Leave me alone."

Vivi Ann took another deep breath. They'd been down this road before, talking around Dallas. She never knew what to say. "Before I leave, I have to pass along the good news that you're going to flunk English, which means you won't go on to high school in September."

That got his attention. "What?"

"Lucky for you, Mrs. Ivers has agreed to give you a second chance. She's going to let you write in a journal for her this summer. You'll meet with her Monday morning before school to discuss the details."

"I hate writing."

"Then I hope you enjoy eighth grade better the second time."

She left him alone to mull that over.

Who Am I?
Only a totally whack old lady like Mrs. Eyesore would give such a stupid assignment. She thinks I care about passing Language Arts. Like I'm going to need THAT after I graduate from high school. Yeah, right. Screw her and her last chance. I'm not gonna do it.

They suspended me.
Fuck.

Who Am I?
Why does Mrs. I. think that's such an awe-some question? I'm nobody. That's what I'll tell her. Oh wait, I don't have to tell her because she's not going to READ MY PRIVATE STUFF. Like I believe her when she says she's just going to skim over it to see if I'm not copying other people. Yeah. I so totally believe that.

I should tell her. Blow her mind. I DON'T KNOW WHO I AM.

How could I?

I don't look like anyone in my family. Everyone says I have my mom's eyes, but if I ever look that sad I'm gonna blow my brains out.

That's my answer this week, Mrs. I. I don't know who I am and I don't care. Why should I? No one else in this town does. I eat all my lunches alone at the table with the other dorks and losers. No one ever talks to me. They just laugh when I go past and whisper shit about my dad.

Chapter Nineteen

Winona's life was proof positive that if you got a good education, worked hard, and kept believing in yourself, you could succeed. She gave this inspirational speech—the story of her triumphs—all over the county, to church groups and classrooms and volunteer organizations. They believed her, too, and why not? The measure of her success was visible to the naked eye: she lived in a gorgeous, flawlessly remodeled Victorian mansion, drove a brand-new, totally-paid-for ice-blue Mercedes convertible, and periodically bought and sold local real estate. Her client list was so extensive that in non-emergency situations, people often had to wait two weeks for an appointment. And best of all, her neighbors had grown accustomed to taking her advice. She'd proven, over time, to be right about almost everything, and it was flattering to know that her calm, rational decision-making skills were recognized and admired. In retrospect, even the ugly business with Dallas had bolstered her reputation. Everyone ultimately agreed that she'd been right not to represent Dallas, and Vivi Ann had come back to the family, just as Winona had hoped. Now they were together again; sometimes the ragged seams showed or buried resentments poked through, but they'd learned how to ignore those moments and go on, how to change the subject to something safe. All in all, Winona felt they were as strong a family as most and better than plenty.

Not everything was perfect, of course. She was forty-three years old, unmarried, and childless. The children she'd never had haunted her, came to her sometimes in her dreams, crying to be held in her arms, but as much as she'd wanted that fairy tale, it hadn't happened for her. She'd dated plenty of nice men over the years (and a few real losers), and she'd often hoped. In the end, though, she'd remained alone.

Now she was tired of waiting for the life she'd once dreamed of, and had decided to try another road. Career had always been her great strength, and so she'd try to find fulfillment there.

With this shiny new goal in mind, she stood on the sidewalk, studying the booth she'd just erected and decorated. It was really just four card tables tied together and draped in red fabric that fell almost to the cement. Behind it was a huge banner, strung between weighted poles, that read: THE CHOICE FOR MAYOR IS CLEAR. VOTE GREY. On the table were hundreds of brochures, complete with photographs of her great-grandfather standing by a handmade OYSTER SHORES POP. 12 sign, as well as a detailed description of Winona's political position on every issue. Other candidates could blow hot air about their beliefs; not her. She intended to crush the competition with the force of her convictions. Two large glass bowls held hundreds of VOTE GREY buttons.

Everything was ready.

She checked her watch. It was 7:46 in the morning.

No wonder she was out here pretty much all alone. The Founders Day festivities didn't start until noon and none of the businesses were open yet. She leaned back against the streetlamp and looked up and down the street. From her vantage point in front of the Sport Shack, she could see everything from Ted's Boatyard to the Canal House Bed and Breakfast. The usual Founders Day signage was in place—banners decorated with covered wagons set against a beautiful ocean-blue backdrop, hand-painted pioneer-themed artwork on the glass storefronts, and blinking lights twined around the streetlamps.

As she stood there, the clouds overhead thinned out a little and the shadows lifted. By eight o'clock the rest of the vendors had shown up, waving at Winona as they passed, in a rush now to get their stalls ready by noon, and by nine o'clock the stores were beginning to open. All up and down the street one could hear the tinkling of bells that meant doors were opening.

Memorial Day Monday had always been the start

of the week-long celebration. The same street vendors showed up year after year, selling the same things: homemade scones with jam, churros, fresh lemonade, oyster shooters, barbecued oysters, and the ever-popular Conestoga wagon hand puppets. All day long, throngs of people would fill this one street, walking from booth to booth, eating food they didn't need, and buying junk they didn't want, and come nightfall a bluegrass band would set up in the Waves Restaurant's parking lot, position speakers in the corners, and everyone from five to seventy-five would dance. It was the unofficial start of summer.

She walked down the street and bought herself a latte. By the time she got back to her booth, Vivi Ann, Noah, and Aurora were there. No doubt Vivi Ann was afraid to leave her delinquent son home alone.

"We're ready to help," Vivi Ann said, smiling.

"I was hoping you'd show up," Winona said.

"Hoping?" Aurora arched one perfectly plucked eyebrow. "I know an order when I hear one. What about you, Vivi?"

"Oh, she definitely ordered us here."

"I don't know why. You two are total bitches." Winona grinned. "Thank God you're cheap labor."

Aurora studied the booth and frowned. In her trendy low-rise designer jeans with stiletto-heeled sandals and a fitted white blouse, she looked more like a celebrity than a small-town doctor's ex-wife.

"I can't believe you put pictures of the flag all around your banner. Rectangular shapes are bad for women; everyone knows that. And your slogan: Vote Grey. Seven years of college and that's your best shot?" She turned to Vivi Ann. "Fortunately originality isn't valued in a politician."

"I suppose you could do better," Winona said.

Aurora made a great show of thinking. She frowned deeply, tapped one long, acrylic-tipped nail against her cheek. "Hmmm . . . it's difficult, I'll agree. I mean, your name is Win. But how, oh, how could you use that?"

Winona couldn't help it: she burst out laughing. "How could I miss that?"

"You've always been a see-the-trees, miss-the-forest gal," Aurora said. "Remember when you took your first driving test? You were so busy looking ahead to the stoplight and calculating how many feet it would take you to stop at that speed and wondering when to hit your turn signal that you drove right through a four-way stop."

That was the thing about family. They were like elephants. No one ever forgot a thing. Especially a failure, and a funny failure was as durable and reusable as plastic.

She was about to offer to get coffee for everyone when she noticed Noah going through her purse. "Noah," she snapped. "What are you doing?"

He should have looked guilty, but that was the thing about Noah: he never behaved as you expected. Instead, he looked angry. "I need a pen to do my homework."

My ass, Winona thought, but said, "How very enterprising of you." She plucked a pen off the table and handed it to him, then retrieved her purse.

For the next eight hours, she and her sisters handed out brochures and buttons and gave away candy. Sometime after three, Aurora disappeared for half an hour or so and came back carrying quart-sized margaritas in Slurpee cups. After that they really had fun. Winona wasn't exactly sure whose idea it was, but after they'd given away all the promotional items, while the other business-oriented booths were shutting down for the night, the three of them ended up standing in the middle of the street, arms slung around shoulders and waists, doing the cancan and singing, "Can can can you vote for Win?"

Laughing, they walked back to the booth, where Noah sat like a little black rain cloud.

"Could you be *more* weird?" he said to Vivi Ann, who immediately lost her smile.

It pissed Winona off. The last thing her sister needed was an angry, maladjusted kid to hurt her feelings. "Could you?" she asked Noah.

"Who wants another drink?" Aurora said quickly. "Everyone? Good. Come on, Noah. You can help me carry them back. It'll be good practice for senior year."

After they were gone, Winona went over to Vivi Ann, who was standing by the banner's stanchion, looking out across the crowded street. Through the colorful, moving blur of people, Winona knew what her sister was staring at. The corner of the ice-cream shop and the start of the alley.

Cat Morgan's house was long gone, of course; now that clean, well-tended alley led out to the Kiwanises' park. But no matter how many signs they erected or ads they placed in the newspapers, to the locals it would always be Cat's alley.

"Are you okay?" Winona asked cautiously.

Vivi Ann gave her one of the Teflon smiles she'd perfected in the past few years. "Fine. Why?"

"I heard Noah got in a fight again."

"He says Erik, Jr., and Brian started it."

"They probably did. Butchie's kid has always been a bully. The apple doesn't fall far from the tree."

"I gave Noah the benefit of the doubt the first few fights, but now . . . I don't know what to do with him. Even if he's not starting the problem, he's finishing it, and sooner or later he's going to hurt someone."

Winona considered her words carefully. Of all the land mines buried in the dirt of their past, none was more easily triggered than discussions about Noah's problems.

The past year had changed everything; it had

happened almost on the day of his thirteenth birthday. In one summer he'd gone from being a skinny, smiling Labrador retriever of a boy to a sullen, sloop-shouldered Doberman. Quick to anger, slow to forgive. He'd caused talk in town with his temper. Some even whispered the word *violent,* usually paired with *just like his father.*

Winona thought he needed counseling at the very least and possibly placement at a school for troubled teens, but offering Vivi Ann that advice was problematic. Especially coming from Winona. Their reconciliation was complete, but a little conditional. Some things were just out of bounds. "It's not surprising that he'd have trouble dealing with . . . stuff," Winona said. She never mentioned Dallas's name if she could avoid it. "Maybe he needs counseling."

"I've tried that. He wouldn't talk."

"Maybe get him into sports. That's good for a kid."

"Could you talk to him? You remember what it was like to be picked on, don't you?"

Winona didn't want to agree. The truth was that she didn't like Noah lately. Or, maybe that wasn't quite accurate.

He frightened her. No matter how often she told herself that he was just a boy and that he'd had a rough shake and that the teen years were hard, she couldn't quite make herself believe it. When she looked at him, all she saw was his father.

Dallas had almost ruined this family once, and she was terrified that his angry, violent son would finish the job.

"Sure," she said to Vivi Ann. "I'll talk to him."

I can't believe I used to like Founders Days. What a joke. Like people don't think I'm enough of a loser already, I have to sit in Aunt Winona's "campaign center" and hand out cheap buttons to old people.

When they started that stupid kick dancing in the street I wanted to hurl. Of course that's when Erik Jr. and Candace Delgado walked by. I totally wanted to smash his grinning face, and Candace looked like she felt sorry for me.

I HATE THAT.

I'm so sick of people thinking they know something about me just because my dad shot some lady. Maybe she gave him one of those you're scum looks. Maybe that's why he shot her.

I've tried to ask my mom about it, but she just looks like she's gonna cry and says none of that matters anymore, that the only thing that matters is how much she loves me.

Wrong. She has no clue how I feel. If she did she'd take me to see my dad.

That's the first thing I'm gonna do when I get a license. I'm gonna drive to the prison and see my father.

I don't even want to talk to him. I just want to see his face.

You probably want to know why, don't u, Mrs. Ivers? U think I'm being an idiot to want to see a murderer and you're wondering if I'll steal a car to do it.

Ha ha.

You'll have to wait and see.

In June, the Bits and Spurs 4-H Club was having their first official get-ready-for-the-fair meeting. The girls, and several of their mothers, were in the cottage, seated on the floor, on the sofa, on the hearth. The pine-plank floor was dotted with blank squares of poster board. On each white sheet sat a bucket of supplies. Colored markers, rulers, glitter paint, decorator scissors, Scotch tape; more than twenty years of experience had taught Vivi Ann exactly what they would need. Trends came and went, the words changed with the generations, but how girls expressed themselves remained the same: with bright colors and glued-on glitter.

Vivi Ann stepped around the room, positioning each of her girls in front of a piece of poster board. "Go ahead and begin," she said finally. "Start with your horse's name. It's his stall, remember, and neatness and spelling count. The barn judges will read every word." She stepped over one girl's outstretched legs and sidled past another. At the dining room table, she paused. From here, she could look out through the old, rippled kitchen window and see the shingled exterior of the addition.

Noah's light was on.

To the girls, she said, "Excuse me for a minute," and walked into the new wing of the house. To the left lay her bedroom and bathroom. She turned right and went down to the end of the hall. She hadn't found the time yet to pick out carpeting for this area, so her cowboy boots creaked on the springy plywood flooring.

She knocked on Noah's door, got no answer, and went inside.

He was on his bed, knees drawn up, eyes closed, rocking out to music on his iPod. White wires snaked down from the buds in his ears and plugged into the thin silver player.

At her touch he flinched and sat upright. "Who said you could come in my room?"

Vivi Ann sighed. Did they really have to have the your-room-my-house conversation every day? "I knocked. You didn't answer."

"I didn't hear you."

"That's because you listen to music that's too loud."

"Whatever."

She refused to take the bait. Instead, she reached out to tuck the hair behind his ear the way she used to, but he shrank back from her touch. "What happened to us, Noah? We used to be best friends."

"Best friends don't jack your Xbox and TV out of your room."

"You got suspended from school. Was I supposed to send you flowers? Sometimes parents have to make hard decisions to do what's best for their kids."

"I don't have parents. I have you. Unless you think Dad is making hard choices about me in his cell."

"I don't know why you're so angry these days."

"Whatever."

"Please stop saying that. Come on, Noah, how can I help you?"

"Give me back my TV."

"That's it, that's your answer. You get in a fight at school and—"

"I *told* you it wasn't my fault."

"Nothing ever is, is it? You're like a fight magnet, I guess."

"Whatever." He glared at her. "You know everything."

"I know this: you're a member of the Bits and Spurs 4-H Club, and as such, you're supposed to be making a poster for your stall."

"You're crazy if you think I'm showing at the fair this year."

"Then I'm crazy."

He jumped off the bed. His iPod swung from his earbuds and then fell, clattering to the plywood floor. "I won't do it."

"What's the alternative? You going to sit in this room all summer, staring at where your TV used to be? You don't do sports, you won't do chores around here, and you don't have friends. You can damn sure go to the fair."

He looked so hurt that Vivi Ann wanted to apologize. She shouldn't have said that about his lack of friends.

"I can't believe you said that. It's not my fault I don't have any friends. It's yours."

"Mine?"

"You're the one who married a killer and an Indian."

"I'm tired of this same argument, Noah, and I'm tired of you sitting around doing nothing and feeling sorry for yourself."

"I'm not showing at the fair. Only girls show horses. I take enough crap already. All I need is Erik, Jr., to see my pink and blue glitter why-I-love-my-horse poster."

"That was a great poster. Everyone loved it."

"I was *nine*. I didn't know any better. I am not showing at the fair this year."

"Well, you're not sitting home all summer."

"Good luck with making me move," he said, putting his earbuds back in.

Vivi Ann stood there, staring at him. She could actually feel her blood pressure elevating. It was amazing how quickly he could get to her. Finally, remaining silent by force of will, she left his bedroom, slamming the door behind her. A juvenile show of irritation that nonetheless felt good.

In the living room, she paused. "I'll be right back, girls. Keep working."

Grabbing a sweatshirt off the sofa, she left the cabin and walked down to the barn. It was full of trucks and trailers.

Inside the arena was carefully controlled pandemonium. Kids and dogs ran wild through the bleachers, chasing the barn cats around. Several women and girls were riding in the center of the arena, practicing flying changes. Janie, back from college, was working her mare along the rail, and Pam Espinson was leading her grandson on his new pony.

Vivi Ann scanned the crowd, finding Aurora in the stands watching her daughter. She put her hands in her pockets and walked over to her sister. All around her was the blurring movement of people on horse back, the vibrating thunder of hooves on dirt. She moved easily through the crowd and took a seat by Aurora. "It's nice to see Janie riding again."

Aurora smiled. "It's nice to see her again, period. The house is awful quiet these days."

"I wish," Vivi Ann said.

"Noah?"

Vivi Ann leaned against her sister. "Isn't there a rule book for raising teenagers?"

Aurora laughed and put an arm around her. "No, but . . ."

"But what?" Vivi Ann knew what was coming and tensed up.

"You'd best do something before he hurts someone."

"He wouldn't do that."

Aurora looked at her. She didn't say anything, but they both knew she was thinking about Dallas.

"He wouldn't do that," Vivi Ann said again, although her voice wasn't as strong this time. "I just need to find him something worthwhile to do."

Traffic on First Street was stop-and-go on this last day of school. No doubt all the graduating seniors in town were in their cars right now, honking to one another and high-fiving out their car windows as they passed. She saw a few yellow high school buses caught in the snarl, too, and could imagine their tired drivers' reaction to all this.

If she'd left ten minutes earlier or later, she wouldn't be stuck here. It wasn't as if she were on a tight schedule—or like she didn't have access to a calendar.

It was summer on the Canal now, on the very June day that most of the county's schools ended for the year, and those two details combined to make a perfect storm of traffic. One blocky motor home after another inched down the winding road. Most of them were hauling other vehicles—boats, smaller cars, bicycles, Jet Skis. Nobody came to the Canal in these golden months to sit inside, after all; they came to play in the warm blue water.

Out on the highway, she drove past Bill Gates's gated compound and the gorgeous lodge and spa called Alderbrook, where yuppies congregated for wine tastings, weddings, and hot stone massages.

As she drove, the Canal bent and curved beside her; sometimes the road was inches from the water and sometimes there were acres in between them. Finally, as she neared Sunset Beach, she slowed and turned onto the sloped gravel driveway that led to the house she'd purchased only last week.

Her newest project was a sprawling 1970s rambler, originally built as a summer home for a large Seattle family. There were six bedrooms, one bathroom, a kitchen the size of a toolbox, and a dining room that could comfortably fit a motorboat. A huge covered deck jutted out over the Canal, and to its right, stairs led down to the two-hundred-foot-long dock that was white with bird droppings. Every square inch of this place was dilapidated or rotting or just plain ugly, but the property made it all worth it. Along the road, huge cedars shielded the property and ringed the flat grass patch like a protective circle of friends. In front of the trees, in full bloom now, were giant rhododendron bushes and mounds of white Shasta daisies. The two-acre parcel sloped gently down to a sand beach. White pieces of opalescent oyster shells decorated the shoreline, interspersed with beautiful bits of gem-colored glass. A hundred years ago this stretch of sand had been a dumping ground for broken bottles. Time had taken that trash and turned it into treasure. Every time Winona looked at that impossibly colored beach, she thought of her mother and smiled.

She parked in the grass, grabbed a Diet Coke out of the cooler in the backseat, and considered how best to redesign the house. Obviously she was going to use the building's footprint and remodel extensively. It was the only way she'd be able to have a house so close to the water these days. She could, however, go up a floor. That meant opening up the downstairs, making sure every room had a view, and creating a master suite, master bath, and office upstairs.

Perfect.

She retrieved her meatball submarine sandwich and her note pad from the car. Sitting on the front lawn, she ate her lunch and began drawing out interior plans. She was so enmeshed in the scale of rooms and the positioning of doors that she didn't even notice that she wasn't alone until Vivi Ann said her name.

Winona turned. "Hey. I didn't even hear you drive up."

"I didn't mean to startle you." Vivi Ann crossed the lawn toward her as Noah exited the passenger side of the truck. Making no move to join them, he stood there, hands in his baggy chewed-up jeans, shoulders slouched, hair in his face, looking put-upon and pissed off.

"You came out to see the new house, huh?" Winona said. As a rule, she ignored Noah's presence whenever possible. It made life easier. "Can I show you around?"

Vivi Ann's gaze swept the place. "What do you have to do before you begin tearing down walls?"

"Oh, lots. There's always prep work. You should see the dock. Forty years' worth of seagull crap takes a while to wash off."

"That's perfect!"

"I know. A dock adds over one hundred thousand dollars' worth of value to this place." Winona frowned. "Is that what you meant?"

Vivi Ann glanced over at Noah, who was studying his dirty fingernails as if he might find gold in there. "Noah doesn't want to be in 4-H anymore and he's refusing to show at the fair."

"Uh. Duh. He's a boy. Maybe you want him to take ballet, too."

"I'm glad to see you understand the problem. It wasn't quite so clear to me."

"Of course it wasn't. You were beautiful and popular. If you wanted to play football, the guys would have said it was cute. Hell, if you threw up at homecoming, the boys would've lined up to hold your hair and still thought you were adorable. A kid like Noah has to be careful: no math or computer clubs, no chess, and certainly no 4-H. He's trying to make friends, not lose them."

"And you said he shouldn't be sitting around all day."

"Did I? I think I said he needed counseling, too. He seems . . . angrier than normal."

"What he needs is a summer job. And not at the ranch. We don't need something else to fight about."

"That's a great idea. It would use up his time and give him self-esteem and . . ." Winona stopped. "No," she said to Vivi Ann, shaking her head. "You aren't thinking—"

"It would be perfect. He could clean up the dock. Eight hours a day, five days a week. You can pay him by the foot. If you pay him by the hour I think you'll go broke and your dock won't ever get cleaned up."

"I'm supposed to pay him, too?"

"Well, he'll hardly do it for free. And you're rich."

"Look, Vivi Ann," Winona said, lowering her voice. "I don't know about this."

"Tell her you're scared of me, Aunt Winona," Noah yelled. "Tell her you think I'm dangerous."

"Shut up, Noah," Vivi Ann snapped. "She certainly isn't afraid of you." She looked back at Winona. "I really need your help here. You're so good at solving problems. Aurora thinks it's a great idea."

"You ran it past her?"

"Actually, it was her idea."

Winona was screwed. Any idea that had been vetted and approved of by half the family was a done deal. "He has to pull his pants up—I don't want to look at his underwear all day—and he washes his hair on the days he works for me."

Noah grunted. She didn't know if he'd agreed or not.

Winona walked over to him, hearing Vivi Ann following her. "How does eight bucks a foot sound?"

"Like slave's wages."

Vivi Ann cuffed the back of his head. "Try again."

"It sounds fine," he grumbled, shoving his hands deeper in his pockets.

Winona was actually afraid his jeans would fall down in a heap around his ankles.

This was a bad idea. The kid was just like his dad: trouble. But she had no way out. "Fine. He's hired. But if he screws up once—*once*—you get him back, Vivi. I'm no babysitter."

Vivi Ann looked directly at Noah. "If you fire him, he's competing at the fair. Is that understood?"

Noah didn't answer, but the look in his eyes was pure teenage rage.

He understood.

Chapter Twenty

WHAT DO I CARE ABOUT?

Another totally useless question, Mrs. I. What do you do, sit around reading some old teacher's handbook on how to get bad kids to talk? I can tell you what I don't care about. How's that? I don't care about Oyster Shores or the kids in my class or high school. It's all just a big waste of time.

And I don't care about family suppers. We had another rocking good time at the Grey house last night, btw. It's always the same. Aunt Aurora bragging about how perfect her kids are. Ricky the perfect college student and Janie the girl wonder. And Grandpa sits there like a rock while Aunt Winona tells us all how perfect her friggin life is. No wonder my mom used to take a bunch of pills to get through the day. I'm not supposed to know about that. They think I'm an idiot. Like because I was a kid I didn't notice that she used to cry all the time. I tried to help her—that's what I remember most about being little. But she used to either push me away or hold me so tight I couldn't breathe. I got so I knew what her eyes looked like when she was drugged up and I just stayed away. Now she pretends everything is okay because the medicine cabinet is empty and she never cries.

I found something else I don't care about. Aunt Winona's dumb old dock. It's covered with bird shit, so naturally I'm the one that gets to scrape it all off. You should see the way she watches me. Like I'm going to blow any second or come at her with a knife. She used to like me, too. That's another thing I remember from when I was little. She'd read me bedtime stories when Mom was gone and watch Disney movies with me. But now she stays away, staring at me when she thinks I don't notice.

I think she's scared of me. Maybe it's because of that time I got pissed off at a family supper and threw my glass at the wall. That was the day Erik Jr. told me my dad was a half breed murderer. I didn't believe him and when I got home, I asked my mom and she talked and talked and talked and never said anything.

And everybody wonders why I get pissed off. What am I supposed to do when Brian calls me injun boy and says they shoulda fried my dad for what he did?

The next Friday teased them with the promise of summer. A pale, pretty sun played hide-and-seek with the clouds; light came and went across the yard like a capricious child, until finally sometime just past noon it came out and stayed.

Winona was busy scrubbing the kitchen floor when she noticed the change in the weather. At first she thought nothing of it, figured, in fact, that it was just as likely to begin raining as not, and kept working. But when she started to feel heat prickle on her forehead and form tiny moist beads in the curl of her back, she climbed to her feet and pulled off her rubber gloves. If it was actually going to stay nice out, she knew she should power-wash the deck. You didn't squander sunlit days in June around here.

She changed into shorts and a baggy, thigh-length T-shirt. As she pulled her hair back into a ponytail, she peered through the cloudy glass of her bedroom window and saw Noah down on the dock, supposedly scraping bird poop off the splintery wooden rails.

Honest to God, the dead moved faster.

And his pants were so low she could see the waistband of his blue boxer shorts.

He'd been working for her for five days and she could barely identify his progress. He got here promptly at nine o'clock every morning and went down to the dock without saying a word to her. On the days she went into the office, leaving him here alone, she had no doubt whatsoever that he was sitting on his ass.

"This is so not working out," she muttered, grabbing a roll of duct tape.

She marched out onto the deck, letting the door bang shut behind her. Enough was enough. She might have to employ him, might have to ignore his surly attitude and his dirty hair, might have to pretend he was working, but by God, she didn't have to look at his damn underwear.

She walked down the dock. The tide was low, so the ramp down to the dock was steep and springy beneath her. She held tightly to the bird-ruined handrails, looking carefully for bare wood places to touch, as she made her way cautiously down to him. "Noah."

He'd been so busy doing nothing that he was startled by her voice. He flinched, dropped the metal scraper. "Jeez. Yell, why don't yah?"

"Duct tape is a remarkable invention. It can be anything. Did you know that?" She unwound a length about as long as her arm, tore it off, and then carefully folded it in half lengthwise.

"I don't think about tape much, but I'll believe you." He reached down for the fallen scraper. "Unless you want to tell me something about . . . I don't know, maybe yarn? I think I'll get back to work."

"We both know what a joke that is. Here." She handed him the strip of silver tape.

"What is it?"

"Your new belt. Put it through the loops—you do

know how to do that, don't you?—and tie it in a knot. I do not want to see even a strip of your boxers."

"You've got to be kidding me."

"Do I look like I'm kidding?"

"This is the style," he said stubbornly.

"Oh, yes, you're a real Giorgio Armani. Put on the belt. If you'll remember, it was a condition of this ridiculous enterprise you and I pretend is employment."

"And if I don't?"

She smiled. "You know what I loved about the fair? The way my chaps and hat and gloves all matched. They were all the same blue. Your mom called it dressing to win. And everyone I knew was there, seeing me dressed like a fat blueberry."

Noah said nothing.

"I'm sure you'll be very handsome in whatever outfit she's made. She *is* still making your riding clothes, isn't she?"

"Give me that," he said, grabbing the makeshift belt. It took him a while to thread it through the loops and pull it taut, but when he was done his pants were pulled up to his waist. The knot was as big as a fist. "I look like a total dork."

"You won't find any disagreement here. If you'd buy pants that fit it would help."

"Whatever."

"That is such a useful word. I notice you're par-ticularly fond of it. I'd appreciate it, as your employer, if you'd speak in complete sentences."

He glared at her. "Whatever . . . Aunt Winona."

"And progress is made." She started to explain to him yet again how to scrape the dried bird crap off when she heard a truck drive up. She tented her hand over her eyes to block out the sun and saw a large yellow moving van pull into the driveway next door. "I wonder who bought that place," she said. "The construction crews have been there for weeks."

"Tell me something I don't know."

"As easy as that would prove to be, I'm going to check out my new neighbors." She made her way up the steeply pitched ramp and cut across her shabby yard. Everything on this edge of her property was overgrown, almost primeval in size. Giant rhododendrons, sprawling junipers, hedges gone wild. She peered through the narrow break in the foliage and tried to see the house. Unfortunately, the moving truck was directly in front of her. Disappointed, she returned to her house and began power-washing the deck.

She was halfway through, covered in water and sweat, standing in rivulets of blasting water, when she realized that a man was standing just beyond her deck, smiling hesitantly. He was tall and stocky, with a pleasant face and hair that was actively in retreat. He was dressed in an expensive silk Hawaiian print shirt, khaki shorts, and leather flip-flops, and she knew instantly that he was a summer person, here for what tourists ridiculously called the season. Probably from Bellevue or Woodinville. No wonder he'd been able to pour so much money into remodeling the old Shank place without bothering to oversee construction. Beside him was a pretty red-haired girl of probably twelve or thirteen.

Winona flicked off the machine and set the sprayer down. It occurred to her in a flash that she looked like hell—old shorts, baggy, splotched T-shirt, damp hair falling out of its ponytail. The sight of her thick fish-belly-white legs was an image she tried to block from her mind. "Hello there," she said, forcing a smile. "You must be my new neighbors."

The man advanced toward Winona, his big hand outstretched. "I'm Mark. This is my daughter, Cissy."

Winona shook his hand. Good, strong grip. She liked that. "I'm Winona."

"Nice to meet you, Winona." He took a deep breath and exhaled, looking around. Oddly, she was reminded of a king surveying his holdings. "It's stunningly beautiful here."

She pushed the sweaty hair out of her face. "I never get tired of the view."

"It's not one you forget, no matter how far you go."

Winona saw Noah coming up the dock and figured that it must be noon. The kid might not grasp the idea of working, but break times he understood. At the top of the ramp he paused and then slowly shuffled toward them, shoulders slumped, hands in his pockets, hair in his eyes.

"Is that your son?"

"No," she said quickly.

Noah gave her a sullen look.

"This is Noah. My sister's son. Noah, this is Mark and Cissy."

Noah jutted his chin an almost imperceptible amount. "What's up?"

Only it sounded more like *whasup?* Winona fought the urge to roll her eyes. He looked like a homeless person with his dirty, baggy pants and duct-tape knot at his waist. His ridiculously big skater's shoes bloomed up around his feet like baking bread.

No doubt Mark would pull his preciously pretty girl close and run back to his house.

Instead, he said, "Cissy and I were going to take the boat out this afternoon, maybe do a little waterskiing. Would you two like to join us?"

Winona was surprised by the invitation. "Your wife—"

"I'm divorced."

Winona saw him in a whole different light suddenly. He was older than she was, by five or ten years probably, but he had a really nice smile. "Unfortunately, I don't think Noah has any shorts."

"I got 'em on," he said. "Under my cool duct-tape belt."

"You're wearing trunks?"

He shrugged. "I swim sometimes."

Mark smiled. "It's settled, then. We'll go get stuff ready and meet you on our dock in, say, thirty minutes?"

"Sure," Winona said. The minute they left, she went into the house and looked at herself in the mirror. "Oh, God." It was worse than she'd thought. She looked like the love child of Demi Moore and the Michelin Man—plump white legs, fleshy arms, tangled, frizzy hair, sweat- and water-stained T-shirt. She flew into the shower, washed her hair, shaved her armpits and legs. There was no time to dry her hair, so she French-braided it and put on makeup.

Then she looked at her one-piece bathing suit. It was a size twenty and unless she missed her guess, she'd barely fit in it. Perfect. The first reasonably good-looking single guy she'd met in almost a year and she was supposed to show off her body on day one? That would guarantee that he never asked her out on a date.

"No swimming for you, fat girl." Instead she chose a pair of black capris and a long white tank top.

At precisely twelve-thirty, she was in the yard, carrying a cooler full of beers, Cokes, and munchies. Cute boating clothes might be a problem for her, but food she always had.

Noah was milling aimlessly around the deck, and she called him inside. When he stepped into the kitchen she was momentarily taken aback. He'd stripped down to a pair of blue board shorts that hung low on his narrow hips. When had his shoulders filled out like that? And his arms. He had the lean, defined build of a runner.

"Sit down," she said, waiting impatiently for him to do as she'd asked.

"Why?"

"That girl was pretty cute. I saw the way you were looking at her."

"Whatever."

She gave him the look.

"Whatever, Aunt Winona."

"She might actually think you're cute if you quit sulking around and hiding behind your Morticia hair."

"My what?"

"Do you want her to think you're cute?"

"Hot," he said, eyeing her mistrustfully. "Puppies are cute."

"Whatever. You want her to think you're hot?"

"You mean 'whatever, Noah,' right?"

She almost smiled. "Hot or skanky. What's your choice?"

"Hot," he finally said, sitting in the chair she'd indicated.

"Good." She brushed his hair with deep, brutal strokes, untangling it until it fell in soft, straight strands to his shoulders. "Your mom shouldn't have let you grow it this long. I guess she always liked it that way, though. I remember . . ." She realized what she'd been about to say and shut up and put his hair in a ponytail. "There."

He looked up at her, said quietly, "Could you tell he was a killer, right from the start? I know he fooled Mom, but everyone says you're so smart . . ."

Winona took a deep breath. Vivi Ann would want her to ignore the question, but she couldn't do that. "No. I didn't know."

"He won't let me visit him."

"I think that's probably for the best."

He looked young suddenly, and vulnerable. "How come no one cares what I think?"

Before Winona could answer, there was a knock at the door, and she went to answer it.

Cissy stood there, wearing a string bikini the size of a postage stamp. "My dad said to tell you he's ready."

Noah got to his feet and walked toward them.

Winona watched Cissy stare at her nephew. She might not know the words the kids used these days—hot or cute or bootylicious or whatever—but she damn sure knew what it meant when a girl looked at a boy that way. "What grade are you going to be in, Cissy?" she asked.

"I'll start ninth."

"Really? That's the same as Noah." She turned to him, saw the blush on his sharp cheeks. "I guess you better work hard on that English assignment this summer."

He blushed harder and mumbled something.

"Do you like school here?" Cissy asked him.

Noah shrugged. "It's okay."

"My grandmother says I won't have any trouble making friends, but I don't know . . ."

"Who is your grandmother?" Winona asked. "Do you have family in town?"

Cissy was so busy staring at Noah that it took her a second to answer. "My dad went to high school here. Our whole family is from Oyster Shores."

"High school in Oyster Shores? You're kidding. I should know him, then."

"You probably know my grandma. Myrtle Michaelian. She lives on Mountain Vista."

"Yeah," Winona said, wondering if Noah recognized the importance of that name. "I know Myrtle."

The summers were easiest on Vivi Ann. She woke early in the mornings, well before dawn, and began the long string of chores that occupied her days. There were lessons and clinics and jackpots to organize and run, animals to feed and exercise, horses to train, the fair to prepare for. She was busy from morning to night, moving too fast to think about much of anything, but even in the busiest of seasons there would sometimes be nights like tonight, when the ranch was quiet and dark and the sky overhead was a riot of stars, and she couldn't help remembering how it had felt to sneak out of her bedroom and run across the grassy fields to this cabin. How it had felt to be alive, a being made of sunlight instead of shadow.

"Hey, Renegade," she said, walking up to the fence.

The old gelding limped over to her, nickering a velvety soft greeting. She gave him an apple and scratched his ears. "How you feeling, boy? That arthritis acting up? Do you need some bute?"

Behind her a car drove up; twin headlight beams flared through the darkness, startling Renegade, who moved away.

Vivi Ann turned in time to see Winona and Noah getting out of the car. They walked close together, talking. Winona said something and pushed him away. He stumbled sideways, laughing.

Vivi Ann couldn't believe her eyes. She wasn't sure she'd *ever* seen those two actually talking, let alone teasing each other.

She walked up to meet them.

"Hey, Mom." Noah grinned, and the sight of it took her breath away. Dressed in board shorts and a sleeveless T-shirt, with his hair drawn back in a ponytail, he looked relaxed. Happy. "I learned how to waterski today. It was totally awesome. It took me a long time to get up, but once I did, I was *great*. Wasn't I, Aunt Winona?"

"I've never seen so much natural ability. He was crossing the wake like a pro."

Vivi Ann felt a smile start. For a perfect moment, everything was right with her world. "That's great, Noah. I can't wait to see you do it."

"I'm gonna write about it in my journal," he said. "Thanks, Aunt Winona. That was awesome."

Vivi Ann watched him disappear into the house, then turned to her sister. "Where's my son and who was that boy?"

Winona laughed. "He was actually a lot of fun."

Vivi Ann slung an arm around her sister. "I'm buying you a beer. Come on."

They got two beers out of the fridge and went back outside. Sitting in the porch swing, side by side, shoulders touching, they stared out across the sleeping ranch.

"It's like a miracle, seeing him laugh again."

"He's a pretty decent kid, under all that attitude." Winona paused. "He's got a lot of questions about his dad."

"I know."

"It's hard enough to be a teenager without also looking different, feeling different, and hearing all the time that your dad . . . you know."

"I've always been afraid of that conversation. I know why we have to have it. He'll ask me if Dallas did it, though."

"What will you say?"

"If I say his father did it, then Noah's the son of a murderer. If I say Dallas didn't do it, his father is rotting in prison for another man's crime, and injustice is hard to live with. Believe me: I know. So, you tell me, Obi-Wan, what's the right answer?"

Winona seemed to think about that. "When I was a kid, Mom used to tell me that I was big-boned and beautiful. I knew it wasn't true: I had a mirror. But I also knew she believed it, and that was what mattered. I knew she loved me." She turned to Vivi Ann. "Let him know he's a good person in spite of what people may think. Tell him it doesn't matter who his dad was. What matters is who *he* is."

Vivi Ann leaned against her big sister. It was times like these that made her glad she'd chosen all those years ago to forgive Winona. "Thanks."

"You're welcome. What should I do if he asks me stuff?"

"Answer him, I guess. Maybe it'll help."

Winona stared down at her beer.

"Okay," Vivi Ann said when they'd been quiet awhile. "Spill the beans."

"What do you mean?"

"You're never quiet that long. What are you trying to figure out?"

"The guy we went skiing with today is Mark Michaelian. Myrtle's son. He graduated about five years before me."

"Oh." Vivi Ann took a long drink of her beer.

"He asked me out on a date. Do you care if I go?"

Vivi Ann leaned back and pushed off; the porch swing glided back gently.

The familiar sounds of the ranch were all around—the distant purr of the waves and the clomping of horses in the field and the creaking of the metal chains behind them.

"If you want me to cancel the date, I will," Winona said.

Vivi Ann knew it was the truth. One of the things about their past was this: the baggage might be stored in the dark, but it was still in the house. They were all very careful not to haul it out. The same mistakes couldn't be made again. "You haven't dated anyone seriously in, what, two years? Not since that marine biologist was here for the summer."

"Thanks for pointing that out."

"I didn't mean that. I meant . . . sure. Go out with Mark. You have my blessing."

"Really?"

Vivi Ann nodded. "Really."

It felt good, that decision, made her feel as if she'd finally let go.

"Are you sure?"

"I'm sure. It's all in the past."

Today was such a totally tight day that I don't even need one of Mrs. I.'s dorky questions. I feel like if I don't get all this down on paper I'll forget it and I DON'T EVER WANT to forget.

It started out sucky. I totally didn't see how anything was ever gonna change. I showed up at Aunt Winona's house and she acted as stuck up as ever, all up in my grill, giving me that I just ate a bad piece of fish look. I pulled my pants down as far as I could just to piss her off and it musta worked cause at about lunchtime she came running down to the dock with this long piece of duct tape that I was supposed to use as a belt. I would have told her to take a flying leap but she started talking about the fair and the riding outfit my mom made me wear last year and I chickened out. I pictured Erik Jr. and Brian and all the rest of those assholes seeing me showing horses with a bunch of little girls and I figured the duct tape was better. I felt like a total loser after that but so what? I'm sorta used to that and no one was there to see anyway. I slowed down my bird shit scraping, tho, just to piss her off, which I know it does. Sometimes I see her standing up there on her crappy deck watching me work and I can practically hear her grinding her teeth. She wants to fire me but she can't and that's cool.

Anyway, I was just smoking along, doing practically nothing when I looked up at the house and saw some strangers in the yard, talking to my aunt. That was weird, so I put down my scrapey-thing and went up, even tho my aunt hates it when I stop working.

When I got close I could see that it was an

old guy with the kind of hair you should just shave off and quit trying to save. He was dressed like a bartender, but he isn't the one I stared at.

She was the most beautiful girl I'd ever seen in my life. The most amazing part was that she didn't look at me like I was just that indian. When her dad took us out waterskiing she wanted to sit by me and everything. She told me that she and her dad had been traveling around the world for a year and now they'd come back to Oyster Shores and she was bummed cause all her friends were in Minnesota. Then she asked me if I wanted to hang out with her tomorrow. I know she won't stay friends with me when she hears all the shit in town and finds out that no one likes me. I don't even care.

When we got home Mom was so cool with everything that she even left me home alone while she went to the Outlaw with Aunt Winona. She NEVER does that. I think she's afraid I'll smoke crack or burn the house down but tonight she said I was growing up and making good choices and I'd earned this chance.

My mom just got home from the Outlaw and she was laughing and happy. I haven't seen her look that way in a long time. She even sat down *with me on the couch and put her arm around me and told me she was proud of me and that she was sorry. She didn't say what she was sorry about but I knew it was about my dad and how screwed up everything is so I told her it was fine. I know it was dumb, but I liked it when she said she was proud of me. It was kinda cool.*

Chapter Twenty-one

A ll right, we're here. What's the emergency?" Winona turned around to face her sisters, who were standing by the front door. "It's a fashion 911. My date with Mark is in an hour and somehow I need to lose forty pounds and buy a new wardrobe. And I think I need microdermabrasion."

"Take a deep breath," Vivi Ann said.

"What is she, in labor? Breathing never works. I say we get her a straight shot," was Aurora's advice.

"We are not getting her drunk before her date." Vivi Ann laughed. "Besides, lately that's your advice for everything."

"Consistency is a virtue," Aurora said primly. "I'll be right back." She left the house and was back in a flash with her makeup kit (housed in a designer case that was as big as a tackle box) and a pretty pink box from the clothing store on Main Street.

"What's all that?" Winona asked. "I only called you guys fifteen minutes ago."

"We were waiting for it," Vivi Ann said. "Remember when the banker from Shelton asked you out? You were a wreck."

"And that teacher from Silverdale. I think you actually puked before he got here," Aurora added.

"She did."

Winona collapsed onto her garage-sale sofa, realizing for the first time that it kind of smelled like gasoline. "I'm hopeless."

Vivi Ann sat down beside her. "No. You're hope*ful*. That's your problem. Maybe this guy is finally the one. Your Neo."

"Do you have to use the word *finally?* And I hated those Matrix movies, you know that. They made no sense."

"She's looking for Tom Hanks in *Sleepless,*" Aurora said. They all knew—but never said—that since Luke had gotten married seven years ago, Winona had grown increasingly despondent over her romantic future. Her self-esteem—never high when it came to men—had fallen below sea level. "Come on, let's get this intervention going. Ricky is coming home from school this weekend, and I want to make his favorite enchiladas."

Winona let herself be carried away by their enthusiasm and self-declared proficiency. Vivi Ann painstakingly straightened Winona's long hair, layer by layer, until it fell in silken columns along her face. Aurora applied makeup with a surprisingly restrained hand—smoky violet smudges beneath her mascaraed lashes, a sweep of rose-hued blush, a lipstick just bright enough to bring out the color of her eyes.

"Wow," Winona said, smiling at her reflection. "Too bad he can't just take my head out to dinner."

Aurora came up behind her, holding a gauzy black sundress with a plunging vee bodice and crinkly skirt that fell from an empire waist.

"My arms will show," Winona said.

"So will your boobs," Aurora said, helping Winona out of her T-shirt while Vivi Ann helped her out of her sweatpants. "Did you shave?"

"I'm not a complete moron."

"I don't know about that. Here."

Winona let Aurora pull the stretchy dress over her head. It fell easily into place and she turned back to the mirror and tried to see herself through his eyes: a tall, big-boned woman with a pretty enough face and flabby arms wearing a black, summery dress that showed off her cleavage. Absent liposuction, this was as good as she was likely to look. "Thanks, guys."

Aurora studied her. Removing one dangling red earring and then the other, she handed them to

Winona. "Wear these. And try not to talk about your campaign."

"Why not?"

"You can't avoid going into mind-numbing detail. Especially when you start talking about refurbishing downtown. Trust me. Zip it."

Winona looked to Vivi Ann for confirmation. "Really?"

Vivi Ann grinned. "Really."

Aurora looked at her watch. "It's five forty-five. I gotta go." She hugged them both and left.

"Don't freak out about this one, okay?" Vivi Ann said. "He's lucky to have you."

"Thanks," Winona said, wishing she could believe it. "Noah asked if he could work till nine. Is that okay with you?"

"Sure. I'll come back and get him when he calls. He's been great to be around the past few days. Actually *smiling*. It's like he's gone back to the kid he was before the hormones hit. And I think a lot of it is thanks to you."

"I haven't done anything major."

"Winona Grey not taking credit for something? Is there a new world order?"

"Very funny."

Vivi Ann gave her a big hug, kissed her on the cheek, told her goodbye, and went outside, where she talked to Noah for a few minutes longer, and then left.

Winona immediately began pacing. She was like

one of those polar bears in the zoo, wearing a groove into the ground at the fence line, slowly going mad. She hated first dates; there was so much hope. And God knew she'd learned how dangerous that crystalline emotion could be. Every time she met a new guy, she thought: *Maybe he's the one; maybe he'll finally make me forget about Luke.*

"Aunt Winona?"

She stopped pacing, thankful for the distraction. "You don't have to keep working tonight, you know."

"I want to. Otherwise I'd just chill in my room and play Xbox." He grinned. "Oh, that's right. My insane mother took my Xbox when I got suspended from school."

"So you're saying that scraping poop off wood is all you have to do on a Saturday night?"

"Jeez. Way to make me feel like a loser."

"Sorry."

He nodded and stood there, staring at her. It occurred to her that he'd cleaned up—his shiny hair was in a ponytail and his sleeveless T-shirt and board shorts actually fit him. He was still wearing those ridiculously swollen skateboarder's shoes, but not all fashion battles could be won at once.

"You look like you want to say something."

He sat down on the arm of the sofa. "What do you do when you like someone?"

"I tend to vomit," she said, laughing. Then she looked at him. "Oh. You mean it. Well . . ." She walked over and sat on the old-fashioned milk crate she was using these days as a coffee table. "Different people will give you different answers, and I'm certainly no expert, but what I care about most are honesty and respect. If a guy gives me that, I'm happy."

"Have you ever been in love?"

The question surprised her. No one had asked her that in a long time, and it wasn't something she asked herself, and yet once the words were in the air she couldn't pretend not to have heard. As expected, the image of Luke came to her mind, more clearly than it had any right to. She wished she could just forget about him, but she couldn't. He was The One for her. As Vivi Ann would say, her Neo. He was the yardstick by which all other men were judged. And he'd never loved her in return. How pathetic was that? "A long time ago, yeah," she answered.

"What happened?"

She wanted to lie, say nothing, or make an excuse, but when she looked into her nephew's earnest eyes, she was reminded of the thing she'd learned because of Luke. Lies and omissions had a way of expanding; like too deep a layer of fertilizer, they could kill everything beneath. "He didn't love me back."

"That blows."

She couldn't help smiling. "Yes, it does. He's married now. With two little kids."

"Maybe he still thinks about you."

"Maybe." Winona got up, suddenly eager to end this conversation. "Well. It's six. Mark should be here any minute. I'll leave the house open for you just in case you need to use the restroom. There's plenty of food in the fridge."

The doorbell rang.

"He's here," Winona said nervously. "So scat. And stay out of my booze," she teased, watching him leave. As soon as he was gone, she went to the front door, opening it.

Mark held out a bouquet of flowers. "Is this cliché? Do guys still give flowers on a date?"

She saw that he was as nervous as she was and it calmed her down. "The good ones do. Come in while I put them in water. Can I get you a drink?"

"I don't drink."

She turned to him. "Is there a story there?"

Without looking at her, he nodded. "Are you okay dating a dry alcoholic?"

"I look forward to it."

He took her elbow and guided her out the door and across her bumpy, untended yard, through the freshly clipped arch in the hedge, and into his beautifully restored home. Everywhere she looked there was something exquisite: a massive marble hearth, hand-cut and brought over from Italy; a four-hundred-year-old silk prayer rug from Iran, mounted on black velvet and framed in gold; hand-blown glass light fixtures from Venice.

She followed him down to a toffee-colored media room, full of overstuffed furniture and dominated by a big-screen TV. Cissy sat curled up in an upholstered chair, eating ice cream and watching a movie.

"Hey," she said, hitting the pause button. The image on-screen froze. Hugh Jackman as Wolverine was caught in midair.

Mark leaned down and kissed the top of her head. "I'll have my cell phone on. We should be home about ten or eleven."

"Call me when you leave the restaurant so I know when to expect you. Otherwise I wouldn't know when to panic."

Winona smiled. It was the kind of thing she would have said to her sisters.

Mark led Winona back upstairs and out onto the deck. There, he grabbed a cooler and a blanket.

"Are we going camping?" she asked.

"Follow me."

He led her down to his dock and out to the ski boat, where he settled her into the seat beside him.

They puttered away from the dock, motored through the flat, calm water. Every now and then a water-skier or a Jet-Skier would zip past, causing a wake to rock the boat, but for the most part it was peaceful on this blue June evening. There were no clouds in the sky, nothing to cast a shadow on the water. It was a deep, rich green at this time of the day, flat calm.

Winona studied the houses along the shoreline, noticing how many newer, bigger houses had sprung up in the last few years. She wondered how long it would take for this whole area to be changed beyond recognition. Mark maneuvered the boat up to the Alderbrook Lodge's long public dock, tying up next to a gorgeous old wooden yacht called *The Olympus.*

He helped her out of the boat, paid the dockmaster a moorage fee, and together they headed toward land.

The newly redone Alderbrook was a full-service resort built on the foundation of what had once been a quaint family-owned lodge. On a stunningly gorgeous stretch of beach that overlooked the placid Canal and the sawtooth range of the Olympic Mountains, every room and cabin was exquisite. Built of stone and wood and glass, it was a perfect expression of new upscale Northwest chic.

At the restaurant, the hostess seated them at a table along the window, and almost from the first moment they were talking. Mark told her about the year he and Cissy had traveled the world, and the amazing things they'd seen. He'd described Thailand and Angkor Wat and Egypt in the kind of detail that made her yearn to go.

"I would love to see those places," she said when dinner was over and they were sitting in big plastic Adirondack chairs on the resort's grassy lawn.

Night was falling finally; the sky was a brilliant smear of striated hues—orange, pink, lavender. The water had gone black, with only the lapping sound of the waves to remind you that it was alive and awake.

"Have you ever traveled?"

"No, not really."

"Why?"

Winona shrugged. "My mom died when I was fifteen and I had to grow up fast. After law school, I came back here to practice because my sisters and my dad needed me."

"Your sisters were lucky to have you. When my wife left, poor Cissy had no one but me."

It was a topic he'd danced around all night but never quite addressed. She wanted to ask him about his ex, but things were going so well she didn't want to jinx it.

For the next few hours, they sat in the Adirondack chairs, staring out at the dimming view and talking with the ease of old friends. Winona couldn't remember when a first date— especially a dinner date—had gone so well.

Finally, at eleven, he said, "We'd better go. I don't like to leave Cissy alone too long."

And he was a good parent, too.

"Sure," Winona said, smiling at him.

After a quick call to Cissy, they motored home slowly beneath a dome of starlight and pulled up to the dock. As they walked up to her house, he held her hand, and their first kiss was everything she'd imagined: tender and firm and filled with longing. Winona's long-dormant passion came alive, reminding her forcibly that kisses weren't enough.

Suddenly he drew back.

"What's wrong? It's me, isn't it? You aren't attracted to me."

"It isn't you. It's me."

A George Costanza line. She'd expected more from him; that had been her mistake. "Okay." She sighed and turned away.

"Win." He reached for her hand and forced her to look at him.

"You don't have to put on a big show. It's fine. I get it, believe me. I just thought we were getting along, that's all."

"That's the problem."

"You lost me."

"My wife. Ironically, her name was Sybil. I should have seen that as a sign instead of a joke. Anyway, I love her." He paused, glancing out at the water as he whispered, "Loved her."

"And?"

He shrugged. "I wish I knew what happened. That's what kicks the shit out of me. I thought we were happy. Until I came home to an empty house and a *Sorry, Mark* note. She fell in love with her Pilates instructor and she was gone. Just like that. Cissy and I didn't know what hit us."

"That must have been terrible."

"Don't give up on me. Can I just say that? I know I have no right to ask, but I am anyway. Don't give up."

"Believe me, Mark. Giving up isn't something I know how to do."

"Okay, then."

"Okay."

"I'll call you."

"You know where I am," she said, then watched him leave her. He walked across the deck and over to his property line, where he disappeared into the dark black hedge.

She couldn't help wondering how long she'd have to wait for his next call.

Last night was el primo night of my life. As soon as Aunt Winona and Mark left on their date, I walked up the ramp to the yard and waited. My heart was beating so hard I thought I was gonna puke. I can't describe how it felt to see her coming through the opening in the hedge and know that she wanted to be with me.

I asked her if she wanted to watch a movie, but she said it was such a pretty night we should just lay down in the grass and talk. And that's what we did. I brought a blanket from Aunt Winona's guest room and spread it out over the bumpy grass and Cissy got us some Cokes and chips from her house and we laid down right beside each other and talked about stuff.

It was so awesome. She told me how her mom just left one day and didn't come back and never even called, and how her dad started drinking when it happened. She started crying when she was talking and I didn't know what I should do. I wanted to say the right thing only I know there's nothing you can say. Maybe that's why my mom never talks about my dad. Sometimes shit just hurts and that's the way it is.

She made this little sound when I touched her, kinda like a tire going flat, and I could tell that she'd stopped looking at the sky and was staring at me. Thanks, she said, I been hoping you'd do that.

What about you? she said later, what's the story of your life? I know she's gonna hear it all sooner or later, so I tried to tell her, but couldn't. I looked into her eyes and saw how much she liked me and I just couldn't ruin it. So I told her other stuff. Like how Brian and Erik Jr. talk trash around me and sometimes I lose my temper and how I've been suspended a couple of times for fighting. I even told her I started some of them.

I waited for her to say what everyone says which is what were you thinking? Like I'm an idiot. No one gets how I feel when Brian calls me injun boy. It's like that time I was riding Renegade and we turned a corner and saw a cougar. Renegade spooked and reared so fast I was lucky not to fall off. That's what happens when I hear shit like that—I spook. And instead of running, I fight.

So I waited to hear what Cissy would say. I didn't want her to think I was a chicken or a bully. I was so worried I barely heard her say I know how you feel.

The worst part, she said, was pretending it didn't hurt all the time.

That's when I kissed her. I didn't even think about it. I just saw her start to smile, and I knew how she felt and how I felt and I kissed her.

Of course that was exactly when my mom drove up. Cissy and I were laughing as we grabbed our stuff and put it away—all without Mom seeing anything. She honked her horn when I was out on the deck with Cissy. I almost said I love you but I knew she'd laugh at me, so I just said Later instead, and she said Later back.

But when I was practically up at the truck, I heard her whisper my name and I turned.

Meet me tomorrow, she said.

Where?

My mom was inside the truck, waving at me, like I hadn't seen her in a year.

At the state park, Cissy whispered, after lunch.

It was a good thing I put a seatbelt on when I got in the truck, cause I felt like I'd just fly away.

You look happy, Mom said when she turned onto the highway. That's what this feeling is, I guess.

Winona couldn't sleep. Turning on the light in her bedroom, she slipped into her favorite pink terry-cloth robe and went to the kitchen.

Nothing in the fridge appealed to her, so she made a cup of herbal tea and carried it outside. Leaning up to the railing, she stared out at the inky water. A slivered moon hung suspended above the invisible mountains, casting almost no light. After all her years in town she'd forgotten how dark it was among the trees and along the shore. If not for the water breathing along the sand there would be no sound at all.

It made her feel even more alone, all this quiet darkness. At her house on First Street, she often went onto her back porch in the evenings. There, she could sit in her glider and look out over the Canal House Bed and Breakfast and the beach park parking lot. Even in the dead of winter on a cold and frosty night, there was light and movement, and she was, however tangentially, a part of it.

Here, there was nothing. Just mountains unseen, black water, and distant stars.

"Hey, Winona."

She turned toward the sound, trying to see him, but it wasn't until he came closer, until he stepped onto the wooden deck, that she could make out more than his shape among the shadows. "Mark," she said, uncertain of what to add.

"I saw your light come on through the trees."

"I couldn't sleep."

He moved closer, stepping at last into the pool of light cast through the kitchen window. "Me, either."

She could see now how disheveled he looked, how ill-put-together. Like a man who'd been pacing for hours, running a hand through what hair he had until it stood up in all different directions. His shirt was buttoned wrong, too. "Is something wrong?" she asked.

"My whole life is wrong."

"I know that feeling."

"Do you?"

"Sure," she said quietly, putting her tea down on the table behind her. "I'm forty-three years old, Mark. I've never been married and it's probably too late to have kids now. And you may have noticed that my weight is a problem. So, yeah, I know about life not being what you thought it would be."

"I had such a great time with you tonight," he said. "It freaked me out."

"It's okay. We have lots of time."

He shook his head. "That's the thing I've learned

this past year. You think you have all the time in the world, but shit happens."

"What are you saying?"

He moved closer. "I'm saying I want you, Winona."

She felt a little thrill move through her, and as intoxicating as it was, being wanted, she couldn't be completely swept away by it. Her body might be aching for his touch, but her brain was up and working, too. "You're not ready," she said.

"I know I'm not."

"You could have denied it."

He put his hand around the back of her neck. His fingers felt warm and solid against her skin. She leaned back just a little so that she felt anchored by him, held close.

"Do you want me?" he asked.

She felt the softness of his breath against her lips. She wanted to close her eyes or look away; anything that would allow her to pretend. But the truth was in his eyes, as clear and visible as a starfish at low tide. He was still in love with his wife.

But she'd been lonely for a long time, and now that opportunity had drawn so surprisingly close, she couldn't make herself push it back. She moved closer and looked up at him. "I want you."

His kiss was a cool glass of water to her parched soul and she drank greedily. When they finally drew back, she saw her own desire reflected in his eyes.

"Come on," she said, taking his hand, leading him into the house and down the hall and into her bedroom. Without turning on the lights, she stepped out of her robe and nightgown and pulled him into bed.

He kissed her until she begged for more, and when he finally made love to her, she clung to him with all the desperate passion of a woman who'd been alone too long. Her release was an exquisite blending of pain and pleasure, and she cried out, almost weeping at the emotions that came with it.

"That was great," he said, lying back into the pillows and pulling her close.

She lay beside him. It had been so long since she'd been in bed with a man, she'd forgotten how much space men took up, how heavy their legs felt, how nice it was to have someone kiss your bare shoulder for no reason at all.

Long into the night they talked and kissed and later they made love again. At around four o'clock, Winona finally put on her nightgown and went into the kitchen. When she returned to the bedroom, she held a tray of food—Denver omelets, sourdough toast with fresh local honey and orange juice she'd squeezed herself.

Mark sat up in bed, letting the covers fall away from his naked chest.

She climbed in beside him.

"It's been a long time since someone cooked for me," he said, and then leaned sideways to kiss her.

The truth was that she had at least a thousand recipes in her card box at the house in town. She'd been collecting them for years, perfecting them all alone, waiting for someone to cook for. She ate her breakfast, listening to him as he talked. He told her about the countries he'd visited and the problems he'd had raising a teenage girl alone for the past year, and how happy he was to be starting over in Oyster Shores.

After breakfast, he pulled her into his arms and kissed her. When he let go, they were lying on their sides, their legs entwined, their heads on separate pillows, staring at each other.

"How come you never came home for Christmas or anything like that?"

"I left at eighteen, remember? All I wanted back then was to get the hell away from the small town where everybody knows your business. When I married Sybil, my mom and dad came out to the wedding, but it was the only time they ever visited, and I couldn't get Sybil west of Chicago."

"Did you and your mom talk?"

"Some. That's a strange question."

Winona chose her words carefully. This was a conversation they had to have, and there was danger in it. "A long time ago there was a murder in town. It was a big deal around here."

"I remember hearing about it."

"Dallas Raintree." She paused, then said, "He

was married to my sister, Vivi Ann. Your mother testified against him."

He frowned. "Yeah. I guess I knew all that. Is it important? Does your sister hate my mom or something?"

"You know Oyster Shores. Nothing is ever out in the open, but I've seen your mom cross the room after church to avoid having to talk to Vivi Ann. And vice versa."

"It's all gossip to me and I don't see . . . Wait a minute, are you talking about Noah's father?"

"Yes."

"Do I need to worry about Cissy around him?"

"A week ago I would have told you to keep Cissy away from him. He's had some trouble in school— you'll hear about that pretty soon, I expect. Some people think he's trouble waiting for a place to happen, but actually, I think he's okay."

"That's good enough for me. And now, how about some more small town gossip?"

"What?"

He craned his neck forward just enough to kiss her chin, her cheek, her lips.

She felt his hand slide down her back, across her butt, and slip between her legs.

"I hear Mark Michaelian is sleeping with Winona Grey."

She shivered at his touch. "From what I hear, they're not doing a lot of sleeping."

Chapter Twenty-two

This has been the best summer ever. Cissy and I have learned a hundred ways to sneak off and be alone. Even at my birthday party, we figured out a way to hang out without anyone seeing us. It's not that we don't want people to know we're together, it's just that in secret we have all the privacy we need. No one worries about how much time we spend together cause they don't know about it and Mark doesn't think he has to tell Cissy why I'm not good enough for her. I know she'll hear all that when she starts school, but I'm trying to keep it away for now.

The Fourth of July was especially tight. Everyone was busy with their own shit—Mom had the parade and the 4-H car wash to worry about, Aunt Winona was running her campaign booth, and Mark spent the whole day waiting for her to be done.

I took the money I'd saved this summer and spent at least half of it at the fair. I played games until I won Cissy the giant giraffe, and I kissed her on top of the ferris wheel at least ten times. When I was out of money, we went up to the hill by the horse barns and made out and talked. Best of all, I beat Mom home by about ten seconds. She found me in bed, reading, and said I'd missed a really cool time at the fair. She didn't know I still had my clothes on under the blankets!

July and August have been the best months of my life. I don't have time to write now (Cissy's waiting for me at Twanoh State Park), but I'll write soon . . .

Mark and Aunt Winona are going to Sol Duc hot springs for an overnight trip and they invited me and Cissy along! We know they did it because they want to pretend they aren't having sex all the time. Like Cissy and I are blind AND stupid, but we so don't care. When they said they were going, I totally acted like I was bummed but that I was down with doing a favor for Aunt Winona. Cissy acted the same way with her dad.

We all piled into Mark's Escalade last night. Mark and Aunt Winona were talking so much in the front seat that they never noticed Cissy and me were holding hands. At the camp-ground, we roasted hot dogs and made s'mores and played cards. At night we all slept in our own sleeping bags in a big orange tent. The worst part was being about ten feet away from

Cissy. I could hear her breathing but I couldn't touch her or kiss her or really even talk to her.

On Saturday we all woke up early and had breakfast at the lodge, which was cool. The place has this HUGE swimming pool that's filled with water from the hot springs, so it's like 100° or something. You can float in the hot water and then run over and jump into a regular swimming pool, which feels freezing. Aunt Winona and Mark were in the hot springs so long I think they kinda melted. When they got out, they were both trying to touch each other secretly—as if Cissy and I couldn't see exactly what was going on. They came over to the edge of the cold pool and called for us.

Anyway Cissy is a freaking GENIUS. Cause she swam right up to them and said she wanted to hike up to see the falls.

I swam up beside her and complained that the falls were like ten miles away, even tho I knew it wasn't that far.

And then Mark goes Noah, why don't you hike up to the falls with Cissy, and Cissy groans and Aunt Winona (who has to solve every problem) says that's a great idea, Noah. You two will be safe together.

Cissy and I got to hold hands all day and hike up the wide trail. The trees around us were gigantic. Everything was big—the rocks, the plants, the trees. Even though it was a hot day in August, there was practically no sunlight on the trail. Cissy got cold so I took off my shirt and gave it to her and even tho I was freezing I didn't care.

We could tell when we were getting close. It was loud, like a train running through the trees, making everything shake. We crossed over this rickety old bridge and kept going until we saw the falls.

It's magic Cissy said, holding my hand. I kissed her for a long time and it was the coolest thing ever. The ground was shaking and the spray was everywhere and it was so loud you couldn't hear anything, but when we stopped kissing, I saw the sunlight shining on us—just us—not anything else.

I said I love you without even thinking about it and she started to cry.

I said I was sorry and started to pull away but she wouldn't let go of me. She said Don't be an idiot. I'm crying because I love you, too.

She said it was destiny, us meeting, and maybe she's right. I mean, if we hadn't kissed by the falls or hadn't said we loved each other, or if the hot sunlight hadn't landed on us right then, maybe I wouldn't have taken her by the hand and pulled her into the shade beneath a huge cedar tree, and if I hadn't taken her there, maybe I wouldn't have seen it.

But there it was, just waiting for me. Carved

into the tree's shredded-looking brown bark was a smooth, perfectly formed heart. Inside the heart were two sets of initials and a date.

D.R. loves V.G.R. 8/21/92

Today was the 20th.

I sat up so fast Cissy kinda fell away.

What is it? she asked.

I wanted to tell her, I really did, but I couldn't talk, couldn't think. All my life I'd thought of my old man as nothing but a killer. Practically an animal.

But suddenly I thought of him as a guy who'd taken his wife here, to the exact spot I had picked for my girl, and I was scared.

What if he wasn't an animal? What if he was just a guy who got spooked one day and did something stupid?

And for the first time I knew that all those people who gossiped about me might be right.

Maybe I was just like my father. And he was just like me.

Look at that, Cissy said when she saw the carving, it's so romantic. I wonder who they were.

I took out my phone and took a picture of the carving. I can't remember what excuse I made to Cissy. From then on I was totally freaked—I don't even know how to put it—I sat there by the fire, totally tripping, waiting to get home so I could finally ask my mom who the hell Dallas Raintree was.

The worst day of the year for Vivi Ann was August 21. Sometimes she saw it coming for weeks, bearing down on her like a semi truck with bad brakes, and sometimes she was startled by its sudden appearance in the midst of an otherwise ordinary week, but either way the effect was the same: a pale gray depression. Years ago the pain of this day had been sharp, almost unbearably so, but time had sanded away its edges. It had gone from unbearable to bearable; that was the arc of her progress. She hoped she lived long enough to see it become just another day on the calendar.

She woke up late and fed the horses and steers, and then joined her father for coffee. They talked for a few moments about things that needed to be done, and then went their separate ways: him to Seabeck to look at a used Bush Hog, and her to her chores. For the rest of the day she worked tirelessly, careful never to slow down, until the effort exhausted her. Finally, as sunset drew near, she sat down in the rocking chair on her porch and dared to close her eyes.

Within mere moments she was where she wanted to be: lost in the land of memories. In some cool, rational space of her mind, she knew she shouldn't want to be here, but that voice was small and easily ignored. On this of all days, she couldn't help herself.

"Vivi Ann?" Winona said, walking toward her. "Are you okay?"

"I'm sorry, I guess I dozed off," Vivi Ann said. She got to her feet slowly, feeling a little unsteady. Memories were like alcoholic drinks; too many too fast could ruin your equilibrium. "Where's Noah?"

"I'm right here, Mom," he said, getting out of the shiny black SUV.

Mark got out of the driver's side. "Hey, Vivi Ann," he said, taking Winona's hand. "Thanks for letting us take Noah along. He was a lot of fun."

"Thanks for taking him. That was very generous of you two."

Mark smiled. "We thought we'd buzz down to the fish shack for dinner and then have some ice cream."

I was at the ice-cream shop, working late, when I saw Dallas come out of the alley . . .

"You want to join us?" Winona asked.

Vivi Ann smiled as brightly as she could. "No, thank you. Not feeling good," she added as an afterthought.

"I think I'll stay with Mom," Noah said. "Thanks for the trip, though." He went back to the car, said something to the girl in the backseat.

Winona let go of Mark's hand and moved toward Vivi Ann. "Are you really okay?"

Some days Vivi Ann loved the way sisters could read each other, and some days—like today—it pissed her off. The only good news was that

Winona would never take the time to figure out the importance of this date. "I'm fine. Really. Go have fun."

She watched her sister walk back to the expensive black car/truck and climb inside. As they drove away, Noah walked across the lawn and up onto the porch. "Today is August twenty-first," he said. "Does that mean something to you?"

Vivi Ann's whole world was momentarily upended. "W-what do you mean?"

"Don't," he said sharply.

Where only moments ago his expression had been blank and demanding, she saw now that he was nervous.

"We were up at Sol Duc," he said, coming nearer. "Cissy and me—"

"Cissy and I."

He rolled his eyes and went on. "We hiked up this long trail to the waterfall and then we sat down for a while to look at it. I saw this carving on a tree."

"A carving," she said, unable now to look her son in the eyes.

"It said, *D.R. loves V.G.R. August 21, 1992.*"

Vivi Ann felt the last bit of her resistance fall away. She was so tired of evading her son's questions. God knew he had a right to ask. She reached out for her chair and sank into it. The pain she tried so hard to outrun sat down beside her, taking up too much room.

"Mom?" he said; pleaded, really.

She nodded at him finally, revealing the fullness of her emotions for the first time in years, holding nothing back. "Today is our wedding anniversary. Your daddy carved that on our honeymoon."

"You never call him my daddy."

"It hurts too much."

"Will you answer my questions?"

"The ones I can. Come on, let's go inside. This may take a while." She got up and followed him into the house and poured herself a glass of white wine, then sat down on the sofa, tucking her bare feet up underneath her.

Noah sat in the chair opposite her. "Tell me about the crime."

"That's what you care most about? Hmm. Well, a woman was murdered—a friend of your father's, actually. I think the police suspected your father right away."

"Did he do it?"

She'd steeled herself for this question, knowing it was coming for more than a decade, and yet now that it was here, she wasn't sure what she should say. "Your dad had trouble controlling his temper."

"Like me?"

"Nothing like you," she said firmly.

"Did he kill that woman?" he asked again.

She knew he'd keep asking it until she answered, so she sighed and told him the truth. "I don't believe he did."

"Did you love him?"

Vivi Ann felt tears fill her eyes. There wasn't a damn thing she could do to stop them. "With all my heart."

"Why did you divorce him, then?"

"He divorced me, actually, but that's not what you really want to know. You're asking why I . . . gave up on him." Even after all this time, it hurt to remember that, to think about the way she'd let him go.

"It was so painful; hanging on, year after year, hoping. Every time the news was bad, I lost it. You remember some of that time. I took a lot of drugs and drank too much. I was a bad mother. I think your dad loved me so much he forced me to let go. And after we hit that tree in Grey Park—you remember that? It scared me, what I'd almost done to you. I knew I had to move on. *We* had to move on. You and me."

"How could you do that to him?"

She closed her eyes. It was a question that haunted her. How many times had she longed to go back in time and say, *No, Dallas, I won't walk away. I won't sign your papers.* "I just had to, that's all. But to tell you the truth, I don't think I'll ever forgive myself."

He got up and came around the coffee table. Sitting down by her, he laid his head in her lap the way he used to. She immediately began stroking her fingers through his silky hair.

So much like his father's . . .

"Did he love me?" Noah asked in a voice so quiet and hesitant she knew why he'd come over here. He didn't want her to see him cry.

"Oh, Noah," she said, leaning forward to whisper, "he loved you so much. That's why he wouldn't see you. It would have broken his heart to look at you through prison glass."

"That makes him a coward."

"Or human."

"Could I write him a letter?"

"I don't think he'll answer you. Could you handle that?"

"I think it's better than not trying."

Vivi Ann used to think like that; now she knew that trying could sometimes hurt more than giving up. "Okay, then. You give it a try. I love you, Noah. And I'm so proud of you."

"I love you, too, Mom." He wiped his eyes in a casual way, as if he thought she wouldn't notice his tears. "It was kinda cool, you know. That carving in the tree."

"Yeah," she said, remembering. "It was."

I thought talking about my dad would answer my questions, but all it did was make more. I kept remembering that carving in the tree. I know how he felt when he did it, so it's like I know a part of him now and it makes me want more.

417

I tried to hide it from Cissy. The next time we got together was Tuesday while Mom was giving an equitation clinic and Aunt Winona and Mark were gone to Seattle. Cissy and I spent the day on a big blanket in her back yard. I tried to pretend that everything was the same as before, but she knew something was wrong. I guess love gives you Xray vision or something. I was just sitting there, drinking my rootbeer when she said I know you're keeping a secret from me and I don't like it.

I told her she wouldn't like the secret, either, and she said if we really loved each other we wouldn't have any secrets.

I do love you I said.

Prove it.

I could have made up something else, maybe told her that I might not pass Language Arts or some other bullshit, but the truth was I wanted to tell her. I'm afraid, I said.

Of what?

I told her she wouldn't like me anymore once she knew the truth, but I knew that school was starting in ten days anyway, so I might as well tell her. Brian and Erik Jr. and the rest of them would do it for me.

She said she didn't like me, she loved me and nothing I said could change that.

So I told her everything, how my dad was Dallas Raintree, half Native American and half white, how he came to town looking for work and found a job at Water's Edge, and how he married Mom even though no one wanted him in the family. I told her about his temper and all the fights he got into. And I told her he killed a woman and went to prison for it. When I was done I couldn't even look at her. It was the longest I'd ever talked about my dad and I felt sick.

She moved closer to me on the blanket and tried to get me to look at her, but I couldn't do it. I just stared out at the canal as if I'd never seen it before. She reached over for my shoulder and pulled me down to the blanket so that we were lying down, facing each other.

I know all that, she said. My dad told me everything a long time ago. Did you know my gran testified against your dad?

It's weird how a word can surprise you sometimes. I've thought about my dad in prison all my life. I've imagined what he looks like and how he lives behind bars and what he thinks about me, but until Cissy said that thing about her grandmother, I never once thought about how he got to prison. How they proved he was guilty.

Do you think he did it? she asked.

I didn't know how to answer that. How could I? He's like this ghost to me. When I tried to remember real things there was almost nothing—a dirty pair of cowboy boots, a white hat I used to play with, a voice saying something in a language I didn't understand.

You should go see him, she said.

That's when we came up with The Plan.

On the last day of the fair, Vivi Ann cleaned up the barn and told her 4-H girls goodbye, and then walked down the grassy hill toward the glittering midway.

Aurora was at the ticket booth, waiting for her. "You're late."

"The girls just left. And we said four o'clock. I practically made it." She snagged a chunk of pink cotton candy from her sister and popped it in her mouth.

"Winona better not bail on us," Aurora said, putting one hand on her slim hip.

"She's in love. We all bail when love comes along."

Aurora frowned at her. "What's wrong with you? You seem happy."

"And that's wrong? I've had a good week. Noah and I finally talked about Dallas. It felt good."

"Where is the little delinquent, off smoking crack?"

"Why, is Janie back in town?"

Aurora smiled grudgingly. "I'm glad you talked about it, and I'm glad you're happy, but where is that bitch sister of ours?"

"There," Vivi Ann said, watching Winona and Mark come toward them.

"She brought a *date?* To girls' night? That is such a low blow," Aurora said, throwing the rest of her cotton candy in the trash.

"Thank God," Winona said, breathing hard as she came to a stop in front of them. "I've been calling you for an hour, Vivi."

"I don't get reception at the barn. You know that. What's up?"

Mark stepped forward. "I can't find Cissy. She was supposed to be at the house all day. Win and I were on our way to Seattle, but the Bainbridge ferry was a mess so we turned around. When I got home, the front door was standing open and Cissy was gone."

"You've tried her cell?"

"Of course," Winona said. "She's not answering. And we found this in her room." She held out her hand. In her palm lay a strip of photo-booth pictures. In it, Noah and Cissy were smiling, laughing, kissing. "It explains why my dock is still covered in bird shit. They've been together all summer. Unsupervised."

Mark looked like he was going to be sick.

"Let's not assume the worst," Aurora said, and Vivi Ann could have kissed her sister for her sensible voice. "We'll find them. That's the first thing. Then you can get to the bottom of how far they've gone."

"Where should we look?" Winona asked.

"I used to take girls to the beach park at night," Mark said. "There was that tree swing at the far end. And the logging road out by Larsen's Turnoff."

"Perfect," Aurora said. "I'll check out the far side of the fairgrounds, especially behind the grandstands."

"I'll ask around the midway, check the empty horse barns, and go home," Vivi Ann said. Flipping open her phone, she called Noah's cell and got no answer. She left an urgent message, then did the same thing on the home number.

"I'll help Vivi Ann," Winona said to Mark. "My sisters are right. We're panicking over nothing. Chances are they're at the fair."

Mark didn't look convinced, but to his credit, he nodded and gave out his cell number.

"We'll meet back at your house in an hour," Winona said.

At that, they dispersed in different directions.

Winona and Vivi Ann hurried down the busy midway, looking everywhere, calling out for Noah and Cissy. When they'd covered every game and ride and food booth, they separated and did it again.

"This is impossible," Winona said. "They could be anywhere. Hell, we used to hide from Mom and Dad when they came looking for us at the fair, remember? All we had to do was see them coming and duck into the shadows. What if they're doing that?"

"It makes sense, especially since they didn't want us to know they were together."

"Should we just go home and wait for them?"

Vivi Ann thought about that. "Why don't you go to my house? Make sure they aren't there and see if Noah left a note? I'll make one more run through here. I'll be a little quieter, though."

"Okay."

After that, Vivi Ann combed the midway and the empty horse barns but found no trace of the kids. Finally, she climbed in her truck and drove home.

Winona was waiting for her on the porch.

Vivi Ann knew instantly that this news was not going to be good. "What did you find?"

Winona held out a brochure. "It's a bus schedule. In the corner Noah has written, Cissy/1:00."

"Which bus leaves at one?"

"There's no way to know. The Mason County transit system hooks up with Kitsap and Jefferson. From Belfair, they can go almost anywhere."

Vivi Ann ran into Noah's room and went through his closet and drawers. "All his stuff is still here."

"Thank God," Winona said. "That means they're coming back." She flipped open her phone and called Mark with the news. "He's not happy," she said when she hung up.

Vivi Ann felt seared by disappointment. "Yeah," she said. "I'm not happy, either."

"Let's be logical. We're pretty sure they're together and that they took a bus somewhere. They must have planned to be home before us, and Mark told Cissy he'd be home at nine. There's a bus stop about one hundred yards from my beach house, but how would Noah get home? Would he hitchhike?"

"Since I would have said he wouldn't sneak around all summer with a girl or take a bus out of town without telling me, clearly I'm no authority on what he would do. Doesn't Mark have a boat?"

Winona nodded. "We spent all summer teaching them both how to run it."

"She could drop him off at Water's Edge and be back in ten minutes."

"In the dark? Could they *be* that stupid?"

"A question that hardly needs to be answered. Come on, let's wait at Mark's house. We can scare the shit out of them."

Vivi Ann, Aurora, and Winona all pulled into her driveway in a line. They parked on the shabby grass and walked next door through the hedge. Mark was pacing back and forth on the expensive flagstone path in his yard.

"Beautiful house," Aurora said, looking around at the carefully planned landscaping and copper outdoor lighting.

Mark didn't even acknowledge her comment. He just kept pacing and muttering to himself.

"This is pretty much a rite of passage, Mark,"

Aurora said. "Every kid sneaks out at least once. Janie snuck out and went to the Tacoma Dome to see Britney Spears. I didn't know whether to punish her for sneaking out or for making such a poor musical choice."

Mark turned to her. "Do you really think that situation is like this one?"

Aurora frowned. "You're right. My kid was driving. At least Noah and Cissy were smart enough to take the bus. Look on the bright side; they didn't steal a car."

"She's fourteen years old, for God's sake. We should be calling the police."

"Calm down," Winona said.

Mark wrenched away from her and called Cissy on her cell phone again. When she failed to answer, he walked up to the road and looked out. He stood there so long night started to fall. The sky turned orange and then lavender.

"Parenting is going to be tough on that one," Aurora said, shaking her head. "He's wearing a groove in the lawn."

"Shut up," Winona said. "He has reason to be upset."

"Yeah, but . . . I'm afraid his head is going to pop off. Let's hope she never tries drugs. He won't be able to handle it."

By the time Mark came back, Aurora was on the porch, sitting in a beautiful cushioned ironwork chair, Winona was standing by the custom stone obelisk fountain by the walkway, and Vivi Ann stood near the hedge. "It's seven thirty-nine," he said. "I think we should call the police."

"They'll be here within the hour," Winona said reasonably. "If they aren't, we'll call Al."

"People couldn't wait to tell me what a bad seed Noah was, but I gave him the benefit of the doubt and look where it got me. He's taken my Cissy God knows where. I'm afraid—"

Up on the road, a bus pulled to a wheezing, clanking stop and then started up again. Its head-lights shone through the twilight.

Vivi Ann took a step forward. She noticed that Mark did the same thing.

Noah and Cissy were so intent on talking that at first they didn't see the people waiting for them. Heads bent together, hand clasped, they walked down from the road.

"Cecilia Marie Michaelian," Mark shouted. "What in the *hell* do you think you're doing?"

Noah and Cissy stopped in their tracks.

Winona came forward first. "We've been worried about you guys."

"I'm sorry," Cissy said; her voice was barely a whisper.

"It showed really poor judgment, running off like that," Winona went on. "Where did you go?"

Noah took a deep breath and looked from Vivi Ann to Mark. "We went to the prison."

For a terrible moment no one spoke. The only

426

sound was the sea, washing onto the pebbled shore and then retreating.

"Unbelievable," Mark said finally. "Get in the house, Cecilia. We'll discuss this privately. And *you*," he yelled at Noah, "you will never see her again, you understand me?"

"Daddy," Cissy said, surging forward. "It was my idea. I talked him into it. Please, don't—"

"In the house," he said. "Now."

"Mark," Winona said, "certainly it was poor judgment, but—"

"Are you *insane?* Poor judgment is riding a bike without a helmet or skipping your class when you forgot about a test. This was dangerous and it's *his* fault. Cissy," he said firmly, "get in the house. And Noah, you can get the hell off my land." He looked at Vivi Ann. "I'm sorry. Really. But I can't let him endanger my daughter." On that, he turned and walked into his big new house, herding his sobbing daughter in front of him. The door slammed shut behind him.

"Well," Aurora said, "he was pleasant."

"Shut up, Aurora," Winona snapped. To Noah, she said, "What in the *hell* were you thinking? And how could you lie to me all summer? I trusted you. I told Mark Cissy was safe with you."

"I would never hurt Cissy," Noah answered stubbornly.

Vivi Ann recognized the look on his face: he was hunkering down emotionally, preparing to deflect

427

every word hurled at him. Nothing said here and now would get past that armor. "Come on, Noah," she said. "Let's go home."

She didn't bother saying goodbye to her sisters, or even thank you. She was too drained, and too scared, to expend any more energy than absolutely necessary. The worst part was how disappointed she felt, and how stupid.

"Say something," Noah said in the car. "How come you aren't yelling like Mark?"

"Would you rather I yelled at you?"

He shrugged. "Whatever."

"Let's not go there, okay? You know I hate it when you act like you don't care. We both know that's not really your problem."

"No, it's yours."

"Another misfire, pal. This is not about me." She turned off the highway and drove through Oyster Shores.

"So you love her, I guess," Vivi Ann said a few minutes later.

Noah looked at her. "Are you going to make fun of me? Or tell me I'm too young to know what love is?"

"No." She pulled up to the cottage and parked. "One thing about love is its recognizability. When you're in love, you know it. No one else's opinion matters. But Noah, this is something I learned the hard way: love doesn't exist in a vacuum. Other people matter. And you just screwed the pooch,

428

pal. You made your girlfriend's father mistrust you. I don't think he'll let you see her now."

"No one can keep us apart."

"Okay, so now is when I'm going to tell you you're young and make fun of you. If Cissy is the girl I think she is, she's going to want to make her father proud of her."

Noah looked desolate. "So what do I do?"

"First why don't you tell me about today, then we'll figure out tomorrow."

"We wanted to see Dad."

Even though Vivi Ann had expected those exact words, still they hit her like a slap. "Would he see you?"

"They wouldn't let us go in. You have to be eighteen or have an adult with you."

"Oh."

"But I want to try again. I know he'll want to see me."

Vivi Ann heard every nuance of emotion in her son's voice—bravado, fear, anger, and worst of all: hope. She hated to see Noah take that path, but how could she advise her child against hope?

"And I'm sorry about tonight. I should have told you about Cissy. It was just so cool to keep it to ourselves."

Vivi Ann knew that feeling. She was the last person to deny someone the right to be in love. Such emotion was too rare to handle it roughly.

Vivi Ann reached out and touched Noah's hair,

moving her fingers through it. "I understand why you did what you did. Maybe I even have a little responsibility for it. And I noticed that you didn't lose your temper tonight. That's good."

"But I fucked up."

She gave him the bad-language look. "You lied to me and Mark and Aunt Win. You took advantage of my trust in you. Worst of all, you just showed Mark that he was right to believe the worst of you."

"What do I do to fix it?"

"You were smart enough to come up with your master prison plan. I'm sure if you try, you can come up with a redemption plan."

"I will."

"And while you're figuring it out, factor in that you have to do it without leaving home, because you're on restriction until school starts. You can leave this ranch to go to church and to see Mrs. Ivers, but for no other reason."

"Aw, Mom . . ."

"Believe me, there's a price to be paid for love. You might as well learn that now."

Chapter Twenty-three

When I was little, we had this old mare named Clementine's Blue Ribbon. Mom used to put me up in the saddle while she was pulling weeds and Clem would just stand there with me on her back. She followed me around like a puppy in the fields and sometimes at night, she'd trot up as close to my window as she could and whinny. Mom said it was horse talk for goodnight special boy. And then one day Mom told me Clem had gone to Heaven. I went out to her stall and it was empty.

That was when I learned you could lose what you loved.

That's how I feel now. Ever since I wrote to my dad, I've been—I don't even know what word to use anymore. Not sad, not even pissed off. Empty maybe. I go to the mailbox every day and nothing ever comes.

Cissy hasn't called or emailed or texted me either. It's like she fell off the planet. I know what happened. My mom was right. She picked her dad's side. I even understand it. But it hurts so much that sometimes I don't want to turn on the light in my room or get out of bed.

She's all I think about. I remember how she came up with the plan, saying no one has a right to keep you away from your own dad. She held my hand on the bus rides to the prison and back. All the way home she was saying how cool it would be to actually talk to him someday.

She knew how much I needed that.

Maybe that's who I am, Mrs. Ivers, a guy who needs things he can't get. I need Cissy to love me again and I need to talk to my dad.

Which pretty much means I'm screwed.

Today I registered for high school. Mrs. Ivers told mom I passed Language Arts with flying colors. Whatever the hell that means. It made my mom happy, and me too, I guess. It means I'll see Cissy on Wednesday when school starts.

How will I look at her without being a total dork?

I know Erik Jr. will glom onto her. She's so smoking hot he'll want her to be his girlfriend. If I see that how will I keep from going postal?

Maybe I'll pretend to be sick all year.

I was going to quit writing in this book Mrs. Ivers gave me, but today was so amazing I don't want to forget a single thing.

So there I was, standing out by the flag like a

total loser while everyone else yelled and screamed about how cool it was to see each other. Being alone in a crowd is the worst, I think. Everyone belongs somewhere except you. Last year that would have pissed me off. I would have looked around and seen all those smiling kids and I would have hated them. If someone had looked at me sideways I would have flipped him off. There are different ways to start a fight. I guess I know that now.

Anyway I was standing there, wishing I'd worn my old favorite Vans instead of these dorky Nikes my mom made me buy, when I saw Cissy. She was with Principal Jeevers. They were next to the blue metal doors and the principal was yakking on. There were kids everywhere. Laughing, talking, playing hackey sack, listening to their iPods, talking on the phone. All the usual first day of school shit.

Still she saw me right away.

I waited for her to smile. When she didn't, I walked away, went over to this alley between the gym and the auditorium, where it was quiet and dark.

I was there, with my eyes closed, leaning against the warm brick wall when I heard her say my name. I wanted to ask her what she wanted in a voice that made me sound tough, as if I didn't care, but I couldn't do it.

I missed you she said.

I don't even remember what I said. All I know is one minute I was in the shade by myself and the next minute she was there with me.

SHE STILL LOVES ME!!!! ☺

I can't believe I doubted it. She says it hurt her feelings that I gave up so easily and I don't know what to say to that. I guess when your dad's in prison you learn to give up easily. My mom is the same way I think. But I won't be like that anymore.

From now on I'm gonna be a believer. Cissy says all I have to do is choose to be one and it'll happen.

That was when she gave me this copy of Seattle magazine.

I knew right away it was going to cause trouble.

Winona stood in the small avocado-colored bathroom, peering between a pair of geometric-patterned curtains. From here, she could see most of the beach house's backyard—brown now from the heat of August and early September—and dashes of the highway beyond the trees.

She saw Cissy at the end of the driveway next door, waiting. When the yellow school bus drove up and stopped, the girl went up the steps and disappeared inside.

Winona backed out of the bathroom, put on the slippers by her bed, and went next door. Upstairs, she found Mark in bed.

"You're late," he said, putting his newspaper down.

"I'm fat. I can only run so fast. You could always come to my house, you know." She flicked off her slippers and climbed into bed with him. Snuggling close, she began unbuttoning his pajama top and kissing the hairy chest beneath.

In moments they had taken their clothes off and started to make love.

It was their new Monday morning routine, and Winona looked forward to it all week. After the fiasco with Noah and Cissy, she'd been afraid that Mark would leave her. He'd even tried, although that attempt wasn't something they brought up. After two lonely weeks, he'd come back and now they were better than ever. They just didn't talk about their families. Instead, they created a bubble world where they alone existed. Saturday nights, Monday mornings, Thursday afternoons; these were their times. Winona hoped like hell that Cissy tried out for soccer.

They lay entwined after sex. She kissed the curl of his shoulder and closed her eyes, almost falling asleep.

"It's a long time until Thursday," he said.

"You made the rules," she murmured. "I say we tell Cissy we're still together. All this sneaking around is ridiculous."

"You haven't seen her lately. She's like some walking zombie. She's never stayed mad at me this long. Not even when I was a drunk."

"I hear Noah is pretty much the same way."

"Don't mention that kid's name to me. Cissy asked my mom last week if she was totally sure she saw Dallas that night. Mom was so upset she had to take a pill to sleep."

"Young love. It's a durable thing, I guess."

"Love. Christ. They're fourteen years old. They're too young to know what the hell love is." He threw the covers back and got out of bed. "I need to go to work."

When he left, she lay there for a few more moments, staring out the windows at the sunlit Canal. Finally, she got out of bed herself, slipped her nightgown and slippers back on, and followed him to the bathroom.

He put down his electric razor. "We know better than to talk about that."

"I know. See you Thursday?"

"You bet."

For the next seven hours, she focused on work. Clients came to her office, one after another, complaining mostly about each other and counting on her to sort through all their confused emotions and find a common ground.

Her last scheduled appointment concluded at just past four o'clock, and she kicked off her pumps, took off her navy blazer, and reached for her mayoral debate file. The town meeting was currently set for early November, and she intended to blow her competition out of the water with her well-reasoned, perfectly considered plan for running this town. She was adding thoughts to her speech file when her intercom buzzed.

"Winona?" Lisa said through the small black speakers. "Your nephew, Noah Raintree, is here to see you."

"Send him in."

Noah walked into her office and smiled at her. A ragged backpack hung negligently from one shoulder. He'd changed so much this summer that sometimes she was caught off guard by his appearance, even going so far as to be proud of him until she remembered how he'd lied to her. "Have a seat, Noah."

He sat down across from her, let his backpack slump to the floor. "I need to hire a lawyer."

"What did you do?"

"Jeez, Aunt Winona. Way to think the worst of me."

"I did trust you, remember? You made me look like an idiot in front of my boyfriend."

"Yeah, well. Your boyfriend is a dick."

"And God knows your high opinion of him is so important to me. Why do you need a lawyer?"

"If I hire you, everything we say is confidential, right?"

"Have you been studying law in social studies?"

"When I was on restriction, I watched a lot of TV. *Law and Order* is awesome."

"Okay, yes. Our communications are confidential."

"And if you take my case, you have to do your best, right?"

"I would hardly do less. But you'd have to pay me a retainer, of course. Two thousand dollars is standard for me."

He pulled a one-dollar bill out of his pocket and set it on her desk. "There's a family discount, I hope."

She glanced down at the wrinkled, wadded-up dollar, and then up at Noah. Whatever this was about, he took it seriously. She knew she should send him on his way, but her curiosity was piqued. There were few things she hated more than unanswered questions. So she took the dollar bill and put it in her desk drawer. "Okay, Perry Mason. Hit me with your best shot."

He leaned sideways and pulled a magazine out of his backpack. He put it on her desk and shoved it toward her.

She saw the lead article's headline. *Seattle's Best Lawyers*. It was *Seattle* magazine's yearly listing of the state's top legal eagles. "Is this your subtle way of telling me that I'm not universally lauded by my peers? Because believe me, Noah, when a lawyer opens up shop in Oyster Shores, she pretty much knows her place on the food chain. And P.S., it's near the bottom."

"Turn to page ninety."

She did. Beside an ad for one of the city's newest high-rises, she saw a gloomy photograph of a man standing in front of a prison guard tower. The headline read: *Innocence Project Northwest Works to Exonerate the Wrongly Accused.*

"It's about DNA testing," he said.

"Noah," she said gently, "that's all water under the bridge with your dad. It's over."

"It's not," he said, stubbornly jutting out his chin. "They never tested his DNA. Mom told me."

"Yes, they did."

"No, they didn't."

She thought about that, scrolled through the facts she could recall. "Oh. That's right. The sample was too small."

"Maybe the tests are better now."

"Look, Noah—"

"I got to know you this summer," he said, leaning forward. "No missed spots, you always said, no rushed jobs. Remember? You hate things that aren't done right."

She sat back, surprised. She would have sworn he hadn't listened to her. "Your dad won't agree to this, you know. Why would he? Guilty people don't want their DNA tested."

"If he doesn't agree to the test then I'll have an answer, won't I?"

Winona felt a headache start behind her eyes. These were dangerous waters suddenly. "Your mom and I have . . . history with your father . . ."

"Please, Aunt Winona," he said. "You're the only one I can trust with this. If you tell me it's nothing,

439

I'll believe you. I just want you to tell me if a new test would give him a chance."

"Does your mother know you're here?"

"No."

"I couldn't keep this from her."

"I didn't ask you to."

She didn't see how she could say no. It was so little to ask, and once she had an answer for him, maybe he could finally—finally—let this go. God knew that would be best for Vivi Ann, for Noah. And besides, she knew for a fact that Dallas wouldn't go along with it. "Fine. I'll read the article and look through the record. But no promises."

He smiled so brightly she had to turn away. How many times and in how many ways was Dallas Raintree going to hurt the people who cared about him?

More firmly she said, "No promises."

A week later, as autumn leaves fell in a flurry outside her window, Winona closed her office door, told Lisa to hold all her calls, and settled down to read the transcript she'd ordered. Drawing the seventeen-hundred-page document onto her lap, she put on the drugstore magnifying glasses she'd recently begun to need and began the slow, arduous task of reading the testimony given at his trial.

It was like opening a door on the past. The words brought the whole experience back to her, the sensation of sitting there, hearing one damning fact after another, of watching Vivi Ann try so hard to be strong, and listening to the prosecutor, so certain she had truth on her side of the courtroom.

Winona didn't need to take notes. It was all exactly as she remembered—the foundation of Cat and Dallas's friendship, the naïveté Vivi Ann showed in letting that relationship continue, the convenience of Dallas's so-called fever hitting on the exact night Cat was murdered. And then there was the forensic evidence apart from the DNA: the hairs found in Cat's bed, microscopically consistent with Dallas's, and his fingerprints on the gun. There had been no doubt left after all of that, reasonable or otherwise.

Noah didn't understand. Dallas hadn't been railroaded or subjected to prosecutorial misconduct or improper police technique. A jury of his peers had found him guilty based on the totality of the evidence presented. It wasn't some small-town miscarriage of justice. It was a verdict rooted in fact, and of the evidence, certainly Myrtle's eyewitness testimony had been the most compelling.

Winona reread that section of the transcript, although she remembered it pretty clearly.

HAMM: And where is the ice-cream shop in relation to Catherine Morgan's home?
MICHAELIAN: Down the alley. You go right past us to get to her place.

HAMM: Please speak up, Ms. Michaelian.

MICHAELIAN: Oh. Yes. Sorry.

HAMM: Were you working at the ice-cream shop on Christmas Eve of last year?

MICHAELIAN: I was. I wanted to make a special ice-cream cake for the evening service. I was running late, as usual.

Winona skipped down.

HAMM: Did you see anyone that night?

MICHAELIAN: It was about eight-ten. I was almost ready to go. I was putting the finishing touches on the frosting when I looked up and saw . . . saw Dallas Raintree coming out of the alley that leads to Cat's house.

HAMM: Did he see you?

MICHAELIAN: No.

HAMM: And how did you know it was the defendant?

MICHAELIAN: I saw his profile when he passed under the streetlamp, and I recognized his tattoo. But I already knew it was him. I'd seen him there before at night. Lots of times. I'd even told Vivi Ann about it. It was him. I'm sorry, Vivi Ann.

Winona put the doorstop-sized pile of paper aside and got up from the couch, stretching to work out the kinks in her back. "Thank God."

No DNA test was going to save Dallas Raintree at this late date. That was for innocent men.

Feeling better (she hated to admit it, but Noah had planted a tiny seed of doubt and that didn't sit well with her), she wandered back into the kitchen and stared into her fridge. There was plenty of food there, but none of it appealed to her. A quick glance at the clock on the stove told her it was eight o'clock.

Maybe she should walk down to the ice-cream shop. The idea of Myrtle's famous Neapolitan cake had whetted her appetite.

On this early evening, it was quiet in town. Labor Day was the official end of summer around here, the day tourists packed up their motor homes and drove away. Without their loud voices, you could hear the water again, and the mournful call of the wind through the trees. Locals loved these first weeks of September best of all: the sun was still shining, the days were still hot, and the Canal was theirs again.

Winona went up to the window at the ice-cream shop and ordered a piece of Myrtle's Neapolitan ice-cream cake from the pimply-faced girl working the take-out counter.

While she waited, Winona pictured Myrtle at the window, looking out as she spread frosting on her frozen cake. The shop was elevated; Myrtle would have had a clear view of the start of the alley.

Winona turned toward it. A black ironwork

streetlamp was right there, standing sentinel, throwing a net of warm golden light down onto the sidewalk.

The girl came back to the window, said, "Here you go, Mrs. Grey. That'll be three dollars and ninety-two cents."

"Ms. Grey," she muttered, paying for her cake. When she'd gotten her change, she turned back toward the streetlamp. It was in the perfect spot; Dallas would have been easily identifiable by Myrtle, who knew him. True, he was never facing the ice-cream shop, but a profile was plenty in good light, when you knew the person.

"I'll explain it to Noah," she said to herself. "Maybe I'll even bring him down here to show him. He'll know I took him seriously."

She crossed the street, taking a bite of cake, remembering Myrtle's testimony in detail.

I'd seen him there before.

I recognized his tattoo.

Winona stopped. Turning slowly, she walked back down Shore Drive, past the souvenir shop and the fish bar, to the ice-cream shop.

From this vantage point, Myrtle saw Dallas's right side.

Winona had always had a photographic memory, and she'd noticed Dallas's tattoo when she hired him. She would have sworn it was on his left arm.

She must be mistaken. A flurry of people had gone through this evidence, the prosecution team, the police, even reporters. No way a fact like this got overlooked.

Of course, the cops and the prosecution wouldn't have been trying to discredit Myrtle. Only the defense team would have looked that closely. The defense attorney, she corrected. There had been no team, but surely Roy had done it.

She started walking toward home, but when she got to Viewcrest, instead of turning into her yard, she kept going, past the historical society museum toward Water's Edge.

At the door to the cottage, she finally stopped long enough to think about what she was doing.

She didn't want to tell Vivi Ann about Noah's quest for DNA testing if she didn't have to.

But that seed of doubt was back, and she had to eradicate it.

She knocked; Noah almost immediately answered.

"Hey, Aunt Winona," he said. "Did you read the article?"

Vivi Ann's voice came from the kitchen. "Who is it, Noah?"

"Aunt Winona," he yelled back.

Winona leaned toward him, whispered, "I need to know which arm Dallas had his tattoo on."

"I don't have a clue."

Vivi Ann came into the living room. "Hey, Win. This is a nice surprise. You want some tea?"

"Sure." She followed her sister into the small, cozy

living room of the cottage. Gone were the dingy pine wooden walls; in their place, everything was white—the walls, the peaked ceiling, the trim. Twin sets of small-paned French doors looked out over the back deck and the horse pastures below. The overstuffed furniture was upholstered in country French fabrics of marigold and Wedgwood blue.

What now? Noah mouthed.

Winona shrugged. *Ask her.*

Me?

Vivi Ann brought her a cup of tea. Winona sipped it while her sister built a fire in the river-rock hearth.

Noah cleared his throat. "Hey, Mom. I've been thinking about something."

"That sounds ominous."

"What do you think about tattoos?"

Vivi Ann backed away from the fireplace and turned around. "I think everyone knows that I'm not anti-tattoo . . . for adults."

"What if I wanted to get one?"

"I'd say the law is that you can get a tattoo at eighteen."

"Sixteen, with a parent's consent."

"I see. And did you turn sixteen without my knowledge?"

"I'm just thinking ahead."

"Really?"

"If I *did* get a tattoo, I'd want it where dad has his. Which arm was that?"

446

Vivi Ann looked suspicious. "You've never mentioned your father's tattoo before."

"Which arm was it on?"

"Why do you want to know?"

"See, Aunt Winona?" He walked out of the living room, muttering something about the Spanish Inquisition and slamming his bedroom door.

"What the hell was that about?" Vivi Ann asked.

"Where was Dallas's tattoo?" Winona asked quietly.

"His left bicep. Why?"

"You'd better start talking," Vivi Ann said a moment later. The sudden silence felt weighted. Dangerous. "What's this about Dallas?"

"It's about Noah, really. He came to my office a week ago, said he wanted to hire me."

"He's in legal trouble?"

"That's what I thought. It's why I took his case. But . . ."

"But what?"

"It turns out he was interested in his father."

Vivi Ann nodded. "He's been obsessed with Dallas lately. Why did he need you to find out that tattoo thing? I would have told him if he'd asked. Or is he afraid to ask me? Is that it? It is, isn't it? He thinks I don't want to tell him anything about Dallas."

"He wants me to petition the court for a new DNA test. The methods are better now. But we both know Dallas won't agree to it," Winona added quickly.

It was like getting smacked in the chest when you weren't expecting it. Vivi Ann stood up slowly, unable to quite look at her sister. It took everything she had inside of her not to run. "I need to go talk to Noah. You should leave."

"We're okay, aren't we?" Winona asked, rising.

"Sure."

They both knew it was a lie, and a necessary one. Their reconciliation had always demanded a certain fiction, a tacit pretense that Dallas hadn't really come between them. Now, of course, he was back, between them as clearly as if he'd been standing in the room.

Without saying more, she headed toward Noah's bedroom. At his door, she knocked hard a couple of times. There was no answer, so she went inside.

He was sitting on his bed, with his knees drawn up to his chest and his eyes closed, rocking out to some music on his iPod. She couldn't see the headphones hidden within his ears, but she could hear the tinny echo of music played much too loudly.

She went over and tapped him on the shoulder.

He reacted like a startled horse, shying away from her hand, but she could tell by the wary look in his eyes that he'd expected her. He pulled the earbuds out and tossed the tiny silver player on his bed.

She went to the end of his bed and sat down opposite him, leaning back against the footboard. "You could have come to me with this, you know."

"How?"

"You just walk up to me and say, 'Mom, I have something I need to do.'"

It was a long moment before he looked at her and said, "Most kids remember their moms reading them to sleep. I remember running to get you toilet paper and crawling up into your lap to wipe your eyes. I thought I was bad, that it was my fault. It was Aunt Aurora who told me that my daddy had broken your heart and that I needed to be strong for you. I was six years old when she told me that."

"Oh, Noah." Vivi Ann had blocked out so much of that time; it was what she'd ultimately had to do: forget and go on. "I never knew you and Aurora even talked like that."

"She was the one I went to when I had questions. She was the only one who'd tell me the truth. You acted like he was dead."

"I had to," was all she could say.

"But he's not dead."

"No, he's not."

"And I have a right to try and help him."

Vivi Ann almost smiled. Usually she saw Dallas in Noah; just now, she saw herself. "I know how you feel, believe me. I should have seen it coming and helped you. I'm sorry."

"You won't stop Aunt Winona?"

The question was like an undercurrent in calm water; it came suddenly and sucked her under until she could hardly breathe. It had almost killed her, the hope necessary to do battle with the justice system. She'd believed in the law at the beginning. But if she tried again, failed again, she was certain she'd drown. "I won't stop you. But . . . I don't want you to get your hopes up. Disappointment can be toxic if you aren't careful. And your dad . . . might not agree to the test."

"So you *do* think he did it."

Vivi Ann looked at her son, hating the heartbreak that was stalking him. Quietly, she said, "Dallas trusts the courts even less than I do, and he's even more afraid of hope. His whole life the system let him down. That's one of the reasons he might say no."

They both knew what the other reason was.

"It'll be over then, won't it?" Noah said.

If there was one truth Vivi Ann knew to her bones, it was that loss, like love, had a beginning but no real end. "Yes," she lied, "I guess it will be."

Chapter Twenty-four

On the long drive to the prison, Winona rehearsed what she would say to Dallas. *I'm here on behalf of your son. You do remember—Idiot. Don't bait him,* she admonished herself.

I'm here on behalf of your son. He wants to petition the courts to test the DNA found at the crime scene. Surely, if you weren't there that night, you'll want to do the same thing.

She glanced down at her watch when she pulled up to the prison. It was one forty-five. If everything went well, she would be back at Mark's house in time for dinner.

She drove up to the guard tower and gave her name into the speaker beside her window. While waiting for approval, she looked out over the forbidding gray stone, chain-link fence, and razor-wire world of the prison. She could see the armed guard in the tower, and as she drove through the gates and into the parking area, she couldn't suppress a shudder of apprehension. The gate clanged shut behind her.

She forced a straightness into her spine, surprised by how frightening it was to simply visit here. How had Vivi Ann done it every Saturday for years?

451

She entered the administration building and was immediately struck by the noise. Although there weren't a lot of people around, the walls vibrated with sound. The place seemed at once both eerily empty and bizarrely crowded.

At the desk, she signed in, got an ID badge, stowed her purse and coat in the locker room, and went through the metal detector.

"Usually lawyers request a private meeting with their clients," the guard commented as he led her down the corridor. The echoing din grew louder. "You new?"

"This meeting won't take that long."

At last he came to a door and opened it.

Winona walked slowly into the room, feeling acutely conspicuous in her expensive wool pantsuit. Taking an empty seat, she stared through the fingerprint-smudged Plexiglas, afraid to touch anything. She could hear snippets of conversation going on around her, but nothing was really distinct. All up and down the row, people were pressing hands to the fake glass, trying impossibly to connect, to touch.

Finally the door opened and Dallas was there, in his baggy orange jumpsuit and his worn flip-flops. His hair was longer now, well past his shoulders, and his face had hollowed out. The darkness of his skin had paled somewhat; still, there was a frightening intensity about him, a barely checked energy that made her think he could come through this flimsy Plexiglas barrier and grab her by the throat.

He picked up the phone, said, "Is Vivi Ann okay?"

"She's fine."

"Noah?"

She heard the emotion in his voice; saw a vulnerability in his gray eyes. "Noah's fine. In fact, he's the reason I'm here. Sit down."

"Say something worth sitting down for."

"I'm here on behalf of your son. He wants to petition the court—"

Dallas threw down the receiver so hard it cracked against the Plexiglas. Then he turned and walked away. The guard opened the door for him, and without looking back, he disappeared into the buzzing, thudding growl of prison life.

"You've got to be kidding me," Winona muttered. She sat there a long time, staring at the smudged glass, waiting for him to return. Finally, a woman came up to her, touched her shoulder, and asked if she was waiting to see a prisoner. "I guess not," she said, scooting her chair back.

When Aunt Winona got home from the prison, I was waiting for her on her front step. It was raining hard and I was totally soaked, but I didn't care. I saw her drive up and get out of her car and walk up the path.

She was by the dorky mermaid fountain when she saw me standing there in the rain.

I'm sorry she said.

I asked what he said, what excuses he gave, and Aunt Winona said he wouldn't even talk to her about it. She said, I told him what you wanted and he just got up and walked out.

It made me want to scream or cry or punch someone, but I knew what a waste all of that was. So I thanked her for trying and walked home.

By the time I got to our house, the rain was falling so hard I sucked in water when I breathed. I opened the front door and saw my mom. She was sitting on the coffee table, trying to look cool, but I could tell that she was worried. She got up and came toward me, saying something about my wet clothes.

All I got out was the word Dad and like a total zero, I started to cry.

She hugged me and said It's okay a bunch of times like she used to, but I know it's a lie. I miss my dad, I said, even tho I don't know who in the hell he is. Even tho he's a murderer.

He's more than that, Mom said. She told me to remember that she'd loved him and he'd loved me.

I told her I would but it was bullshit. I'm not gonna remember that he used to love me. That's exactly what I'm gonna try to forget.

October was a month of gray days, cool nights, and thready, inconstant rain. The shorter days were busy for Winona as she prepared for the coming election.

From the outside looking in, anyone who was casually watching Winona would surely have seen nothing out of the ordinary. She was at her desk answering phone calls and seeing clients by eight o'clock in the morning. At lunch, more often than not, she could be found at the diner or at the Waves, treating some influential town citizen to a working lunch. After work, as the darkness fell, she tended to sit in her bed, watching her reality TV shows and mailing out promotional items. Her crisp linen envelopes read: *Go with a Winner! Vote Winona Grey this November.*

All of that, combined with church, the monthly family supper, and her dates with Mark, filled her time. She couldn't remember when she'd been so busy or so happy. Individually and collectively she loved all of the things that commanded her time and attention. She and Mark had finally gone public with their romance in late September, and since then everyone seemed certain that it was only a matter of time before a wedding took place. Even Winona was beginning to hope. They weren't head over heels in love, it was true, but she was old enough to recognize the reality of life. Besides, she'd truly loved a man already in her life, and look at the mistakes she'd made in the name of that unreliable emotion. It was better to play it safe. Thinking this, she often found herself at the magazine aisle in King's Market, flipping through the latest *Brides* magazine.

The only fly in this beautiful, intricate web was Dallas.

It stuck in her craw that he wouldn't see her, wouldn't even listen to her. Both Vivi Ann and Noah had dropped the whole thing when Winona told them of Dallas's reaction. Vivi Ann had sighed and said sadly, "That's that, then." Even Noah had accepted it, muttering thanks as he walked away.

But Winona couldn't let it go. She went to the prison once a week—always on Saturday. Hour after empty hour, she sat in that molded plastic chair in front of the dirty Plexiglas. Week after week, Dallas didn't show.

Each time she left the prison, Winona berated herself for her poor judgment and vowed not to return, and every week she broke that promise.

She couldn't pinpoint the source of her obsession. Perhaps it was the mysterious tattoo (surely Vivi Ann was mistaken and it was on his right bicep; nothing else seemed truly possible), or the way Noah had smiled when she agreed to take this ridiculous case, or the way Dallas had asked about Vivi Ann and his son. Or maybe it was what Vivi Ann hadn't said and should have: *I asked you to help him twelve years ago.*

Whatever it was, she knew that she couldn't let

go of this until he gave her an answer. That was all she needed, just a simple, *No way, Win. A DNA test doesn't make much sense to me. You know why.*

She'd imagined that exact answer from him so many times that sometimes she woke up from a restless night thinking he'd actually said it to her.

"Okay," she said aloud, "it's time to do something else." She glanced at the clock. It was 4:20 on Thursday afternoon. Mark would be here in ninety minutes to take her out to dinner and to a movie. She got out a piece of her special *Winona Elizabeth Grey, Esquire,* stationery. Beneath her imprinted name, she began to write.

Dear Dallas:

You win. I have no doubt that you could continue this little game of ours forever. Surely you cannot believe that I would attempt to see you again after all these years on a lark. Obviously I have business of a serious nature to discuss with you. That being said, I will only put forth so much effort. You are—as you no doubt intend—making me feel like a fool. It is in both of our interests—and certainly your son's as well—that you accept my invitation to talk. I will be there Wednesday during the 4–6 visiting hours for your cell block. It will be my final attempt to see or speak to you.

Sincerely,
Winona Grey

She folded up the letter, sealed it in an envelope, stamped it, and carried it immediately out to the blue mail drop on the corner.

She was done now. It was in Dallas's hands.

On Wednesday, Winona carefully packed up her desk, put everything away, and went out to tell Lisa that she'd be gone for the rest of the day. "If anyone calls, I'm in a meeting. Take a message and I'll call back first thing in the morning. And before you leave tonight, will you water the plants in the sunroom? They're looking a little wilted."

"Sure."

Winona went to her car and drove out of town.

It lightened something in her, this thought that it would finally end today. She had just recently realized how much Noah's request had been weighing her down. Now, though, she would be out from under its pressure. Whatever sin she may have committed by omission at the first trial, she'd atoned for it in the past six weeks. Six times—seven, including today—she'd driven to the prison, waited for a man who never showed, and gone home. Each sojourn took up at least six hours of her time.

By now she knew many of the faces along the way and she smiled and made small talk as she checked in. It had all become so routine that when the officer handed her her name tag and said, "A private meeting, huh? That's new," she was too shocked to answer.

"Here you go. This is one of the lawyers' visiting rooms."

Winona nodded and went inside. It was a small room, with a big, scarred wooden table and several chairs scattered about. The walls were an ugly brown; the paint was worn through to show the concrete beneath. A uniformed guard stood in the corner, staring straight ahead, his hands clasped behind his back. Under his watchful eye, she took a seat at the table.

The door opened and Dallas hobbled in, his wrists and ankles shackled, his head bowed forward as he moved.

He sat down across from her, thumping his shackled wrists on the table between them. "What does my son want?"

She heard the way his voice caught on the word *son*. "I'd like to ask you a few questions. May I?"

"Like anyone could ever shut you up."

She bristled at that, remembering in a rush how much she'd once disliked this man. Now that she was with him, she just wanted to be gone. "What arm is your tattoo on?"

He looked surprised by that. "My left. Why?"

Winona cursed under her breath. "Did Roy have an investigator, someone to go to places, check them out; you know, dig deep?"

"There was no money, you know that. He did the best he could."

"Why didn't you testify?"

"Jesus, Win. This is old news. I didn't testify because of my criminal record."

"People wanted to hear your side of it."

"No, they didn't."

"Your son wants me to get your permission to run a new DNA test on the sample left at the crime scene. The technology is better these days. The sample may be large enough to exonerate you."

"You think I'm innocent suddenly?"

"I think this test would give us the answer once and for all."

"No."

"Am I to assume you don't want the test for obvious reasons?"

"Assume what you want. You were always good at that."

Winona leaned forward.

"I read the transcripts, Dallas. Myrtle Michaelian saw you coming out of the alley. You stepped into the light from a streetlamp and she saw your profile and your tattoo."

"Uh-huh."

"But the tattoo she saw had to be on the man's right arm. He was walking away from her."

"Yeah. So?"

"You aren't even surprised. Why not?"

He stared at her, saying nothing.

The answer to her question washed over her like an icy breeze. "You aren't surprised because you weren't there that night. You always knew Myrtle saw someone else."

"Go home, Winona. You're closing the barn door years too late."

"Are you telling me you didn't do it?" Winona felt sick at the thought.

"Go away, Winona."

For the first time she saw it in his gray eyes, the pain she was causing him. "Why did you stop seeing Vivi Ann?"

He pushed back in his chair and glanced over at the door. "Did you ever see her when she brought home one of those abused horses?"

"Of course."

"That was how she started to look when she came to see me. I knew she wasn't sleeping, wasn't eating. Believing in me was killing her, and I knew she'd never let go."

"So you made the choice for her." Winona sat back in her seat, stunned. It was like suddenly seeing one of those images hidden in a kaleido-scope of shapes. Once you saw it, you wonder how you could have missed it. He'd divorced Vivi Ann because he loved her.

"I didn't say that. You did. What I said was, 'Go away.' None of this matters now. Vivi Ann's gone on with her life and Noah will, too. It's best if we just leave them alone."

"You think Vivi's gone on?" she said, staring at him.

In his gaze she saw a yearning that was like nothing she'd ever seen in her life. "Hasn't she?"

"She hasn't rescued a horse since the day she got the divorce papers. I guess all that took a kind of optimism she doesn't have anymore. In fact, she's like one of those horses now; when you look her in the eye, all you see is emptiness."

Dallas closed his eyes slowly. "No DNA test will save me, Win. Say the test comes back negative. They'll just claim I didn't have sex with Cat before I killed her."

"But there's a chance. It's not a slam dunk, you're right—other facts convicted you—but I'm sure it will get you a retrial."

He looked at her, and it was terrible, the despair she saw in his gray eyes. "And my son wants this."

"He needs you, Dallas. You can imagine what they say about him. Butchie and Erik's kids taunt him all the time. And he has your temper."

Dallas got up and hobbled around, pacing along the table, chains clattering on the floor. "It's dangerous to do this," he said.

"Not if you're innocent."

He laughed at that.

She went to him, came up behind him. She would have touched his shoulder, but the guard was eyeing them suspiciously. "Trust me, Dallas."

He turned. "Trust you? You must be kidding."

"I misjudged you. I'm sorry."

"It wasn't about you misjudging me, Win. You

462

were so jealous of Vivi Ann it made you blind."

She swallowed hard, knowing that accusation would stay with her for a long time. "Yes," she said. "Maybe that's why I'm here now. As atonement."

That seemed to surprise him. "I don't want to hurt her, or Noah."

"I don't know about love or damage or hurting, Dallas, but I do know that it's time for the truth."

It was a long time before he said, "Okay," and even then, when he'd agreed, he looked unhappy, and she knew why. He knew this legal system—and love—better than she did, and he knew the price they all could end up paying for the hubris of hope.

Chapter Twenty-five

In a lightly falling rain, the Grey family walked home from church. On this first Sunday in November, the town looked dull and a little forlorn. Bare trees lined the empty sidewalks, their rough brown trunks blurred by the misty haze that rolled in off the water.

From a distance, the family would have looked like a black caterpillar, huddled as they were beneath their umbrellas, winding their way up the hill and down their long, uneven driveway.

This was always the worst part for Vivi Ann. She was okay with the Sunday morning walk to town, the service, and the refreshments. It wasn't until now, the walk down the driveway, that she remembered that it was Dallas who'd planted these trees. They'd been tiny, spindly, untried things back then; the ground at Water's Edge had nourished them, made them grow strong. Once, she'd thought she was like those trees, rooted here, planted firmly enough to grow and flower forever.

By the time they reached the house, piling their rainy outerwear and rubber boots by the door, Vivi Ann's mood was as gray as the weather. It wasn't that she was unhappy or depressed; rather, she felt listless. Out of sorts.

And she wasn't alone in this. Noah had been moping around for weeks now, too, quick to slam doors and disappear into his music.

Vivi Ann tried to put all of that out of her mind on this Sunday afternoon as she led the way into the kitchen and started dinner.

"You do realize that the sherry-Parmesan-cream sauce and pie dough defeat the healthiness of the veggies?" Aurora said as Vivi Ann put three home-made chicken potpies in the oven.

"It's a Paula Deen recipe," Vivi Ann answered. "Be glad there's no mayo or sour cream involved. Besides, you could use a few pounds."

"I get more stuck in my teeth than she eats," Winona said.

"Ha ha ha," Aurora said, pouring herself another glass of wine. "That's so funny I forgot to laugh."

It was a remark plucked directly from the grassy field of their childhood, and Vivi Ann found herself smiling for the first time in days. Picking up her wineglass, she said, "Let's go sit on the porch. Supper won't be ready for forty minutes."

They all went out onto the porch and sat down. Leaning back into the frayed white wicker chair that had been Mom's favorite, Vivi Ann put her feet up on the railing and stared out over the ranch. A silvery curtain of rain fell from the eaves, blurring the green acreage, making everything look distant and insubstantial. The beach-glass wind chimes clattered musically every now and then, a reminder of who should be here and wasn't. It made her wonder suddenly what this family would have become if Mom were still here. *When you hear the wind chimes, remember my voice,* Mom had told them all on the night before she died. Vivi Ann didn't remember much from those last few months, had blocked out most of it, but she remembered that night, with the three of them clustered around Mom's bed, holding hands, trying not to cry. *My garden-girls. I wish I could see you grow.*

Vivi Ann released a heavy sigh. What she wouldn't give for one more day with her mom. She tapped the wind chimes, listening to their sweet clatter. For the next half an hour, they talked about unimportant things; at least she and Aurora did.

"You're awfully quiet today, Win," Aurora said from behind her.

"You sound surprised," Winona said.

"It's Mark, isn't it?" Aurora asked. "Has he said he loves you yet?"

Winona shook her head. "I think true love is really rare."

"Amen to that," Aurora agreed.

Vivi Ann hated how bitter Aurora had become since her divorce, but it was understandable. Love could reduce you to rubble; lost love most of all.

"You found true love, Vivi Ann," Winona said, looking up finally. "You and Dallas gave up everything for each other."

"Winona," Aurora said quietly, "what are you doing? Are you drunk? We don't talk about—"

"I know," Winona said. "We pretend he was never here, never a part of us. When we see Vivi Ann struggling, we ask about the barn or tell her about the new book we're reading. When we see Noah bruised and bloodied for being Dallas's son, we talk to him about self-control and sticks and stones that we pretend can't break our bones. But they can, can't they, Vivi? Why don't we ever talk about that?"

"You're too late, Win," Vivi Ann said, striving to keep her voice steady.

"Definitely," Aurora said. "Bones are supposed to stay buried."

"But what if the person isn't dead? Should he stay buried then?" Winona asked.

"Let it go, Win," Vivi Ann said. "Whatever your new obsession is, drop it. I forgave you a long time ago, if that's what this is about."

"I know you did," Winona said. "I don't think I realized how generous that forgiveness was."

"Until you fell in love?" Vivi Ann said, understanding now. Her sister had finally fallen in love, and with that emotion came a better understanding of how deeply Vivi Ann had been hurt.

Winona took a deep breath. "Until I went to—"

Behind them, the screen door banged open. "The oven is beeping, Mom," Noah said.

Vivi Ann got quickly to her feet, thankful for the distraction. "Thanks, Noah. Okay, everyone to the table." She hurried into the kitchen and got everything organized—the salad, the cornbread muffins, the potpies.

Right on time, she served dinner and took her seat.

At the head of the table, Dad bowed his head in prayer, and each of them followed suit, intoning the familiar words of faith and gratitude.

It wasn't until the prayer was over and Vivi Ann opened her eyes that she noticed Winona, standing off to the left, holding a sheaf of papers to her chest.

"Don't make us listen to your speech again," Aurora said. "It's my birthday dinner."

467

Winona moved forward awkwardly; it was almost as if she'd been pushed. "I went to the prison last week and saw Dallas."

The room went silent, except for Noah, who said, "What?" in a loud voice.

Winona handed Vivi Ann the papers. "It's public record now. I filed at the courthouse on Friday."

Vivi Ann's hands were shaking as she read the document. "A petition to retest the DNA found at the crime scene."

"He agreed to the test," Winona said.

Vivi Ann looked at her son, saw the way he was smiling, and she wanted to cry.

"I knew it!" Noah said. "How long will it be before he can come home?"

Vivi Ann pushed her chair back and got to her feet. "You think he's innocent, Winona? *Now?* You didn't say a thing when it mattered." Her voice broke and she stumbled backward.

Dad banged his palm on the table so hard the silverware and dishes rattled. "Stop it, Winona."

"Shut up," Aurora yelled at her father. She looked up at Winona. "Are you saying we were wrong?"

Winona looked at Vivi Ann. "Not all of us. She knew."

"Do you know how many times I heard about motions or tests or petitions that would save him? I can't take it all again. Tell her, Aurora. Tell her to back off before Noah gets hurt."

"You can't mean that, Mom."

Aurora got up slowly and stood by Winona. "I'm sorry, Vivi. If there's a chance we were wrong—"

Vivi Ann ran out of the room, out into the yard. Rain slashed at her face and mingled with her tears. She ran until she was out of breath, and then collapsed onto the wet grass.

She heard Winona coming up the hill toward her. Even in the symphony of the rain, the drops hitting the fence posts and leaves and the grass, her sister's heavy breathing stood out.

Winona sat down beside her.

Vivi Ann didn't move. All she could think about was how much she wanted to believe in all this again, and how much her sister's support would have meant to her twelve years ago. For a moment, she hated Winona, but then even that emotion faded. Slowly, she sat up. "It will fail, you know. You'll get all our hopes up, and drag us through the mud again, and in the end Dallas will stay where he is and Noah will know how empty life can feel." Her voice fell to a whisper. "So just stop, okay?"

"I can't do that."

Vivi Ann had known that would be the answer, but still it hurt. "So why tell me? What do you want from me?"

"Your blessing."

Vivi Ann sighed. "Of course you have my blessing."

"Thanks, and just for the record, I—"

Vivi Ann got to her feet and walked away. In the cottage, she closed the door behind her, went to the kitchen and downed three straight shots of cheap tequila, then laid down on top of her bed, heedless of the dampness of her clothes or the fact that she still wore her dirty boots.

"Mom?"

She hadn't even heard Noah come into the house, but he was here now, beside her bed.

"How can you not be happy?" he asked.

She knew she should say something to him, prepare him for the devastation that came in the wake of false hope. That was what a good mother would do.

But she had nothing inside of her right now, no spine, no spirit, no heart.

She rolled onto her side and tucked her knees up into her chest, staring at the stark, soft white mound of her pillow, feeling the unsteady beat of her heart, and remembering all of it. Most of all she remembered signing the divorce papers. Leaving him there alone, with no one to believe in him. For years she'd been telling herself it had been the right thing to do, the only way to survive, but now the excuse rang hollow. In the end, she'd given up on him. Left him all alone because it was too hard for her to stay.

When she heard Noah back up and walk away, and close the door behind him, leaving her alone with her memories, she didn't even care.

• • •

Winona walked back into the farmhouse, leaving a trail of rainwater behind her. She stood there, alone, watching her sister do the dishes in the kitchen. Dad was in his study, with the door closed, of course; the Grey family signal for I'm-pissed-off-and-drinking-my-way-through-it.

Behind her, the door banged open and Noah came running back into the house.

"You so totally rock, Aunt Win." He ran for her, threw his arms around her, hugging her as if it were already over and he'd gotten his life's wish.

Noah drew back and immediately frowned. "What is it?"

Winona didn't know what to say. The magnitude of what she'd done uncoiled, swelled. She prayed she was doing the right thing for the right reason.

"I need to talk to my sister, Noah," Aurora said, coming into the living room. She was drying her hands on a pink towel.

"But I have a ton of questions," he said stubbornly, "and my mom is just lying in bed. Big surprise."

"Cut her some slack. Now go."

Noah made a great show of dramatic disappointment—including slamming the door behind him—and left the house.

Winona glanced at the closed study door. "Did Dad say anything?"

"A rusted pipe makes more noise than he does.

He's a mean, pitiful old man and I don't give a shit what he thinks. More's the pity that you do." Aurora moved forward. "Here's what I need to know, Win. Is this for real?"

"What do you mean?"

"I love you. You know I do. But you've always been jealous of Vivi Ann."

Dallas had said essentially the same thing. It shamed her to realize what people thought of her. And even more, to know that she deserved it. "I'm afraid he's innocent. Is that what you want to know?"

"And can you really get him out of prison?"

"I don't know. All I can do is try."

Aurora said, "God help you if you fail in this, Win. She might not survive a second time."

"I know that."

"Okay," Aurora said at last. "What can I do to help?"

"Be with her," Winona said. "She won't want to see me for a while, and I don't want her to be alone. And Aurora?" she said when her sister turned away. "Pray for me."

"Are you kidding? After tonight, I'm praying for us all."

I don't know how I'm supposed to feel right now and there's no one to ask. Big surprise. I wish it was a school day so I could talk to Cissy. She would know what to say.

472

It all started at the family dinner we had last night. Everything seemed totally normal until Aunt Winona wouldn't sit down for prayers. That totally pissed Grandpa off.

Then she gave Mom some papers and said Dad had agreed to the DNA test. I couldn't believe it! I wanted to laugh out loud, but all hell broke loose. Grandpa slammed his hand on the table, and then Mom totally spazzed out and Aunt Aurora agreed with Aunt Winona.

Mom screamed something at Aunt Winona and ran out. I thought that would be the end of it, but Grandpa went totally postal. He got up so fast his glass fell to the floor and broke and he said you will not do this thing, Winona. Enough is enough.

And then Aunt Aurora said he was a mean old man and he ought to be proud of Winona for being able to see a mistake and to want to fix it.

Aunt Winona tried to explain that it wasn't a choice she was making, that some things were the right thing to do, and he went into his study and slammed the door shut. I ran up after Mom and tried to talk to her, but she just curled up on her bed like a snail and stared at the wall, and when I went back to the farmhouse, Aunt Aurora threw me out. She didn't even let me ask any questions. And Aunt Winona looked like she was gonna cry. It's all a big mess. No one cares at all how I feel.

But I don't care what any of them think or say, I'm gonna believe in my dad, and if that pisses off my mom, too bad.

On the morning of the mayoral debate, Winona woke well before dawn and couldn't go back to sleep. For a long time she lay in her bed, staring out the small panes of the French doors at the gray November morning.

At eight o'clock, she finally threw the covers back and got out of bed. Padding barefooted downstairs, she made a pot of French roast coffee, poured herself a big mug, and carried both the coffee and her debate notes upstairs.

For the next four hours, she sat in bed, reading and rereading her notes. She made sure that every necessary fact was firmly in her head—the population projections for Oyster Shores, the environmental concerns over the slow death happening in the waters of the Hood Canal, the socioeconomic hardships faced by residents as the salmon and timber industries lost viability. She wanted her neighbors to leave this debate with an absolute belief in her ability to manage their community. She wanted folks to say that she would undoubtedly become the best mayor ever. That was goal #1. Goal #2 was actually being the best mayor in modern memory.

At two o'clock, Aurora showed up, armed with her big makeup case and a new outfit for Winona. Vivi Ann was conspicuously absent.

Aurora pushed her way into the house. "I couldn't stand seeing you in one of your boxy blue double-breasted suits."

"Hey. They're expensive."

"That's hardly the 'A' answer. Look, I've brought you this lovely Eileen Fisher outfit. It's flowy but professional. And how about a necklace a little trendier than Grandma's pearls?"

Winona sat down on the end of her bed. "I'm in your hands."

"Perfect."

"How's Vivi?"

Aurora combed her hair out, began straightening it with a flat iron she'd brought from home. "Quiet. Afraid, I think. Noah is certain his dad will be coming home any day." She leaned down. "You're sure about this, right? The court will test Dallas's DNA against the sample and let him out if there's no match, right?"

Winona squirmed beneath the weight of that question. "All I know is I can't sleep since I found out he might be innocent. You should see the prison . . . and Dallas. He looks as beaten as Vivi Ann does."

"Yeah," Aurora said, gently pulling Winona's hair back into a pretty filigree barrette. "I always wondered . . . I mean, he loved Vivi Ann so much.

I never believed he was sleeping with Cat. I should have said something back then."

"I wouldn't have listened to you. No one would have."

"But it would have helped Vivi to know she wasn't alone."

Winona thought about that. It was true that sometimes the support of only one person could make a difference.

For the next hour, they left the topic of Dallas Raintree alone. They talked about the debate and next week's election and the upcoming holidays. Aurora bitched about Ricky's infrequent and rushed phone calls, while Winona studied her notes.

By the time they finally left the house, Winona knew she looked as pretty as was possible. Aurora had straightened her hair and done her makeup to perfection, emphasizing her brown eyes and pale skin. The outfit she'd brought was an unconstructed jacket made of a soft burgundy fabric and matching pants, with a black scoop-necked tank.

"Ready?" Aurora asked when it was time to go.

"Ready."

They went outside and walked down to the high school. There, they ducked into the girls' locker room to await the start of the event.

"Thanks, Aurora," Winona said, hugging her sister. "Your support really means a lot to me."

"Knock 'em dead, sis."

Winona watched her sister leave the locker room, then sat down on one of the slick wooden benches to study her notes one last time. She was so deep into the facts and figures that she was startled when someone came to get her.

"It's time, Winona."

She laughed, feeling nervous and excited. Almost giddy with anticipation. She'd never been more ready for anything in her life.

Maybe she'd even go on from here.

Senator Grey.

Why not? She followed the council member out to the gymnasium, where hundreds of her friends and neighbors sat in folding metal chairs on the basketball court. In front of them, two podiums with microphones had been set up.

At her entrance, the crowd fell silent, watching her in what could only be described as awe. Their respect washed over her, gave her strength. She went up to one of the podiums and took her place behind it. A moment later her opponent strode into the room; he was grinning like a Cheshire cat. "You look mighty pretty tonight, Winona," he said, extending his hand to shake hers.

"Why, thank you, Thad. But looks aren't what matters here, you know."

"Since I've been mayor for eight years, I imagine I know more about what matters than you do, but don't let ignorance stop you from speakin' your mind."

Winona smiled brightly, thinking, *I can't wait to kick your ass,* while she said, "We'll see soon enough."

Then, like a fighter in the ring, Thad went to his corner—the podium—and she stayed where she was. Between them, the man who'd been mayor ten years ago, Tom Trumbull, stepped up to the microphone and introduced the two candidates and outlined the rules for the question-and-answer debate format.

"We'll direct the first question to Mayor Olssen. Thad, you'll have two minutes to answer, and Winona, you'll have one minute to rebut his answer. Shall we begin?"

Erik Engstrom immediately stood up. "Mayor Olssen. We all know that the mayor's office is in charge of overseeing local law enforcement. How will your administration help make us citizens feel safer?"

It was a ridiculous question asked by an idiot, but there was nothing she could do about that. Smiling, she scanned the crowd, looking for friendly faces. Aurora and Noah were right up front; they nodded encouragement at her. Vivi Ann and Dad sat stiffly beside them; neither was smiling. Of course they'd be here. Dad wouldn't let the town know there was discord at Water's Edge. People would talk. For once she was grateful that he cared so much about appearances.

Mark and Cissy were seated in the back, with Myrtle.

"Your turn to respond, Ms. Grey," Trumbull said.

Winona didn't miss a beat. "Local law enforcement needs financial support and careful monitoring, but they certainly don't need more government pressing down on them, making it harder to do their job. As mayor, I would make it my duty to aid Sheriff Bailor and his deputies, not to get in their way."

Aurora and Noah clapped loudly in response.

Winona felt a trickle of anxiety when she looked at the rest of the audience; they were sitting with their hands in their laps.

Myrtle Michaelian stood up. "Winona," she said in a halting voice. "I'd like to know how you think it's staying out of the police's way when you accuse them of being stupid."

"I'm sorry, Myrtle. I don't know what you're talking about."

"I hear you suddenly think Dallas Raintree is innocent. So that means the police and the jury were either stupid or wrong. And I guess you figure I'm a liar."

Winona understood the long faces looking up at her now. News of her petition had gotten out faster than she'd expected.

She took a deep breath and began to explain, forming each word with exquisite care, but as she looked out over the crowd, she knew. Her words might be perfectly chosen and elegantly, passion-ately strung together, but in the end they were weightless things, bits of sound and breath that disappeared like soap bubbles into the air. No one cared about remedying a long-ago mistake.

No one cared about Dallas Raintree.

Halfway through her explanation, Trumbull cut her off, saying, "Your time is up, Winona."

And the people applauded.

Chapter Twenty-six

This is the worst Christmas ever. We went to church but I guess all that talk about forgiveness and faith is a bunch of shit. I mean, hardly anyone in town will talk to Aunt Winona and all she's trying to do is tell people that maybe they were wrong about my dad.

He's not helping either because he STILL WON'T SEE ME. Aunt Winona says he doesn't want me to see him in handcuffs and behind bars but that is so lame. I know all this would be easier if I could just hear him say he didn't kill that woman.

I tried to talk to Cissy about all of it but even that isn't working like it used to. We talk at school and stuff, only people are watching us now, pointing and whispering. At the winter break assembly I couldn't find her anywhere. I know she was hiding so she didn't have to be seen with me. The worst part is I get it. I know how mad her dad is at Aunt Winona. And Cissy says her grandma just cries all the time. It totally pisses me off. Why does everyone care so much about my dad being a murderer? It's like just the IDEA of him being innocent makes everyone crazy. Aunt Winona says it's because people need to believe in the law and the cops and we're scaring them, but that's totally bogus.

I tried to talk to my mom about it on Christmas night, after we got home from Grandpa's. I could tell she was sad and she's doing what she always does when something bugs her, she gets all quiet and stares out the window as if she's waiting for something. But she has a chance to believe in my dad again, maybe even to hope that he can come back to us and she acts like Aunt Winona is ruining our lives for even trying.

So tonight I asked her. I said why don't you want Dad to come home to us?

And she DIDN'T EVEN ANSWER ME. She just walked into the kitchen like I was invisible. So I went into my room and slammed the door shut behind me.

What an excellent Christmas.

P.S. And Aunt Winona lost the election by a landslide. Rumor is that only Aunt Aurora and Mom voted for her.

Vivi Ann heard Noah's bedroom door slam shut. She bowed her head, releasing the breath she'd been holding. This couldn't go on any longer. Straightening her spine, trying to simulate a strength lost long ago, she went into the hallway and walked down to his room. Even as she knocked and heard his irritated, "Come in. I can't stop you," she wondered what exactly she would say. Opening the door, she went inside, pretending to study the posters and pictures tacked up onto the walls.

"You asked me why I don't want Dallas to come back."

"And you stared out the window."

She turned to him finally. "Yes. Can I sit by you?"

"I don't know. Can you?"

She went over to his bed, said, "Move over," and then sat down beside him. "Remember when you were little, before the electricity was done in your room? I used to sit here with you and read by flashlight. You loved *The Dark Is Rising*, remember?"

"Just answer the question, Mom."

She leaned back against the wobbly headboard and sighed. "I never should have let you hang out with Win. You've learned her Doberman techniques."

"Don't say anything bad about her. She's the only one in this stinking family who cares about my dad."

"Believe me, Noah. I care about your father."

"Coulda fooled me. You never talk about him. There aren't any pictures of him in the house. Yeah, you really care. You're not even *hoping* he'll get out of prison."

"You're young, Noah, so hope seems shiny to you, and I'm glad of that. I really am. But I've learned differently over the years. It can be dark, too."

"So? You don't just give up on someone."

Vivi Ann closed her eyes in pain. "That's an easy thing to say, Noah. You have no idea what we lived through, Dallas and I."

"Did you ever ask him if he did it?"

"No," she said quietly. "I believed in him. I believed and believed and believed . . . then his last appeal was denied and he stopped coming out to see me. By then I was a mess. You remember that day we got in the car accident?"

"Yeah."

"Waiting for him to come home almost killed me. I don't want you to go through what I did."

"I have to believe, Mom," he said.

"A son *should*. And the man I married, the one I loved, is worth everything you're feeling. That's the man who is your father, not the killer you've heard about all your life. But try to . . . understand why I can't stand beside you on this. I'm just not strong enough. I am ashamed of that."

Noah reached over and held her hand. "You were alone, though. I have you."

Winona stood at the window of her beach house, watching the road above. It was the ninth of January, a cold and blustery day that hinted at a coming rainstorm. The low gray sky matched her mood, made everything outside look faded and soggy. An inauspicious start to the new year.

The school bus came into view above the trees, stopping for a few minutes at the top of Mark's driveway. When it drove off again, she stood there, still staring out at the bare, wintry backyard, feeling a rush of loneliness on this Monday morning.

Last night she'd lain in her lonely bed for hours, trying to figure out how best to proceed with Mark. She'd given him time to come to his senses, assuming he'd walk over here one night and say he was sorry, but it hadn't happened. November had rolled into December, and then into a new year, and still he hadn't walked from his house to hers. She made sure to be here a lot, to keep her lights on late into the night, and still, nothing.

Last night, for the first time, she'd wondered if he was waiting for her. She was the one who'd made the mistake (she hadn't told him about the petition; she should have; she saw that now), so maybe he was waiting for *her* apology.

The more she thought about it, the more likely it felt.

Dressing carefully, she bundled up in her wool coat and headed next door. With only a moment's hesitation, she went up the flagstone steps and rang the doorbell.

He answered quickly, coming to the door in his slippers and robe, with his hair still wet from the shower. "Hey," she said, smiling uncertainly. "I thought maybe you were waiting for me to say I'm sorry."

The smile she needed so desperately didn't arrive. "Winona," he said in an impatient tone, "we've had this discussion before. Too often."

"I know you love me," she said.

"No, I don't."

"But—"

"Did you even speak to my mother? Did you warn her that this firestorm was coming down? Reporters call her every day. She barely leaves the house anymore, she's so upset."

"I never said Myrtle was lying on the stand."

"Oh, really?"

"Eyewitness mistakes are common. I've been doing research—"

"Either way you're saying it's her fault, and everyone in town knows it."

"You don't understand."

"*You* don't understand. You're hurting everyone with this crusade. Do you really expect us to just accept it?"

"I thought *you* would, Mark. You know me. I wouldn't be doing all this for no reason. It's the right thing. I should have done it a long time ago."

"That's the thing: I don't know you. Obviously I never did. Goodbye." He stepped back and closed the door.

All the way back to her house, in her car, and into town, Winona replayed his words: *No, I don't.* She wasn't sure which hurt more: the idea that he didn't love her now or the unsettling truth that he never had. For the first time in years, she longed to talk to Luke, to sit down with him as they had when they were kids, and ask him what was wrong with her, why she was so easy to discard and so difficult to love, but in the years of his absence, their friendship had faded. He called once or twice a year and they talked mostly about his children and her career.

In town, she pulled into her garage and walked around the side of the house and through the front door.

Lisa was at her desk, typing at her computer. "Your father is in the sunroom. He was here at eight when I got in. Sitting on the porch."

"Thanks." Winona took off her coat and went back toward the sunroom.

He sat stiff-backed in the antique white wicker

chair by the French doors, with his boots firmly planted on the floor. His gnarled, bony fingers lay splayed on his jean-clad thighs; there was the tell-tale tremble in his hand. His white hair was thin and unkempt-looking beneath his brown, sweat-stained cowboy hat, and even in profile she could see the tension in his jaw.

"Hello, Dad," she said, coming forward.

He pulled his hat off and set it on his lap, pushing a hand through his hair. "You got to stop this, Winona."

She sat down on the plush sofa opposite him and knew this was her chance to make him understand. "What if we were wrong?"

"We ain't."

"Maybe we were."

"Drop it, Winona. People are talking."

Winona got to her feet. "That *would* be what you care about. The great Grey family and our precious reputation. You'd rather have an innocent man rot in prison than admit to making a mistake. You don't care about anyone but yourself. You never have."

He got to his feet in the gradual, rickety way that had become normal for him, but there was nothing frail in his eyes. The look he gave her was cold and dark. "Don't you talk to me that way."

"No. Don't *you* talk to me that way." She almost laughed, but was afraid it would sound hysterical. "Do you know how long I've waited to hear you say you were proud of me?" Her voice trembled on that, caught on the sharp point of a need that began a lifetime ago, almost before she could remember. "But that's never going to happen, is it? And you know what? I don't care anymore. I'm doing the right thing with Dallas, and if I discover I'm wrong, I'll live with it, but I won't spend the rest of my life thinking I made a mistake that mattered."

On that, she turned and walked out of her sunroom and went upstairs to her bedroom. There, she went to the window and stared out, watching her father make his slow, shuffling way out to the sidewalk toward his truck. Without even a backward glance, he drove away.

Chapter Twenty-seven

The late winter and early spring of 2008 was one of the wettest on record in Oyster Shores. Rain fell almost constantly from mid-February to late March, turning the ground into a spongy, muddy mass of green and brown.

Winona's life had changed so much in the last five months that it often felt unrecognizable. Fighting an unspoken battle had had unforeseen consequences.

It made no sense to her. To her mind, she was so clearly doing the right thing that any other view was ridiculous. Quite simply, if there was even the smallest hope that a mistake had been made with Dallas, it needed to be explored. How could the people she'd lived among for all of her life not see that?

There was support for her efforts, to be sure, but most of it was voiced quietly. Aurora and Noah were her front line; her foot soldiers in this battle. Vivi Ann was neither fully in nor fully out; that was one of the worst things about this quest. The tiny flicker of hope had burned her sister to the bone and left her once again lethargic and a little numb.

And Dad was just plain pissed off. He considered Winona's efforts a public embarrassment. Just last week in the Eagles Hall he'd been heard to say, "She's always needed to be in the spotlight, that girl. You'd think she'd put her family first."

That had hurt most of all, since she was doing all of this for Vivi Ann and Noah, and at night, when she lay in her bed, emptier somehow without Mark than it had been before, she knew her desire to free Dallas was about redemption. For all of them, perhaps; her most of all.

And so she sucked it up. She accepted that many of her friends and neighbors disagreed with her choice, that her father despised it, and that Vivi Ann was frightened by it. These were the burdens

Winona willingly carried as she waited for the court's response.

By April, though, the waiting had grown difficult. She'd lost clients and often spent whole days in Seattle, researching at the University of Washington's law library.

On Thursday, the third of April, she worked in Seattle all day and drove home slowly, in no real hurry to arrive. She passed her beach house with barely a glance at the FOR RENT sign. Since the breakup with Mark, she spent most of her time at her house in town; to be honest, it was too difficult to be so close to him and not see him.

Instead of turning into her own driveway, she headed for Water's Edge. She was tired of being alone.

For a moment, when she stepped out of her car, it wasn't raining, and the beauty of this place in sunlight hit Winona anew. The fields were lush as green felt, the fences had all recently been painted black, and the trees along the driveway—Dallas's trees—were in full cotton-candy-pink bloom. A few errant blossoms floated on the air around them. Success had come to this ranch in the past decade and with that success came much-needed repairs. Everything, every building, was now well maintained. The parking area was a huge patch of jet-black asphalt; usually it was full of trucks and trailers, but just now, in the late afternoon pause between day and night, the place looked empty.

Winona walked toward the light she saw on in the barn.

Vivi Ann was alone in the arena, struggling with a big yellow barrel, rolling it awkwardly into position.

Winona stepped into the light-as-air dirt and called out, "Hey. You need some help with that?"

"Stay there. You'll ruin your shoes." Vivi Ann muscled the barrel into its place at the peak of an imaginary triangle, then wiped the dirt from her gloves and headed toward Winona. In the pale light—dimmed by dirt on dozens of overhead bulbs—she looked both immensely tired and inexpressibly beautiful. The years had taken a toll on Vivi Ann, made her leaner and hollowed out her face, but even the crow's-feet around her eyes couldn't deface her beauty. She was one of those women like Audrey Hepburn or Helen Mirren who would be a beauty at every age. Once, that would have made Winona jealous; but now she saw more than the perfection of her sister's face: she saw the pain in those green eyes.

"Barrel-racing practice tonight?" Winona said.

"Every Thursday for fifteen years." Vivi Ann pulled off her brown leather work gloves and tucked them in her belt.

As they walked up past the barn, it started to rain again. Winona felt the cool drops hit her face, blur her vision, but they didn't walk faster. They were local girls, tougher than a little rain.

Inside the cottage, Winona took off her coat and heels and sat down on the sofa in the living room. It had been a long time since they'd been in a room together, she and Vivi Ann. Just the two of them. Since the filing of the petition, probably. Winona understood why: Vivi Ann was too fragile to talk about the proceedings and too invested in the outcome to talk about anything else, so she stayed away from Winona. As she'd done for years, Vivi Ann buried her fear and sorrow and pain in the rich brown arena dirt and kept going.

Vivi Ann stared out the window at the falling rain. The window reflected her face, softening it into a watery smile. The gentle pattering noise on the roof substituted for conversation. Winona could have let it go, said nothing and just listened to this familiar symphony, but she couldn't stand it.

"I should have taken Dallas's case in the first place, Vivi," she said. She'd been waiting for a chance to say it.

"That's old news, Win."

"I'm sorry at how much the new petition has upset you, you have to know that."

"But not sorry you took the case on?"

"How can I be sorry for that?"

Vivi Ann turned at last. "How is it that you're always so damned certain of yourself? Even when you're wrong."

"Me, certain?" Winona laughed. "You must be kidding."

"You go into the china shop like a bull every time."

Winona looked at her sister, seeing the vulnerability in her eyes, the pain. "And I break everything. That's what you're thinking, isn't it?"

"No," Vivi Ann said, but it wasn't the answer in her eyes.

Before Winona could reply, her cell phone rang. She pulled it out of her coat pocket and saw that it was her office. "This is Winona."

The cottage door burst open and Noah ran inside, his clothes splattered with rain, his hair wet, his backpack dragging on the floor beside him. "Aunt Winona's car—"

"Shoes," Vivi Ann said tiredly.

Noah dropped his backpack and kicked his big shoes off; they flew into the dining room, hit the wall, and thudded to the floor. "Did we hear something?"

Winona held up her hand for silence, listening to Lisa on the phone. "Thanks," she said finally, and hung up.

"Well?" Noah demanded.

Winona's heart was beating so fast she felt lightheaded. "They granted our motion," she said, rising in anticipation. "They're going to test the DNA sample found at the crime scene."

Noah let out a whoop of joy. "I knew it! You did it, Aunt Win."

"We did it," she said, still a little unable to believe it.

"Tell him," Vivi Ann said in a voice as cold and brittle as a sheet of ice. She was clutching the sofa table tightly.

"Tell him what?" Winona asked, frowning.

"The thousand things that can go wrong from here. Don't you *dare* let him go to bed thinking this was easy and dreaming of what he'll say to Dallas when he's free."

Winona wanted to take her wounded sister in her arms and comfort her the way she used to, so long ago. Instead, she gentled her voice. "Let him enjoy his victory."

"You don't know what you're talking about. But congratulations," she said. "Dallas is lucky to have you." Then she walked past them, went into her bedroom, and slammed the door.

"Ignore her," Noah said. "Everything either pisses her off or makes her cry these days. It's pathetic. So if the DNA isn't Dad's, they'll let him come home, right?"

"It's not certain like that. Just a chance."

"You mean he could still end up staying in prison for life? Even if it's not his DNA?"

"Yeah," she said, looking at her sister's door. The whole landscape had changed with this ruling. A denied petition would have moved them all back to Start; in time, they would have reconciled and moved on, as they'd done before. This, though, was something else. This was the beginning of a new and specific hope. And suddenly she understood every word Vivi Ann had said to her.

She hadn't been fully listening before: her twin flaws, ambition and certainty, had deafened her. She'd focused on undoing a wrong, righting her own mistake; redemption. Now she saw how Vivi Ann had been trying to protect her son. Her sister had understood all along that they could win the battle and lose the war.

Winona often wondered in the next few months how Dallas was holding up in prison. Waiting for the test results was like having a faucet drip constantly in the back of your mind. She knew Noah was as unnerved by it as she was. As Vivi Ann had predicted, he was falling apart a little more each day: getting in trouble, skipping class, failing tests.

But it was Dallas she really worried about. She made a point of visiting him every other week; more and more often, they sat there with nothing to say. April faded into May, which blended into June. The tourists came back to Oyster Shores, bringing noise and money and traffic with them, but here at the prison, nothing ever changed. Life could be vibrant and bright outside of these walls. It was always gray and dark within.

"You need to get some sleep," she'd said to him on her last visit. It had been the only time he'd smiled that day.

"I guess I should have thought of that before we started this thing."

"Are you scared?" she'd asked.

"Scared is a fact of life for me," he'd answered, flicking the dirty hair from his eyes.

Winona had had nothing to say in response. So she'd changed the conversation, adding hope to the list of topics to steer away from.

How much the landscape could change in a week and a half. That was what she thought on this Wednesday afternoon as she followed the guard down to her meeting with Dallas.

Once in the room, she waited impatiently for his arrival, moving from one foot to the other, too excited to sit down.

Finally the door opened and Dallas was there. His hair was dirty and lank, his face was pale, and he moved awkwardly, as if his whole body hurt. As always his ankles and wrists were shackled. "Hey, Winona," he said.

"You sound sick. Do you need a doctor?"

He laughed at that. The sound dissolved into a cough. "It's just June. I'm allergic to something around here. Razor wire, maybe."

"Sit down, Dallas."

He stopped moving and lifted his chin to move the hair from his eyes. She knew he hated to do it with his hands—the shackles rattling in front of his face, the obvious awkwardness of the movement. Once he'd asked her to do it, and she'd found herself almost trembling as she reached forward. It had been the one and only time she'd looked into

Dallas's steely gray eyes and seen a glimpse of the abused boy he'd once been. The way she'd put his hair behind his ear was perhaps the gentlest she'd ever been with a man. "I'll stand," he said.

"We got the test results back. The semen isn't yours." She smiled, waited for him to do the same, but he just stood there. "Did you hear me? The DNA found at the scene wasn't yours."

"Now what?"

"You don't look very happy."

"You forget, Winona. I always knew it wasn't my DNA."

The power behind those few words struck her hard, and for a moment, she truly imagined what life had been like for him all these years. An innocent man in prison. Her voice softened when she said, "I've already called the prosecuting attorney's office. I've asked them to join me in vacating the judgment and dismissing the case."

"You're kidding me, right?"

Winona frowned. "I know I could make the motion myself, but they'll fight me on it. If we can get them to see the evidence, agree with our argument, and believe in a miscarriage of justice, we could do a joint recommendation for release. That would be a slam dunk."

"You're as naïve as Vivi Ann. Here's what's going to happen: they'll admit I didn't have sex with Cat, but maintain that I killed her. Maybe they'll say suddenly that I had an accomplice.

497

What they won't say is, *Gee, Winona, good save.*"

She sat down on the hard chair. "If you believed all that, why did you let me start this?"

"For Noah," he said simply. "He's like his mom, I guess. I knew he couldn't let go without trying."

"So you let Noah and me start this thing, believing in your innocence, and then you say *hasta la vista* and go back into your cell until you die? *That's* your plan?"

"That's the way it is, Win. If you'd bothered to ask Vivi Ann, she could have told you what would happen. We've been here before, remember?"

"I don't believe it. I don't accept it. You're wrong."

"Later," he said softly, "when you've figured this whole thing out, do me a favor, okay?"

"What?"

"Tell Noah I did it. Otherwise he'll drag me around in his head. He doesn't need that."

"I will not. I *won't.*"

He nodded, said, "Thanks, Win. I mean it. If it was redemption you needed, you've earned it. Now go home and take care of my family." Then he left the room.

She stared after him, feeling a hot, impotent rage bubbling up.

"He's wrong," she said to the guard, who didn't respond at all. "I didn't go through all of this to have it mean nothing."

She left the prison and went to her car, muttering. "He's a cynic. Of course he thinks the worst, with what he's been through." Already she was figuring how to prove what good news this was.

Noah would be thrilled.

She'd concentrate on that: the good. Optimism was always a choice, and her will would not fail her now when she needed it so much.

She was halfway home when her cell phone rang. It was Lisa, calling to tell her that the prosecuting attorney had just called to say that she'd seen the DNA results and was willing to concede that Dallas had not had sexual relations with the decedent that night, but reaffirmed her certainty that he'd murdered her. They'd be filing their motion to uphold the conviction this week.

Perhaps, the prosecuting attorney had opined to Lisa, Dallas had had an accomplice.

Vivi Ann was in the farmhouse's kitchen, making a casserole for dinner, when the story came on TV. She wasn't really listening, was humming along to a song in her head ("Mamas, Don't Let Your Babies Grow Up to Be Cowboys," but it was best not to think too much about the song itself), when she heard Dallas's name.

She turned slowly, bumping the oven door shut with her hip. As she walked through the living room, she told herself it was her imagination, running like a colt through new grass, but when she stepped into the family room and saw the look on her father's face, she knew it had been real.

Saying nothing, Vivi Ann picked up the remote and hit the back button, thankful for the first time that Winona had talked her father into getting a DVR.

When she hit play again, a local newscaster was on-screen, standing in front of the forbidding gray prison walls. A snapshot of Dallas—his mug shot—hung suspended in the corner.

". . . DNA test results indicate that Dallas Raintree was not the last man to have sexual relations with the victim, Catherine Morgan. Defense Attorney Winona Grey was unavailable for comment, but Prosecuting Attorney Sara Hamm is here with us now."

Sara Hamm filled the screen, looking older and even more regal. "This is all just legal wranglings. Mr. Raintree's conviction was the result of a great deal of physical and circumstantial evidence. The DNA evidence wasn't even used at trial, so it could hardly have convicted him. Thus, this test result changes nothing. Except that local law enforcement is actively investigating the chance that Mr. Raintree did not work alone the night he killed Ms. Morgan."

The newscaster came back on. "That was Sara Hamm—"

Vivi Ann flicked the off button and the screen went black.

Her father went back to drinking. Ice rattled in his glass as he lifted it to his lips.

"I guess that's that," she said, feeling as if something were draining out of her, leaving her smaller. But that was ridiculous. She'd expected this. Prepared for it.

"Thank God. He done nothing but ruin us."

"What if we ruined him?"

Dad waved his gnarled hand impatiently. "He killed that woman, plain and simple. And his son ain't much better."

Vivi Ann felt as shocked by that as when he'd slapped her all those years ago. She stared at this man whom she'd once loved as much as Dallas, as much as Noah, and felt as if she were seeing him for the first time. Had she imagined him once or had he changed, been twisted into who he'd become by loss or disappointment? She knew how that could happen, how emptiness could reshape you. "That's my son you're talking about. Your grandson." She moved toward her father, studying him. The lines on his face had become deep valleys; heavy lids hooded his dark eyes. "When Mom died, I saw you crying," she said quietly, feeling the memory of that night all around her. "You were by her bed."

He said nothing, didn't admit or deny, and suddenly Vivi Ann questioned the validity of a memory she'd always taken for granted.

"All these years I thought it was romantic, but the truth was right in front of me all the time. Aurora saw it first. Winona tries not to believe it.

And airheaded Vivi never saw it until now. If you *were* crying, it wasn't for the reason I thought. You don't know a damn thing about love, do you?"

"If you're talkin' about that Indian—"

"Enough," Vivi Ann snapped at him, surprised to see him recoil at the force of her voice. "I won't let you talk about him."

Before Dad could answer, the door burst open. She heard footsteps thundering through the house and a voice calling out her name.

Aurora came into the family room. "Vivi Ann," she said. "I just saw the news. Are you okay?"

Vivi Ann looked at her father, and in that last, quick glimpse, she felt the final brick in her childhood wall tumble free. For the first time, she wasn't just looking at him; she was seeing him. "I feel sorry for you," she said, noticing how he flinched.

Walking past him, she linked arms with Aurora. Together they walked through the house and out into the salmony-pink early evening.

"What the hell was that about?"

"He's an asshole," Vivi Ann said.

Aurora grinned. "It's about time you figured that out."

"How did I miss it?"

"We see what we want to see."

Vivi Ann hugged her sister, whispering, "Thanks for coming over."

"How are you?"

"I knew this would happen. Hoped otherwise, maybe, but I knew."

"And Noah?"

Vivi Ann sighed. "He won't handle the news well. He let himself believe."

"What will you say to him?"

The idea of the conversation was overwhelming. "I don't know. Words are cheap when you're waiting." She cut herself off, unable to finish that thought. "I guess I'll tell him I love him. What else is there?"

I hardly had time to get amped up over the news that my dad's DNA didn't match the sample from the crime scene when Aunt Winona tore the shit out of everything by saying that the prosecutors were fighting to keep him in prison.

But he's innocent, I said.

If the DNA had convicted him, maybe it would have freed him, she said, but there had been lots of evidence against dad.

It's still going forward. Aunt Winona filed her motion and the prosecutors filed theirs and next week we'll all be in court to see what happens, but I can tell what's what. Aunt Winona has talked to lots of lawyers and they all say the same thing: keep trying but don't hold your breath. The prosecutor told the newspaper that maybe dad killed that woman in a jealous rage cuz some other guy banged her.

They have a guilty answer for everything.

It's funny, Mrs. I., even though you haven't been reading my stuff all year, I still feel like you are. I'd give anything right now for one of your dorky questions like Who am I? or What do I want out of life? Or How do you make friends?

All that school shit is way easier to think about than my real life. I wish I could sit down and talk with Cissy. She always makes me feel better about this crap. But her assface dad still thinks I'm this terrorist and won't let us hang out after school. It makes the time go slow between school days.

The good news is I don't lose my temper any more. At least I didn't when I figured my dad was getting out of prison.

Who knows what I'll do now?

Tonight when I was feeding the horses, Renegade came up to the fence and shoved me with his nose and made me fall. It was totally bizarre cuz usually he just stands back and watches me throw the hay to him. He's the only horse we have that doesn't seem to care about food. After he knocked me into the mud puddle, I yelled at him and threw a flake of hay right at his face.

That's when my mom walked up to me. I told her that horse was a whack job, and she said,

Did I ever tell you about the day I rescued Renegade?

You said he was all starving and shit, I said. I was still pissed off about everything, about the sucky courts and my dad who wouldn't see me and the horse that knocked me on my butt. I was mad at mom for lots of stuff. I guess I've been mad at her for a long time.

She rested her arms on the fence's top rail, looking at that raggedy black horse as if he were something special. Your dad could make that horse dance Swan Lake if he wanted to, she said. I never saw anyone who was better in a saddle.

I wish I knew the right word for how it felt to hear that. All I know is that it was like seeing the next generation of a video game before anybody else. I said You never told me that before and she said there were lots of things she should have shared with me.

She told me that when I was little I would cry every morning until my dad picked me up. He whispered something to you, she said. I never knew what it was, but you waited for it. Mom was smiling when she said that everyone used to call me a daddy's boy, and that she didn't think that had changed.

I said I guess he wasn't going to get out of prison and Mom just nodded and so I asked her if she'd known that all along. She said it was the kind of thing you could never really know but that she was proud of me for trying so hard.

So how come I feel so crappy, I asked, if I did the right thing?

Mom put her arm around me and said life was like that sometimes.

We stood there for a long time and just stared at Renegade, who never even moved toward his hay.

Why doesn't he move? I finally asked. Why is he so crazy?

He's spent a long time waiting for Dallas to come home.

It was totally bizarre, but when she said that, it was like I already knew it, and when I looked at the horse's face, I saw something like sadness in his eyes.

That's why he's so banged up, Mom said quietly. It takes a toll on you, waiting.

I said I wish I knew how to stop.

Mom said me, too, little man. Me, too.

Chapter Twenty-eight

Winona was a wreck. For the past twenty-four hours she'd been working nonstop: rereading the transcripts, rehearsing her oral arguments, getting ready for what could well turn out to be the single most important day in her life.

Even a month ago, she would have been certain about the outcome of today's proceedings. Then, she'd had the kind of confidence that came from a belief that the world worked in a predictable way, that endings could be foreseen based on an understanding of the events that came before.

Now she knew better. The prosecution's dogged determination to preserve the conviction had proven Vivi Ann's point. They had even thrown in a ridiculous argument about the requisite finality of verdicts—as if reliability were somehow more important than fairness. There might be an animal called absolute truth, but it couldn't be caged and certainly didn't roam the halls of justice. In her research for Dallas's case, she'd read about more than one hundred men who'd been freed from prison in the past five years based on DNA testimony . . . and even more who hadn't. Those unfortunate souls were all too often in Dallas's position:

DNA evidence neither tied them irrefutably to the crime nor wholly exonerated them. It amazed—and shamed—Winona how inflexible district attorneys and police could be once they decided on a defendant's guilt. Often no amount of evidence could dissuade them, and so they kept fighting, making specious, ridiculous arguments that kept innocent people in prison for decades.

"Breathe," Aurora commanded beside her.

"I'm going to faint."

"No, you're not. Now breathe," Aurora said again, more gently this time, as she guided her to the long, low table on the left side of the courtroom. "Good luck," she whispered, and she was gone.

Winona sat down, looking through glazed eyes at the yellow legal pads, boxes of files, and stacks of pens in front of her. An open laptop stared bleakly back at her. She could hear the courtroom filling up. She wanted to turn and look, but knew it would only heighten her anxiety. Too many of her friends and neighbors would be there; they'd come to be calmed, to be told that the system had worked.

Then she heard a door open and the rattle of chains. The courtroom went quiet.

Winona finally stood and turned.

A pair of uniformed guards were leading Dallas toward her. He was dressed in the new blue suit she'd purchased for him, with his hair drawn back into a loose ponytail. Even in chains, with his steps shortened and his wrists manacled together, he managed to look defiant. It was those pale gray eyes that did it. She saw the way he searched the faces in the crowd until he saw Vivi Ann; only then did his angry defiance soften.

Vivi Ann stood perfectly erect, her shoulders drawn back, but when she saw Dallas, everything about her melted. It looked as if only Aurora and Noah, who held her tightly between them, kept her from sinking slowly to her knees.

Dallas shuffled up to Winona, shackles clanking, and sat in the chair beside her. "She looks . . ." His voice trailed away. "And Noah . . . my God . . ."

"Do you want me to bring them here to talk to you? I'm sure—"

"No." It was barely spoken. "Not like this."

Winona touched his hand, and he flinched, reminding her how long it must have been since someone last touched him in an attempt to comfort.

The judge strode into the courtroom, taking his seat at the bench. "Be seated," he said, putting on his glasses and glancing down at the papers. "We are here for oral arguments on the defendant's motion to vacate the judgment and sentence and to dismiss the case."

Sara Hamm stood. "Sara Hamm for the state, Your Honor. That is correct."

"I'll hear from the defense," the judge said.

Winona released her hold on Dallas and stood

up. "Winona Grey for the defendant, Dallas Raintree. As you can see from the pleadings, our motion is based on new evidence, specifically the testing of DNA found at the scene of the crime. At trial . . ."

For almost an hour, she pled her case, citing legal precedent as well as moral imperatives. In conclusion, she said, "It is a travesty of justice, what our legal system has done to Dallas Raintree. It's time to right an old wrong and exonerate him."

The courtroom erupted into noise. Everyone was talking at once.

The judge hit his gavel and said, "Silence." Then he looked at Sara. "The state's response, Ms. Hamm?"

The prosecuting attorney stood up, looking as calm as Winona looked harried. "Your Honor, the record in this case is clear and cogent, and no interpretation of this DNA evidence can lead to exoneration of the defendant. If it did, we would have joined the defense's motion. The state has no interest in keeping innocent men in prison. Quite the contrary, but in this case, a jury studied the evidence in its totality and found Dallas Raintree guilty beyond a reasonable doubt. And what was that evidence? Let me go through it."

For nearly two hours, Sara Hamm wielded her evidence like a blunt object. When she was done, she looked up at the judge. "So you see, Your Honor, the right man was convicted in 1996. The state asks that the conviction be upheld."

Winona's throat was dry. It took remarkable effort to sit there in silence, watching the judge read through the pleadings.

Finally, the judge turned the last page and looked up. "I see no reason to take this under advisement. The facts and arguments seem clear. The defendant's motion is denied. Prisoner is remanded into custody." He banged his gavel; it sounded like thunder. "Next case."

The courtroom erupted into noise again.

Winona sat there, stunned.

"Nice try," Dallas said. "Tell Vivi—"

And then the guards were there, taking him away again. She could hear Noah calling out; he was probably trying to push through the crowd, but it was too late.

Slowly, she turned around and saw Vivi Ann, holding Noah. Both of them were crying.

Winona sank onto her chair and sat there, staring dully at the bench. Behind her, she could hear the courtroom emptying out, hear the raised voices of the spectators, who said *I knew it* to one another. She knew Aurora would be confused right now, her loyalties split, her mind questioning which sister needed her more. In the end, though, it would be Vivi Ann who seemed the more broken, and thus would Aurora's choice be made. As it should be.

"You were fantastic."

She was so desperate for comfort that she'd gone

a little mad, imagined his voice. Expecting nothing, she glanced to her left.

Luke stood there, not quite smiling as he reached down and offered his hand. "Come on."

Thirty years ago, he'd done exactly the same thing, and it had been the beginning for them. *It gets easier,* he'd said then, and those few words had been a bit of Styrofoam to keep her afloat. And here he was again, just when she needed a friend. She picked up her heavy briefcase and directed Luke to help her with the boxes. For nearly an hour they loaded and unloaded the useless notes and files she'd accumulated in her quest to exonerate Dallas, saying nothing. When it was all done, she led him back to her house, made two drinks, and followed him out into the backyard, where they sat in the porch swing.

"Do you want to talk about it?" was the first thing he said when they were in their seats.

"There isn't much to say. Vivi was right. In the end, all I did was hurt them." She glanced at him. "I suppose you'll say I was always like that."

"No."

Something in his voice surprised her; a sadness, maybe. "Why are you here, Luke?"

"I thought you needed a friend."

She could tell by looking at him there was more. "And?"

He smiled at that. "And I needed one, too."

"Trouble with the wife?"

"Ex-wife."

Winona frowned. "When did that happen?"

"Three years ago."

"And you never told me? Why?"

"I was embarrassed. I think I told you once she was my soul mate."

"More than once, actually."

He smiled ruefully, looking like a kid again, caught red-handed. "I guess my soul mate had itchy feet. She went to the store one day and didn't come back. We signed the papers last week. The worst part is that she doesn't even want to see the girls."

"Oh, Luke. How are they doing?"

"Not so good. At four and six, they can't understand all this; they keep asking when she'll be back. It isn't good, maybe, to stay in a house that holds so many ghosts."

"Or a town," Winona said, wondering how long it would be before she stopped thinking about Dallas every time she drove down Shore Drive, or into Water's Edge. She leaned back, staring out at her yard. In the falling night everything looked silvery and a little surreal. "Maybe you should go see Vivi Ann. She could use a shoulder these days."

"You're the one I came to see," he said quietly, and the whole of their past was between them suddenly, the light spots and the dark. He reached over and took her hand. "I was proud of you today."

"Thanks," she said, surprised by how much the

simple compliment meant to her. In all the emotion and loss she'd stirred up recently, she'd forgotten how much it meant that for once, she'd done things for the right reasons. Too bad that only made it hurt more.

I never even got to talk to him. It all happened so fast. One minute we were sitting there, listening to that bitch lie about my dad and then it was over and everyone was moving and they were taking him away in chains.

Mom said don't worry Noah, you'll get through this I promise. But how am I supposed to not care that he's in there alone?

My mom was right. I wish I'd never started all this. It hurts too much.

"How is she?" Winona asked.

"You know Vivi. She's being extra quiet and not going out much. I hear Noah is getting in trouble at school again." Aurora paused in her work. She was busy creating a counter display for the store. "But they'll be fine. It's only been a week. She'll get better again."

Winona turned away from the gentle understanding in her sister's gaze. She walked idly around the empty store, pretending to study the pretty trinkets for sale—the blown-glass wind chimes, mother-of-pearl earrings, pretty stained-glass windows that depicted the Canal and the mountains.

514

"Maybe we can get her to come to the Outlaw this weekend," Aurora said, coming up behind her.

That was how it would be done, the reparation; they would go back to their routines and in time, this failure, too, would be forgotten. Almost. "Sure."

Behind them, the tiny brass bell above the door made a tinkling sound.

Aurora elbowed Winona in the side, and she turned.

Mark stood beside a glass display full of local pearls. He looked exactly the same—touristy clothes, balding head, broad shoulders—and that surprised Winona somehow. With all that had happened lately it felt as if they all should look different.

She saw surprise register in his eyes and she didn't move, didn't even smile. An awkward hesitation seemed to fill the tiny gift shop, and then Mark moved toward her, smiling uncomfortably.

She met him halfway, forced a smile, and said, "Hey, Mark."

"I've been meaning to call you," he said. "You never come to the beach house anymore."

"I've got it up for rent."

"Yeah." He glanced at Aurora, then back at her. "Can we talk?"

"Sure."

She caught Aurora's quizzical look, shrugged a little, and followed Mark to the door.

Outside it was a beautiful day. They walked down Shore Drive to the beach park and sat on an empty picnic table. Normally Winona would have filled the silence with nervous talk, saying anything to avoid nothing, but in the past months she'd learned a thing or two about words. Sometimes you needed to wait for the ones that mattered.

"I was wrong," he said at last. "I still think you should have warned my mom and me, but I should have known you had to do what you did."

"It didn't end up meaning anything."

He didn't seem to know what to say to that, so he said nothing.

"I appreciate this," she said.

"For what it matters, my mom is certain it was him."

"And I'm certain it wasn't. But I know your mom isn't lying. Please tell her that. I just believe she's mistaken."

"That won't help, but I'll tell her."

Winona nodded. She couldn't think of anything else to say, so she got up. "Well, I—"

He took her by the hand. "I miss you. Do you think we could try it again?"

Winona was surprised by that. She turned slightly and looked at him, really looked, and what she saw was a man she'd liked once, and wanted to love, but never had. It freed something in her, that unexpected realization. She'd seen love in that courtroom when Dallas looked at Vivi Ann, and

Winona knew that was what she wanted. She wouldn't accept a watered-down version ever again. "No," she said, making her voice a little soft. "We didn't fall in love," she said. "But I want to be friends, if you do."

He smiled, maybe even looked a little relieved. "Friends with benefits?"

Winona laughed at that, thinking how good it felt to be wanted, and how empowering it was to say quietly, "I don't think so."

Winona stared down at the latest court case on the unreliability of hair analysis, wondering if it was enough for an appeal.

Her intercom buzzed.

"Winona? Vivi Ann is here to see you."

Winona sighed. "Send her in." Getting up, she went over to the window and stared out. The back-yard reflected the change in seasons. Deep autumn jewel tones had replaced the summer's brightness. The petunias were ragged and tired, the roses leggy and untamed. Summer was gone and she'd hardly noticed.

In the months since her loss in court she hadn't noticed anything, really. Instead of curing her obsession, the loss had inflamed it. She couldn't seem to let go of the image of Dallas in prison. And her weekly visits weren't helping. Dallas had given up completely, if in fact he'd ever actually believed in hope.

"Hey, Win."

"Ironic that my nickname is Win, don't you think?" she said, not looking at her sister. She should have picked up her office. Now Vivi Ann was seeing the reams of Post-it-tagged paper, the file folders lying open.

"This all about Dallas?" she asked.

Winona nodded. Lying was something they didn't do anymore. "Transcripts, police reports, depositions, interrogation notes." She knew she should shut up, but that was the problem with an addiction: you couldn't control it or yourself when under its influence. "It's everything. I've read it all so many times I'm going blind. There's so much that was wrong—the tattoo, the lack of real investigation, the rush to judgment, Roy's ridiculously inadequate defense, the DNA—but none of it *means* anything legally. Even though it means everything."

"I know."

"You knew it all along."

"I didn't just give up on him," she said quietly. "I spent years believing in a good ending."

Winona finally looked at her sister. "I failed him. And Noah. And you."

"You didn't fail him," Vivi Ann said. "Sometimes we just can't save the people we love."

Winona didn't know how to live in a world where that was true; she also knew she had no real choice. "How is Noah doing?"

"Not good. He keeps skipping school. Last week he flipped off his science teacher."

"Mr. Parker?"

"Of course. If I remember, Aurora once did the same thing."

"I'll talk to him."

"And tell him what?"

"That I'm not giving up."

"You think that's what he needs to hear?"

"What would *you* say? Walk away? Just give up and let your dad rot in there alone?" Winona knew the minute she said it she'd gone too far. "I'm sorry. I didn't mean that."

"You're always sorry lately." Vivi Ann released a heavy sigh. "Do you think I don't dream of going back in time, of standing beside him?"

"I know you do."

"Part of me is grateful I didn't get to talk to him in court that day. How could he ever forgive me?"

"He loves you," Winona said.

Vivi Ann flinched at that, but like a fighter taking a blow, she kept moving. "He's in there and you and I and Noah are out here. That's the way it is. The way it's going to be."

Winona could tell what was coming and she shook her head, as if the movement could deflect incoming words.

"I'm here to tell you what you once told me: it's time to let go. The DNA test was a good move, and you took it and it failed. We both know it was all over for Dallas years ago. It doesn't matter whose DNA was left behind."

"I can't—" Winona stopped suddenly. She looked up at Vivi Ann. "What did you say?"

"It's time to let go. It doesn't matter whose DNA it was."

"Jesus," Winona said, rushing back to her desk. She began pawing through the paperwork, looking for the DNA lab work. Finding it, she grabbed the file and then pulled Vivi Ann into her arms, kissing her hard on the lips. "You're a genius."

"What—"

"I've got to go. Thanks for stopping by. Tell Noah I'll come visit this weekend."

"Are you hearing me? I'm trying to help you."

"And I'm trying to help you," Winona said, and then ran out of her office.

"Gus tells me Noah is a crappy employee," Dad said to Vivi Ann as they stood near each other on the porch on a cool September morning. Dawn was breaking across the ranch, setting the arena's metal roof on vibrant silver fire.

"He's having some trouble dealing with all this. He really thought Winona was going to get Dallas released."

"Winona," Dad said, and Vivi Ann heard the poison tip to his voice. Had it always been there when he mentioned his eldest daughter? The more she saw of him lately, the farther she pulled back.

She could go whole days without talking to him at all. It wasn't that she was angry with him; quite the contrary. But now that she'd seen the bitterness inside him, she had trouble seeing past it.

She looked up and saw Noah come out of their cottage. He moved down the hill in that lanky, loose-hipped way that always reminded her of Dallas. Her son was growing by leaps and bounds. Since his fifteenth birthday, he'd begun to look down on her—when he looked at her at all. Up on the hill, he walked over to the paddock, stood at the rail.

Renegade turned to face him, whinnying, but he didn't move forward, even though Noah was offering him a carrot.

"Ain't never seen a horse turn down food," her dad said.

"Some hearts can be broken," Vivi Ann said, hurting for her son, knowing what he needed right now . . . knowing that she couldn't provide it. No mother should ever have to feel so helpless with her child. She pushed away from the wall and headed for the steps.

It was time to say to Noah what she'd said to Winona.

"I'm taking a day off, Dad."

"What about your lessons?"

"I only have a few. I'll cancel." Without waiting for his permission, or even his agreement, she muttered goodbye and walked up the hill, through the dewy grass. Tucking her work gloves into her belt, she came up beside Noah.

"How do we tell him Dad won't be coming back?"

Vivi Ann stroked her son's silky black hair. "I think if Renegade knew that, he'd lie down and die."

"I know how he feels."

Vivi Ann stood there with her son, staring at the black horse. The white lines of his long-ago abuse were faded, visible only if you knew where to look. Scars were like that, she thought; they faded but never went away completely. "Get your coat. We're leaving now."

"School doesn't start for another hour and a half."

"I know. Get your coat."

"But—"

"I'm taking you out of school for the day. Do you really want to argue?"

"No way."

They went their separate ways for fifteen minutes and then met back at the truck.

"This is totally cool, Mom," Noah said as they drove past the high school.

For the next two and a half hours, they talked about little things: the ranch, the mare that was ready to foal, Noah's paper on the Civil War.

It wasn't until Vivi Ann turned off the highway and began the long, slow climb into the Olympic

National Park that Noah seemed to take stock of his surroundings. He straightened in his seat, looking around. "This is the road to Sol Duc."

"Yes, it is."

Noah turned to her. "I don't want to do this, Mom."

"I know," she said. "I've been running away from it, too, but some things have to be faced."

By the time they reached the main lodge, it was just past nine o'clock in the morning. The parking lot was nearly empty on this mid-September day.

She parked the truck and got out, putting on her Windbreaker and zipping it up. It was sunny at the moment, but this was deep in the heart of the rain forest, where the weather was fickle.

Noah stood by the truck, watching her as she came around to his side. "I can't go up there."

Vivi Ann took his hand, as she should have done so long ago. "Come on." She tugged on his hand, felt him resist for the merest of time and then relent.

They hiked up the trail that was bordered by towering cedars on either side, into a world of impossible vibrance. Everything was green and rich here, and oversized. The trail wound deeper and deeper into the forest, taking her into her own past.

At the falls, they were alone, just the two of them: mother and son, as once it had been husband and wife. The area thundered with the sound of falling water; spray flew everywhere, stinging their cheeks and blurring their vision.

Noah stood at the railing and looked out at the falls.

Vivi Ann put her arm around him. "He loved it here, just like you do."

Noah jutted his chin in answer. She knew he was afraid his voice would crack or betray him if he said more.

She held her hand out; spray fell like diamonds into her palm and turned instantly liquid. "He called this *skukum lemenser*. Strong medicine." She touched her wet fingertips to her son's temple as if it were holy water she'd gathered. "I should have taught you so many things about him and his people. But I never learned enough. Maybe we could work on that. Go to the reservation or something."

He turned, wiping his eyes—whether from tears or spray, she couldn't tell—and went to the small bower beneath the cedar tree.

Vivi Ann had prepared herself for this during the long drive, but now that the time had come, she was afraid. She followed Noah, sat beside him. As before, the waterfall sounded like an army thundering through the trees. Droplets of water fell from the boughs.

D.R. loves V.G.R. 8/21/92. She stared at the carving in the tree, remembering everything about that day. The girl who'd been here had believed in love and happy endings. She'd been strong and sure of herself, having married the man she loved even if the whole world despised her for it. That girl, like her son, would have fought for the DNA test and dared to believe in the truth. "I was wrong and you were right. You can't run away from what's in your heart. That was the mistake I made."

"I know why you didn't want Aunt Winona and me to reopen everything. I get it now." Noah leaned against the tree. "He's never getting out, is he?"

Vivi Ann put her hand on his cheek, seeing Dallas in his son's face. "No, Noah. He's never getting out of prison."

Chapter Twenty-nine

For most of her life, Winona had been sure of one thing: her intellectual superiority. She might worry about her weight, or bend over backward for her father's approval, or worry that no man would ever truly love her, but from her earliest memory, she'd felt she was the smartest person in any room.

That certainty had been one of the many recent casualties. Now she agonized constantly, second-guessed herself, wondered what she'd overlooked, how she'd screwed up. The memory of her day in court, when the judge hadn't been moved enough by her argument to take the matter under advisement, rankled.

All her life, people had said she barreled forward, her eyes always on the prize, her hands outstretched to grab hold of what she wanted.

This year, however, had taught her caution. And humility. Even fear. She wondered sometimes at night how it would feel if this was her new life; if caution and anxiety were to be her companions from this year on. How would she handle never being certain again?

She sat in her car now, staring through the rainy windshield at the county courthouse. An American flag hung listlessly against the pole, the only splash of color amid all the gray: the sky, the clouds, the building. A mist rose up from the road, blurring it, too. Across the street, the autumn colors were muted and obscured by the weather.

Winona reached for the briefcase beside her. Clutching the leather handle, she left the safety of her car and walked forward, feeling as if every step were taking her into enemy territory. She tried to salvage some of her former confidence, but it was slippery in the rain.

At the desk, she said, "Winona Grey to see Sara Hamm. I have a ten o'clock appointment."

The receptionist nodded and set Winona on her way through the layers of security that had become commonplace in even the most out-of-the-way counties. She put on her visitor's tag, went through the metal detector, showed her ID twice, and was escorted to the prosecuting attorney's office.

It was a cool, professional-looking space, with no plants in pretty pots, no family photographs on the desk. A big window looked out over the parking lot.

But it was the woman sitting behind the desk who commanded Winona's attention.

The years had been kind to Sara Hamm. She was tall and thin, with the wiry look of a long-distance runner. Winona pegged her as the kind of woman who, when stressed, reached for her running shoes instead of the refrigerator handle.

"Ms. Grey," she said, pushing back from her desk. The wheels of her chair rumbled on the hard-wood floor. "This is a surprise. I didn't expect to hear from you again."

Winona sat down. "I appreciate your willingness to see me on such short notice. I couldn't have made too good an impression the first time we met."

That seemed to surprise Sara. Her perfectly arched eyebrows drew slightly together. "On the contrary, I found your passion impressive, even if it was misplaced. You're his sister-in-law. I'd expect no less. May I ask why you didn't take his case initially? Since you obviously care so much."

"The easy answer is that I'd had no criminal experience to speak of."

"And you have more now?"

No wonder this woman had risen in her field; she saw everything. "No." Winona leaned forward. "What did you think of Roy's defense?"

"It was competent."

"Barely, and we both know it."

"Are you going to go after him? That's a tough criteria. Basically he needs to have fallen asleep during the proceedings, and I'm not sure even that would do it."

"I know." Winona sighed. "Believe me, I've researched every possible appellate avenue."

"And the DNA was your best shot."

Winona wasn't certain if that had been a question. Perhaps. Either way, this was the moment. She steeled herself and said, "I don't think it was. My best chance, I mean."

Another infinitesimal frown. "Really?"

Winona tried to take a deep breath without being noticeable about it. *Please let me be doing the right thing, in the right way.* She'd floated her new information past the lawyers at the Innocence Project and they'd advised her to handle this motion carefully. If she could convince Sara Hamm—really convince her—a dual motion was the best way to get Dallas's conviction overturned. Any other way would create a fight, and Winona didn't want to fight the state again if she could help it. "Let me tell you what I believe first. Roy was an ineffective counsel at best. He never hired an investigator to study the scene or do background work. If he had, he might have found the discrepancy in Myrtle Michaelian's testimony. She testified that she recognized Dallas's tattoo that night, but she couldn't have. His tattoo is on the left arm—"

"You presented all this in your petition, Ms. Grey. I don't need to hear it again."

"I know. I just want you to keep it in mind. Along with the fact that the DNA sample wasn't Dallas's. And you and I both know that the hair sample was junk science. There has been plenty of precedent set on that issue in the past ten years. If he gets a new trial, I'm certain I could get it excluded."

"A new trial? Am I missing something? This is all old news. It's been ruled on. The court upheld his conviction."

Winona reached down into her briefcase and pulled out a file. Putting it on Sara's desk, she pushed it forward. "This is new."

Sara opened the manila file, reading the top document. "A second petition to vacate the judgment and sentence and to dismiss? And you've included this office? You think I'm going to join you in this motion? You're delusional, Ms. Grey."

"Keep reading," Winona added. "Please." Her last, best chance—maybe her only chance—lay in convincing this woman. If the state agreed to vacate the judgment and dismiss the case, the court would go along.

Sara turned the page and looked up sharply. "When did this come in?"

Winona knew exactly what had gotten the prosecutor's attention. It was the test results she'd waited almost a month for. "Yesterday."

"Oh, my God," Sara said.

"It occurred to me that all I'd done was test the semen sample to see if it was a DNA match with my client's. As you know, it wasn't. I was so inexperienced, I ran with that result, certain it was enough to exonerate him. Then, about a month ago, I was talking to my sister. His wife. Anyway, she made a comment about that DNA and I realized that I'd never checked whose it was. So I sent the sample to the national database, and it matched a man named Gary Kirschner, who is currently serving a nine-year sentence at the Spring Creek Correctional Center in Seward. For rape in the first. Once we had a name, we checked the gun. Remember that unidentified fingerprint?"

"Of course," Sara said, frowning.

"Turns out it belongs to Gary Kirschner, too."

"Why didn't his prints show up in 1996?"

"He hadn't been arrested yet. He was a drifter. Meth addict who made his way through a bunch of towns around here on his way north. And before you ask, I'll tell you that Dallas Raintree has never met Gary Kirschner."

Sara stared down at the papers, reading through

them again. "I'll need to research this. We won't make a snap decision. It may take some time."

Winona stood up. "Thank you, Ms. Hamm."

Sara nodded and kept reading.

Winona let herself out.

The big Halloween carnival at Water's Edge is this weekend. Yippee. I hope you can read my sarcasm, Mrs. I. Not that you're reading this journal anymore. It's weird. I still write it to you. Why is that? I guess it's one of your big life questions. Maybe someday I'll ask you.

Anyway, after school I came right home to help out around the ranch. Some kids would have been pissed off by that, but they're the kids who have friends. When you don't, it's totally okay to go home after school. There's nothing worse than the ten minutes after the bell rings. Everyone meets up then. That can be lonely when you're standing there all by yourself.

The only one I care about is Cissy. Today she almost smiled at me and my heart practically came to a stop. I know I'm totally insane but sometimes I think she still loves me.

Like it matters. She's too scared to go against her loser dad. Oh, who cares anyway?

Winona was on the phone with Luke when her doorbell rang. "Oh, great. Someone is here," she said sarcastically. She'd been in the middle of whining about how long the prosecuting attorney was taking to make her decision. He was the only one she could talk to about it so sometimes she went overboard. Big surprise there. The only real surprise was that he kept calling her anyway. Almost every Saturday night in September and October, like clockwork, she sat out on her porch, or in front of her fireplace, and talked to him about their lives. The easy way of their conversations had come rushing back.

"You have to be patient," Luke said. He'd been saying the same thing to her for weeks. "It's still October. She'll call. I know she will."

"The waiting is killing me," she said. "I'm actually losing weight for the first time since sixth grade. Maybe I'll get lucky and finally get pretty while Dallas rots in that cell."

"You were always pretty, Win."

The doorbell rang again.

"Yeah, right," she muttered. "That's why you fell in love with my sister when I was standing right there. Look, Luke, I've got to go. I'll call you later."

"Okay, I'm officially worried about you now."

"That means a lot to me. Truly," she said, and then: "I've got to go. Call me tomorrow night." Before he could answer, she hung up the phone and headed for the door. "Keep your pants on. I'm coming." She opened the door and found her sisters standing there. Aurora was dressed as if for a walk across the frozen tundra—jeans, winter boots, a big fake-fur-lined parka. In her gloved hands was a big silver thermos. Beside her, Vivi Ann stood holding coffee cups.

"You're coming with us. Dress warmly," Aurora said.

"No, thanks," Winona said. In truth, she was too anxious lately to behave normally around her sisters.

"She's confused," Aurora said, shooting an I-told-you-so look at Vivi Ann. "That's often the case, lately. I said, you're coming with us. Get dressed."

"What's in the thermos?"

"Irish coffee. Now hurry."

"Fine. But I'm taking my phone," Winona said. She hadn't been away from her phone for more than ten minutes since her meeting with Sara Hamm.

"Who are you? Condoleezza Rice?" Aurora muttered.

Winona left them in her entryway and went upstairs to change her clothes. Five minutes later she came down dressed in old jeans tucked into ice-blue UGG boots, a heavy Irish cable-knit sweater, and her coat. Her purse (with the phone in it) was slung over her shoulder.

"Where's Vivi Ann?" she asked Aurora when she was coming down the stairs.

"Bathroom." Aurora waved her over, whispered, "Hurry." At Winona's arrival, she said, "Spill it. Now."

"What?"

"You've been avoiding Vivi and me for weeks. I know you. That means you haven't let it go."

"It?" Winona said, stalling.

"Don't make me hurt you."

Winona took a deep breath. "I found some new evidence. I'm waiting to hear if it will matter."

"If it does?"

"He could get out."

"And if it doesn't work, he stays put." Aurora crossed her arms. "Thank God you didn't tell her. She's hanging on by a thread as it is. But don't keep me out of the loop, damn it. I want to help."

Winona hugged her sister. "Thanks."

Vivi Ann returned just as they drew apart. "Okay," she said, "let's go."

Winona followed them out to Aurora's car and got into the passenger seat. Now that she was out of the house, it felt good. She couldn't really remember the last time she'd gone somewhere for fun. "Where are we going?"

Aurora turned into the ranch's driveway.

"This is our big outing with a thermos of caffeine and booze?"

Aurora pulled up into the driveway and parked. She got a blanket, two small boxes, and a boom box out of the trunk. Then the three of them started walking: past the ghost-and-witch-decorated barn, past the automatic walker draped in faux spiderwebs.

Winona knew immediately where they were

going. It was a small rise beyond Renegade's paddock, a grassy hillock positioned beneath a huge old madrona tree. From there, one could see almost all of the ranch, the flat waters of the Canal, and the distant mountains. A salmon stream ran alongside it, changing course with the seasons and changing strength, but like every aspect of Water's Edge, its existence remained constant.

Aurora laid a blanket on the grass, and as they'd done so many times as girls, they sat down side by side. The madrona tree, stripped bare of leaves by the autumn cold, created a canopy over their heads; a network of black, spiky branches splayed like reaching hands across a starry lavender sky. Below them, huddled in the shadows, lay the small patch of ground that had once been their mother's garden. None of them had ever had the courage to mow it down or replant it, and so it had simply grown wild.

"We haven't come out here in a long time," Vivi Ann said, pouring the hot spiked coffee into mugs and handing them out.

"We're sisters," Aurora said, and there was an unmistakable gravitas to her voice as she spoke. "Sometimes we have to be reminded of that." She reached over for the two boxes she'd brought along. "These are for you two."

Winona pulled the small, unwrapped box into her lap. Opening it, she stared down at the gift. It was crumpled, confused-looking, but she knew what it was, and the knowledge caused a tightening in her stomach. Slowly, she lifted the wind chime up from its resting place. It was a collection of stunningly beautiful opalescent shells, strung together with nearly invisible silver line. It made a sweet clattering sound as she held it.

Vivi Ann's chimes were different, made of tiny, misshapen bits of jewel-toned blown glass. Even in the fading light, the colors shone as if with some inner brilliance.

"They're beautiful," Winona said, remembering her mother and that last time the three of them had stood around her bed, holding hands, taking strength from each other. *Stay together,* Mom had whispered, crying for the only time in all those months. *My garden-girls . . .*

"We're sisters," Aurora said again. "I just wanted to remind you. No matter what happens, what choices we make"—at this her gaze cut to Winona—"we stick together."

Winona clanked cups with her sisters and took a drink. Then, reaching into her purse, she pulled out a photograph and showed it to her sisters. In it, her father was laughing and handsome, with his arm slung possessively around Mom.

Aurora and Vivi Ann huddled close, studying this picture as if it were a great archaeological find, which, in a way, it was. Pictures of Mom were few and far between. Winona often thought that Mom had edited herself from their family memories—

taking away photos where she looked old or tired or heavy. She couldn't have known that she had so little time with them.

But it wasn't Mom that caught their attention in this picture. It was Dad. He looked vibrant and handsome.

Happy.

"I don't remember him like that at all," Winona said.

"Me, either," said Aurora.

"I do," Vivi Ann said softly. She almost sounded regretful when she said, "See the way he's looking at her?"

"Why doesn't he love us that way?" Winona asked the question, but she knew they all were thinking it. Of course, there was no answer.

"Where did you get the picture?" Aurora asked.

"You should have been a prosecutor," Winona muttered. "You don't miss a thing."

"Except my husband's affair," Aurora answered, taking a sip. "I actually brought the woman muffins when she was sick."

Vivi Ann slung an arm around Aurora. "He was a prick."

"And boring," Winona added.

"Don't forget hairless," Aurora said, finally smiling. She took another sip. "So, where did you get the photo?"

"Luke."

No one responded right away. Winona understood why. Luke was like a forbidden pool in a fairy tale; it might be beautiful, but there was danger beneath the surface of the water.

Aurora knew to say nothing, to let Vivi Ann answer first.

Winona should have done the same—waited—but the silence unnerved her. "He came to see me after the hearing. He'd read about what was going on and thought I might need a friend."

"He's a nice guy," Vivi Ann finally said, looking at Winona. "Do you still love him?"

Winona didn't know how to answer that. "Compared to you and Dallas . . ." She shrugged, unable to find the words.

"It's not a competitive sport," Vivi Ann said, touching her arm. "Love just . . . is."

"It's too late anyway. We missed our chance. Or maybe we never had one. I don't know."

Vivi Ann's look was pure sadness. "You don't know about too late. If there's even a chance, Win, you take it. For all the pain with Dallas, I thank God I loved him."

Winona put down her coffee and lay back on the blanket, staring up through the skeletal tree at the Milky Way. "I'm afraid," she said quietly. She didn't think she'd even said those words out loud before. She'd always been afraid that simply naming her weakness would compound it, but now she needed her sisters to help her through.

"Fear is the mind-killer," Vivi Ann said, and

even in the darkness, Winona could tell that her sister was smiling.

"Great. I bare my soul and you give me geek-girl sci-fi psychobabble."

Vivi Ann laughed. "Yeah, but it's great sci-fi. Legendary. And it's also true. You can't go through life afraid."

"You're one to talk," Aurora said.

"Touché," Vivi Ann answered.

"What would you do if you could go back in time with Richard and get another chance?" Winona asked.

"I've thought a lot about that," Aurora said, drawing her knees up to her chest. "But even when I'm the loneliest, I know I didn't love Richard enough. I want what Vivi had, and if I don't get it, I'm cool with being alone. No more compromises for me."

Winona closed her eyes, listening to the sounds of her youth—the horses walking in the fields, the waves washing on shore, the rushing of the water in the salmon stream. For the first time, she appreciated the constancy of this place, the predictability. In a month or two the orcas would come back to the Canal, and for a few magical weeks, it would be the talk of the town. On the Canal road, cars would stop suddenly, park right in their lane while their drivers rushed out to watch the black and white giants breach and play. Later, when spring came, the frogs would return, rib-biting so loudly at night that people would stumble out of a sound sleep to close their windows.

In a place like this you always knew what to expect, and if you were careful, and you looked closely, you could see your future as clearly as your past. "I've never figured out how to stop loving Luke," Winona said. It took an act of pure courage to say the words, but she was glad she did it.

"Yeah," Vivi Ann said. "Love is like that. You're lucky, though. All you have to do is pick up the phone and ask him out. The worst that can happen is he says no."

"It's not like you're worse off," Aurora agreed.

Winona imagined herself taking the risk, asking him out; she couldn't help but think about the other time, when she hadn't been brave enough to confront Vivi Ann with her longings, and how that lie of omission had changed everything between them, made their relationship fragile.

Winona was doing that again, wasn't she? Although her motives were better, she was still hiding a truth from her sister. "You know I love you, Vivi, right? I would never want to hurt you again."

"I know that. And believe me, nothing about you and Luke can hurt me."

Winona sat up. "About Dallas—"

Aurora elbowed her. "Enough about men. This is a sisters' night." She poured three more Irish coffees from the thermos and then held out her mug. "To us," she said, and they drank. In the long silence that followed, as they sat there, leaned against each other, on this blanket that had once graced their grandmother's bed, Winona said, "Maybe we should replant Mom's garden."

"Yeah," Aurora and Vivi Ann said at the same time, their voices blending together in the night. "It's time," one of them said; Winona wasn't even sure which one had spoken, but she nodded just the same. "It's time."

I NEVER KNEW LIFE COULD CHANGE SO FAST!!!!

I have to put my pen down for a second. My hand is actually shaking. Okay, here's what happened. I'm going to write it all down so I NEVER FORGET A SECOND.

Yesterday was a regular, boring old school day and Mom woke me up early. Lucky me. We were in the kitchen, eating breakfast when Aunt Winona walked into our house. She didn't knock or anything. She just said I need my nephew for the day.

But it's a school day, my mom said, and the Halloween carnival is in two days. I need his help on a thousand things.

Please Aunt Winona said. I'll owe you one. Mom did her famous eye roll and said you already owe me a ton, go ahead and take him. He's skipping all his classes anyway.

Just like that I was free. Aunt Winona looked

at me and said go take a shower and put on pants that fit. I don't want to see your underwear. I started to say no way but she gave me the hand and said Then stay here and go to school.

So I dressed nice.

We got in Aunt Winona's car and drove away. All the way along the Canal I was asking where we were going and she wouldn't tell me, but I could tell she wanted to. She was smiling big time.

I was so busy asking her that I didn't notice when we got off the freeway. And then I saw the sign for the prison.

Are you kidding me? I said. Before I'd been laughing and poking her when I asked, but when I saw the sign it was like my blood froze.

I didn't want to tell your mom, just in case something went wrong, Aunt Winona said. She gave me a Look. Things can always go wrong at the last minute. That's one thing I've learned.

How? was all I could say.

I had the lab run more DNA tests and we found out who was really there that night at Cat's house.

It wasn't your dad, she said. So the prosecuting attorney joined in my motion to dismiss.

By tomorrow, she said, the newspapers will have the story, so I'm taking you to see him now before cameras will follow you around.

But what about mom? I asked.

Don't worry about her, Aunt Winona said.
Aurora is going to keep her busy all day and
keep the ranch gate shut and unplug the phone.
I don't want your mom to know about this until
he's out. Just in case. She can't take another
disappointment.

We drove up to the prison and it looked like I
remembered, all gray and ugly. At the parking
lot, we stopped and got out. In the guard tower,
a guy with a gun walked back and forth.

I forgot my student i.d. I said suddenly. Will
they let me see him? Before Aunt Winona could
answer, a buzzer sounded and the big black
gates started to swing open.

And I could see him. My dad. He was
walking out of prison with a huge guard beside
him; he was wearing black Levi's that were too
big and a wrinkled black shirt. I couldn't tell
how long his hair was cuz it was in a ponytail.

I walked toward him, just staring at the face
that was so much like mine. Noah, he said, and I
realized I'd never heard my dad's voice before.

You're really here, he said, and he was the
one of us who cried first. He said something I
didn't understand but the sound of it was so
familiar. And I knew: it was what he used to say
to me when I was a baby, the thing my mother
didn't know. It was just ours, me and my dad's.

It means Ride Like the Wind in my mother's
language he said. God, he said next. I left a

little boy in his mom's arms and now here you are, a man.

Then he pulled me into his arms and said I missed you little man.

Chapter Thirty

There were literally a hundred things to do between now and the start of the Halloween carnival on Friday. Without Noah, Vivi Ann was going to have a hell of a time getting everything done. After breakfast, Dad went off to the loafing shed for his tractor and the ranch hands set off to feed the steers.

Aurora showed up around noon, and although she wasn't much help, she shadowed Vivi Ann for most of the day, and then sat with her on the porch until nightfall. The white railings were decorated with colorful shells and rocks and bits of beach glass; generations of Grey women and children had marked their territory with treasures taken from their own shores. Vivi Ann still had the last scallop shell her mother had given her, and although she no longer carried it around with her, it was always here, waiting for her on this porch.

For the next few hours, they sat there, sometimes talking, often laughing, occasionally falling silent.

In fact, the whole ranch was surprisingly quiet today; not a truck had driven down the driveway and not a call had come in. Finally, at around nine o'clock, Aurora looked at her watch and said, "Well, I think I've been here long enough. I'd better get going."

When Aurora left, Vivi Ann went back inside to call Noah. Unable to get a dial tone, she did a quick search and discovered the source of the problem: her phone was unplugged. Irritated, she plugged it back in and called Noah on his cell. After several rings he answered.

"Hey, Mom. I've been trying to call you."

"I know. I'm sorry. Somehow the phone got unplugged. Are you on your way home? It's a school night."

"Uh. I've . . . been helping Aunt Winona carry stuff down from her attic all day and we're still not done. Can I spend the night? She'll take me to school tomorrow."

"Let me talk to her."

Winona came on the line. "I'm really here and everything's fine. I'll get him to school on time."

Vivi Ann wanted to say no, demand that her son be returned to her, but it was only because she felt lonely, so she said, "Okay, then. Tell him I love him."

"You bet."

She curled up on the sofa, put in her headphones, cranked up the volume, and listened to music on her iPod. Finally, when she couldn't keep her eyes open any longer, she went to bed. It felt strange to be alone in the house. She heard all kinds of new noises. For the first time, she imagined how it would be when Noah was grown and gone. How quiet this cottage would be.

Sighing at that, she drifted off to sleep.

Sometime later, a steady *ka-thump, ka-thump, ka-thump* wakened her. The muffled beat was regular and even, like the movement of a rocking chair in soft dirt. Or of a man riding a horse in the darkness.

Dallas. She gave in to the memories, let them wash over her . . .

Then she realized it wasn't a dream. The noise was real. She woke up and threw back the covers and got out of bed, reaching for the robe draped on the foot rail. Putting it on, tightening the frayed belt around her waist, she walked through the quiet house, listening.

Opening the French doors, she stepped out onto the porch and closed the doors behind her. A pearl-white full moon hung suspended above the distant mountains. Its bright light illuminated everything, turning the fields into patches of midnight-blue velvet.

Moonlight shone on the man riding the horse without saddle or bridle.

She was losing her mind finally; after all these years it had just snapped.

She moved to the railing, not caring if she was mad, loving it, in fact. From here, all she could see of him was his white T-shirt; it glowed as if under one of those black light bulbs from her youth. Beneath him, Renegade was all but invisible in the darkness, but she could see that he moved in a flowing, rocking lope, his steps as fluid as long ago, when he'd been a champion. Another fact of her madness: Renegade was healthy again. *Of course.*

She tried to stay where she was, but like on a night sixteen years ago, she was powerless to resist. Her footsteps creaked on the wooden slats of the porch as she stepped across it.

She walked down the grassy hillside, careful not to slip in the dew-wet grass, and came up to the paddock fence.

They glided past her, made a circle in the paddock, and then they were in front of her, stopped. Renegade's heavy, snorting breathing seemed to be the only sound for miles; even the sea seemed to have stilled in anticipation.

"Vivi," Dallas said, and the sound of his voice made her feel so unsteady she clung to the top rail of the fence.

"You're not really here . . ."

She stopped. Speaking required more substance than she seemed to have right now; it felt as if she were forming the words somehow, creating them from the parts of herself that were fading.

"I am."

He slipped off Renegade, took the time to rub the horse's ears and stroke his muzzle, and then slowly he moved toward Vivi, ducked underneath the fence's lower slats, and came up in front of her.

For the first time in years, there was no one beside them watching their movements, and no dirty glass between them. He looked older and sadder; the lines on his face were deeply etched, as if drawn on by Magic Marker. The ache inside her was so deep it opened up and she fell in. "I left you alone in there. I know you can't forgive me. I can't forgive myself, but . . ."

He moved closer, slipped his hand down her cheek and along her throat and around to the back of her neck. With that one steady hand, he drew her closer.

She felt herself come alive in his arms. She clung to him, afraid to let him go, terrified she'd blink and discover she'd imagined it all.

She touched his face, let her fingertips wipe away his tears. "Dallas," she said. "Don't cry . . ."

He swept her into his arms and carried her up the slippery hillside and across the porch and into the cottage that had once been their secret rendezvous location, and then their home, and now was foreign to him. But their bedroom was still in the same place and he carried her there, kicking the door open.

He lay her down on the bed and knelt beside her. Moonlight filtered through the window and puddled on the white sheets. She came up to meet him more than halfway, desperate suddenly to undress him. Her hands moved furiously to peel off his shirt and unbutton his pants; he untied her robe and pushed the worn terrycloth off her shoulders and away until it became a layer of softness beneath them.

They touched with the kind of desperation that can only come from more than a decade of waiting. Their breathing became ragged and torn, their cheeks were damp with each other's tears as they remembered how easily their bodies had always come together. And when at last he filled her, she cried out the name she'd been holding back for so many long and empty years.

Winona, Aurora, and Noah were gathered around the game table in Winona's family room, playing a lackluster game of Hearts. Mostly they were talking about Vivi Ann and Dallas, of course, but the cards helped to keep them grounded. They were all so amped up on adrenaline it was difficult to stay focused. Winona had just tried—and failed—to shoot the moon when her cell phone rang.

They all threw down their cards and Winona jumped up to answer it. "Hello?"

"Hey, Winona. I'm sorry to call so late."

She heard her Realtor's voice and sighed. "Hi, Candace."

Noah and Aurora both sat back down.

"What can I do for you?" Winona asked, trying to conceal her disappointment. She didn't actually expect Vivi Ann to call tonight, but still . . .

"I just got a call from a doctor who wants to rent your beach house. He's out there right now and wants to see it. Normally I'd drop everything and go, but the kids are in bed. And since we've had so few calls on it . . ."

"I'll go," Winona said. It was just what she needed: something to occupy her thoughts. "Thanks." She put down the phone, made a quick excuse to Noah and Aurora, and went out to her car.

The long, dark drive out there was perfect. As she wound along the familiar streets, seeing the landscape beneath the beautiful glow of a silvery blue full moon, she replayed the day in her mind. It had been unquestionably the best day of her entire life. Never would she forget a moment of it, from Dallas's bear hug, to his quietly spoken *Thank you,* to the way Noah's face had changed when he met his father for the first time in years.

She pulled into her ratty driveway and parked beside a big blue pickup truck. She was still thinking about Dallas when the shadows beside her shifted, broke up, and moved toward her.

Luke.

Suddenly he was there, coming toward her.

"What are you doing here?" she said. "You don't need to rent my house."

"No. I just wanted to see you alone. I drove all day."

She didn't understand. "I told you I'd call you tomorrow, after—"

"When you told me what you'd done for Vivi Ann and Dallas, all I could think about was what it would be like, having you on my side."

She took a step back, frowning. She didn't want to misread what was happening, pour meaning into his words, his look. "I've always been on your side, Luke. Even when I shouldn't have been."

"But I wasn't on your side, was I?"

"No." And there it was: everything that had always been wrong between them. It surprised her that he had been the one to see it.

"I'm sorry," he said simply.

She didn't know how to respond to that. She'd forgiven Luke—and herself—a long time ago. "That's old news, Luke."

He closed the last small distance between them, and when he looked down at her, she saw the whole of their lives in his eyes, everything that had been theirs—the things that had happened between them and the things that hadn't—and in that single look, she saw that she wasn't the only one who'd changed. "Do you believe in second chances?"

"Of course."

He reached down and took her hand, as he'd done at so many of the critical moments in her life. "Would you like to meet my daughters? They've been hearing about you for years."

"When can we go get them?"

Winona had anticipated the question from her

nephew, knew in fact that it would be his first question this morning. She put an arm around him, still smiling from last night. "Soon."

"My dad is cool, isn't he?" Noah said. In the past twenty-four hours, Winona had seen this boy learn how to smile from the inside out. Gone completely was the sullen, hair-in-his-face troublemaker; in his place was a young man who'd been through bad times and come out on the other side. A young man who would always know that, while bad things happened, good could still triumph.

And Winona had given him that.

"Thanks, Aunt Win," Noah said as if reading her mind. She supposed that didn't surprise her, either. She knew what he was thinking these days, too.

"No. Thank you, Noah." She turned to face him. "I made a mistake with your parents. The biggest of my life. Until you came around with your crumpled old dollar bill, I thought an apology was all I needed to offer. All I had. You gave me a chance to change what I'd done. So, thanks."

At about nine o'clock, the first call came in from a reporter. Winona said, "No comment," and hung up, but a few moments later when the phone rang again, she knew their private time had come to an end. She went to her guest bedroom and woke up Aurora, who'd been up late last night listening to Winona talk about Luke. "Come on, little sis. It's time to go. The news is out."

A few minutes later, when Noah came down the

stairs in clean clothes, with his hair washed and dried and tucked behind his ears, she knew it was time. "Let's go tell Dad."

Aurora groaned. "I'd rather remarry Richard."

Winona smiled, but herded them out and into her car. The drive to the ranch took almost no time, and as they'd feared, there were reporters at the closed gate.

"Private property," Winona reminded them as she opened the gate, drove through, and closed it behind her.

"What will Grandpa say?" Noah asked a few minutes later when they got out of the car.

"He'll be glad," Winona said, wanting it to be true.

Aurora laughed.

They walked up the porch steps, knocked on the door, and went inside.

Dad was in the living room, sitting on the sofa. He looked up at them through narrowed, angry eyes. "Is it true?"

"Dallas was released yesterday. He's up with Vivi right now," Winona said.

Dad drew in a deep breath and let it out. "God. What will folks say?"

"They'll say we made a mistake," Winona said.

"And that Winona fixed it," Aurora said, squeezing her hand.

"Fixed it? You think we're better off now?"

Winona had expected this reaction. "I've done a good thing here, Dad. Whether you know it or not, *I* know it. And right now we're going to go up to their cottage as a family and welcome Dallas home."

Her father sat there saying nothing, just clenching and unclenching his crippled hands. She saw the way his mouth tightened in anger, but trembled, too, and how he couldn't look his daughters in the eyes, and for the first time in her life she saw him as Vivi Ann saw him, a man unable to reveal the smallest emotion.

She went to him, knelt in front of him. All her life she had felt weak in his presence; now, though, she knew that she was the stronger of the two of them. Maybe she always had been. "Come with us, Dad. We're the Greys. That matters. Show us your true colors, who you used to be."

He didn't look at her, maybe he couldn't. He just got up, walked into his study, and slammed the door. She didn't need to open it to know what he was doing: standing in his spot, staring out at his yard, his land, making a drink even though it was morning.

Was he crumbling inside or laughing? Did he care about these things he didn't do, didn't say, or was he empty inside? The tragedy was that she didn't know, would probably never know. Whatever he felt or didn't feel belonged to him alone. All she knew was that for once she hurt for him. His choice made him an island, separate and alone. "Let's go," she said, exchanging a meaningful look with Aurora. "He's made up his mind."

· · ·

Vivi Ann and Dallas spent all night making love and getting to know each other again, talking about how Winona had saved them. Finally, when the sun had risen into a cornflower-blue sky, they sat up in bed, the covers puddled around their naked bodies, and talked about the things that mattered.

"Noah is a hell of a boy, Vivi. You've done a great job with him. We spent yesterday together."

"I did a terrible job," she said quietly, ashamed all over again at how she'd fallen apart without Dallas.

"Don't," he said. "We've lost enough time. No regrets. You think I don't kick my ass for not seeing you when you came to visit? I was trying so damned hard to be noble."

"Still, I gave up."

He smiled down at her, pushed the sweat-dampened hair out of her eyes, and kissed her again. "And I gave in. None of it matters anymore."

She was about to ask him something else when there was a knock at the door.

"That will be Dad," Vivi Ann said. "Wondering why the hell there's no breakfast."

She climbed out of bed, put on her robe, and went to the door, opening it.

Her whole family was standing there, smiling at her. Well, almost her whole family. Her father wasn't there. The pain of that pinched a little, reminded her of things she'd rather forget, a relationship that had been lost or never formed.

Even now she wasn't sure.

"Hey, Mom," Noah said, drawing her gaze back to the people standing in front of her.

She looked at Winona first, loving her so much she couldn't hold it all. "You're my hero," she said, losing it just a little. She surged forward and hugged her sister fiercely, whispering, "Thank you." When she stepped back, they were both crying.

Dallas came up beside her, sliding a hand possessively around her waist. The movement was like a release switch. They all came together at once, crying and hugging. And when it was over, Vivi Ann found herself standing in the grass of Water's Edge, holding her husband's hand, staring through tears at this family of hers—the Greys—and the land that defined them. From here, she could see the mighty evergreens shooting up behind the cabin, their roots driven deep into the fertile soil, and the rolling green fields, dormant now in this cold autumn month, but ready to grow again when the spring sunlight returned. Below the barn lay the house where she had grown up, a girl among girls, knowing always how it felt to belong. It was something she would pass on, not just to her son, but to her husband, who didn't yet understand that he belonged here, on this land, in this place. It would be their gift to him, the thing this generation of Greys passed on to the next: the knowledge that it wasn't property lines or markers on a man's land that outlined the boundaries of a home. It was who you were that mattered, how you stayed together in hard times, the people you held in your heart.

You probably don't even know how you saved me with your stupid questions, Mrs. I.

Who am I? That was the one that got me. I didn't know in ninth grade who I was or who I wanted to be and I sure as hell didn't want to ask. But now I do.

When my dad came home, everything changed. Almost as soon as we got to Water's Edge, people started showing up. First, it was Myrtle and Cissy Michaelian and her dad.

We all just stood there for a minute. It was like some weird, quiet game of Red Rover, Red Rover, with them by the truck and us by the arena. Then Myrtle walked up to my dad and said: I was wrong, I guess.

It's okay, he said real quiet.

I saw what it meant to Cissy's grandmother, his forgiving her, and for the first time in my life I knew how it felt to be proud of my dad.

Then he went over to Cissy and said, So you're the girl my boy loves.

And Cissy nodded and started to cry and said, I hope I am.

You started it all, dad said. Thank you.

After that, Cissy came over to me and kissed me and it was like it all hadn't happened, only it had, and I was glad because right then, with all of that going on, I thought: this is who I am.

I'm a Grey and a Raintree and this land I never cared about is where I belong, and this town isn't what I thought. Oh, some people don't believe in my dad or me—and maybe they never will, but that's okay. Because we believe, and we're here together. And lots of people came over to tell my dad welcome home. Except grandpa of course. That really pissed me off, but when I said something to dad, he just smiled kinda and said, I get it. Cut the old man some slack. So I'll try.

And that night, when everyone had gone, and it was just mom and dad and me in our house, I looked out the window, and I saw Renegade staring up at us. Dad came up beside me and put his arm around me and said, I thought about you every night, Noah. Every night.

That's when mom came up and stood beside us and said, What are my boys doing over here by themselves?

And I said the only thing I could think of: waiting for you.

That's done now, my mom said. This family's waited long enough. Who wants to play cards?

And my dad said, Yeah. It's about time I taught my son to play poker.

His son.

That was when I had my answer, when I finally knew who I was.

Acknowledgments

Again, to Kany Levine, for his help in legal matters, large and small.

To Holly Bruhn, thanks for answering all my quirky horse-related questions, and for reading so closely for mistakes. I owe you one.

To Andrea Cirillo and the phenomenal team at the Jane Rotrosen Agency. How could I get through all of this without your support and encouragement?

To the amazing team at St. Martin's Press: Thank you for everything.

And to the various Innocence Projects around the country, who fight for justice one case at a time. I salute you.

Center Point Publishing
600 Brooks Road ● PO Box 1
Thorndike ME 04986-0001 USA

(207) 568-3717

US & Canada:
1 800 929-9108
www.centerpointlargeprint.com